SPARRING WITH REMBRANDT

BY MONROE KATZ

SILVERADO BOOKS

—Napa, California—

Manufactured in the United States of America

Published by
Silverado Books, Napa, California
First Printing

Cover Photography by Christophe Genty
Cover Design by Robert Bruno and Gary Strommen
Cover Layout by Gary Graybill
Interior Design & Layout by Gary Graybill

First Edition

Library of Congress Catalog Card Number 2010931746
ISBN 978-0-9817425-4-0 (trade paperback)

Library of Congress Cataloging-in-Publication Data

SB-10-TF1001

This book is dedicated to
my daughters,
Minette and Katherine

Acknowledgements

My thanks to these good people:

My friend and writing guru, Paul Chutkow, for reading countless versions of these chapters, giving me solid literary advice, and encouraging me when the going got rough.

The love of my life, Joan Handrich, for her numerous readings and slashings of redundant copy. She says I tend to say the same things twice. She says I tend to say the same things twice.

Ev Parker, a retired New York City police inspector and now a Napa Valley Register columnist, who refreshed my memories of rough city neighbourhoods and baseball.

Julie English, the artist who painted my portrait on the back cover and who speaks the language of art, for her inspiration and astute artistic observations.

"Never permit a dichotomy to rule your life, a dichotomy in which you hate what you do so you can have pleasure in your spare time. Look for the situation in which your work will give you as much happiness as your spare time."

Pablo Picasso

PROLOGUE

I'm standing at my paint-spattered easel, putting finishing touches on fishing boats I painted yesterday after the fog cleared at the Napa Marina. Up on blocks in the boatyard sit two faded wooden hulks with warped planks and rusted fittings. Those seventy-year-old boats needed some respect, so on canvas I repaired planks, replaced frayed rigging, shined the metal, and put them in the water to wait their turn at the gas dock. I painted in another fishing boat, daubed on some red to harmonize with the red gas pump, and added white clouds to the clear sky. I painted out a fisherman on one boat and added him to another. And to not be too photographic, I fuzzed out sharp edges of the hulls.

Now I'm painting highlights on portholes and adding little dabs of color that take the eye from place to place. These are artist's touches that Rembrandt taught me.

This is happening in my dental office.

My dental assistant knocks on the door to tell me that a patient is here. I put down my brush and scrub up.

Across the hall, sitting in a dental chair, is Mrs. Montgomery, pinched-faced, with tiny Chicklet upper denture teeth all the same size and color. She's sixty-one years old, but with lips sunken in, she looks eighty. I've designed a denture that will make her look more attractive. A stone model of her toothless upper jaw is on the counter, and mounted on it is a wax horseshoe with acrylic denture teeth pressed on just where I want them. She doesn't remember what her real teeth looked like, and she doesn't have any smiley photos, so I had to use my own judgment. Since she's quite busty, I gave her large central incisors. That's my rule. And I insisted that the shade be darker than the refrigerator-white teeth I'm replacing. When the wax try-in is inserted into her mouth, her lips are neither sunken nor pooched out, her bite is opened just enough to eliminate wrinkles at the corners of her lips, and when I ask her to say Mississippi, she doesn't lisp.

Before sending her case to the lab to be finished, I add one more artist's touch—a slight twist to the lateral incisors in the wax to make them more feminine.

If Aunt Manya were alive, she might say, "An award-winning artist and a successful dentist? Dentistry is an art? What a ridiculous notion. Who does Norman think he is?"

Imagine my childhood. Little Norman, nurtured by a proud, honest Jewish aunt in Brooklyn who would let nothing stand in the way of his future success. His own bedroom filled with books on planets and constellations, airplanes, and baseball players. An easel, paint, brushes, drawings hanging on the walls. A bat, a ball, a glove. Hugs, kisses, validations of his art.

Sounds like a fairy tale, doesn't it? But it didn't happen that way.

CHAPTER 1

CRAYOLAS AND WAR

I'm warm and wet. I've done it again.

From the army cot squeezed between Cousin Sarah's bed and the window, the outline of the apartment house across the alley is visible in the moonlight. Sarah is asleep. She's eleven years older than me.

I dreamt I was standing over the toilet, but Aunt Manya never believes me. She says a boy who's almost five shouldn't pee in bed. She tells Uncle Irving I'm too lazy to go to the bathroom in the middle of the night, that I do it on purpose to spite her.

In the morning, when she wakes me for breakfast, she feels the bedding and says, "I'm hanging these stained sheets on the fire escape. I want the whole neighborhood to know."

All day long, while I'm playing on the sidewalk with my friend, Joey, I keep looking up at the fire escape, but luckily, Aunt Manya doesn't hang the sheets there. I wish she wouldn't holler on me so much for things I can't help, like peeing in bed, or stuttering, or blinking.

Today my fuzzy face is looking up at me from the shiny yellow floor. So is the reflection of the ceiling light. The waxy floor smells nice, so do my crayons. I like the warm kitchen, the humming refrigerator, the gurgling radiator, and the clatter of the dishes Aunt Manya is washing in the sink. This is my home. These sounds and smells make me feel safe.

A door slams at Mrs. Katzman's apartment across the hall. Running feet. No one ever runs in the hallway. It's not allowed. No one ever knocks that loud.

"Yoohoo, Manya, Manya, let me in."

Mrs. Katzman never shouts.

"Manya, the Japanese have bombed Pearl Harbor!"

"*Oy gevald.*"

My aunt's face turns white. She drops a soapy dish back into the water, rubs her hands on her apron as she runs five steps to the door, stands on tiptoes, and reaches up with shaky fingers to undo the silver chain.

"We're at war, Manya. Turn on the radio. We're at war."

My aunt, racing to the radio in the dining room, steps on my coloring book, slips on my Crayolas, catches herself at the table, turns on the Philco, and fumbles with the knobs.

"*Swarms of Japanese aircraft came out of the sun at 7:50 am Honolulu time in a sneak attack, sinking the USS Arizona and capsizing the USS Oklahoma.*"

Mr. Schepsel Mirsky, our landlord, runs up the stairs to see what the commotion is.

"We're at war, Schepsel. Our country's at war," Mrs. Katzman cries. The creases around her brown eyes are wet.

I get up off the floor and tug at the edge of Aunt Manya's apron. Something terrible has happened, something very frightening.

Mr. Mirsky throws his chubby arms into the air and speaks to the ceiling, "God protect us!" He runs back down the stairs, calling to his wife and daughter.

There's shouting outside. I lean on the cold windowsill, rub frost off the glass, and see people at their open windows, yelling the bad news across the alley. Aunt Manya is teary. Mrs. Katzman bends way down and puts her arms around my four-foot-eight aunt. I shove the broken crayons back in the box.

"Aunt Manya, are the Japs going to bomb our house?"

"No, *tatelah*, New York is too far away."

President Roosevelt says on the radio the next day, "*Yesterday, December 7, 1941—a date which will live in infamy—the United States of America was suddenly and deliberately attacked by naval and air forces of the Empire of Japan.*" He sounds like a kind but powerful man.

When Uncle Irving comes home from his daily prayers at the *shul*, his eyes are red. He takes off his black overcoat and furry Russian hat, hangs them in the hall closet, and puts on his black *yarmulke*.

"Manya, the Senate voted eighty-two to zero to make war on Japan. The House voted three hundred eighty-eight to one."

"Someone voted not to make war?"

"A woman from Montana, Jeanette Rankin. She voted no."

"Rankin? I never heard of her. Is she Jewish?"

"*Ich veys nisht.* The radio said she did the same thing in 1917. This time she hid in a telephone booth and had to call the congressional police to rescue her from the other congressmen."

"She should only get consumption, this Jeanette Rankin, Jewish or not." Aunt Manya shakes her fist.

"For voting what her heart tells her to vote, she should die?"

"It's an expression of mine. I don't mean she should die."

"I'm worried for Nathan and Sol."

"God willing, it'll be over soon. Maybe they won't have to serve... Oh my God, isn't Benny's son stationed in Hawaii?"

"Benny who?"

"Norman's father, Benny, who else? His son, Melvin, by his first marriage, is in the Navy."

Uncle Irving turns to me. "Norman, you know about Melvin?"

"Yes. He works on a big ship with guns on it. He blows a silver whistle and bosses other sailors around."

"*Oy*, what a *pisk*, what a mouth on him."

Today is February 2nd.

"Time to get up. Happy birthday, Norman."

"Thank you, Aunt Manya."

There's the nutty odor of kasha cooking. News about the war in the Philippines crackles on the radio. I roll out of bed. Aunt Manya feels the sheets to see if they're wet. I squirm as she scrubs my face with a blue washrag and Lifebuoy soap.

"Your ears are so dirty, I can plant potatoes in them. Hurry up, get dressed, or we'll be late for your first day of school."

I tuck my shirt in as I walk to the kitchen.

"Here's your cod liver oil. Lick the spoon clean."

"Yum. I like it."

"Is there anything you don't like?"

"Yes. Milk of Magnesia."

"An answer for everything, like your father."

She slices two pats of butter, drops them into my bowl of kasha, and I stir them until they melt. She shakes a quart bottle of milk that has cream in its neck and sets it on the table. I pull off the round paper stopper, lick the cream that's stuck to it, and pour milk into the kasha to make it slushy.

The radio stops crackling, and the announcer says, "*Punxsutawney Phil emerged from his burrow this sunny morning, saw his shadow, and scurried back inside. What this means, folks, is that we'll be having six more weeks of winter.*"

I'm more interested in hearing about the groundhog than about the war.

After breakfast, my aunt bundles me up in a blue-plaid lumber jacket, blue woolen hat with earflaps, and rubber boots with metal clasps.

"Here. Put on this muffler so you won't catch cold."

While she puts on her coat and babushka, I use my finger to draw her face on the frosted kitchen window that leads to the fire escape.

Down in the foyer Mr. Mirsky is polishing the brass mailbox.

"*Gut morgen*, Schepsel. *Vos far a veter hoben mir haynt?*"

She's asking him what the weather is like today. I can understand just about everything Aunt Manya says in Yiddish.

"*Es iz a frost*, Manya."

"Today is Norman's birthday. He starts kindergarten."

"So quickly he turns five. Happy birthday, Norman."

"Thank you, Mr. Mirsky."

On the sidewalk are cinders that Mr. Mirsky has sprinkled on the ice.

"It would kill the other landlords to make their sidewalks safer?" Aunt Manya complains as we walk down the block, holding hands to keep each other from slipping on the cratered ice. "Only last week, Mrs. Gibalowitz fell on the ice in front of her apartment house and a cast they had to put on her arm."

We follow a crowd of children to PS 165. My cheeks sting. The plow has piled the snow on the curb so high that I can't see over it. I run my wool mitten over it. It's too icy to make a snowball.

"*Gut morgen*, Manya. Happy birthday, Nor-Man."

Steam is coming out of Henry's mouth. He's our black neighborhood handyman, and he knows Yiddish. He always says my name the same way: Nor-Man. His voice is very deep. Aunt Manya says he's a basso profundo. I say his name the same way he says mine: Hen-Ry. Cousin Sarah says I'm a squeaky profundo.

"*Vos machst du*, Manya?"

"*Vos zol ich machen?*" By me there's always some aggravation. I'm worried that any day now they'll draft my Nathan or my Sophie's Sol. We have to go. Norman starts school today."

"Goodbye, Hen-Ry… Aunt Manya, how did he know it's my birthday?"

"The *Schvartze* knows many things."

We pass Gussie's delicatessen in the middle of the block. Her window is icy around the edges. Inside the glass door, hanging from a string, is a hand-written sign that says "closed," but Gussie is inside, plopping a big spoonful of mustard onto a square piece of yellow waxed paper and rolling it into a cone.

"Look Aunt Manya, that's where Joey got his tongue stuck on the doorknob."

"Good. So now maybe you won't try it."

The thermometer in the window of Berg's corner grocery says 15 degrees, but I'm sweating in all my clothes. Mr. Berg is opening his store.

"*Gut morgen*, Manya. You're out early."

"Norman starts school today. It's his birthday."

"Happy birthday, Norman. You'll come by after school, I'll give you a slice of halvah. I know how crazy you are over halvah."

"Thank you, Mr. Berg."

"Such a polite *boychik*, Manya. His mother, may she rest in peace, would have been so proud."

"I am, too. What's not to be proud?"

"Tell me Manya, the father visits?"

"Once in a blue moon."

"He pays a little for Norman's upkeep?"

"*Gornisht*, a nickel on a dollar."

"*Gotenyu*. I'm sorry, Manya."

We wait for the crossing guard to blow her whistle. Girls giggle, boys push, children shout to each other. I wish my aunt wasn't with me. Some of the boys are taller than she is. Tweeet. We cross Amboy Street, huddle against the wind, walk by the black iron bars of the school fence. A boy in a red woolen cap cuts in front of us, runs alongside the fence, clapping the bars with a ruler. A coal truck drives by, and its tire chains jingle.

We get to the main entrance and hold onto the brass railing as we climb up the front steps. Together, we pull open the heavy front door. The building is as hot as Coney Island in the middle of summer. On a big gray mat we stomp snow and ice off our boots, then walk on a shiny wooden floor down a long, pea-green hallway that smells waxy. Our clopping footsteps echo.

At the counter in the waiting room, a lady tells us to take a seat and listen for my name to be called. Children are sitting with their mothers on long wooden benches. When a name is called, mother and child go into the principal's office. A girl in a pink coat is whining that she doesn't want to go to school. I can't wait. When my name is called, I run in ahead of my aunt.

"Happy birthday," the principal says when we sit down. Mr. Cohen's crew cut is gray. He wears round wire-rimmed glasses over baggy eyes. "I like to meet all new students and welcome them to PS 165."

"I like starting school. The groundhog saw his shadow today, and we're gonna have six more weeks of winter. It's so hot in here."

"I'll ask the janitor to turn down the heat a little."

"I should be so lucky, Mr. Cohen. By me, I have to bang on the radiator so Mr. Mirsky will turn up the heat a little."

"I sympathize with you, Manya. My Clara has to bang on the radiator, too. Such a happy occasion, the first day of school. Too bad our children have to be subjected to war."

When I walk out of Mr. Cohen's office, my friend, Joey Goldberg, is sitting on the bench next to his mother. Joey has dropped his red plaid jacket on the floor, and his mother is shaking her finger at him. If they were out on the street, she'd be hollering.

"Hello Joey's Mother. Hello Joey. Mr. Cohen is a nice man. He has a big box with a bunch of vanilla folders in it, and my name is on one of the folders. He knows when my birthday is, and he knows that my mother died when I was three days old."

"Your Norman is very observant, Manya."

"Thank you, Rifke. With his mouthpiece, *keyn eyne hore*, he should become a lawyer some day."

Aunt Manya says *keyn eyne hore* a lot so that no evil eye will befall me.

"My Joey wants to be an artist."

"An artist?" Aunt Manya makes a *farcrimpte pawnum,* a face that's even sourer than usual. "Tell me Rifke, an artist makes a living?"

"Money, schmoney. As long as he's happy, I'm happy."

"He looks, *keyn eyne hore,* so thin."

"My Harry, may he rest in peace, was thin too. But I'm not worried. Joey eats like a horse."

"He eats like a horse? He has a tapeworm maybe? What does Doctor Apfel say?"

"Manya, *dreyt mir nisht keyn kop!*"

"I'm not trying to make you crazy. I'm just concerned."

"Joey is all right."

"I believe you, Rifke. Ah, they're calling for you, Joey. Wipe your nose before you see the principal."

"Not on your sleeve!" his mother hollers.

I can count, tell time, and read easy words in English and in Yiddish, so why did they make me start out in kindergarten? My seat is in the back of the classroom. When pencils or crayons are passed back, by the time they get to my seat there aren't any left. Every Tuesday morning, musical instruments are handed out, but all that's left when they get to me is the triangle. Joey, up front, got to pick out a horn.

I'm in the lavatory, on the seat. Ring, ring. Ring, ring. Ring, ring. An air-raid drill! I finish, flush, pull up my knickers, frantically tuck in my shirt, cinch my belt, button my fly, start for the door, then remember to wash my hands with soap and water. Even if it weren't a drill, even if Japanese or German planes were actually bombing PS 165, Aunt Manya would holler on me if I didn't wash. I dry my hands on a brown paper towel and use the same towel to turn the doorknob, as if my aunt were looking over my shoulder.

Back in Room Number One, thirty-nine children are crouched under tables. There's space under the first table by the door, but Max is there, and I don't want to get punched. There's Judy. I can squeeze next to her.

"I'm scared, Norman."

"It's only for practice, so we'll know what to do if the Germans bomb us."

"I'm still scared."

"Don't be a fraidy cat. I'll hold your hand 'til the drill is over."

"Norman's in love with Judy, Norman's in love with Judy," Linda sings.

The whole class copies her.

The bell rings twice, and the drill is over.

Judy lives three doors down the block from me in a ground floor apartment next door to Gussie's delicatessen. She isn't allowed to play outside, and I'm not allowed in her house. After school, when I walk past her window on the way to the playground, I stop to listen to her practice the piano. Her window shade is always all the way down. I don't know the pieces she plays, but I play along with her anyway on my imaginary piano even if people on the street are looking. I can tell when she hits a wrong note.

"You're really good at the piano," I tell her at school.

"Thank you, Norman. I play the violin, too."

"Really? You're lucky. I love violin music on the radio. I asked my aunt if I could take violin lessons, but all she did was shrug her shoulders and say no."

"Norman, watch out for fish bones. Sarah, remember when you got one stuck in your throat?"

"Don't remind me, Mamma… " My cousin turns to me. "Norman, how do you like school so far?"

"I'm disappointed… "

"Don't talk with your mouth full… Okay, so now talk."

"I'm disappointed with kindergarten."

"Disappointed?" Uncle Irving asks, "How can a five-year-old boy be disappointed with kindergarten?"

"My teacher told me I'm very good at drawing, but I heard her say the same thing to Judy, and she doesn't draw very well."

"Listen to Norman, Irving. Such a mouth on him."

"Norman, the teacher is being diplomatic. She doesn't want to discourage Judy."

"But Uncle Irving, how do I know if my drawings are really good?"

"You have a good point there, Norman."

"Yes he does, Pappa. Have you ever seen a five-year-old who draws as well as he does?"

Aunt Manya pounds her fist on the table. Dishes rattle. "Enough Sarah. Enough already with drawing. What I care about is that Norman should be good at reading, writing, and arithmetic. By me, drawing is a waste of time."

It's Friday. Uncle Irving has the day off. After he comes home from shul, we walk to Gubernick's pet store on Church Avenue to buy new fish for his ten-gallon aquarium. Uncle Sam posters are in store windows. Uncle Sam is pointing his finger and saying, "I want you." The table on the sidewalk in front of Golda's is piled high with women's things on sale. Two ladies are having a tug of war with a girdle. It stretches back and forth, back and forth, until there's a loud rip. They look to see if Golda is watching and hurry off in opposite directions. We laugh. Two Hasids in black hats and long black coats are laughing, too.

"Here's Yellin's, Norman. We'll take home a *challah*."

There's a long line inside. Customers are talking about the war. *Challah*, pumpernickel, and rye fill the shelves. The smell makes me hungry. In the back room a fat man dressed in white scoops a handful of runny chocolate out of a giant pot and lets it drip onto a white cake. Sweat from his forehead drips onto the cake, too. He keeps on scooping and dripping until the cake is frosted.

I give Uncle Irving half of a macaroon. "When I come here with Aunt Manya, Mrs. Yellin always gives me a cookie. But I don't want any chocolate cakes from here."

The street is buzzing. Hollering, arguing, haggling over prices. Shopkeepers are calling to us. Babies are crying. I smell perfume, coffee, bubblegum, exhaust fumes, and cigarette smoke. The green trolley cars make an electric whine.

People on the sidewalk are reflected in store windows. It looks like there are twice as many ladies with shopping bags, carriages, and complaining children. There we are, *schlepping* up the street. I like to *schlep* with Uncle Irving, to have time to enjoy everything around me. When I'm with Dad, everything's a blur. Dad's always in a hurry, and I have to run to keep up.

We pass a candy store that sells charlotte russes, a radio store, a jewelry store, the Waldorf theater, and across the street, my favorite Chinese restaurant. Sarah and her friends, Peppy and Gladys, take me there after the movies and treat me to chicken chop suey, which I love. But all they ever talk about is boys. Except once they were talking about how Aunt Manya could be sweet as pie one minute, and the next minute, explosive. Sarah told them that Aunt Manya can't help it; she's a neurotic. Well I sure hope it's not catchy, because I wouldn't want to be that way.

At Gubernick's, fuzzy brown, black-nosed puppies are crawling over each other, tails wagging. I hold my nose as we walk by their cage on our way to the fish tanks. Water is gurgling. Bubbles rise to the surface. I stand on a stool next to a huge tank, pick out an orange swordtail, catch it with a net, and dump it into a white bucket with a wire handle like the ones at the Chinese restaurant.

"Uncle Irving, look at that fat guppy in the other tank. It's gonna have lots of babies." I drag a stool over and climb on. A skinny lady comes over, plops her net into the water as if I didn't get here first. We chase the speedy guppy with our nets. She cuts me off, pushes her net in front of mine, and closes in. Her net is half way around it. I flip my net out of the water so fast that water splashes in her face. She drops her net in the tank, takes out a hanky, and wipes her eyes. Meanwhile, I wait with my net in the corner and scoop up the guppy when it passes by.

"Sorry about getting you wet, lady."

"I know you did that on purpose."

On the way home with the *challah*, the fish, seaweed, and also two snails that will clean the sides of the aquarium, I ask, "Can I have a chocolate ice cream cone?"

"Only if I can have a bite."

Uncle Irving is a whole lot nicer than Aunt Manya. She never buys me an ice cream cone, a knish, a charlotte russe, or a Mounds bar. Every time I ask, she says, "You can't have everything you want. There's a war on." Dad says she's stingy, but he hardly ever gives her money, and he almost never comes to visit.

Uncle Irving took me to see *Pinocchio* at the Waldorf last week, but he let someone sit in my seat when I had to go to the bathroom. Dad wouldn't let that happen, but then, Dad never took me to a movie.

Back home, Aunt Manya says, "Irving, when are you going to get rid of the aquarium already? It stinks, and it takes up too much space in the dining room."

"What are you talking? It gives me pleasure. I'll change the water."

Aunt Manya never watches the swordtails, black mollies, fat guppies, and blue and red neon tetras that everyone in the family enjoys so much. She's a sourpuss.

Cousin Nathan and his girlfriend, Debbie, are the first to arrive for our Friday dinner. Debbie hands me a thick green book. "This is for you, Norman."

"Wow. A picture book about North American animals. What a great present, and it's not even my birthday."

Nathan gives Uncle Irving a bottle of Manischewitz wine. Nathan is Aunt Manya's middle child. He works in Manhattan in the garment district, pressing clothes. Debbie helps Aunt Manya with dinner whether she wants help or not.

"Nathan, look at the guppy I caught."

"It's a fat one. Pappa told me how you got it. I wish I could have seen the lady's face when you splashed her."

"When the guppy has babies, they'll hide in the seaweed until they grow too big to be eaten by the bigger fish. Uncle Irving was smart to buy seaweed for the tank."

Nathan smiles.

"The fish swim around and around all day long. It must be boring for them. Wouldn't it be nice if they could swim in the ocean and be free?"

Sarah comes home from her girlfriend's house.

Sophie, Aunt Manya oldest daughter, and her fiancé, Sol, are the last to arrive. Sophie puts the Pyrex casserole dish she's carrying on the white metal cabinet by the sink. I love Friday evenings when the whole family is together. The warm apartment smells of roast brisket, chicken soup, garlic, horseradish, candied yams and Sophie's potato kugel. The kitchen window is steamed up.

"Sit already," Aunt Manya says. "You're all standing in my way. Norman, take your book off the table, it's time to eat." When we're seated, Aunt Manya lights the Sabbath candles, covers her eyes, and recites the *Kiddush*, "Blessed are you, Lord, our God, sovereign of the universe Who has sanctified us with His commandments and commanded us to light the lights of Shabbat. Amen."

Uncle Irving, wearing his *yarmulke*, is at the head of the table by the window. The table is set for eight. Earlier, I had laid out the silverware that I took from the white metal cabinet, not the silverware in the drawer attached to the table. That's only for dairy foods that Aunt Manya calls *milkhidik*. The *challah* is on the cutting board. We recite the blessing for bread. "*Boruch ataw adonoi elohainu melech ho' olom ha'motzi lechem min h'oretz.*" I say it the loudest.

As Nathan passes the kugel to Debbie, he tells everyone what I said about the fish being free.

"*Oy*, Norman the philosopher," Debbie says. She passes the kugel to Sol.

"He's such a smart little boy, my cousin," Sarah says.

"Too smart for his own good," Cousin Sophie says.

She never says anything nice about me. Now she puffs out her chest and looks at her engagement ring. The smirk on her face is like the one the skinny woman at the pet store had.

I remember when Cousin Sophie got the ring. She strutted into the kitchen like a movie actress and stretched out her arm to show it off. We crowded around her.

"Hoo hah."

"It's about time."

"My sister is getting married."

"Congratulations."

"*Mazel tov.*"

Aunt Manya told me to go next door and get Mrs. Katzman so that she too could see the ring. When Mrs. Katzman followed me in, Sophie just about poked her finger in the woman's eye so she'd look at the diamond. I squeezed between Mrs. Katzman and Sophie and asked if I could see, too.

"Okay already," Sophie said, "but don't touch it."

"What, he'll break your diamond?"

"No, Mrs. Katzman. I don't want him to get it dirty."

"It'll get *schmutzik*, you'll wash it. It won't melt."

"My hands aren't *schmutzik*."

"Enough, Norman," Aunt Manya said. "Don't touch the ring."

"When the light hits it, it twinkles like a star," Sarah said.

"It must have cost a pretty penny." Mrs. Katzman, holding Sophie's finger close, examined the diamond like the Hasidic jeweler I saw through the window on 47th Street when Aunt Manya took Sarah and me to Times Square.

"Sol won't say how much, only that it's a blue-white, a gemstone, and it's a whole half of a carat."

"A whole half of a carat!" Mrs. Katzman said. Her eyes were wide.

"Gemstone, schmemstone," Aunt Manya said. "If you ask me, a smaller diamond would have been more sensible. The money could have been better spent on practical things, like furniture."

"Well, Manya, you're certainly sensible," Mrs. Katzman said.

"And practical too," Uncle Irving added.

"Norman, quit daydreaming," Aunt Manya says. "Eat, eat, enjoy. Who knows how much longer the family will be together."

"I love your candied yams, Mamma," Sol says.

"Listen to Sol, Manya," Uncle Irving says. "Already he calls you Mamma. Here, try the horseradish. It has beets in it."

"I helped Uncle Irving grate it by the kitchen window. It made us cry, so we went out on the fire escape to grate it in the fresh air. When our horseradishes got real small, we had to be careful not to grate our fingers. I cut my finger. Then I put it in my mouth and burned my tongue. Then I rubbed my eye, and it burned."

"Take just a little bit of horseradish, Norman, or again you'll be crying," Aunt Manya says.

"The brisket is heavenly," Deborah says.

"From what Manny the butcher charges, it should be heavenly. But I only get meat by him. Always fresh, not like on East 98th Street. Manny's mother and father, may they rest in peace, were from Pinsk."

"Better to be from than in."

"Why, Uncle Irving?"

"Well Norman, my mother and father, may they rest in peace, suffered under the Czars. Nicholas I, may he roast in Hell, decreed that every Jewish man had to serve in the Russian army for twenty-five years."

"Twenty-five years, Pappa?"

"Yes, Nathan."

"I spit on the Russian government," Aunt Manya says, spitting on two fingers and wiping them on her apron. "They tried to rob us of our heritage. A policy they had, convert one third of the Jews, let another third die, and let the final third emigrate. As if this would solve their social problems."

"Poverty, persecution, and terror Jews had to live with. Death Jews had to live with."

"And even from World War I the Russians didn't learn, The defeated White Russian Army took out its frustration by slaughtering Ukranian Jews."

"And now again they kill Jews. This madman, Hitler, may God curse him for eternity, is worse than the Russians. Rabbi Zimmerman says German Jews are being sent to gas chambers! Yes, you heard right, gas chambers."

The hairs on my arms prickle. Before I can reach over to hold Debbie's hand, she puts her arm around me, squeezes me tight. There's the catching of breath around the table. Tears come from Aunt Manya's eyes.

"My children, and Sol, Deborah, Norman, you don't know how lucky you are to be born in America. I've lived through a nightmare. To watch your own father knocked to the ground by a Cossack. To run to his side. I still dream of this. I wake up at night, my heart pounding in my ears, and I realize I'm safe here in New York City, in America, the greatest country in the world."

"What about your father, Uncle Irving? Was he okay?"

"From the horse, a broken arm. From the Cossack, a slashed forehead, a broken heart."

"That's why I want to sign up for the service," Sol says.

"No, I won't let you. Don't you dare."

"But Sophie, what if I'm called up?"

"Drafted? That's another story. Then you'll have to go, of course. But you haven't received your notice yet, knock on wood."

"*Shah*, don't tempt the devil."

"Debbie's right," Aunt Manya says. "Some things, *keyn eine hore*, are better left unsaid."

"They should only lose the boys' addresses."

"Not much chance of that, Pappa", Nathan says. He reaches into his pocket. "I got this in the mail this morning. It's a letter from the President of the United States. It says, 'Greeting: You are hereby directed to report for pre-induction physical examination at…'"

CHAPTER 2

COUSIN SOPHIE'S WEDDING

I undo the chain, and Sophie bumps into me as she comes through the door. "Mamma, we set a date."

She unrolls her calendar, sets it on my drawings, and knocks crayons off the table. Like Aunt Manya, she has trembly lips and a permanent frown. Pointing to days marked with red X's, she says, "Here's when Sol is on leave. I called, and the hall will be available, on a Saturday night no less. Harry will be best man. Gloria will be maid of honor." She points her finger two inches from my nose, screws up her face as if I were a cockroach, and says, "He can be our ring bearer."

"You hear that, Norman? Sophie wants you to be in her wedding."

"What's a ring bearer?"

"A boy who carries the wedding rings on a satin pillow."

Am I supposed to be happy? She never even talks to me, and she's my Godmother. I like Sol. He's blond and has a dimple in his chin. If I have a scraped knee, he holds me on his lap and makes the pain go away. He can sound like the wolf or the little girl or the grandmother when he reads a bedtime story. It would be nice to be Sol's ring bearer.

For weeks, my stomach hurts when I think about the wedding. What if I trip? What if I drop the rings? Well, it's too late to change my mind. The wedding's today. Aunt Manya raps on the door and hollers, "Get out of the tub and dry yourself, and I don't want to see one speck of dirt in your ears." I make sure I'm really clean, because her face-washings feel like she's rubbing my skin off.

Uncle Irving combs my hair, buttons my shirt, stands behind me to tie my bow tie, and I put on the tuxedo jacket.

"Hoo Hah. Come look in the mirror." In the bedroom. Aunt Manya is safety-pinning her slip so it won't show. "Here, try the *hett*," Uncle Irving says. My aunt laughs when she sees me in a top hat.

"Aunt Manya, is Dad going to be at Sophie's wedding?"

Her neck muscles tighten and her lips purse.

"He was invited."

It's been over a month since he visited me. He could be here real quick if he wanted to. Manhattan is less than an hour away on the subway. I turn to the right and to the left in front of the mirror. I want Dad to see me dressed like this. He'll say I look like a million bucks. That's the way he talks.

"Do you remember what Rabbi Zimmerman told you to do?"

"When he nods, I walk down the aisle and carry the rings to Sophie and Sol."

Sarah comes upstairs. "Mamma, the taxi's here."

It's parked on Herzl Street, in front of Gibalowitz's drug store, a yellow DeSoto with shiny chrome bumpers and grille. Cousin Nathan, in his khaki uniform, is sitting on the jump seat. "Sit on my lap," he says. Sarah is on the other jump seat. We're facing Debbie, Uncle Irving, and Aunt Manya, all snuggled into the plush rear seat. Nathan's lap is okay, but I wish I were in the back seat. I'd rather see where I'm going than where I've been. Next to the driver is Uncle Irving's cousin, Fat Annie. I heard she weighs two hundred and ninety pounds. That's a hundred pounds more than Debbie weighs. Alongside Fat Annie is her husband, Jacob. He's a sourpuss. They live across the street, on the third floor of the five-story apartment house my best friend, Joey, lives in. They smell like wet chickens.

Fat Annie strains to turn her head around.

"*Oy*, look at Norman, so handsome in a tuxedo."

"Thank you, Fat Annie."

Nathan's hand is over my mouth. "*Shah*," whisper Aunt Manya and Uncle Irving, bringing their fingers to their lips. Sarah and Debbie smile. When Nathan lets go, he smiles, too.

The family talks in English and in Yiddish as we ride up Herzl Street. We pass the *shul*, the apartment house Rabbi Zimmerman lives in, and Sam's Fish Market where Aunt Manya shops for carp. People are on stoops and on folding chairs on the sidewalk. They turn to watch our taxi.

A pink Spaldine thuds into the windshield. Fat Annie throws her hands forward. The driver stops on the narrow street, shakes his fist at the stickball players.

"You coulda broke my windshield!"

"Sorry mister cab driver." It's my friend, Joey.

"Norman, is that you all dressed up?"

"Yeah. I'm the ring bearer at my cousin Sophie's wedding."

The driver honks the boys out of the way.

A couple of boys on roller skates stand between parked cars, waiting for us to go by. Girls are playing potsy on the sidewalk.

"Such a smooth machine," Uncle Irving says.

"For what this taxi costs, it should be smooth," Aunt Manya says.

Her face is powdered, her mustache is gone, and she's wearing gold earrings. She looks a little bit like one of the photographs of Mother.

The taxi stops in a parking lot behind a stone building on Eastern Parkway. Big windows are on the second floor. We walk up a staircase and go into a red-curtained room in back of the hall. Uncle Irving adjusts the tilt of my hat and picks a piece of lint from my coat. He pulls back the curtain and we peek out at a roomful of family and friends who are moving their arms and hands a lot, each talking above the other. "Hoo hah," Uncle Irving says. "The *gantse mishpokha* is here."

That means the entire family, but I don't see Dad anywhere.

At six o'clock sharp, the rabbi's wife, Mrs. Z, raises her bracelet-covered arms, brings them down on the keyboard of the Steinway baby grand, and the wedding march begins. I pay attention. I don't want to miss Rabbi Zimmerman's signal or stumble on the carpet. There it is! Toe by toe I walk to the *chuppah*, carrying a white satin pillow in the palms of my hands, my eyes darting to the right and to the left, searching for Dad. I want him to see me in tails and a top hat. Even though I'm in the middle of the *gantse mishpockha*, I feel lonely without him.

There's Fat Annie. Her husband is asleep on his feet, as Uncle Irving would say. Mr. and Mrs. Mirsky smile at me. It's the first time I've ever seen them smile. Mrs. Katzman is so tall, she's easy to spot. Sarah blows me a kiss. Debbie winks. The music stops. The people in the hall sit down on cushy red folding chairs.

Uncle Irving stands by Sophie and Sol, in front of Rabbi Zimmerman. Holding up one of the *chuppah* poles is Cousin Nathan, who has on his army hat instead of a *yarmulke*. Sol's brothers, I can't tell them apart, are holding up the other three poles. A decanter of wine is on a low table by the rabbi. Pots of pink, red, and white roses are under the canopy. Blue-striped and black-striped prayer shawls are draped over it.

Sol is sharp and serious in his tuxedo. Sophie is pretty in her lacy wedding gown with its long train. Pink roses are in her dark hair, and she's smiling for a change. Most of her smiles are put-on, but today it looks real. Aunt Manya hardly ever smiles. She's in the first row on the aisle with a hankie in her hand.

When she touches my elbow, I stop squirming. While Rabbi Zimmerman speaks, I stand on one foot and then the other, waiting for the ceremony to end. I think about sitting on the floor, but when he looks at me, I freeze. His blue eyes are penetrating. His beard is long and black with flecks of gray. If his beard were white, he'd look like God.

I wish they had given my job to someone else. Where's Dad? He's never around when I need him. He's not near the piano. A giant wedding cake is there, with a bride and groom on top. It's on a table surrounded by presents tied with blue and gold and red ribbons. My stomach is growling. Sophie turns her head and glares at me. Now she looks exactly like her mother. They both get aggravated if I forget to turn off a light, or leave the radio on, or slam the door.

Sol takes the white cushion from me, lays it on the table, and puts the littlest ring on her finger.

"*Har'ey aht me'kudeshet li b'taba'atzo, k'dat Mo'sheh v' Yisroel.*" He translates the Hebrew into English. "With this ring, you are consecrated unto me according to the law of Moses and of Israel."

Sophie puts the other ring on his finger and repeats the sentence but changes the word *aht* to *ahtah*. She says, "*Ah'nee l'dodi v'dodi li,*" and translates it into English. "I am for my beloved and my beloved is for me."

Sol puts the cloth-covered wineglass on the floor, stomps on it with his right foot, and kisses Sophie. The guests shout, "*mazel tov!*" I go looking for Dad.

There's something I've never seen before! Sophie and Sol are being carried around the room on chairs. Four men are holding up each chair.

There are many people in the crowded room that I don't know. I'm patted, pinched and spoken to in Yiddish. A happy lady in a blue dress leans over and presses me against her chest, knocking my hat off.

"I'm Bessie. We're second cousins. My, how you've grown. You look just like your mother, may she rest in peace."

"I remember you, Bessie. Have you seen my father?"

"No, I haven't. If I see Benny, I'll say you're looking for him."

"Thank you, Bessie."

Sarah takes me to the banquet table, where I sit between her and Debbie. My favorite foods: steaming roast beef, chicken, kishka, potato kugel, noodle kugel, yams, the works, but nothing tastes as good as Aunt Manya's cooking.

There are speeches. People laugh at things I don't think are funny. I get silly and laugh at things other people don't think are funny. At last, they cut the giant wedding cake that's covered in creamy white frosting. Each tier has seven layers of white and chocolate cake.

A klezmer band sets up, and the floor is cleared for dancing. The five musicians have on blue vests. Their gray pants are tucked into shiny black boots. They look like happy Gypsies.

Fat Annie says to Uncle Irving, "By me, I prefer a piano. In one instrument you have a whole orchestra."

"By a klezmer musician from a *shtetl* near Pinsk, a flute or a fiddle is preferable. Can you run from a pogrom carrying a piano?"

The fiddler raises his bow, and the band plays a waltz.

Sophie gathers up her train and dances with Sol. Around and around the room they go.

"Hoo Hah," Uncle Irving says "They're a regular Ginger Rogers and Fred Astaire."

He raises his wine glass toward them and smiles a long, happy smile. The dance ends.

"With a grand dip, no less," Aunt Manya says.

They bow to the audience, and the audience claps. This is all new stuff. I feel like I'm in a Fred Astaire movie.

Sophie and Uncle Irving dance next. He's stiff at first, but he loosens up by the time the dance is over. Now Sol takes Aunt Manya's hand. She gets all red in the face and pulls away.

"But it's tradition, Mamma."

She shakes her finger at him. "All right already, but no dip at the end. Nothing fancy schmancy."

"That's my Aunt Manya dancing with Sol," I say to a woman I've never seen before. "They're a regular Ginger Rogers and Fred Astaire."

Almost everyone is dancing, but I don't know how. It looks like fun, though. Sarah comes off the dance floor, pulls me close.

"This is how you dance, Norman: Put your left arm around my waist. Hold my hand. Don't back away, I'm not going to pinch you. Now, one two three steps to the right, one two three forward. Good, you're getting it. Take bigger steps. That's right, Norman. One two three to the left, one two three back."

"Dancing is easy to do."

"Sure it is. Now let's try it on the dance floor."

I get bumped and stepped on. People are in the way of my one, two threes.

"I'm getting a little dizzy, Sarah."

"You should have listened to Mamma when she warned you not to drink so much wine."

I squeeze through the dancers. Fat Annie is heading straight at me. I spot Bessie at the last second.

"I promised Bessie I'd dance with her."

Fat Annie fades into the crowd with a hurt look.

Bessie crushes my nose into her perfumed chest again and dances me around the floor.

"You're a fast learner, Norman. I saw Sarah teaching you. Tell me, did you ever find your father?"

"No, Bessie."

I look at every face on the dance floor, every person sitting on chairs around the room. The room keeps twirling after Bessie leaves me to dance with someone else.

Guests are dancing the *Hora* to *Hava Nagila*, even Aunt Manya, who is actually smiling. She pulls me between Debbie and her. I don't have to ask how to do it, I just do what they do. We hold hands, go round and round in a circle, go to the middle of the circle, raise our hands in the air, and go back. People keep joining us. Fat Annie gets between Debbie and me. She still smells like a wet chicken, but at least I don't have to put my arms around her, just hold her damp hand. Now our circle gets so big that it breaks up into a second circle inside of ours. It's going around in the opposite direction.

The room is spinning. I walk off into the coatroom and lie down on a pile of fur coats that stink of mothballs. I'm mad at Dad. He promised to take me to Yankee Stadium to see Joe DiMaggio play. He promised to take me to the circus, the Statue of Liberty, and the Bronx Zoo. He should have seen me dance. I like weddings and cake and klezmer bands and people who like me.

I fall asleep and dream that Mother's face is inside my new marble.

She's talking, but I can't hear what she's saying. I dream I'm on the ocean in a fishing boat like the one in the watercolor painting hanging on the white wooden wall in our bathroom. It's heading home to Sheepshead Bay, not too far from Coney Island. I have to pee, so I stand in back of the boat and hold on to the railing.

In the morning, the sun streaming through the Venetian blinds wakes me up. I'm on my army cot, my pajamas and sheets are drenched, and there's a strong smell. I'm in bad trouble now.

CHAPTER 3

MY MOST IMPORTANT POSSESSION

"Get away from me, Prince. Stop licking my face. Make him stop, Sarah."

"Okay, but first let go of those bars."

"No. I won't let go. I d-d-don't wanna go. I really d-d-don't wanna go."

My face is wet from Prince's tongue, and everything is blurry from these stupid tears. I can barely see my school, PS 165, on the other side of the fence.

"Stop tickling me, Sarah. Get off me, Prince." Sarah shushes Prince away, grabs my hand, drags me along the grass backward to the sidewalk. My heels scrape the concrete. "Okay, you win, I'll go already."

Up Lott Avenue we run, hand in sweaty hand, to catch up with Aunt Manya and Uncle Irving, who aren't aware that we've fallen behind them.

"I wish I could stay home."

Uncle Irving says softly, "The dead can't hurt you." I lean on his smooth camel's-hair coat. He slips a hand into his pocket and passes me a hard red candy wrapped in clear cellophane.

Aunt Manya, wearing a flowered babushka and an ankle-length gray wool coat, turns her head. "You know, Norman, it's a sin, a true sin not to want to visit your own mother's grave."

"Is it really a sin, Aunt Manya?"

No one answers. Even my legs don't want to listen. They don't want to walk fourteen blocks from our Lott Avenue flat to the New Lots Avenue train station in East New York.

Joey is on the sidewalk, riding the scooter I helped him build. All you need is a vegetable crate, a two by four, and roller skates.

"Hello Norman," he says as he whizzes by.

"Watch where you're going with that noisy contraption," Aunt Manya hollers and shakes her fist at him.

Girls are playing hopscotch in front of Sal's. His red-and-white barber pole makes me dizzy as it spins round and round. Sal's Italian. The Sons in

Service flag on his window has a gold star on it. I feel bad that his son was lost in the war. Comic books are stacked on the floor in big piles, and Sal lets me read them even when I don't get a haircut. I could be in there now with the latest *Superman* comic book on my lap.

"I'm tired, and my legs hurt."

"Stop your *kvetching*, Norman. We're almost there."

Almost there? I wish we weren't going to that awful place. Here's the station. Here's my chance. I try to pull away from Sarah, but she's strong. She squeezes my hand, pinches my arm, gives me a jerk.

"No fighting, Norman."

Aunt Manya is like my teacher, Mrs. Dixel. She's got eyes everywhere they shouldn't be.

Sarah drags me up steep stairs. Candy wrappers stick to my Buster Browns. I step on a yellowed *Daily Mirror*.

"Go under the turnstile," Aunt Manya says. "Just duck. Go under."

"How old is the boy?" asks the man in the change booth.

"Five."

"I am not. I'm seven."

Aunt Manya unsnaps her black leather coin purse, fishes out another nickel, drops it into the slot. She leans down and growls, "You should only get consumption with your big mouth." Her eyebrows are squiggly, her lips, tight together. It's the same face she shines on Dad when they're talking about the gazillions of dollars he owes her.

The empty station smells like stale bread. Cars are honking on the street below. A Manischewitz wine poster, curly around the edges, looks like it will fall off the wall. There's a map of the BMT subway system, each route a different color: red, yellow, blue, green.

"Look, Uncle Irving, here's where we are. See? New Lots Avenue. We're on the Fourteenth Street-Canarsie line."

"You can read that map better than I can. In New York, you'll never get lost."

"There's a dead bird between the tracks."

"Don't get too close, Norman, to the edge. The train is coming. Sarah, pull him back."

She pulls me over to the middle of the platform by my coat collar. The train whooshes past like thunder, shaking the station. When the door opens I jump on, find a seat that faces the front of the train, and scooch over to make room for Sarah. The doors hiss closed.

With my nose on the window, I look down at the brick buildings flying by.

The train slows and shudders to a stop at Sutter Avenue, Atlantic Avenue, and now, Broadway Junction. A woman with flowers in her arms gets off.

"Look! Out the window! A cemetery. Is Mother there?"

"No, Norman. That's the Most Holy Trinity Cemetery. A *goyische* one. See the crosses?"

"What does trinity mean, Aunt Manya?"

"It means… oh, don't worry about what it means."

"Uncle Irving, what's that big building over there?"

"Trommer's Brewery. Give a *schmeck*. Do you know what you're smelling?"

"Beer."

"Actually it's malt. They use it to make beer."

"My Uncle Tim drinks a quart of beer at a time. He smells like this smell."

"I know. I know. I met your Uncle Tim."

"He poured me a glass last time I was there with Dad. He taught me to chug-a-lug it down my hatch."

"What else did Tim, the clown, teach you?"

"Card tricks, how to play gin rummy."

"Enough already about your Uncle Tim," Aunt Manya says, and I know she means it.

The train goes underground. Lights off, on, off, on. Electric flashes from the third rail light up the tunnel walls. Dad told me that electricity from the third rail makes the train go. He knows everything.

There's not much to see except the Bromo Seltzer, Ipana Toothpaste, and Lucky Strike signs above the windows. Dad smokes four packs of Luckies a day. He smokes a cigarette down to almost nothing, then uses it to light another. His finger tips are yellowish-brown.

"Here's our stop, Manya. Come Sarah. Come Norman."

"I'm glad we're getting off. These banana-yellow seats make me sick."

Lots of stores are upstairs on the street, and two movie houses. Horns are honking. The sidewalk is jammed with people. Trains are zooming overhead on the Myrtle Avenue El. This is the good part of the trip. I smell knishes, hot dogs, and pastrami from Gottlieb's deli.

"Uncle Irving, can I have a knish?"

"Leave him alone with knishes. He's not made of money. There's a war on."

"I'll buy him one, Mamma."

"No, Sarah. He doesn't need a knish."

"I d-d-do too need one."

"Enough, Norman. Don't argue with your aunt," Uncle Irving says.

The trolley stop is on Palmetto Street. Trolleys are fun.

"That big gray building, Uncle Irving. What is it?"

"The New Ridgewood Grove."

"Oh yeah. I heard about it. There's wrestling there on Thursdays. Fights on Saturdays."

"How, may I ask, does a seven-year-old boy know of such things?"

Before I can answer Uncle Irving, Aunt Manya sticks out her hands, palms up, tucks in her chin.

"From who else? His father the gambler, of course."

I blink, step back, blink some more. Whenever Aunt Manya talks about Dad her face screws up like she's just tasted something sour. I can't shut up.

"Billy Graham, he's a middleweight. He boxes there. Dad says he's not with the mob."

"Enough already with fights and mobs. I don't want to hear such talk out of you."

It doesn't take much for Aunt Manya's face to turn from white to red.

Ding, ding. Ding, ding.

The trolley wobbles from side to side, creaks along like it could fall apart, then squeals to a stop. I'm first on again. Oh, oh, that skinny woman on the seat behind the motorman. She has on a black dress and a black veil. Shining out through the veil are bright red lips. A big silver cross is hanging from her neck. Scary. I go past this Cross Lady fast as I can, sit down in back of the trolley, slide over for Sarah. I wiggle close to her, put my arms around her neck, give her a squeeze.

"That Cross Lady, is she the Angel of Death?"

"No, Norman, no. She's just a gentile, that's all. A gentile."

"*Shah!*" hisses Aunt Manya from the other side of the aisle. "She'll hear."

Aunt Manya stares straight ahead. She's awful quiet. Could she be thinking about Mother? Can't tell, can't ask. Might make her mad. Sometimes she gets mad even when I say nice things.

Side to side, side to side, the trolley sways along the tracks. I peek at Cross Lady. She sees me seeing her.

"Don't watch her!" Sarah pulls me closer.

"Look, look! St. Nicholas. Seneca. Onderdoonk."

Funny street names. Even Aunt Manya laughs. But the houses around here are not funny at all. They're all just the same, three stories tall.

"Cold water flats," Uncle Irving says, pointing out the window. "See the women scrubbing their stoops? I've heard they all do that in this neighborhood."

Church steeples poke into the sky. I hold Sarah tighter, rest my head on her shoulder as we clack, clack, clack our way along the tracks.

"You know, Sarah, this trolley is a lot better than those green ones that go up Church Avenue near our house."

"What's so bad about the Church Avenue trolleys? You don't like streamlined?"

"They look like green sow bugs."

"And this trolley?"

"It's square. It looks like a real trolley. Maroon and cream colors, shiny wooden seats. It feels good to ride on this one."

"It's good that you notice these things. You could be an architect when you grow up and design things with your own shapes and colors."

"Those streets that we passed, the ones with the funny names. They could sure use some color. And I'd make every house different. Different sizes, different windows, different doors."

The trolley creaks and groans like Uncle Irving when he sleeps. The motorman pulls on a rope, the bell clangs, and people and cars get out of the way fast. Aunt Manya and Uncle Irving bump against each other like they're in a stagecoach in a cowboy movie. Her face looks all melty now.

Screeeeech. The trolley stops. People get off. Some head for the cemetery just outside my window. There are crosses on them like the one Cross Lady is wearing. I know for sure that Mother isn't in this cemetery.

"Sarah, look at those little white buildings. What's in them?"

"Dead people."

"Why? Why aren't they buried in the ground?"

"The aboveground burials are for people with lots of money."

My arm hairs prickle. Dead people above the ground? I dig in my pocket and take out my marble. It's my special shooter, and I've won lots of games with it. It's big and smooth and clear except for the tiny bubble like a baby marble inside. It's my most important possession. It's so important that once, when a boy bigger than me grabbed it and ran off, I chased after him with a stick and threatened to hurt him if he didn't give it back.

It's also a tiny crystal ball like Aunt Lilly's real one. She's Dad's sister. Ladies come to her house to have their fortunes told in her kitchen. I've been there lots of times. It smells from that incense she burns and the icky perfume she splashes all over herself. She reads magic tea leaves and the lines in people's palms. She has these tarot cards, too. Scary. Some fell on the floor once, and she asked me to pick them up. I told her, "I'm not touching those cards. I'm never gonna touch them, 'specially since you told me that one of them is the death card."

Aunt Manya says Aunt Lilly is a Gypsy. She's warned me to never, never let her tell my fortune. So when she took my hand and rubbed it with her finger, I pulled it back and told her I didn't want to know my future.

She could tell I really meant it.

I roll the marble around in my hand. We're passing trees and telephone poles now. Sparks from the sun fly into my marble and make it easy to see what's inside. It's Mother. She's beautiful. I know she is. Those pictures prove it, the tiny ones mounted on the black pages of Aunt Manya's family album. Little black triangles on the corners hold the pictures in. Aunt Manya has to use a magnifying glass to see them okay, but not me. I can see them just fine. The best one is of Mother, wearing a flowered white dress with a big bow.

I asked Aunt Manya, "What color is the bow?"

"Blue. Green. I don't remember. Don't bother me with colors."

"I wish these pictures were in color, like in the movies, like in Bambi."

"Someday they'll all be in color. You wait and see."

I didn't have to ask about the color of Mother's hair. Black, just like mine. Everyone says so. In the picture, her hair is short, parted on one side, and her head is tilted. She's smiling. It's just like my smile when I look at her. And she isn't mean.

Aunt Manya scrunches her face into a frown, and she has a moustache. She wears thick glasses and has to put drops in her eyes bunches of times a day. Sometimes, she makes me do it.

Behind Mother in the picture is a boxy Ford sedan with thin tires. It's parked at the curb. Way back, a big sign says *The Trust Company of New Jersey*. Aunt Manya thought the picture had been taken in Atlantic City. Uncle Irving thought the West Side, near the Hudson River. They argued about that picture, raising their arms and shaking their fists in the air. Everyone in my family and in my neighborhood argues about something, about nothing, about everything.

Aunt Manya pointed to Mother's round stomach and said, "See Norman, that's you inside." Then she pushed the chair back hard and hurried into the bathroom. I knew she was crying.

I took my marble out of my pocket and rolled it all over Mother's face, all over the face that's my face, too. I played like I was seeing her in Aunt Lilly's crystal ball. Maybe she would talk to me so I could hear her sweet voice. It had to be sweet. She'd talk, and I'd talk. I'd tell her how Aunt Manya squashes up my drawings and throws them in the garbage.

"Mother-in-the-marble, I wish you were here."

"Norman, put your marble away, we're almost there."

Mt. Hebron Cemetery has an iron fence around it like the one at PS 165. Stars of David are on the tombstones. There are no crosses, no statues with halos. This is the right place for Mother.

I hold Uncle Irving's hand down the aisle and the steps of the trolley.

"Such a handsome young man," Cross Lady says.

No one answers. I peek at her before the door closes.

"I'm glad she didn't get off here with us. She's the Angel of Death."

"Enough already, Norman. Get going. We haven't got all day."

We walk through the main gate, past a stone building with ivy all over it. Three old men in long black coats are standing in front of the door. They wear black hats and have fluffy white beards. They look at us hard, just like the shopkeepers on Pitkin Avenue look at us, so we'll buy something.

A very old one walks over, and Uncle Irving pulls his hand away from mine. He needs both hands to talk. I take Sarah's hand. Uncle Irving and the man argue in Yiddish. It doesn't seem right in a cemetery. I shuffle my feet. Aunt Manya groans. Uncle Irving tries to walk away, but the man tugs on his coat.

"Momma, I'm gonna give that man a *klop* in the *kop* if he doesn't let go of Pappa."

"*Shah*, Sarah, he'll hear you. Be nice now."

"I know where all the graves are," says Prayer Man.

"I know, too, the way to the graves. Our families are buried here."

"I'll make prayers for your dead."

"I'll make my own prayers, thank you."

Uncle Irving turns away from Prayer Man, takes out his tattered book. Bookmarks stick out everywhere. For Jews, there are prayers for just about everything.

"Manya, every time we're here, it's the same *mishugas*. These people can't take no for an answer?"

Aunt Manya shrugs. Prayer Man follows us down the path, his thick soles clopping on the pavement loud enough to wake the dead, as Aunt Manya would say. I wish he could wake up Mother.

Prayer man is at least a hundred years old. His beard is more yellow than white. His hands are wrinkled and spotted. His crooked fingers have thick, chalky white nails. He follows us all the way to Mother's grave then stands there, still as a gravestone, his arms folded.

"Irving, let him say a prayer already. A prayer out of respect for the Jews of Pinsk."

"How do you know he's from Pinsk, Aunt Manya?"

"By his accent, his expressions. That's where our family is from."

The gravestone is very tall, very black, and Mother's name is on it in big letters. NORMA. On top are six stones.

"Aunt Manya, why are those stones there?"

She takes one out of her coat pocket and puts it on the gravestone. "Each time I come, I leave one. Look around you. Everyone leaves stones."

"Norman, put on your *yarmulke*."

I take it out of my pocket, put it on my head. Sarah moves it around, tucks in some hairs, kisses me on the cheek. I wipe her kiss off.

Prayer Man mumbles a prayer at Mother's grave. Then we shuffle off to the nearby graves of Mother's mother and father, who died before I was born. Aunt Manya puts stones on those gravestones, too. Prayer Man doesn't hurry through the prayers like I thought he would. His eyes fill with tears. He pulls a wrinkled handkerchief from his coat pocket, starts swiping at his eyes. Why is he crying? They're not his relatives.

After he says the prayers, he freezes up again.

"Here. Here you go. Take this." Uncle Irving puts a quarter in Prayer

Man's hands. The old man closes his fingers, walks away.

"Who is he, Uncle Irving?"

"Who knows? A rabbi. A *shammes*. He's a professional mourner trying to make a few bucks to feed his family."

"Well, I'm glad he's gone. I don't care if he is from Pinsk. I don't want a stranger saying prayers for Mother 'cause you know how to say them. You say good prayers."

"Listen, would you, to Norman. He talks like a Philadelphia lawyer. So tell me, *Groysa Knacker*, you're still scared to visit your mother?"

"No, not really. I like being near her."

"At home you're also near her. Everywhere you are, she's by your side, so no harm can come to you."

I know Aunt Manya's trying to be nice. I wanna believe her, but I don't. If Mother were everywhere, really protecting me, she wouldn't let Aunt Manya holler on me, tear up my pictures, and throw them in the garbage.

Uncle Irving is saying prayers for my grandparents, and he's rocking back and forth like he does in *shul*. He pronounces every word perfectly, not mumbly like Prayer Man. When he's done, we walk back to Mother's grave. I read the date when she died, February 5, 1937. I was three days old. Uncle Irving reads a long musical Hebrew prayer. He sounds like the cantor in *shul*. Aunt Manya stands next to him, on the left side of Mother's grave. She bends down and picks some weeds. Sarah is on my right. They're both crying. I should be, too. I tighten up, squint my eyes. No tears. Nothing. Why can't I be like Prayer Man? He says prayers for people he's never met, and he cries. I'll spit on my fingers and wipe them on my eyes. No spit. Nothing. No stone, either. Nothing on the ground, or anywhere. Snatch a stone from somebody else's grave? It's not nice, but I have to.

Uncle Irving claps his book closed.

"Come, Norman. Time to go."

Sarah takes my hand, pats me on the head, kisses my cheek.

We walk down the path that leads to the main entrance. I'm very sad. I wish I hadn't taken that stone. I wouldn't want anyone to take one from Mother. We're a long way from the grave now. I can see the ivy-covered building up ahead.

"I'll be right back." I spin around, pull away from Sarah, and run to Mother. The sun is down a little. There's slanty light that's like the light that comes in through the window of the *shul* on Saturday mornings, shining on the Holy Ark. This cemetery is holy, too. Every grave, every tree, every bush is holy, even Prayer Man. I'm not afraid anymore.

I put the stone back where it belongs. I'm alone with Mother now. Nor-Ma, Nor-Man. Nor-Ma, Nor-Man. She's a Ma, a Mother. I'm a Man, a boy. I reach into my pocket for my perfect marble. It's warm in my hand. I kiss it and put it on Mother's gravestone.

CHAPTER 4

GRAND THEFT

The Saratoga Avenue elevated station in Brownsville shudders as the express barrels in and screeches to a stop. Doors open. Aunt Manya and I scramble aboard. I put my satchel on the floor, climb up on the seat, and press my nose against the window, but not for long. After the next station the train goes underground into the cool dark tunnel. Utica, Kingston, Nostrand, Franklin. I know the names of the stations all the way to Aunt Lilly's house in downtown Brooklyn.

Aunt Manya calls Aunt Lilly a bohemian. She has names for Dad's four other sisters, too. She's not crazy about any of them. But that doesn't stop her from leaving me with Aunt Lilly for two weeks every year so she and Uncle Irving can go to the Catskills, which Cousin Sarah calls the Jewish Alps. Sarah will stay with Cousin Sophie. I'm glad I don't have to stay there.

Above the window is an advertisement for Carter's Little Liver Pills. At school we call them Carter's Little Farter Starters. It's fun to read the signs.

"You like going to your Aunt Lilly's, don't you?"

"Yes. She'll be telling people's fortunes, and I'll get to play gin rummy with Uncle Tim. He knows magic tricks, too."

"Remember what I told you this morning?"

"Yes. I shouldn't eat *traife*, I shouldn't drink out of Uncle Tim's glass, and I should brush my teeth after every meal so I won't need to get false teeth like you have."

In downtown Brooklyn, we push through black turnstiles and walk up a steep stairway into a sunny street with shoppers, honking horns, and policemen blowing whistles. Even though it's early, this street is hot. We walk block after block past buildings that all look the same, go into the dark foyer of Aunt Lilly's apartment house, and take the stairs to the third floor. I run ahead of Aunt Manya so I can ring the bell like Dad does: two short rings-wait two seconds-then two more short rings. It's his special signal. When Aunt Lilly opens the door, I smell lilacs.

"Hello, Norman. Hello, Manya. Come inside."

"I can't stay, Lilly. I have to get back. How's Tim?"

"Coughing, always coughing. If only he'd see a doctor. I beg him until I'm blue in the face."

"I bet if he saw my doctor his cough would go away real fast. Dr. Apple is the best doctor in Brooklyn."

"I'm sure he is, dear."

Aunt Manya leaves without reminding Aunt Lilly not to give me *traife*, but that's okay. I'll remind her myself. Aunt Lilly is my favorite. She hangs my drawings on the walls.

"Is Uncle Tim here?"

"No dear, he's at work. He'll be home later."

Two of my pictures are still taped to the cupboard by the stove. They're greasy like everything else in the kitchen, including Aunt Lilly. She picks up the cups and saucers, puts them in a sink piled with dirty dishes, and sits at the table to write a letter.

The air is hot. My shirt is soaked. Sweat is trickling down her face and dripping on the letter. She's always writing letters. She starts off with her right hand then switches to her left. By the time she's done she's switched hands a bunch of times. Uncle Tim says she's ambidextrous. He can't read what she writes no matter which hand she uses. I wish he were here. I explore the living room. More of my pictures are on the walls. I can draw even better ones now.

I'm allowed to go into every room of the apartment and sit wherever I want. Uncle Tim's red leather easy chair isn't as comfortable as it looks. Springs are sticking through the seat. The ceilings are real high, the windows are blurry, and chunks of plaster are coming off the walls, exposing strips of wood. In the bedroom, I have to walk over piles of dirty laundry. *Shmutz* is everywhere. I draw faces on the dusty lamp tables with my finger.

In the hallway, I dance around, waiting to use the toilet they share with the next apartment. It flushes, and Mrs. Feldman comes right out. I know she didn't wash her hands. I hold my nose, lock the door, and remember what Aunt Manya told me. "At Lilly's, be sure to put toilet paper on the seat. Who knows what kinds of diseases you can pick up from strangers."

A bare yellow bulb is on the ceiling, and a window that I can't see through is held open by a brick. Hanging high over the toilet is a wooden tank, gurgling as it fills with water. Attached to the tank is a brass chain for flushing. The small sink is stained brown. The walls are dingy yellow. I imagine faces in the plaster.

In the kitchen, my aunt is still writing.

"Aunt Lilly, do you have any games?" "Can I blow up that white balloon on your lamp table?"

"I have an idea, Norman. Why don't you play on the fire escape? Here's a writing tablet and a pencil. Draw me a picture. Draw me a whole bunch of pictures."

Oh boy. Aunt Manya gets mad when I ask to go out on her fire escape. Climbing out, the windowsill burns my thighs. The alley is a long way down. The black bars are rusty. What if the fire escape pulls away from the building and crashes to the alley? But Uncle Tim is out here every day, and he goes up and down the ladder a lot. I'll hold onto the windowsill just in case.

Two women are smoking on the fire escape across the alley. Owwr. Owwr. A pigeon is on the landing above me. When I look up, the building seems to fall toward me and makes me dizzy. I hold on to the windowsill for a long time. There's nothing to do inside, and it's kinda nice out here. I quit holding on.

Telephone poles are jungle trees. Fire escapes are tree-house porches. Clotheslines crossing the back yards are vines for Tarzan to swing on. Garbage cans in the alley are jungle drums. Horns and sirens are screeching monkeys and chirping birds.

For two days, I draw my fabulous tenement jungle, filling two pads of writing paper on both sides of each page. "Aunt Lilly, do you have any crayons? Aunt Manya forgot to pack them in my satchel."

"No, dear. I'll get some when I go shopping."

A week later, I still don't have any. None of my aunts on Dad's side ever keep their word.

Aunt Manya would have a conniption fit if she knew I just about live on the third-floor landing of this rusty fire escape. She wouldn't like it if she knew that Aunt Lilly gives me coffee and peanut butter and jelly sandwiches every morning for breakfast. At night, after I get tired of connecting the dots of light in the sky, imagining animals that Uncle Tim told me are there, I sleep curled up against the cool black bars.

I never run out of things to draw from the fire escape. The farther away the buildings are, the fuzzier they get, and colors become lighter and bluer.

Uncle Tim is home a lot during the day, sitting on his big chair, drinking Schlitz, smoking Camels, and coughing. It's not like the four-pack-a-day Lucky Strike cough Dad has, but a softer blood-on-the-handkerchief cough.

"Timothy, let me take you to see my doctor. He's very good."

"I'll not be going to any doctor, thank you kindly. They're all a bunch of charlatans."

"But you're sick, Timothy."

"Lillian, I refuse to see any doctor. Now where was I Norman? Oh yes, I'm goin' to show ya how to tell the number of days there are in each month by using yer knuckles. Put yer fists side by side in front of you, lad. That's the ticket. Now, the knuckle of your left pinky is January, a long month. The space between the pinky knuckle and the knuckle of your forth finger is February, a short month. The next knuckle is March, another long month. See how it goes? Now try it yerself. Atta boy."

Uncle Tim shows me stuff no one else knows about.

The thermometer nailed to the kitchen cupboard says ninety-four degrees. I'm sitting in an iron bathtub that I helped Aunt Lilly slide out from behind the curtain under the kitchen sink. Aunt Lilly and Uncle Tim had to go to Manhattan, so I'm the only one in the house and I'm taking a bath because she told me to. It's nice, soaking in cool water. Reaching over to the towel lying on the sink counter, I pat my hands dry, pick up a pad and a pencil, and draw the faces I can see on the rough-plastered walls. I draw them with big noses, small noses, long chins, short chins, and no chins. It's fun to exaggerate. If clouds stood still, I'd be able to draw their faces, too. The drawing paper is used up. By the time I dry off and get dressed, I'm so sweaty that I feel like jumping back in.

Something is always going on in this noisy neighborhood. From the fire escape, I can see boys play kick-the-can. There are police cars, taxis, fire engines, horse-drawn ice wagons and delivery trucks. People argue in foreign languages. I smell garlic from Rita's apartment next door. She's seven, too. Sometimes we play together on the fire escape. She lets me climb from the fire escape into her living room.

Her apartment is a different country. The Puerto Rican music makes me feel good. She says it's *borinqueño* music. Her roly-poly mother, Concha, has on a flowered yellow dress. She hugs me, tells me to pull up a chair at the kitchen table, and sets a bowl of steaming chicken and rice in front of me.

"It's *Asopao.* Eat, eat, eat."

She scoops up a ladle full of *habichuelas*, plops them on my plate. I like these beans. Then she fries in butter some giant black bananas that Rita calls plantains. It's great to have dessert without having to eat bread with it.

"*Despidida* is playing," Rita says. When she turns up the radio, her mother doesn't holler on her.

"I love this song, Norman."

"What's it about?"

Rita's mother understands my question, answers it in Spanish. Rita translates. "The singer is Daniel Santos. He's a famous balladeer, and his song is about a man who's saying goodbye to his friends, because he's going off to fight in the war."

"To fight the Germans and the Japs?"

"Si, Norman."

Concha kisses my cheek, making me feel important. Between her facial expressions and the way she moves her hands, she's easy to understand. I wish she were my aunt.

Rita and I play on the fire escape every day now. We wave hello or goodbye to Uncle Tim, who uses it more than the front stairs.

Aunt Lilly married Uncle Tim after he came to New York from London, where he was a famous circus clown. They worked in Aunt Dolly's traveling carnival. She's Dad's youngest sister. Aunt Lilly and Uncle Tim lived in a tiny trailer and traveled all over the country. Aunt Manya said that they were the *gonifs* who ran the midway games and made Aunt Dolly rich. Dad says Aunt Dolly gave me my first bath. I don't remember the bath, but I do remember that every time I see her, she promises to take me to see her carnival but never does.

Aunt Lilly and Uncle Tim might be crooks, but they're nice to me. She lets me drink coffee. When Uncle Tim drinks beer, he pours me a glass, and I chug-a-lug it. When I was four, he taught me to tie my shoes. The day I ate a whole package of Ex-Lax, he said to me through the bathroom door in the hallway, "Did the same thing once myself I did and had to sit on the can for hours. Life can certainly be the shits." How could something that tasted so good do that?

It's raining. Aunt Lilly comes home from the store with liver, onions, two bottles of Schlitz, a carton of Camels, but no crayons. After she puts everything away, she says, "Let's look at my album."

There are pictures of Uncle Tim in his curly white wig and wide clown shoes, Aunt Lilly in a halter and shorts, Dad in a World War I army uniform with medals on his jacket, and Melvin, my half-brother, who survived Pearl Harbor. He's in the Pacific, fighting Japs. He's wearing a white sailor suit and hat. In another picture, Uncle Tim is young and doesn't have any wrinkles. The picture is loose, and underneath it is one of Aunt Lilly without any clothes on! She closes the album.

"You weren't supposed to see that."

Aunt Lilly lets me look through a cardboard box she keeps under their unmade bed. In it are wigs, earrings, necklaces, Tarot cards, and a crystal ball. I don't see what she sees inside it.

"Can I play with your crystal ball?"

"One doesn't play with a crystal ball."

"Can I look in it?"

"Sure, but you don't exactly *look* in a crystal ball either. You gaze in it."

"Isn't that the same as looking?"

"Gazing is looking intently."

"Oh, like when Aunt Manya checks my ears after I wash them, to make sure potatoes aren't growing inside."

"Be careful, don't drop it, or you'll destroy its magic."

Her Tarot cards are creepy. In the movies, the fortuneteller is serious, her face is grim, and the cards she turns over are always bad. But I feel okay with a crystal ball. They're in funny movies, like ones with Abbot and Costello, and the fortuneteller is silly. But Aunt Lilly is serious about her fortune telling.

After she rubs off my fingerprints with a dishtowel, I gaze into her crystal ball and see blurs of color from chipped blue dishes piled high in her sink. I see the reflection of laundry still hanging from a clothesline in the rain. I put Melvin's picture behind the crystal ball. His eyes follow me when I move it. He looks "hard as nails." I got that expression from Dad.

"Melvin, did you kill any Japs at Pearl Harbor? Can I go to California to see you after the war is over and we win?"

I can see my reflection. Since everyone in my family says I look like Mother, I pretend that my face is her face.

"Aunt Manya always hollers on me. She won't let my friends in the house. I can't help peeing in bed when she makes me drink a glass of milk every night before I go to bed. She says bad things about Dad."

Mother doesn't answer no matter how hard I try to hear her. But I know that if she could speak to me, she'd be angry, because Dad almost never visits.

It's still raining, so I have to sleep on the couch. It's hot and I'm drenched. Aunt Lilly and Uncle Tim must be miserable, too. Their bed squeaks for a long time before they get to sleep.

Today is Uncle Tim's day off. We have to be real quiet, because Mrs. Zaleski is in the kitchen, and Aunt Lilly is gazing into the crystal ball. She talks with a deep Gypsy voice.

"Yes, I can see it. A house in the country, children at play, a puppy."

"I hate dogs."

"I said guppy. Children at play, a guppy swimming in a fish bowl."

Uncle Tim and I put our hands over our mouths.

"Your aunt is as full of shit as a Christmas goose," he whispers.

When Mrs. Zaleski leaves, I ask if I can invite Rita over.

"Of course you can, dear."

She climbs in from the fire escape, and we watch as Uncle Tim, wearing a red rubber nose, looks in a mirror and paints black around his eyes, white on his cheeks, and red lips with a happy smile. He puts on a yellow wig and grins and frowns and laughs. He baas like a goat, clucks like a chicken, neighs and roars. I laugh until my nose runs. He paints our faces and puts an orange wig on my head with long hairs sticking out like porcupine quills. We all laugh when I step into his polka-dot clown shoes and clomp around the room, making silly faces.

Best of all is the trick Uncle Tim taught me. I turn around so no one can see, remove the aces and a few extra cards from the deck, and set them aside. I put a rubber band around the deck and cover the sides with the extra cards so the rubber band doesn't show. I push the aces all the way in, stretching the rubber band down inside, and squeeze the deck tight.

"Okay, ready." I face my audience, hold the deck way out in front of me with my right hand, and make a big arc in the air with my other hand, like a real magician. "Abra cadabra, let the aces appear." When I release the pressure on the deck, the aces pop up, and everyone claps.

On the fire escape next morning, Rita shows the trick to her mother, but she releases the pressure on the deck too fast, and the aces fly up in the air, over the railing, and flutter down to the alley.

I wish Uncle Tim could stay home the whole day and play with me, but he's a janitor for Mr. Johnson, who manages the tenements. He lives downstairs, in front, on the first floor. Aunt Lilly calls him a slum landlord. My Uncle Tim used to be a famous clown. He'd never live in a slum. We play cards and drink beer in the morning.

"Gin, I win."

"You lucky little bas... rascal."

Knock, knock.

Aunt Lilly and Uncle Tim put their fingers to their lips to shush me. She cracks open the door as far as the chain will allow.

"Good day, Mrs. O'Connor. Is Tim at home?"

"Oh no, Mr. Johnson. I haven't seen him all morning."

He puts down his beer and laces up his boots.

"I thought I heard his voice a moment ago."

"You're mistaken, Mr. Johnson. I'm sure he's down in the basement tending to the boilers."

He tucks his shirt in his pants and cinches up his belt.

"Are you sure he's not at home, Mrs. O' Connor?"

"Am I sure? Sure I'm sure. I'm very sure."

She blows a kiss to Uncle Tim. He tiptoes to the open window and climbs out on the fire escape. I start to follow, but she grabs my arm.

"Let me see for myself, Mrs. O'Connor."

"You've got to be kidding. Not on your life, Mr. Johnson."

As Mr. Johnson walks down the creaky stairs, she whispers to me, "Never follow Uncle Tim."

Now, I want to follow him all the more.

In the afternoon Rita and I are playing on the fire escape. Uncle Tim climbs out the living room window, pats me on the head.

"Bye, Norman. Bye, Rita." And he's off down the ladder.

If it can hold him, for sure it can hold me.

"Bye, Rita." I pat her head and follow him down, holding tight to each rail and stretching to reach the rungs. I climb down slow and say hello to the woman on the second-floor landing. She stops washing her window and stares at me. I love Uncle Tim and worry about him climbing the fire escape when he's staggering. I walk around potted plants on the first floor landing and climb down the last long ladder to the alley.

Uncle Tim is out of sight. Rita waves and points down the alley. I run by smelly trashcans, cardboard cartons, bundled newspapers, flat white balloons, and a pair of pink panties. At the end of the alley, I turn right toward Livingston Street. I stand behind a woman until the light changes, cross the street with her and look through the open door of a saloon that smells of cigarettes and beer, expecting to find Uncle Tim sitting on a stool with a glass of Schlitz in one hand and a cigarette in the other. A waiter in a long white apron, with a tray of four foamy glasses of beer, serves people at a table, but Uncle Tim isn't there.

I walk up the street and go into an old variety store with a stained wood floor and six black fans hanging from the ceiling. I wish I had a dime in my pocket for a model airplane. Aunt Lilly would let me build it out on her fire escape. I pick up a toy soldier. It's heavy, like the ones Sarah bought for me at the Five and Ten. Aunt Manya made her take them back.

Boxes of Crayolas are on a shelf. I open one to look at the colors and smell the wax, but there's not even a nickel in my pocket. That woman over there just slipped a comb into her purse. What a *gonif*. She knows I saw her do it. She's giving me the look, with her finger to her lips.

I really need these crayons. No one's watching. I can just slide the box into my back pocket and head for the door. But what about the Eighth Commandment, Thou Shalt not Steal? What would Aunt Manya say if she knew I even thought about stealing? She'd say I'd roast in hell.

I leave the store and walk past a smelly beauty parlor where women are sitting with things like big football helmets over their heads, reading *Ladies' Home Journals*. There's a shoe store with a rickety table in front, full of shoes. Shiny black high-heeled ones are in the window. I tried to walk in Aunt Lilly's high heels once.

A movie house. The woman in the cashier's booth is asleep. *Sahara*, with Humphrey Bogart and J. Carrol Naish is playing. I saw it at the Waldorf with Sarah. Humphrey Bogart doesn't take any baloney from anyone. He reminds me of Dad. There's a radio store and a tiny shop that sells knishes. I could eat one right now. A newspaper stand, and a nickel on the sidewalk. I dive for it. The man running the stand gives me a dirty look.

"Hey kid, that's my nickel."

"Finders keepers, Mister."

I run down the block and duck into a candy store. A nickel's not enough for a knish, but it's enough for a strawberry ice cream cone. It's cool in here. While the soda jerk scoops ice cream out of a round cardboard container, I try to pick up another nickel from the pink marble counter. It's glued on. He laughs.

Down the street I walk, turning my sugar cone, chewing off big frozen strawberries, licking the melting ice cream before it drips to my hand. My eyes are on the sidewalk, looking for more coins. I run into a baby carriage, fall down, but don't drop my cone. The scab on my knee is torn open.

"Watch where you're going."

"I'm sorry, lady."

I take out my handkerchief and wipe off the blood trickling down my leg.

Uncle Tim isn't inside the next saloon either. It has sawdust on the floor and a dartboard. A man on the radio is singing my favorite song:

> My Mamma don' tol' me
> When I was in knee pants
> My Mamma don' tol' me, son
> A woman's a two-face
> A worrisome thing
> That'll lead you to sing
> The blues in the night.

I sing along 'til the song is over then turn around and bump into a blue uniform.

"Where's your mother?" the policeman asks.

I want to say she's in Heaven, but instead, I tell him what I wish were true.

"She's at the beauty parlor down the block, getting her hair done."

"Well, you'd better get back to her before you get lost."

"Yes Mr. Policeman." I salute, and he salutes back.

I cross Livingston Street, this time with a crowd of shoppers, then run to the alley and turn left toward the row of garbage cans. All the apartment houses and fire escapes look alike. It's as if I'm lost in a real jungle. There's a familiar metallic taste in my mouth, the same one I get when Dad plays tricks on me, losing me on purpose on crowded sidewalks.

An ace of spades is on the ground. I put it in my back pocket and look for the other ones that flew out of Rita's deck. A rat jumps out of one of the garbage cans. I look up, searching for Rita. There were flowerpots on the first floor landing, but every first floor landing has flowerpots on it.

I run around the block to Livingston Street. The fronts of all the tenements look alike, too. Same stoops, same doorways, same dirty red bricks. I know I can sneak on the subway and find my way back to Aunt Manya's, but she won't be home. And it would be too embarrassing to go to Sophie's house and tell her I got lost.

I'm mad at myself. Aunt Lilly told me that when I draw a picture, I don't miss a trick, I see the tiniest detail. Now I wish I had paid attention. I guess I'll have to go in every building until I find the right one. Here's one with a boarded up window next to the front door. Wrong house. Three houses later, I walk into a dirty foyer and read T. O'Connor on the dull brass mailbox. I wipe sweat off my forehead with my arm and walk past a door that says Mr. Johnson, Manager. Will he peek out like Mr. Mirsky does? I climb up dark wooden steps. The blistered paint and dingy green walls make me sad. It was scary not knowing the number of Aunt Lilly's tenement. I'll never make that mistake again.

The door's unlocked. The apartment smells like lavender. Aunt Lilly is in the kitchen. Her deep Gypsy voice is mysterious. I tiptoe past the doorway. It's Mrs. Feldman, the hard-of-hearing neighbor who's always using the toilet when I need it. She's cupping her hand behind her ear, listening to what Aunt Lilly tells her she's seeing in her crystal ball.

"A check is coming in the mail. A large check. I see a house on Long Island."

Aunt Lilly has on a purple dress, a red bandanna, long gold earrings, and dark red lipstick.

I climb out on the fire escape.

When Mrs. Feldman leaves, Aunt Lilly comes to the window to hand me a peanut butter and jelly sandwich and a cup of coffee with the right amount of cream in it.

"Norman, you were so quiet out there. I thought you were sleeping."

"No, I'm drawing a picture."

I show her a cityscape on a big paper bag. I've finished the blue sky and I'm coloring in the brick buildings in the distance with brown, yellow, and blue.

"My goodness, Norman. You've really captured the shapes and colors."

"Thank you, Aunt Lilly."

"Where did you get that box of Crayolas?"

"Uh… Rita. I borrowed it from Rita."

"Which reminds me, I was going to buy you some when I go shopping later."

I'm sure she won't ever do it. I put the colors back in the box. They remind me of the people I've seen today: The policeman is blue, Aunt Lilly, red, Rita, brown, and Uncle Tim, yellow, the color of beer. The box I stole doesn't have white in it, but if it did, that's the color I'd use for the waiter in the saloon.

Next afternoon. I'm on the fire escape, watching pigeons peck at the breadcrumbs I put out on a plate.

Knock, knock.

That's the third time today.

"Tim O'Connor, I know you're in there."

Uncle Tim puts down his brown quart bottle of Schlitz, pulls on his boots, gets up from his big chair, and scrambles out the window. He pinches my cheek and makes a funny face before he climbs down the fire escape. His boots are unlaced.

"He's not here, Mr. Johnson," Aunt Lilly hollers through the door. "He's at work."

"I've been looking for him all day."

"He's certainly not here."

"May I see for myself, Mrs. O'Connor."

"No, Mr. Johnson. Go to the basement next door, and I'm sure you'll find him slaving for you among the trash cans and the rats."

"I'll do that, Mrs. O'Connor. Yes indeed, I'll do that, although I might point out that there are no rats in any of my buildings."

"On the contrary, Mr. Johnson. My nephew saw a rat only yesterday."

"Norman's been here two weeks now, hasn't he? How is the young lad?"

"Fine, thank you, Mr. Johnson. He's going home today, mind you, so don't be thinking of increasing our rent."

"Wouldn't dream of it, Mrs. O'Connor. Just tell Timothy not to trip over the lad on his way down the fire escape."

Aunt Manya will be here any minute to take me home. Aunt Lilly's house is magical, but I'm tired of peanut butter and jelly sandwiches, liver and onions, and canned vegetables. I miss Aunt Manya's cooking. She doesn't use canned food, except for herring in tomato sauce and tuna. I'll miss Uncle Tim's clowning, Aunt Lilly's fortune telling, Rita, Rita's mother, and the fire escape. Even though Aunt Lilly ignores me most of the time, she does hang my pictures on the walls. But Brownsville is my home, with my real family, my friends, and my school. I wish all the good things could be in one place.

CHAPTER 5

BUT AT LEAST SHE LET'S ME DRAW

I'm on the stoop, reading a *Batman* comic book, and I sneeze.

"*Gesundheit*," says Fat Annie from the sidewalk. Wheezing from her asthma, she waddles over to the stoop, climbs the steps, and reaches into her shopping bag. "For you, Norman, a present."

"No thank you, Annie. I haven't used a coloring book since kindergarten."

She sighs and walks back across the street. I should have taken it. I always hurt her.

I remember the day when I quit using coloring books. I was sitting right here when Henry, the neighborhood handyman, came by to fix the hall light.

"What's that you're doing, Nor-Man?"

"Coloring."

"Why?"

"Because it's fun."

"Fun is good, but coloring books aren't."

"Hen-Ry, you sound like Aunt Manya."

"That may be, but we probably have different reasons."

"Why aren't coloring books good?"

"They make you stay inside the lines."

"But you're supposed to stay inside the lines."

"Let me tell you something, Nor-Man. I've known you since you were born, and I knew your mother. Now, there's something called cre-a-tivity. I bet you have it. And I don't want to see it spoiled by lines that keep you shut in. They are barriers to be overcome. So forget about coloring books. Throw them away, all of them. Draw your own pictures even if they aren't as slick as ones in coloring books. If you draw enough pictures, they will be slick by and by."

I colored in one more picture after Henry went inside, but it wasn't fun anymore. On the walkway next to the apartment house, I threw my coloring book on the paper collection pile next to the garbage can.

Sophie rubs her hands over her tummy. Everyone's talking about the baby she's going to have in three weeks. They only notice me when I sneeze.

"Mamma, the baby's kicking even harder now. Come feel."

Aunt Manya puts her rough hand softly on Sophie's belly and waits. "*Oy*, I remember when you kicked."

Uncle Irving feels. "Hoo hah. My Sophie will soon have her baby."

"You, too, Sarah. Put your hand here. Can you feel it?"

"Feel it? I can see it. I'm so excited."

"Can I feel too?"

"Oh… all right Norman, but don't push. I don't want you to hurt my baby."

"Never mind, I don't want to. *Katchoo*."

"Another sneeze? What, is he coming down with a cold? Keep him away from me. I'll kill him if he comes down with a cold."

Next day, I'm in my cot, coughing loud and long. Mrs. Katzman and Aunt Manya are standing by the bedroom door.

"A fine time for him to come down with something. My Sophie is nearly ready to have her baby, and he has to get sick."

"A little cold Norman has. He'll be better by the time the baby comes."

"If he didn't run naked in the street, without a coat on, he wouldn't be sick."

"I hope you feel better, Norman."

I'm glad Mrs. Katzman is my next-door neighbor. She sticks up for me.

The mustard plasters don't work, or the vaporizer, or the chicken soup. The Vaselined thermometer Aunt Manya sticks up my behind says I have a fever, but she knows that just from touching my forehead with the back of her hand. She bundles me up and takes me on the green Church Avenue trolley to Schenectady Avenue.

"On a Friday I have to take you, on a Friday no less. I have cooking, cleaning, shopping, the floor to wash and wax. Today, the busiest day of the week, I have to take you."

"I'm sorry I'm sick, Aunt Manya."

"You're sorry you're sick? I'm sorry you're sick."

We walk a long block to the doctor's brick house on Linden Boulevard. A plane tree takes up most of his front yard. I step over patches of bark on the lawn so I can get a better look at a black squirrel chirping up in the branches.

"We don't have time for squirrels." Aunt Manya yanks me off the grass and then along a concrete walkway to the ground floor office of Aaron Apfel, M.D. Apfel means apple.

On the floor of Dr. Apfel's waiting room is a red oriental carpet like the one in our living room. The shiny walnut walls smell of wax. There are diplomas on the wall. The biggest one says University of Heidelberg. It's in German, with a big gold seal and ten signatures in shades of blue and black ink that look as if they were written by Aunt Lilly.

Aunt Manya has on her thick reading glasses. She's thumbing through a *Life* magazine. The waiting room is clean but not as clean as her house. There's dust on the Venetian blinds and butts in the ashtray. My cough is raspy. The man next to me moves to another seat.

"You should put your hand over your mouth when you cough."

"I did, Aunt Manya."

The door squeaks open. Doctor Apfel calls us into his treatment room. He's short, has a wrinkled face, and wears glasses as thick as Aunt Manya's. White hair fluffs out from under his black *yarmulke*. He reminds me of Grandfather, except Grandfather doesn't wear a *yarmulke*.

I'm sitting on a black stool, with my shirt off, looking at the skeleton hanging in the corner. There's a chart on the wall with pictures of the heart, lungs and kidneys. Aunt Manya watches Doctor Apfel thump my chest and examine my eyes. He listens to my lungs with a stethoscope. The cold gives me goose bumps. He looks at his watch, takes the thermometer out from under my tongue and holds it up.

"Vun oh vun. A zlight fever. How long has Norman been sick?"

"Sneezing and a runny nose for two weeks already. Now all night he keeps us awake with his coughing."

"Ah so. He has had two veeks coryzal zymptoms, und now paroxysmal coughing vit terminal inspiratory voop. Norman has catarrhal stage pertussis. No shkool until I tell you. He needs lots of rest und he should be very qviet."

"Norman quiet? Impossible."

In the late afternoon Uncle Irving comes home from work. "*Gut Shab-bes*, Manya. How is our Norman?"

"He has the whooping cough, as if I don't have enough troubles."

"Dr. Apple says it's going around," I shout from my cot.

"*Shah*, Norman. You're supposed to be quiet." In a loud voice she says, "Our Sophie's going to have a baby any day now, and Norman decides to get sick."

"Enough, Manya. He didn't get the whooping cough on purpose."

I cough fifteen or twenty times in a row all day long. Each time it hurts worse. I sound like a rooster crowing and cough up phlegm. I run into the bathroom, kneel on the cold black and white tiles, hold the rim with both hands, and vomit into the toilet bowl. It's worse when nothing comes up, when I retch and retch and retch and my stomach turns inside out. Sometimes I rest my head against the cold porcelain. If Sarah is home, she wipes my face with a damp cloth.

A blood vessel bursts in my eye, and the white part gets bright red. No one looks me in the eye. I can't stand to look at myself in the mirror.

Aunt Lilly visits. She brings a big teddy bear and lays it next to me on my army cot. I hug it tight. I've never had one.

Aunt Manya snatches it away. "Where am I going to put a teddy bear in this small apartment? Anyway, he's too old for it."

"I'm n-n-not too old."

"Norman's right. No one is too old for a teddy bear."

"Lilly, don't *hok mir* a *chaynik*." Aunt Manya pushes the teddy bear into Aunt Lilly's arms. "Take it to your house. When Norman visits he can play with it all he wants."

Aunt Lilly doesn't stay long.

Dad doesn't visit.

Sophie has a boy, Abraham. When they come back from the hospital, Aunt Manya spends a lot of time at their house, two blocks away. I spend the time alone, drawing and listening to the radio.

After a few weeks, I stop coughing so much, and it doesn't hurt. Aunt Manya takes me to see Dr. Apfel again, and he says I can go back to school. My eye is still red. The kids don't look directly at me. Mrs. Nussbaum, my teacher, turns her head when I talk to her. Judy tells me not to breathe on her.

"But I'm all better now."

"I don't care. My mother told me to stay away from you."

I blow in her face, and she runs away.

At home, if I turn on a light before it gets really dark, Aunt Manya flips the switch, and hollers, "Don't waste electricity. I'm not made of money." I'm lucky she lets me listen to *Superman* and *The Lone Ranger*, but no matter how low I play them, she says, "Turn the radio down." I have to put my ear to the speaker to hear. She watches the clock, and when the programs are over she says, "Enough already, give the radio a rest."

I can't have a friend over or build a model airplane. I'm not allowed to open the refrigerator without permission. The living room, with plastic covered chairs, sofa, and lampshades, is off limits, except on high holidays, when I can sit with guests if I bring in a chair from the kitchen. I'm not allowed to touch the big wooden radio or the polished wood of the lamp table. I do it when nobody is looking. While everybody talks about the baby, I stare out the back window at a brick apartment house, imagining it's a giant piece of brown paper, drawing in my mind the fishing boat painting hanging on the bathroom wall. I've drawn it a lot. There's some sort of magic in it. When I'm in the tub or on the toilet seat, I keep looking at it and always see something I didn't see before.

Today I'm aboard my favorite fishing boat, sailing out from Sheepshead Bay. The smell of salt air and the wind in my face feels good. I have to pee really bad, so I go to the side of the boat and hold onto the wires that help hold up the mast. I wake up warm and wet and smelling of pee. It's already light outside, but everyone is still sleeping. I hop out of the cot, fold it up, and head for the bathroom.

I'm washing up when Aunt Manya bangs on the bathroom door and turns the knob, but I have the hook on. She curses, stomps across the kitchen, stomps back, sticks a butcher knife through the opening, lifts it to unhook the door, bursts in, and with the knife still in her hand, pushes the wet sheets into my face.

"*A fier auf dir.* You should only get consumption."

"I'm sorry, Aunt Manya. I d-d-didn't d-d-do it on purpose."

"I'll fix you good. I'm taking these sheets to your school. It'll be a great show and tell. I'll do the showing, and you'll do the telling!"

While she's putting fresh sheets on the cot, I pick up the butcher knife from the cutting board and rub my thumb over the sharp point. I poke it into my belly. She'll be sorry! I'll make her see what she's done to me. I stick the knife in until it hurts, then change my mind.

All week, I'm nervous at school. Every time the classroom door opens I expect that Aunt Manya will come through it, carrying the sheets. But even if she doesn't come, I'm nervous anyway. I crouch down in my seat and hide behind my reader when Mrs. Nussbaum expects us to answer questions.

"Norman, name the boroughs of New York City."

It's embarrassing to answer questions that have stutter words for answers, like B-B-Brooklyn and the B-B-Bronx.

"Manhattan, Queens, Staten Island. I d-d-don't remember the rest."

"See me after class, young man."

After class, it doesn't take her long to figure out why I keep saying I don't know. She stops calling on me.

Frankie stutters worse than I do. "Hey, N-N-Norman, does your aunt holler on you for stuttering?"

"Yeah, Frankie, all the time, but it doesn't make it go away."

I blink my eyes more and more. I can't make myself stop. It's worse than stuttering. If I don't talk, people won't know I stutter, but everyone can see me blink. Hardly a day goes by without Aunt Manya hollering on me to stop it or someone in school making fun of me.

Before Mrs. Nussbaum comes into the classroom one morning, Max grabs my shoulders so I can't get away and stands in front of me with his face almost touching mine, blinking his eyes. Except for my friend, Joey, everyone laughs, even Frankie.

Now my lips twitch, and I kick my left foot to one side when I walk. I twitch like Charlene, who has cerebral palsy. Izzy says, "Charlene and Norman are twins." Larry shouts, "They should get married." Phillip hollers, "They belong in an institution!" Besides Joey, Charlene is the only one who wants to play with me. I wish Mother hadn't died because of me. I wish Dad would come to see me more often.

"He'll grow out of it," says Cousin Sarah. She heard that from Joey's mother, who hollers on him almost as much as Aunt Manya hollers on me.

"He'll grow out of it," says Mrs. Katzman. "But what would it hurt to take him to Dr. Apfel? Science is always coming up with a new cure."

"He'll grow out of it," says Doctor Apfel, "and sooner if you don't holler at him."

"There's maybe some medicine for the problem?"

"Ja, Ja, there is." Doctor Apfel writes out a prescription with his black broad-pointed Waterman pen. "Take one of these tablets twice a day, Manya. They'll help you to calm down."

She never fills the prescription, and she never stops hollering. But at least she lets me draw. There's something inside me that makes me want to do it. There's a big pencil sharpener in the kitchen drawer. Uncle Irving promised to screw it onto the inside of the hall closet door, but he never did. I guess he's afraid Mr. Mirsky will get mad. It's hard to hold a pencil in the hole and turn the handle at the same time.

At school, Mrs. Carroll, my new teacher, draws Manhattan on the blackboard using only blue, green, and yellow chalk. She doesn't use the blue for the sky or for the East River, but still, the sky, buildings, Brooklyn Bridge, and water look real. I copy the picture in my notebook. At home, I try different color combinations.

After school, I have the honor of carrying Mrs. Carroll's briefcase to the trolley stop on Hegeman Avenue.

"You know, Mrs. Carroll, at first I didn't like the colors you used on your picture, but when it was done, I liked them a lot."

"Did you learn anything Norman?"

"Yeah. I learned that there are different ways to see things."

"Good for you. I enjoy having you in my class."

I ask Aunt Manya for a piece of paper. She throws a brown grocery bag on the table. "Draw on this. It's a sin to waste paper."

I wish there were more Crayola colors. If I were an artist, I'd paint Mrs. Carroll's scene on a canvas. I'd paint everything in oils, like the pictures at the Brooklyn Museum. Sarah took me there, and I saw an artist copying a landscape. He was wearing a brown beret, and he had on a brown smock so he wouldn't get his clothes dirty and get hollered on. His painting looked just like the one on the wall. He was holding a big oval palette with lots of colors on it. His easel had a drawer filled with tubes of paint. He was putting in a speck of red with a tiny brush, and he needed a stick to rest his hand on. That was the greatest day of my life.

I wish I had a drawer full of oil paints. I'd mix other colors into the reds, make them darker or lighter, until they matched a chicken's blood or

Aunt Manya's face when she's raving at me.

Mrs. Carroll points to the cursive letters across the top of the blackboard. She believes in good penmanship. "If you don't want to get a ruler smartly smacked against the back of your hand, you'd better hold your pencil my way. That goes for you, too, Norman."

She's not gonna smack me. I'm her star pupil. But I wish I could write like Dad instead of like Aunt Lilly. Dad has the best handwriting in the world. He writes better than the monks in monasteries did before they invented the typewriter. I'm tired of holding my pen Mrs. Carroll's way. It makes my hand ache. It makes me write worse than Aunt Lilly.

Today the class is learning how to sing. I make believe I'm doing it. Suddenly, Mrs. Carroll is standing right next to me.

"Norman, I can't hear you. Louder, I can't hear you." Everybody stops. "Repeat after me, la, la la la, la la la."

"I can't d-d-do it. I d-d-don't know how to sing."

"Everyone knows how to sing."

"Not me, Mrs. Carroll."

When Sarah's favorite radio station is on, it's fun to sing along, especially since I know most of the songs by heart. Sarah says she doesn't hear me stutter when I sing, but I can't take any chances. Kids will tease me. Joey is behind Mrs. Carroll, drawing his index finger across his throat.

"Let me hear you sing la, la la la, la la la."

"I can't."

You can."

"No, I can't.

She slaps my face. I sing la, la la la, la la la with a choked up voice and never again carry Mrs. Carroll's briefcase to her trolley stop.

Uncle Irving comes home with a package under his arm. He sets it on the table, opens it. "Give a feel, Manya. This cashmere is quality, an end piece left over from Rabbi Zimmerman's overcoat."

I stop drawing to watch Uncle Irving unfold the brown cloth.

"For my grandson, Abraham, only the best."

"Can I give a feel, too, Uncle Irving?"

"Only if your hands are clean."

At the kitchen table, he lays patterns over the material and draws their outlines with tailor's chalk. He hums as he cuts with large shears. He pins the cloth together and handles it as tenderly as if it were Abraham himself. I pick up the scraps from the floor.

I draw Uncle Irving in his black *yarmulke* leaning over his Singer sewing machine, feet treadling, wheel spinning, fingers guiding material under the needle. He's part of his machine. His seams are perfect, like the design of the metalwork on the treadle.

He smiles as he snips off loose thread, re-threads the needle, and re-winds spools. Will he ever sew something for me? A coat, maybe a vest? But he never has.

Nathan is home on leave, handsome in his army uniform with ribbons on his chest. We're sitting on the stoop. His army hat is on my head. He fishes pennies out of his pocket, hands them to me one by one as I read the dates, looking for a 1909-S VDB.

Aunt Manya is watching from the doorway. "Nathan, don't give those pennies to Norman. If you don't want them, throw them away."

When Aunt Manya leaves, Nathan gives me the rest of his pennies. I try not to show that I'm hurt. He takes out his wallet and gives me a dollar bill to go with the pennies.

"Don't tell your aunt… You know, Norman, I'm no stranger to my mother's excitable ways. Sometimes she says something or does something without thinking about the consequences. When I was in high school, she threw a fork at me, and it stuck in my forehead before it fell on the floor."

"I hope she doesn't throw one at me."

"She won't. That was when she was sick. She had a nervous breakdown when your mother died. And I'll tell you what made her better, the movies. Dr. Apfel prescribed frequent movies to take her mind off the tragedy. That's why she goes on Thursday afternoons."

"She sends me on Thursdays when she doesn't like what's playing, 'cause that's when they give away free dishes."

"I believe it, knowing Ma."

Chapter 6

Boardwalk Blues

Dad bends down to kiss me, and I smell Old Spice after-shave lotion. He hasn't been here for six weeks, but I'm so thrilled that I forget, almost, the disappointment I feel every Thursday, when he says he'll be here, when I sit on the stoop and wait for him the whole day. I don't go to the playground, because if Aunt Manya is at the movies, no one will be at home, and he'll leave.

All the windows in the house are wide open. It's hot, but Dad never sweats. He looks like a million bucks in his gray, double-breasted pinstriped suit. He's sitting across the table from me, sipping from the glass of coffee Aunt Manya gave him. I try not to stutter or blink my eyes, but it happens anyway. Dad doesn't say anything about my stuttering and blinking. I gobble a bowl of kasha.

He's my hero. He speaks six foreign languages and English with an Austrian accent. He's funny. When he slides his open palm behind my ear and pulls out a nickel, I giggle, and the kasha slides down my chin and into the bowl.

Dad has perfectly square sideburns, a pencil-thin moustache, and black hair combed straight back. He's built like a jockey I saw in a newsreel, all muscle. He tells me he doesn't take any baloney from anybody. People are afraid of him, but not Aunt Manya. She's standing in the middle of the kitchen bent over her ironing board. There's a glass of water on top. She lifts the glass, sucks up a mouthful of water, spritzes it over Uncle Irving's shirt, and irons it with a sizzling sound.

"Benny, that's a beautiful suit you have on. It must have cost a pretty penny."

"Thank you, Manya. My brother-in-law, Morris, gave it to me. It doesn't fit him anymore."

"Whatever you say. Norman's clothes don't fit him any more either. See what he's wearing? Instead of taking him to Coney Island, you should maybe take him to Pitkin Avenue? He needs shoes, socks, knickers, shirts.

Look at the one I'm about to iron! It's a *schmata*. You'd like I should make a shopping list?"

"Manya, it's a nice summer day. Norman would rather go to Coney Island than Pitkin Avenue."

"Then at least leave some money, and I'll take him."

Dad's jaw muscles twitch. With his back to Aunt Manya, he pulls out a wallet stuffed with money and hands over three ten-dollar bills.

"People haven't been tipping so well this week. I'm a little short of cash."

She snatches up the money, squashes it in her fist, and glares at him. As usual, she doesn't kiss me goodbye when we leave, but I'm with Dad.

Out on the sidewalk he looks sad. He had to give Aunt Manya some of his gambling money.

"Melvin," he says after lighting up a cigarette, "how do we get to Coney Island from here?"

"My name is Norman."

"Okay, how do we get to Coney Island?"

"Follow me."

This is a test. No one can find his way around New York better than Dad. I take him two blocks to Church Avenue, where there's a Mobil gas station with a big red flying horse that lights up at night. We get on the green trolley that goes to the subway station in Flatbush. As it hums along the tracks, I point to the pet store where Uncle Irving buys tropical fish, Yellin's bakery, where Aunt Manya buys *challah*, pumpernickel, and rye bread, and the Chinese restaurant, where Cousin Sarah takes me after movies at the Waldorf.

"Aunt Manya doesn't like us to go to the Chinese restaurant, because the food isn't kosher. She tells Sarah never to eat *traife*, but Sarah eats it and makes me promise not to tell. I don't tell on her, because I don't want to be a squealer and a dirty rat. I get mad when she asks me to try some pork or shellfish and holler on her for even suggesting such a thing."

Dad's not listening to me. He's reading the paper. He reads morning and evening newspapers and knows all about the war, crime in New York City, and horseracing. I don't talk to him anymore until we get to the train station.

On the train, there are lots of families carrying beach stuff. When I go to Coney Island with Uncle Irving, Aunt Manya, and my cousins, we wear old clothes. Nathan carries our big yellow umbrella, and the rest of us lug blankets, sandwiches, lotions, towels, iced coffee, water, and a beach ball. How can Dad play on the beach in a suit and tie? Maybe he's wearing his bathing suit underneath his pants, like I am. Maybe we can go for a swim and then dry out in the sun.

"Coney Island. Here's our stop."

I try to take Dad out on the beach, but he doesn't want to get sand on his Florsheims. So we walk on the Boardwalk, where I have to run to keep up. With him, everything is rush, rush, rush. We can't play with a beach ball on the white sand or swim in the gray ocean.

Boys are working on the Boardwalk, pushing people in yellow, two-seater rolling cars.

"Your brother, Melvin, used to push those cars."

All he can talk about is Melvin. Until he joined the navy, Melvin lived in California with his mother, Renee, Dad's first wife. I saw pictures of him at Aunt Lilly's. He looked like Dad. Aunt Lilly had me look in her makeup mirror and cover my mouth and nose. When she put her hand over the mouths and noses of the pictures of Dad and Melvin and herself, we looked alike. I felt that I belonged to Dad's side of the family, too. I'm glad Melvin didn't get hurt at Pearl Harbor. Maybe some day I'll get to meet him.

"Pushing those cars looks like fun. I wanna do that when I'm old enough." Pushing is a stutter word, but I don't stutter or blink as much when I'm with Dad.

"Did you ever take Melvin swimming?" I'm talking to myself. He's marching ahead of me. I run to catch up, hold his hand, ask him to walk a little slower. He pulls away to light up another cigarette.

Boys are down below on the sand, playing catch with an orange beach ball. Dad never plays catch with me. Cousin Nathan and I used to play on the beach. He carried me on his shoulders into deep water, but I felt safe with him. He bought me ice cream from one of the men, dressed in white, selling Good Humor Bars out of a silver ice chest.

Dad doesn't look back to see if I'm following, and I'm afraid I'll lose him in the crowd. Would he come looking for me?

"There's the bumper cars. There's the bumper cars." I catch up and tug him over to the entrance. "Can we go on them?"

"You're too young."

"No, I'm not. I drive them when I'm here with Cousin Sarah."

We buy tickets and walk into a room as big as the Waldorf movie house. I pick out a bright blue car. Dad climbs in after me.

"I'll show you how to drive."

The power comes on, and the cars buzz. I turn the wheel, smack into a yellow car and send it spinning. Another car smacks into ours. Flashes of blue light arc from the wire mesh ceiling. Sarah explained all that to me, and I explain it to Dad. "That funny smell, it's ozone."

Suddenly, all the cars stop, and the other drivers get out.

"Can we go again?"

"Just once more."

"Hurray! This time I want my own car."

When the power comes on, he doesn't bump his red car into any others, and I don't bump into his, because I don't think it's right to bump your own father. He's not smiling.

A green car, driven by a sailor, crashes into Dad's and bounces off. I'm gonna get that guy. I slam into the side of the green car, give it one, two, three big jolts before the power goes off and the ride is over. I look back proudly at Dad, but his face is stone, just like Aunt Lilly's face when she's telling someone's fortune.

Outside, soldiers and sailors are walking along the Boardwalk. I wish the war would end so I could have Nathan back again from wherever the Army sent him. I always have fun with him. The Boardwalk is crowded and noisy when we get near the Parachute Jump. Riders drift out of the sky, screaming. Boy, it's a long way up there. I don't think I'll ever get up enough nerve to go on that ride.

It's hard to enjoy Coney Island, because I have to keep an eye on Dad. There's so much to do, but he just keeps on walking. I tug on his arm, try to get him to look a man carrying so many red, yellow, and blue helium-filled balloons that he could fly.

There's the smell of hot dogs, cotton candy, warm pretzels, and the creosote from the Cyclone's wooden framework. Riders are quiet on the way up, but they're screaming when they whoosh down the steep slope.

I've lost Dad. There's that metallic taste in my mouth again. It happens when he hides from me. He likes to do that, but I don't care. I know how to get back home. Anyway, I'm not having much fun. There he is! He's not hiding this time. I grab his hand. He looks out of place in a suit and tie and hat. He probably doesn't even own a bathing suit.

A carny with a teddy bear in his hands is standing in front of a shooting gallery, barking at the crowd. He's as tall as a basketball player, and he's got big muscles covered with blurry old tattoos.

"Try your luck?" He holds out the teddy bear for me to take, but Dad pulls me away. "What about the kid? Too cheap to buy him a ticket?"

Dad swings around to face the man. I'm afraid. The carny's a giant.

"What did you say?" Dad's voice is low and sinister, like Sidney Greenstreet in the *Maltese Falcon*. His huge hands turn into fists, and he stares straight into the carny's eyes.

The carny's lips twitch, and his eyes blink. "Here, take the teddy bear, it's for the kid."

Dad grabs the bear by its ears, rips it in half, and throws it at the carny's feet. He grabs my wrist and pulls me along the Boardwalk. I keep looking back, afraid the man might try to shoot him with one of his rifles.

"I wanted that teddy bear."

He doesn't answer, and he doesn't look back.

In a Boardwalk café, I sit across from him, squirting ketchup on a hamburger. He empties a tiny jar of cream into his coffee cup, stirs in two level teaspoonfuls of sugar, then pours some of his coffee into the jar for me.

"Don't tell Manya that I let you drink coffee."

He sees me looking at his large, powerful hands.

"When I used to wring out your diapers, I'd tear them in half."

I don't think he ever washed my diapers. Melvin's maybe, but not mine.

"Did Melvin ever have a teddy bear?"

"I don't know."

"Did Melvin ever see me?"

"When you were a baby."

"Did he ever see Mother?"

"He lived with us in Tuckahoe before you were born.

"Where's Tuckahoe?"

"North of New York City."

"What was Mother like?"

"Smart, good looking, very particular about things. A picture on the wall, for instance, had to be in the right place, to the fraction of an inch."

"Did she go to movies a lot?"

"I don't remember."

"Did she read a lot?"

"I don't know."

"What kind of stories did she read?"

"I don't know. I don't know. You're asking too many questions."

Dad's nicest when he sits at a table in a restaurant, smoking a cigarette, drinking coffee, and talking to me instead of reading a newspaper. But I guess I don't know the right questions, because I'm not getting the answers. I wish he would tell me about Mother.

I'm blinking my eyes now. Maybe teddy bears aren't important to him, but they are to me. I suppose that even if Dad hadn't thrown this one away, Aunt Manya wouldn't let me bring it in the house.

At the trolley stop near home, he kisses me goodbye. He isn't going to face Aunt Manya again today. I go home, thinking we should have gone shopping for clothes on Pitkin Avenue instead.

CHAPTER 7

WAR AND DENTISTRY

I keep my eyes and ears open, as Aunt Manya says, and learn a lot of things besides what I'm taught in school. So much happens in 1944. I hear about places where many of our soldiers died. They have a funeral for Sammy Kaplan, who lived across the street, on the second floor of Joey's building, but his body isn't there. He died storming Anzio Beach on January 22nd. The newspaper said Anzio is twenty-five miles outside of Rome. Men from Brownsville died in the Pacific, kicking the Japanese out of Kwajalein Island on February 6th. Many died when they landed on Omaha and Utah Beaches on the Normandy coast of France on June 6th, D-Day. In Europe they were under the command of General Eisenhower. Dad says Ike is a great general, almost as great as General Pershing, whom Dad served under during World War I. Dad talks about trenches, gas masks, and mustard gas sometimes, but when I ask questions, he changes the subject.

I barely fit under my desk for air raid drills. Sneakers are hard to find. The only ones Aunt Manya can buy for me leave black marks on the kitchen floor, and she won't let me wear them inside. Uncle Irving, Mr. Mirsky, and I stomp on tin cans to flatten them so they can be melted down and reused in the war effort. I collect scrap metal, rubber, paper, and cardboard cartons, haul them in my friend Seymour's red wagon, and add them to the piles by the garbage cans.

In the kitchen drawer, Aunt Manya has books of ration coupons. Today, I'm with her in a long line in front of Friedman's on Pitkin Avenue, waiting to buy nylons, one pair per customer. When we get them, she drags me down the block to the end of the line, and we start over again.

At night, after the war news, Sarah turns the dial to her music station, and I sing with the radio *I'll Walk Alone*, *Sentimental Journey*, *You're Nobody Till Somebody Loves You*, and *You Always Hurt the One You Love*.

"Eat your heart out Mrs. Carroll," Sarah says when I belt out *Sentimental Journey*. "She should *gey in drerd arayn*, a teacher who slaps my little cousin for not singing."

"I think she should go to hell, too, but only for a few weeks."

"Norman, you're too kind."

The dentist's waiting room smells of cloves and cigarette smoke. In the corner, butts stick out of the sand in a tall chrome ashtray. There's a sliding glass window and a frosted glass door with gold letters on it that says Bernard Bass, DDS. A woman with a tummy big enough to hold the Dionne quintuplets is sitting on a brown couch by the window, holding an ice bag to her cheek. When the man next to her looks down at his watch, the ash from his cigarette falls on the floor. The door opens, and a man comes out, biting on a big wad of cotton that has blood on it.

"Aunt Manya, we should come back some other time. It looks like Dr. Bass is very busy."

She keeps thumbing through a two-year old *National Geographic*. I hope my teeth are okay. Aunt Manya and Uncle Irving keep their false teeth in water glasses in the bathroom. When they get up in the morning, they sprinkle Wernet's adhesive powder into their dentures and press them onto their gums. Sometimes Aunt Manya's upper denture slips down when she's talking, and she has to add more powder.

The window slides open, and a girl in a white uniform says, "Mrs. Lipschitz, Dr. Bass will see you now." She pushes herself off the couch and walks in.

At school this morning, I told Joey and Seymour that I was going to the dentist. Joey said, "I'd rather get beat up by Max than go to Dr. Bass for a filling. The pain is gosh awful."

"Getting a tooth pulled is even worse," Seymour said. "That's when Dr. Bass rests his knee on your chest while he yanks out your tooth with a big pair of pliers that has blood all over it. Your blood."

"Look at Norman. His face is white."

The window slides open again, and the girl says, "Norman, Dr. Bass will see you now." Aunt Manya told me that she's the dentist's daughter and assistant. She leads me into a room and tells me to sit in a big, cream-colored chair with a black headrest that looks like Sal's barber chair. She puts a white bib on my chest. The chain is cold on my neck.

Connected to the chair are a tiny white toilet bowl with a gurgling whirlpool of water, a white tray with a tiny mirror and sharp pick on it, and a giant chrome swing-arm with pulleys and a gray cord that's attached to a drill. Out the window I can see my second-floor classroom across the street. I'd rather be at school.

Mrs. Lipschitz's screak from the next room hurts my ears. I start to wiggle out of the chair while I still have the chance, but Dr. Bass comes in and washes his hands in the sink by the door, blocking my escape. He's wearing glasses with a silver frame, a white shirt with a wide collar, and he looks like Spencer Tracy in *Boys Town*. His cheeks are puffy. Maybe his collar is too tight. He speaks softly, like Uncle Irving, but I think he can be "hard as nails" if he has to be. His fingernails are short, and they're clean, too, now that he's scrubbed off the blood. He picks up the mirror and pick, says "open wide," and pokes around in my mouth.

"Does this hurt, does that hurt?" he asks and calls out mysterious letters and numbers for the girl to write in my chart.

"Yeow!" A jolt of pain makes me lean back hard in the chair. A couple of more yeows later the exam is over.

On Tuesday after school I'm not so crazy about going back to see Dr. Bass all by myself, but it's better to be tortured than to get in trouble with Aunt Manya. Another bib, another cold chain. Dr. Bass picks up his drill, tells me to open wide, and starts working on my tooth right away, whistling, actually hissing more than whistling, a breathy "Whistle While You Work" from *Snow White and the Seven Dwarfs* that I'd seen at the Ambassador on free-dish-day. I didn't expect a dentist to whistle a happy tune while he's killing me in the chair. I sink so deep into the headrest that it feels as if it's made of concrete. "Does this hurt?" he asks a bunch of times but doesn't give me a chance to answer. I keep my eyes on the fuzzy connection of the gray cord that goes 'round and 'round, making the drill work. He drills deeper and deeper, and his whistling gets louder and louder. I close my eyes and suffer jolts of electric yellow pain. Tears stream down my face. My back and armpits are wet. When the drilling stops, so does the whistling. I hope the torture is over. Uh, oh. He's picking around on another tooth. He says hmm, and drills and whistles again. More jolts of pain. "Just a little more, just a little more," he mumbles. At last, he hangs up his drill, and the girl wipes my forehead with a damp towel.

"Dr. Bass, could you tell me everything you've done?"

"Sure, Norman. I've drilled out deep decay in K and 19 that was very close to the nerve. Here they are on your chart, in blue pencil. The circles with letters on top are baby teeth. Adult teeth have numbers... Tofflemire, please." He holds it up for me to see. "This band goes around your tooth, like this. I'll snug it up, and so it won't slip off, I'll push this wedge between the band and the tooth next to it with this mirror handle."

Compared to the drilling, the pain from the band and the wedge isn't worth another yeow.

"I don't need to put a band on number 19, because it's a one surface filling... Sedative dressing."

The girl mixes a white paste.

"This has eugenol in it, oil of cloves. It's what gives my office its distinctive smell. I'll *schmear* it over the deepest areas of your cavities. It's soothing to the pulp... Zinc cement."

The girl taps out some white powder on a glass slab, adds a few drops of liquid, and mixes it with a silver tool.

"This cement goes over the sedative dressing. It sets up hard. You need something hard under the filling so it won't break... Hi ho silver."

"Pappa always says that when he wants me to mix the silver and the mercury," the dentist's daughter says.

"Is this okay?"

"It's too wet!" He dumps the blob on a round piece of white cloth and squeezes out drops of mercury that plop on the instrument tray and bounce onto the floor. "Hmm, just right. Now I'll scoop up the silver with this amalgam carrier. See this lever, Norman? When I push on it, the plunger will force the silver into your tooth... like this."

The silver squeaks. After a few minutes, he removes the wedge and the band and carves down the filling. He tells me to bite lightly on a strip of blue paper that looks like typewriter ribbon, carves some more, tells me to bite again, and takes the napkin off my chest.

"Don't eat for two hours."

I wipe my eyes with the back of my hand. "Dr. Bass, what makes the drill go around?"

He lets me step on the foot pedal to make the drill spin. He shows me the bottles of mercury, the silver powder, and the mortar and pestle his daughter used to mix them.

"Mr. Gibalowitz has a mortar and pestle. He owns the drugstore downstairs from my house."

"I know Mr. Gibalowitz. He's my patient."

"I want to be a dentist when I grow up… Can I watch you drill on the next patient?"

"Uh, no, I can't do that, Norman."

"Okay, I'll be back for the other two fillings."

On the walk home, Roosevelt and Dewey pamphlets litter the street like snow. Dr. Bass and his daughter were wearing Roosevelt buttons on their uniforms. My classmates have them on their blouses, and caps, and I have three of them on my shirt.

Today is Election Day. Aunt Manya and Uncle Irving love President Roosevelt. They go to PS 165 to vote first thing in the morning. All day long, people walk by my house on their way to vote. I wish I were old enough. I'd vote for President Roosevelt, too.

This November night, the family sits around the kitchen table and listens to the returns. Aunt Manya shakes her fist at the radio whenever the announcer mentions Thomas E. Dewey.

"I don't like the name, Dewey," she says.

"I don't like his Hitler moustache," Cousin Sarah says.

"Me neither," I say. "Anyway, Dewey is a Republican. We wouldn't like him even if he didn't have a moustache."

"Hoo Hah," Uncle Irving shouts when the announcer says that President Roosevelt wins. I'm happy. Now he can begin his fourth term and end the blackouts, rationing, and gold stars in windows. And I can have Cousin Nathan and Cousin Sol back.

Chapter 8

Serenade Melancholia

I'm nine years old. My eyes still burn. Aunt Manya walked by the bathroom this morning before breakfast, peeked in, and didn't approve of my five-second, two-finger cold water rinse off, so she grabbed my collar, yanked me over to the kitchen sink, picked up a stinky bar of Fels Naphtha soap and a blue face cloth and scrubbed my face her way.

A pot full of salty water sits on the kitchen counter, and next to it is a pile of raw chicken guts. Aunt Manya butchering the chicken, the white feathers stuffed into the garbage bag under the sink, these are great things to draw. Her hands are red. She's pulling eggs without shells from the slippery chicken belly while hollering on me about Dad's... what's that word she uses?... shortcomings.

"He promised to visit every other week. He promised to take you shopping for clothes on Pitkin Avenue. And where's the money for your upkeep?"

I pick up a few grains from a box of Kosher salt on the wooden counter and put them in my mouth to give my mouth something to do. I'd defend Dad, but who knows what she'd do.

When she leaves the kitchen, the chicken's mine to explore. The hen's rough neck looks like her neck. The eggs are squishy, the liver, slimy, the feet, rubbery. I touch the edge of the bloody butcher knife. It's not as sharp as her tongue.

"He should only get consumption, your father," she says when she comes back.

Uncle Irving pokes his head out of the bathroom, his face covered with shaving cream. "Manya, enough already. Leave the boy alone."

"Leave him alone? Who's bothering him? Who's touching him? I can't make a comment in my own kitchen?"

The yellow chicken came from Solomon's butcher store on East 98th Street, six blocks away, where we went early in the morning, after the face washing and after breakfast, so she could pay two cents a pound less than at Manny's butcher store down the street. It embarrasses me to walk anywhere with her because of her black mustache.

"Aunt Manya, I thought you only buy meat from Manny. You said his meat is the best."

"Never mind what I said. Two cents a pound is two cents a pound."

I draw her as she picks up the chicken by its legs and plops it into the black brine pot to soak for hours. I draw her black moustache, thick, silver-rimmed glasses, black hair covered by a pink babushka, her red face, and hands strong enough to lift me up and throw me into the pot of brine.

For dinner, we sit down to a roasted chicken and all the good things that come with it. Uncle Irving is at the head of the table in his black *yarmulke*. He reaches over to dip his fork full of chicken into the big puddle of ketchup on my plate. Cousin Sarah sits next to me, asks me about school, pinches my cheek, tells me what a sweet boy I am. Then she pinches me one too many times, and I pinch her.

"No fighting," Aunt Manya says. She turns to me. "Eat, eat, eat. You're too skinny. To be healthy is to have some meat on your bones."

She smiles when I tell her I like her cooking. But the smile goes away when she talks about Dad.

"Your father, the big spender." Her spit sprays on my food. "He goes to the racetrack with the money that should pay for your dinner, following horses that follow other horses. He should only roast in hell."

I'm not hungry now.

When I think I'll never see Dad again, he shows up, and my unhappiness goes away in a second. We sit on the stoop while Aunt Manya complains about her *tsuris*, her troubles.

"What about your sore ass?" Dad says.

That makes me giggle. Aunt Manya glares at us. I fidget with my feet, waiting for Dad to take me to my favorite Chinese restaurant across from the Waldorf theater where there will be just the two of us, but Aunt Manya keeps complaining about her aches and pains, rising prices, clothes I've outgrown, and money for my care. As she goes on and on my father's jaw muscles twitch.

A fiddler is playing in the courtyard of Joey's apartment house across the street. Aunt Manya stops talking. The music echoes off the brick walls, making me feel peaceful. When he stops, people toss coins from apartment windows. He lays his violin and bow on the ground, gathers the coins into a black leather pouch on his belt, and heads across the street to play for us. His clothes have holes in them. Some of his front teeth are gone. Dad keeps wincing while the man plays even though it sounds good to me. When he's done, Dad speaks to him in Yiddish, and he hands over his violin and bow. Dad practices bowing, turning the pegs until he's satisfied with the sound. Then he plays the saddest music I've ever heard. The fiddler looks at us, nods, and says, "Ah, *Serenade Melancholia*, Tchaikovsky."

Aunt Manya's face softens. She takes out her hankie, wipes her tears. Passersby stop to listen. Their jaws drop like they're amazed, but they're not as amazed as I am—Dad never told me he could play the violin. By the time Dad finishes playing there's a big crown gathered around us. Except for Aunt Manya, we all clap our hands, and I clap the loudest. Dad hands the violin and bow back, takes out his wallet, and gives the man two dollars. Other people give the man money, too.

"*Danke, danke*," the fiddler says and hurries down the street.

"Two dollars?" Aunt Manya says before the man is out of earshot. "You paid too much, Benny."

She suggests that Dad take me to a Jewish restaurant. "You shouldn't let him eat *traife*. He'll get sick like last time, and I'm the one who'll have to sit with him, not you."

"Okay Manya, okay. I'll take him to David's, on Saratoga Avenue."

But we walk to Church Avenue instead.

"Dad, there's the pet store. I wanna show you the swordtails and angelfish."

He follows me inside but isn't interested in tropical fish. He does spend some time scratching the head of a droopy-eared basset hound puppy.

"I wish I had a dog."

He ignores me.

We walk up the street to my favorite Chinese restaurant. He let's me order chicken chop suey and then ice cream for dessert.

"How are you treated at home?"

"Aunt Manya says bad things about you. She hollers all the time. She's always wishing consumption on me. When you're not here, I'm lonely."

Dad doesn't have anything to say about my complaints.

The bill comes. We both add the column of figures in our heads. Dad's faster, of course. He leaves the waiter a big tip and gives me two silver dollars. When he looks at his watch I know it's time for him to go away.

"I'll walk you to the station. You know, I miss you already, and you haven't even left yet."

He doesn't answer.

"When will you be back?"

He shrugs.

"Can you teach me how to play the violin?"

"You're too old. You should have started when you were four."

At the Saratoga Avenue station he kisses me on the cheek, drops a nickel into the slot, pushes his way through the turnstile, and walks up another flight to the tracks without turning around to wave a last goodbye.

I'm always sad when Dad has to go, but this time I'm twice as sad. He played the violin better than the street musician did. I want to be a violinist, too, but it's too late. I feel lonelier than I did before Dad came. I won't see him for weeks. Maybe he'll never come back. Aunt Manya is right to be mad at him, but I wish she wouldn't take it out on me. The other day, I overheard her complaining to Mrs. Katzman that the few good things about him are just for show.

"Strangers he gives tips. For Norman's care he gives *gornisht*, nothing. Norman admires his talent, his manliness, his *chutzpa. Oy*, does he have *chutzpa*. But Norman doesn't see his dark side. He's not here when Norman needs him the most. The boy was broken-hearted when he didn't show up at Sophie's wedding. He wanted Benny to see him in his tuxedo."

Dad keeps promising to take me to the American Museum of Natural History, the Bronx Zoo, and a Yankee's game, but he's like his sisters, he doesn't keep his promises. Thinking about the violin I'll never have makes me cry on the inside.

I stop feeling sorry for myself when I get to the corner of Strauss and Newport, two blocks from home. A boy who can't walk lives here. On warm days, like today, he's on his cot on the wide sidewalk. People are sitting on folding chairs and a couple of them are on the edge of his cot, the same kind I sleep on in Sarah's room. Next to him are a checkerboard, playing cards, and a blue beach ball.

He's looking at me, maybe wishing he could walk, while I'm wishing I had people around me like he does. He turns over, knocks the ball to the ground, and it bounces down the street. I run after it, dribble it back. I want to sit on the edge of his cot, too. I want to talk to him, be his friend, play checkers with him. But everyone's watching. All of a sudden, I'm very shy. I toss the ball to him and run home.

CHAPTER 9

ONE IN A MILLION

Here I am at the Metropolitan Museum of Art with my fifth-grade class and my teacher, Mrs. Glick. When I asked permission to go on this field trip, just to be safe, I told Aunt Manya that we were going to the American Museum of Natural History. I've been here before with Cousin Sarah. We spent five hours just looking at paintings, checking off the rooms on the museum map so we wouldn't miss any. It was one of the greatest days of my life.

Mrs. Glick isn't fun like Sarah. She jerks my hand away from a marble sculpture. While I'm rubbing where her nails dug into my skin, she shoves her wrinkled face into mine and with her teeth locked together hisses, "Don't touch anything, Norman." It's hard for me not to.

She rushes us past interesting stuff, Egyptian mummies and medieval armor and weapons, and spends a lot of time on Greek vases and paintings of Jesus and his mother with gold halos. I don't know why a Jewish teacher is so interested in *goyishe* paintings. Anyway, they sure didn't know how to draw in those days. They made babies look like little grownups. I can draw better babies and better hands. Cousin Sarah says I'm the greatest drawer she's ever seen, for a ten-year-old.

"Hey, Joey, lemme have a piece of paper. I forgot to bring my notebook. And a pencil, too, please."

I sit on the wooden floor, copying a painting done in the fifteenth century. The mother's hands are too long and skinny, and she looks as if she has a stomachache, so I change things. I make the baby look like my cousin Abraham, with chubby arms and legs, and I leave off the halos and make the mother's hands and fingers look real. And I change the expression on the mother's face so her stomachache can go away. At home, I'll pink up the baby's skin with Crayolas, which have become the oil paints that Aunt Manya won't let me use in her house.

There's lots of giggling in the next room. "That lady's naked."

"Seymour," Mrs. Glick says, "unclothed figures in paintings and sculptures are referred to as nudes." She spots Joey with his hands cupped in front of his chest like he's holding two grapefruits. "That will be enough, Joey," she says, pointing her finger at him. Her high-pitched voice makes me hold my hands over my ears to keep the sound out.

There's a landscape with a bunch of cows. I've never seen a live cow, just ones in movies, but these look real enough to moo. Next to it is a seascape by Jongkind that's almost as good as the one hanging on the wall in the bathroom at home. He used the same colors. I wish I could paint like him. His painting makes me smell the salt air.

There's no one in this room any more. Mrs. Glick is hurrying the class through the museum, but I'll take my time.

In the next gallery are the faces Rembrandt painted three hundred years ago. Sarah says he was one of the greatest artists in the world. His paintings are looking at me. When I walk around, their eyes follow. They look like kind people, like Mrs. Katzman and Mr. Gibalowitz. I want to paint like Rembrandt. I want to paint a picture of Mother that looks as if it's breathing. If I could do that, I'd know I was an artist. And I'm gonna sign my paintings with my first name, like he did.

Rembrandt won't let me leave this room. The paint on his self-portrait looks like it's still wet, especially around his eyes. My eyes are wet, too. How can a painting make me teary when I couldn't be teary at Mother's grave? I wipe my eyes on my sleeve. Did Rembrandt's lips move? Did he blink his eyes? I guess I'm imagining things. I'm gonna keep coming here until I find out how he did his magic.

I see *Washington Crossing the Delaware*, *The Horse Fair*, *Sargent's Madame X*. It's more fun looking at the paintings without Mrs. Glick telling me what I should feel or what the artist was trying to say. I'll go to all the museums and art galleries in New York City. I'll go to the Brooklyn Library and read about painting and about artists. I won't let anyone stop me from becoming an artist.

I head back to the lobby. What did I do with my drawing? It's probably in one of the rooms, and it'll take forever to find. It's time to go, and there's no sign of my classmates. I'll run to the subway and catch up with them. If not, I know how to get back to Brooklyn.

After dinner, I flatten a brown grocery bag and draw Aunt Manya, in side view, bent over the sink, washing dishes. I leave out her moustache. If I draw enough pictures, I'll get so good at it that she'll let me paint. This portrait is my best yet thanks to Rembrandt.

Someone comes up the stairs and knocks on the door.

"Who is it?"

"Joshua Mellancamp. I'm with the Metropolitan Museum of Art."

"*Oy*, what now," Aunt Manya mumbles as she reaches up to undo the chain.

"Are you Norman's mother?"

"No, his aunt. He doesn't have a mother. What's the matter? Did he break something? Did he steal something?"

"No madam. I assure you it's nothing like that. I'm a curator. A guard found his drawing in one of the galleries. Your nephew wrote his name on it. I knew that P.S. 165 was at the museum today on a field trip, so I made a few calls and spoke to Mr. Cohen, the principal. He gave me your address."

He takes the drawing from his briefcase and hands it to her.

"Please look at this portrait, madam. Notice the composition, the three dimensionality of form, the quality of line from thick to thin and from light to dark. These are advanced concepts for a ten-year-old. Was his mother an artist? What about his father?"

"No! There are no artists in his family. I can't even stand the word artist."

"But madam, the boy is talented, very talented. He's one in a million if you ask me."

"I didn't ask you. Listen to me Mr. Mellancamp, you've wasted your time coming here. Drawing is a waste of time. Better my Norman should become a doctor, a lawyer, an accountant. Now please go. We're… we're getting ready to eat."

Aunt Manya nudges the man out the door, closes it, and fastens the chain. As he clomps down the stairs, she crumples the drawing in her fist, and throws it in the garbage can under the sink with the chicken bones from tonight's dinner.

"That's what I think of drawing!"

I'm watching from the table. Uncle Irving and Sarah are sitting across from me. They look like they can't believe what they've seen. I can't believe it either. It all happened so fast that I couldn't even open my mouth to stutter out that I'm the boy who drew the picture.

I crumple up the one I just drew and throw it in the garbage. Aunt Manya doesn't deserve a picture. And no sense taking the other one out of the garbage and trying to smooth out the wrinkles I can draw any picture again from memory. I'm one in a million.

Chapter 10

Farsighted

Aunt Manya and Mrs. Katzman are drinking tea. Uncle Irving is treadling his sewing machine and humming the *Hatikva*. I'm at the far end of the table with Aunt Manya's family album open in front of me, copying Mother's face on a brown grocery bag. Uncle Irving stops sewing, puts on a new spool, pulls the end of a long strand of blue thread toward him, turns it into a sharp point with his wet tongue and threads his needle.

"This strudel is delicious, Manya. It melts in your mouth," Mrs. Katzman says.

"It's from Berman's, in Flatbush. Have another piece. By me, you don't have to be polite. You too, Norman. Can you put away your drawing long enough to have a bite?"

"I've never seen a child spend so much time drawing," Mrs. Katzman says. "Let me see your picture, Norman… It's Norma, may she rest in peace. Manya, Irving, look, give a *kook*. This picture is by a ten-year-old boy, a ten-year-old! Such a talent. We have a young Rembrandt in Brooklyn. His mother would have been so proud." She points her finger at my aunt and says, "She would have encouraged him, Manya, encouraged him!"

"She kept pulling the pipes out. Norma wouldn't stop pulling the pipes out." Aunt Manya takes off her glasses, wipes her eyes with the back of her hand.

"Why did Mother have pipes in her?"

"Your mother had a terrible infection," Mrs. Katzman says. "She was delirious and pulled at the tubes that were draining the infection. You know, Manya, I can't get over how much he looks like Norma. And look how he's grown. He's a big boy now."

"He weighed exactly five pounds when he was born. So quiet he slept that I had to look in on him to make sure he was breathing."

"But when he was awake in his crib, he was a little terror with the voice of an auctioneer, pedaling his chubby legs in the air, and scratching me with his sharp nails. Remember Manya when you were changing his diaper in the living room? I was standing in the doorway four feet away, and still, I got sprayed with *pishach*."

"I was there too, Irving," Mrs. Katzman says. "Some of the *pishach* got on me."

I pretend not to hear. When Mrs. Katzman leaves, I throw my drawing in the garbage before Aunt Manya does. There's no room for toys, teddy bears, or drawings in her clean, clean house.

Aunt Manya scrubs the grout between the tiny white six-sided tiles under the kitchen sink with the same stiff brush she threatens to use on me if I don't wash my face good. On her hands and knees, she washes and waxes the linoleum every Friday morning while the chicken soaks in a pot of brine. This is her ritual to prepare for the Sabbath. When I come home from school, the linoleum kitchen and dining room floors are covered with newspapers, and I have to walk on the paper, or else.

Aunt Manya says Cleanliness is Godliness. Friends and family know that in her house you can eat off the floor. But even though she's the cleanest person in Brownsville, or maybe even the world, once in a while I see a cockroach speeding across the tiles under the kitchen sink. It makes her crazy. She runs for her broom, but she's never fast enough to catch the invader. And no type of poison, whether it's powder or liquid, seems to work. She swears that the cockroaches come from her neighbor's filthy houses, but she's never been in their houses, except for Mrs. Katzman's, and her house is as clean as Aunt Manya's, almost.

On a hot Sunday afternoon I'm playing stickball with Joey and Seymour. We're sweaty and thirsty, so we run home for a drink of water. Rabbi Zimmerman's wife is over to pay her respects. She's with Leah Schmall, a lady of the congregation, who once actually paid me a quarter for a picture I drew of her. This made Mrs. Schmall say to Aunt Manya that I'm a professional artist.

They're at the table, gossiping. That's one of my new words. I know what a gossip is in Yiddish, too. It's a *yenta*, and Mrs. Z is the biggest one in Brownsville. In fact, she's a *yenta kvetch*, an expert gossiper. What she hears in the afternoon, everyone in Brownsville knows about by sundown.

They're drinking tea and eating apple turnovers from Berman's bakery. Aunt Manya had given me carfare early in the morning to take the green trolley to Flatbush to buy them. For turnovers, Yellins on Church Avenue isn't good enough.

"Hello Mrs. Z. Hello Mrs. Schmall."

"Hello Norman, the artist. My, how you've grown."

"He's the image of Norma, may she rest in peace."

I'm at the sink, guzzling water and watching Aunt Manya and her visitors. It's a comedy. All three of them, at the same time, sip tea out of their saucers, put the saucers on the table, reach for their turnovers, and lift them to their mustached lips. But I yell, "There's a cockroach."

The ladies think the cockroach is in the pink cardboard box the pastries came in. They drop their turnovers and shriek.

"You're mistaken, Norman," my aunt says calmly, but she's shaking and her face is red. "We don't have cockroaches here… I don't know what I'm going to do with him. The boy has such an imagination… Norman, I think you should stop teasing us. Go back out to play. It's a lovely day outside, and it's a shame to be cooped up in the house."

The ladies must be thinking, "Sure, there are no cockroaches in Manya's house." I'm done for!

"Don't forget to bring back a dish."

It's Thursday. At the Ambassador theater under the Saratoga Avenue elevated station every ticket buyer gets a free dish when she leaves. Aunt Manya already has a lot of them, but she wants enough to serve eight people. Usually, I have to suffer through boring love stories, but today, *The Wizard of Oz* is playing.

I buy a Milky Way and take a seat in the middle of the third row. First on is the newsreel. There's Pope Pius in his white dress and pointy hat. Now he's riding in a convertible, wearing a white yarmulke and waving two fingers to the crowds on each side of the street. Uncle Irving calls him the Nazi pope. I've seen him before in newsreels. He looks as scary as Hitler did on the Flit display that used to be in Mr. Gibalowitz's drugstore window.

After the Mighty Mouse and Heckle and Jeckle cartoons, the show begins. I can't believe it. Up there on the big screen, riding a bicycle, is someone who looks and sounds and acts exactly like Aunt Manya. It's Margaret Hamilton, playing Miss Gulch, and she's as scary as my aunt. Later, when she turns into the Wicked Witch of the West, she's even scarier. I love the Tin Man, the Scarecrow, and the Lion. I'm happy for Dorothy and Toto. I can't wait to tell Aunt Manya that she looks like a movie star.

When I walk into the kitchen, carrying her dish in both hands, the first thing that comes out of my mouth is, "Aunt Manya, you look just like the wicked witch in the movie."

The tendons in her neck pop out. Her hands are fists. Now she is the Wicked Witch of the West. Throwing water on her won't work. I'm trembling like the Cowardly Lion, trying to explain that she looks like Margaret Hamilton. Even the Wizard wouldn't be able to talk his way out of this with Aunt Manya.

I'm in the bathtub, blowing on sails, commanding my five-ship naval armada to attack five pirate ships. I have the same number on each side for a fair fight. My first toy ships weren't seaworthy. The destroyer wouldn't float, the submarine wouldn't sink, and the torpedo boat would only float upside down. So I made my own ships out of walnut shell halves, filling the bottoms with clay and sticking in toothpick masts. Sails, half of them with tiny skulls and crossbones drawn with permanent ink, are made out of pieces of paper from a brown grocery bag. I glued them to the masts. Then I experimented in the bathroom sink to see how many pebbles I'd have to press into the clay to make the ships float straight up in the water.

After my armada sinks the pirate ships, I look up at the fishing boat painting on the wall. The sea is calm. The colors glow. If only Aunt Manya would let me paint in her house. But I don't dare ask her again, especially after the witch business.

Today's Saturday. It's raining cats and dogs, as Aunt Manya would say. "Put drops in my eyes." She takes off her wire-framed glasses, holds onto them, and tilts her head back. "Whenever I lay my glasses down, they run away, and I can't find them."

I pull back her upper lids and put one drop in each eye. I thread her needle, watch her darn my sock close to her face, and listen to her swear in Yiddish when she sticks her finger.

At tea-time, she sometimes pours bubbling hot water on the table instead of in the cup, but I have a dishtowel ready, just in case. She has glaucoma, and her failing eyesight makes her more human.

Today she's relaxed. For sure, she's not thinking about my father. We're drinking hot tea and eating macaroons from Yellin's bakery. She signs my report card.

"Without studying, without ever bringing home a book, he's on the honor roll with straight 'A's."

I don't know why she talks to me as if she's talking to someone else about me, but it's good to hear her say something nice for a change.

"Your mother, may she rest in peace, was also very smart. She would have been proud of you. And a science award, too, for what was it, experiments, something about the sun?"

"Harvesting the sun's energy. Remember that solar generator I showed you with the black and the silver paddles? Dark absorbs light. Silver reflects it, so... "

"I remember, I remember, but I don't understand it. A ten-year-old boy harvesting the sun's energy. Some day, you'll be a doctor, a scientist."

I feel like saying artist, but that would make her mad.

"The rain's letting up. I want you should run around the corner to Horo-witz's Market. Put on a sweater under your raincoat. Where's your rain hat? Maybe you should take an umbrella, too."

"I don't need an umbrella if I have a rain hat."

Put on your galoshes. Here's money, here's a grocery list. Oh, one more thing. You should also buy me a half of a quarter of a pound of Muenster cheese."

"Okay, I'll get an eighth of a pound."

"You tell Mr. Horowitz I want a half of a quarter of a pound, and don't step in any puddles. I don't want a muddy floor."

I run around the corner, past empty lots, to Hegeman Avenue. Inside the store, a big hunk of lox is on the counter. With a long, skinny knife, Mr. Horowitz slices off thin pieces for Mrs. Bloom, the shoemaker's wife.

He removes the bones and fat and wraps the slices neatly in waxed paper.

"Here, Norman, have a piece."

"Thank you, Mr. Horowitz."

I ask him for an eighth of a pound of Muenster cheese and then pick out four apples, four bananas, and a head of lettuce. My picture from last year is still tacked to the wall behind the cash register. I had traded it for a chunk of marble halvah. The drawing is of a green bowl filled with fruit and vegetables next to a cutting board. On the board are a hunk of sturgeon and a knife, the same one Mr. Horowitz just got through using. It took all eight colors in my box of Crayolas plus tan shoe polish and Uncle Irving's white tailor's chalk.

At the cash register, Mr. Horowitz gives me another slice of lox and has one himself. Lox is my favorite food, and Mr. Horowitz has the best in Brooklyn. I run home in a light rain without stepping in any puddles. I take off my raincoat, hat, and galoshes in the hallway so water won't drip on the kitchen floor. Aunt Manya opens the door, grabs the grocery bag out of my hand, and slaps my face hard enough to make me teary.

"I was watching from the window, Norman. You were running through all the puddles on the block."

A week goes by. I still haven't forgotten that slap. Aunt Manya's been hollering on me all morning, because Dad hasn't sent her a money order. Why doesn't she call Dad on the phone and holler on him, instead? She says horrible things about him. Some of them are true. Maybe all of them are true. In the bathroom, I wash her spit off my face. I wish I could take the painting with me.

I stomp out, slam the kitchen door, and run down the stairs. She screams my name. To Aunt Manya, the Japanese attack on Pearl Harbor was a minor event compared to what I've just done. I slam the downstairs door, too. Sophie is coming up Lott Avenue with Abraham. No sense going to her with my problem even though she's my godmother. She sticks up for her mother. I run in the opposite direction. If I were walking, would that count as running away from home?

I run past Mr. Berg's grocery store and think about when I went there to cash in stolen milk bottles to buy candy. I run past Dr. Bass's office and PS 165. I turn left on Hopkinson Street and run past Seymour's house. Seymour has a mother, a father, a sister, toys, games, books, a telescope, his own room. I turn left on Newport Street, run past the lucky crippled boy on his cot on Strauss Street. Now right on Saratoga Avenue to the elevated station. Below is the Ambassador Theater, where I'll never have to sit through boring love stories again to get a free dish. I duck under the turnstile, go up another flight of stairs, and wait for the train to Manhattan. In my wallet is Dad's address written in ink in case of emergency, and this is one.

The apartment house where he rents a room is easy to find. A heavy glass front door. Marble steps to the second floor.

I ring the bell.

"Who is it?"

"Norman. I'm Benny's son! Is he there?"

A gray-haired woman opens the door. "Your father's at work."

I go downstairs and sit on the bottom step to wait. I wish I had brought some comic books. After a long time, the gray-haired lady comes down, passes me, and goes out the front door.

Later, she comes back, carrying a grocery bag. She sees me sitting with my elbows on my knees and my chin in my hands.

"I'm afraid your father won't be back until well after your bedtime."

"But I need to see him. It's important. I'll wait here."

"Suit yourself." She climbs halfway up the stairs and turns around. Tears are running down my cheek. "You must be hungry. Come on up, and I'll fix you something."

Her apartment is modern with a black telephone hanging on the kitchen wall and a silver garbage can that opens when you step on a foot pedal. The ceiling light is on even though it's light outside. She gives me soup and a bologna sandwich. They aren't nearly as good as what Aunt Manya would have fixed me, but I'm so hungry, I don't care. Her husband is watching me eat. Any time now he's going ask me a bunch of questions, like am I in some sort of trouble? Instead, he says, "We're not used to having children here. We don't have any games. Would you like some books to read?"

"I'd settle for a pencil and paper."

I expect he'll give me brown paper bags to draw on, but no, he gives me a pad of stationery, linen stationery no less. It says so on the cover. Am I in heaven? I sit at the kitchen table, draw the woman washing dishes, drying them, putting them in her cupboard, speaking on the phone. I draw the man in his chair in the living room, reading his newspaper. I show him the pictures I've drawn on both sides of every page. He gives me another

pad. I ask for a pencil sharpener, a softer pencil, a mirror, crayons. He actually goes to the store to buy me a box of Crayolas and number-one drawing
pencils.

The woman asks if I'd like cookies and milk.

I feel important, like I do at Aunt Manya's when I'm sick. I look in
the mirror, draw myself. I draw the woman, sitting on the couch, darning
socks.

"You're a talented boy," she says.

"You're going to be a famous artist some day," he says.

She must have called Dad when I was in the bathroom, because he
comes home in the early evening. He doesn't say a word, not one word
about any of my drawings, not even the big one on a paper bag that I colored in. It's the best picture I've ever drawn. I captured the afternoon light,
streaming in through the living room window. It lit up the woman's face
on one side, like in a Rembrandt painting. Dad takes me into his room. It's
very tidy. He takes off his black waiter coat and bow tie and hangs them up.
All of his shirts and coats are hanging the same way in his closet.

"Why did you run away from your aunt?"

"She's mean. She slapped me last week. She always hollers on me."

"Hollers at you, not on you. Quit talking like they do in Brownsville."

"Okay, she always hollers at me. And she says bad things about you. I
hate her. I don't want to live there any more."

"You have to. Where else can I put you?"

"Why can't I live with you?"

"There's no room here."

"I don't take up much room."

"You need someone to help you with your homework."

"No one helps me now."

"I wouldn't be here when you come home from school."

"I'd see you more than I do at Aunt Manya's."

"You need to be in the care of a woman."

"Your landlady could take care of me."

"No, she can't take care of you."

"Why not?"

Dad's answers are not the ones I want to hear.

He lets me stay the night. I like sleeping in his bed, except when he
snores. In the morning, he buys me a bagel and lox at a deli down the

block.

"I gave your landlady my pictures. Aunt Manya doesn't let me keep any of my drawings."

Dad doesn't say anything.

Aunt Manya is standing on the stoop with her arms folded when we walk up to the house. If her face were green, she'd look exactly like the Wicked Witch.

"Run along and play while I speak to your father."

I go to the playground but don't feel like playing. Even if I did, none of my friends are there. I wish Aunt Manya had said that she missed me. When I get back, Dad is gone.

CHAPTER 11

ALLIGATOR SHOES

Joey is taller now and sits next to me in the last row of Mrs. Frankl's class, drawing tanks, anti-aircraft guns, naval battles, and dogfights between Japanese and American planes even though the war ended two years ago. He accompanies his drawings with booms, blasts, and rat-a-tats, and I have to shush him, because you can hear him two rows away. It's contagious. I draw, look out the windows, and pay attention to the teacher at the same time. If I twist my head and look between the tall sycamores, I can see Dr. Bass drilling on patients in his dental office across the street.

Joey's sound effects give us away. Before we can slip our drawings in our textbooks, Mrs. Frankl pounces.

"Go to Mrs. Hartman's room." She lifts her hairy arm and points to the classroom on the other side of the dreary green hallway. We're being sent to the gallows. Mrs. Hartman is a huge, frowning woman, who specializes in discipline. Mrs. Frankl's pet, Morton, says Mrs. Hartman is a *hertzabubba*. When I see her in the hallway, I look down and walk real fast. I've never been to her room, and I'm terrified. Good thing Joey is with me. I understand the meaning of Aunt Manya's saying, "misery loves company."

Mrs. Hartman's arms are as big as wrestlers' in movies. She corrects papers while we tremble at her desk in the empty room. She looks up, reaches for the notes from Mrs. Frankl, and hands us three-by-five cards with long-division problems.

"Sit in the back row but not next to each other. When you finish these, come and get more. I have lots."

On the cards are eight-digit numbers divided by five-digit numbers, and none of the answers come out even, but I don't care. This is fun. I finish the cards and go up for more, but she sends us back to our class. She's not as bad as I thought.

The next time I wind up in Mrs. Hartman's room, it's for the crime of chewing gum. She gives me multiplication problems. I finish them and ask for more cards. She looks at the answer sheet and sends me back to my room.

For the fifth time in three weeks, I end up in the same fix and walk up to her desk to ask for my stack of cards. She tries to stifle a smile.

"Norman, you're the most polite boy in the school. It took me a while to figure out why you've come here so often. I'm giving you a complete set of arithmetic cards to take home. Have fun."

There's not one inch of space that belongs to me, so I can't be a kid in Aunt Manya's house. But that doesn't stop me from buying a model Grumman Hellcat with money I got by borrowing empty milk bottles and turning them in for two cents apiece. It took searching the hallways on each floor of three different apartment houses to get enough bottles. Kneeling on the brick walkway behind Joey's apartment house, and using a vegetable crate as a worktable, I spread out the paper fuselage plan, cut balsa wood struts to size with Uncle Irving's single-edged razor blade, and hold them in place over the plan with pins from Aunt Manya's red pincushion.

Sticking the fuselage sections together with great-smelling airplane glue makes me feel good, but I know it will take days to nibble off the glue that's stuck to my fingers. It's time to cut away the places where the model sticks to the crate and to the plan.

By the time I'm done with the wings and tail, the razor blade is dull, the tube of glue is almost used up, and more apartment house hallways will have to be raided for milk bottles. Better not take any more of them to Berg's Grocery store or Horowitz's Market around the corner. They're getting suspicious. I'll cash them in at Kaplan's on East 98th Street, go to the Five and Ten to buy glue and run home for lunch. If I'm lucky, the model will still be there.

I gobble down a pastrami sandwich and dill pickle, go to the bathroom to take another razor blade, and run back to my model. I cover the wings, the tail, and the fuselage with the blue paper that came with the kit and shrink it with water. It dries fast in the sun. I glue all the parts together and wait for the model to dry before flying it home to show Aunt Manya. Flying is fun. I bank to the right and to the left, dive, and climb above the clouds. There's a Messerschmidt 109 below. I swoop down to get it, making ack-ack-ack sounds with the nose gun, but I lose it in the clouds. The German plane can fly 481 mph. From the cards I've borrowed from Shirley's candy store I know all about warplanes, their speeds and wingspans and how high they can fly. I fly my model up the stoop, up one flight of stairs, and into the kitchen.

"Out of here with that contraption," Aunt Manya hollers from the table. "I told you not to bring junk in the house."

"It's not junk, Aunt Manya, it's a model airplane."

"I don't care what it is. I don't want it here."

"I spent all day building it. Can't I keep it just until Dad comes, so I can show it to him?"

"There's no room in the house, Norman. Can't you take no for an answer?"

"I have an idea. I'll…"

She pounds on the table, rattling the bowl of wax fruit.

"I'll hang it from my bedroom ceiling, on a string, and it…"

She pounds again. "Take it out of my house this minute." A wax pear bounces out of the bowl and onto the floor.

She doesn't have a nice thing to say about my Grumman Hellcat. She's the Messerschmidt 109 pilot, blasting my plane. The left wing is riddled with bullet holes, and black smoke is pouring out. I fly away from her gunfire shouts, dive downstairs, down the stoop, down around the corner, down to the vacant lot on Herzl Street. I can't control the plane. It won't respond. I have to bail out. Goodbye plane. The ground is coming up fast. I pull on the ripcord, and my parachute opens with a jerk. The blue Grumman Hellcat spirals to the ground and crashes. When I land, I take out a pack of matches and set my plane on fire.

It's raining, a good time to go to Joey's. As I walk down his hallway, I smell meat roasting and hear hollering before I get to the front door. It's normal at his house. I knock three times.

"Who is it?"

"It's Norman." The chain rattles. Then Joey's mother lets me in. She's short and wide, a Russian peasant like Aunt Manya. She has a mustache, and a few long hairs are growing out of her chin. "Hello, Joey's mother. Can Joey play?"

"He's in his room. Go play already."

His room has a real bed, books and games. A green P-51 Mustang and a silver P-38 Lightning are hanging from the ceiling. Dodgers pennants are tacked on the walls. There's a bulletin board with Joey's airplane drawings. I have a baseball glove that Cousin Nathan bought me, but I don't have a baseball anymore. It fell on the floor when I was holding it at the kitchen table. Aunt Manya scooped it up like she was Phil Rizzuto, and I never saw it again.

We play chess on Joey's bed. I read a *Plasticman* comic book while I wait for Joey to move. His mother looks in sometimes, because we're quiet. When she leaves the house for the grocery store, Joey shows me his deck of French cards.

The queen of hearts is my favorite.

"Hey Joey, these boobs are bigger than my cousin Sarah's."

"How do you know?"

"I seen her take off her brassiere one night when she thought I was asleep."

We play blackjack with the French cards until we hear Joey's mother unlocking the front door. Joey scrambles to gather them up and stash them in his secret hiding place under a floorboard in his closet. He replaces the floorboard, and I kick the queen of hearts under the bed just before his mother walks in.

"That was a close one," Joey says.

On my way back home, I daydream about Joey's room, the cards, and his secret hiding place. But there's no hiding the way I look. Even with her poor eyesight, Aunt Manya can see that I need new clothes.

"What happened to your jacket pocket?" she asks at the dinner table.

"I was squeezing through the fence to get my ball back, and it got ripped off by a piece of wire."

"You have the pocket?" Uncle Irving asks.

"No."

"You'll find it, I'll sew it back on."

Wow, Uncle Irving is actually going to sew something for me.

On my way to the hole in the fence, I see Joey and his mother in front of Berg's grocery store.

"Let me show you my trick. See that cigarette butt on the sidewalk? Watch this." I press down the toes of my right foot, and the sole of my shoe separates just enough to scoop up the butt from the sidewalk. Then I pick it up and pretend to light it. "Red Skelton did this in a movie."

Joey laughs, but his mother makes a *farcrimpte pawnum*.

Next morning, Uncle Irving and I are at the breakfast table. Aunt Manya sets down my kasha so hard that I think the bowl is going to break.

"What's bothering you, Manya?" Uncle Irving asks. "You couldn't sleep last night?"

"Who can sleep with aggravation?"

"So now what?"

She points at me and says, "To Rifke, the *yenta*, he has to show his trick. Now the whole neighborhood knows about his shoes."

"They know anyway. The rabbi mentioned it."

"*Oy Gevald!*" Aunt Manya raises her fist, shakes it. "I don't understand. With the money your father makes in tips, he can't afford to buy you clothes? It's a sin, a dirty sin. He should only roast in hell."

"*Shah*, enough already. Let the boy eat his breakfast in peace."

I push aside my bowl and go to school. The more Aunt Manya complains about Dad, the more I want him and hate her. I wish she would roast in hell.

Something secret is going on. I know, because Aunt Manya and Uncle Irving whisper a lot when I'm around. Sarah lets it slip out that Aunt Manya has started legal proceedings against Dad with the help of the city welfare department.

The phone rings Wednesday after school.

"It's your father, Norman," Aunt Manya says sweetly as she hands me the telephone.

"Meet me at Flo's this Saturday at ten." Dad talks so loud that I have to hold the receiver away from my ear. Aunt Flo is Dad's sister

I daydream in school for two days. I'm so excited on Friday night that I can't get to sleep. I think about the places we can go to: Yankee Stadium, the Statue of Liberty, the top of the Empire State Building, the Metropolitan Museum of Art. I'd settle for a Dodgers game at Ebbets Field so I can see Jackie Robinson play first base.

Saturday finally comes. After breakfast, Aunt Manya gives me a nickel for the subway. "Norman, don't eat *traife* by your Aunt Florence or you'll get sick."

"I promise I won't eat anything that isn't kosher."

I run to the station, buy a candy bar, sneak under the turnstile, wait for an express, and walk through the swaying train to the first car and stand next to the motorman's compartment. Looking out the front window, I make believe I'm driving the train while it moves through dark tunnels under the streets of the city. Lights flicker and sometimes go out for a few seconds. Cool air blows in from open side windows. I race full-speed past dingy local stations with yellow-tiled walls lit with bare light bulbs. People stand on platforms or sit on benches, reading newspapers. Others look down the tracks for their train. I memorize what I see in one station: three Hasidic Jews standing on the platform, reading a newspaper. I want to draw them later.

The train comes to a curve, slows down. Metallic screeches hurt my ears. An express, coming from the opposite direction, whizzes by. I see a boy like me standing at the front window of the passing train. A local comes alongside mine, going in the same direction. When my train slows down, it feels like I'm going backwards.

I get off at 68th St., near Hunter College, run one block east, and walk up the steep concrete steps leading to the musty foyer of my aunt's gray apartment building. I ring Aunt Flo's bell the same way I ring it at Aunt Lilly's: two short rings-wait two seconds-then two more short rings. When I'm buzzed in, I climb the stairs two at a time and knock on the iron door of apartment 302. Aunt Flo opens the door and hugs me. She stinks from cigarettes, wears bright red lipstick, has penciled on eyebrows, and her white sweater has gray cat hair on it.

Dad is sitting in an easy chair, lighting up a Lucky. The apartment is smoky, the gray walls, greasy. The green couch is covered with cat hair and a sleeping cat. Dad waves me over to give me a kiss.

"Norman's always on time," he says, looking at his watch.

Aunt Flo pours coffee for Dad and herself, lights up a cigarette, lifts the cat onto her lap and sits next to me on the couch. I enjoy listening to them making fun of Aunt Manya until they say things I don't want to believe. "Remember when she got poison ivy at Norma's grave?"

"It served her right. God punished her," Aunt Flo says.

"For making Mother's gravesite pretty?"

"She's old fashioned, and she's a cheapskate," Dad says.

"She's a hypocrite."

"What's a hypocrite, Aunt Flo?"

"What's a hypocrite? It's... It's a person who says or does... Benny, explain to Norman what a hypocrite is."

"A hypocrite is a person who gives a false impression of sincerity."

There's nothing false about Aunt Manya even if she is old-fashioned. Aunt Flo is the cheapskate. She never gives me a birthday present or a glass of milk or a piece of cake. The only thing I ever remember her giving me was pork sausage. I threw up that *chazer traife* on her kitchen floor.

"Tell me about school, Norman."

Aunt Flo's voice is sugary now. It's the first time she's ever seemed interested in me.

"I'm in the fifth grade at PS 165. I won a prize last year for my science project in Mrs. Gold's class. We were studying how to harness energy from the sun, and I experimented with different materials that absorb sunlight. This year I'm working on… "

She pets her cat, rubs its ears. "Pretty kitty, pretty kitty," she whispers as I talk.

Dad looks at his watch, and at last we can leave Aunt Flo's smelly apartment. Downstairs, I see my reflection in the brass mailbox and rub off the red kiss Aunt Flo planted on my cheek. I brush cat hair off Dad's coat.

"I have a surprise for you."

"Really? What is it?"

"You'll see when we go downtown."

Dad stops to buy a paper from a blind man at the newsstand above the station. "Hello, Sammy."

"Benny… Good to see ya. On your way to visit your sister?"

"Just came from there. Meet my son, Melvin."

"Happy to meet you, Melvin." The blind man reaches out for a handshake.

"I'm happy to meet you, too, but my name is Norman. Dad sometimes calls me Melvin. He's my older brother. He lives in California."

"Yes. I remember now. He survived the attack on Pearl Harbor. How is he, Benny?"

"He's doing fine. He has a wife and a daughter. Another child's on the way. He works for his mother in the clothing business."

"Good for him."

"Well, we have to go. I'm taking Norman to the circus."

"You'll love it, kid."

"I know I will. Nice to meet you, Sammy."

"Likewise."

The subway takes us to Madison Square Garden. A big sign in front says Ringling Brothers and Barnum and Bailey Circus, the Greatest Show on Earth. We follow the crowd through the turnstiles, and I feel happy in my stomach. There's sawdust on the floor of the smoky sideshow where things are bigger and smaller than life.

The Fat Lady has on a red tent of a dress. She's twice as big as Fat Annie. She's sprawled on a gigantic easy chair, and her tummy hangs down on her knees.

"I weigh six hundred thirty-five pounds, boy. If you don't believe me, climb up here, and I'll be happy to sit on your lap."

"No thanks lady. I believe you."

I look up, way up, and there, wearing a ten-gallon hat is The Tallest Man in the World.

"Is he really eight-feet one and a half inches tall, Dad?"

"That's what the sign says."

Dad buys me one of the giant's rings for fifty cents. I put three of my fingers in it.

The Sword Swallower turns sideways, tips his head back, opens his mouth, and slides a long sword clear down his throat. He's not coughing or bleeding. He takes the sword out and puts a fluorescent light bulb down his throat. His neck glows pink.

Next to the Midget Family, Aunt Manya would be tall. There are five of them, and they look like elves with ruffled shirts and suspenders. They squeak when they laugh, but they don't look happy. Maybe they think that the gawking people in the audience look stranger than they do.

I hear a roar from Gargantua, the gorilla, who's as fat as the Fat Lady and as tall as The Tallest Man in the World. I'm standing in front of his cage, but he doesn't look at me. Maybe he has more important things on his mind, like escaping. I hope the bars on his cage are strong, because if he got out, he wouldn't go back without a fight. It bothers me that animals are trapped and put on display.

"Dad, I heard that Gargantua is the most ferocious gorilla in the world."

"This isn't the real Gargantua. He died last year."

"Well, if Gargantua was meaner looking than this one, he must have really been scary."

I smell peanuts and elephant poop. A red-haired clown walks through the crowd with a chimpanzee on his shoulders. The chimp has on a blue sailor suit and a silver collar with red jewels. The expression on the chimp's face is like Dad's.

Running through the crowd, a clown tips a big wooden pail to the right and to the left. People jump out of his way. He spins around and dumps silver confetti on us.

I try to hold Dad's hand, but he shakes me off so he can light his cigarette. There's a man on stilts dressed like Uncle Sam, a clown with orange hair on a unicycle, and a juggler keeping five yellow balls in the air. I'd like this more if I didn't have to keep an eye on Dad all the time. He walks faster and faster into the crowd. I have to run to catch up.

"Dad, did you ever take Melvin to the circus?"

"Yes, before you were born. We went with Lilly and Tim."

"Did they have a gorilla? Did they have elephants?"

"Yes. Melvin got to ride on an elephant, because Tim knew the trainer."

"I wanna ride on an elephant, too."

"They don't allow that now."

"Did you invite Uncle Tim and Aunt Lilly?"

"I didn't think of it."

I kick a clump of sawdust.

"ATTENTION LADIES AND GENTLEMEN AND CHILDREN OF ALL AGES. THE MAIN SHOW WILL BEGIN IN TEN MINUTES. PLEASE MAKE YOUR WAY INTO THE ARENA WHERE WE WILL PRESENT THE RINGLING BROTHERS AND BARNUM AND BAILEY CIRCUS, THE GREATEST SHOW ON EARTH!"

We climb halfway up the grandstand. Dad is next to me, and I have the aisle seat. I won't lose him now.

The brass band starts to play, and I keep time by conducting with both hands. A parade comes through a big door and marches around the arena. Tigers, clowns driving little cars that honk and toot and squeak, elephants, prancing horses with silver headdresses, a chimpanzee riding a yellow bicycle, and a ringmaster in a red coat with tails and a tall black hat like the one I wore at Sophie's and Nathan's weddings. He's cracking his whip. Pop,

pop, pop.

"He's the boss of the circus," Dad says.

After the parade is over, and the clowns shovel elephant poop off the floor, a spotlight shines on the ringmaster. He introduces the acts in a booming voice like Dad's. Now, things are happening in all three rings, and it's hard to know where to look.

Eighteen clowns get out of a tiny polka-dotted car. Dad doesn't smile. Sad-faced Emmet Kelly sweeps a spotlight under a carpet. Dad yawns. Ten elephants with riders on their heads prance around the center ring. Dad falls asleep.

I think about Melvin riding an elephant. He's my hero, and I wish he lived in New York instead of California. He'd be more fun than Dad, who is now snoring.

Fiery reds, sparkling golds, metallic blues, silver sequins glittering under the spotlights. It would be fun to work for the circus. When I wasn't doing chores, I'd draw tigers, horses, elephants, clowns, and acrobats. I'd need the world's biggest box of crayons.

Dad opens his eyes for the high-wire act. A man in black tights pedals a bicycle forward then backward across the wire. On the ground below are twelve clowns, carrying a fireman's life net.

"Why is he carrying that long stick?"

"It's a balancing bar."

Two people climb on his shoulders. Two more people climb on and stand on the shoulders of the first two. I can almost feel their weight on my shoulders. A woman in a sparkling silver costume climbs to the top and stands with her arms outstretched. The audience is holding its breath. When the bicycle riders make it to the other side the audience lets out one huge sigh.

After the circus, Dad takes me to a bar and grill. I brush confetti off his coat. He orders a beer and lights up a Lucky Strike. He lets me take a sip but not a puff. The warm wooden counter, dark booths, mahogany walls, the light shining through liquor bottles, they're soothing. Just a few crayons would be enough to show these earth colors.

I tell Dad about all he missed: the trapeze act, the tiger trainer, the man who got shot out of a cannon. I feel important when he listens.

We walk to a pawnshop on Tenth Avenue. Dad introduces me to Sam, the owner, whose eyes dart everywhere, just like the eyes of Mrs. Gold, my teacher.

Dad has me try on lots of shoes, but none of them fit. Sam brings out a pointy pair of alligator shoes, the slickest ones I've ever seen, but they're tight in the heels and much too long. I really want a new pair from a shoe store.

"Don't you like them?" Dad asks.

"Kind of, but they're scuffed."

"They're really fine shoes, Norman. They look good on you."

"Well, if you think they look good then I guess I like them."

Dad picks through a pile of jackets and finds three.

"Try these on."

"I don't like them."

He picks up a blue mackinaw. "This is the warmest one they've got. Try it on... Why the face? What's wrong with it?"

"Don't you think the sleeves are too short?"

"Too short? No, they're just right."

"Well, if you say so, then I guess I like the jacket, too."

I'm afraid that if I tell him what I really think he might get mad and never take me anywhere again. He talks Sam down to three dollars. Then, while I'm looking at a green Lionel train set in a glass display case, Dad gives Sam a ten-dollar bill and tells him to bet it on *Pipe Dream*.

When we leave the pawnshop, I'm wearing my new jacket and pointy alligator shoes. I don't feel like thanking Dad for stuff I don't even like, but I guess I ought to.

"Thanks for the jacket and the shoes, Dad."

"You're welcome, Melvin, I mean Norman. You know, pawnshops are the best places to get bargains. Last week I bought a clock for your grandfather. When Sam wasn't looking I took out a part from the back. I told him that seven dollars was too much, because a part was missing, so he gave it to me for four." Dad grins and pokes me in the ribs with his elbow.

I want to tell him that he's dishonest, but I sneak under turnstiles and steal milk bottles.

As we walk along the street, I keep looking down at my alligator shoes, wishing they weren't so long. I don't want to be a clown. I think about Grandfather, who lives with Aunt Ellie, Dad's sister. I want to ask Dad if Grandfather bought him used shoes at a pawnshop in Vienna when he was ten.

"Dad, do you think Aunt Ellie will ever let me have the train set she promised?"

"I'm sure she will."

"But she promised I could have it when I was eight, and I'm ten now."

"I'll talk to her."

"I'm hungry."

"There's an Automat five blocks from here."

"I hope I can make it. These shoes hurt."

'You'll get used to them. You have to break them in."

At the Automat, Dad gives me two one-dollar bills, tells me to get change. I give the woman at the cash register the money. She dips her hand into a tray full of nickels and plunks exactly two dollars' worth into my cupped hands. I watch other customers get nickels for their dollar bills. Dad says the women who make change in the Automats never make a mistake.

I put nickels in the slots, buy two cups of baked beans, two apple pies, two coffees. Dad reads the paper while we eat. In my mind, I draw the wrinkled face and blue beret of the old man at the next table.

Dad gives me money for second helpings. When I come back to the table, a man is sitting across from Dad, eating a sandwich and reading the *Daily Mirror*.

"Has anyone from the city come around to talk to you about me?" Dad asks, not caring that the stranger can hear.

"No, why?"

"Manya is starting to make trouble."

Now I know why he took me to the circus and the pawnshop.

"If anyone comes around, I'll tell him how mean she is. Then she'll get in trouble. Then I can live with you."

The stranger smiles.

"It might be best to not say anything bad about Manya. That wouldn't be nice."

The stranger frowns. Between my Dad and the stranger, I think I'm in some sort of class that my school doesn't teach.

Dad looks at his watch. I know it's time to go. He gives me two silver dollars, walks me to the subway station, and kisses me goodbye.

I duck under the turnstile and wait for the Brooklyn train. I'm careful not to let anyone step on my alligator shoes. The kids at school will be envious. They're the pointiest shoes in New York City. And my new jacket has two big pockets. Comic books will be easier to borrow.

I get off at Saratoga Avenue. I'd like to buy a candy bar at Izzy's, the store below the train station, but I don't want to spend my silver dollars. I won't try to steal a candy bar there. Izzy caught Joey stealing and called the police. It's easier at Shirley's candy store catty-corner from my house.

My feet hurt on the six-block walk from the train station. There's so much to tell everyone about the circus, and I'm going to be real careful not to say anything that will set Aunt Manya off, like for instance: Aunt Manya, the midgets at the circus are even tinier than you are.

She opens the door, looks at me, and groans.

"Where did your father buy you those shoes?" she hollers and showers me with spit. They're from a *Schwartze*! And that jacket, that *schmata*, the sleeves are too short. Why did you let him buy you those things? Why, Norman? Why? He couldn't have taken you to Barney's Boy's Town to buy something decent? The big spender has to buy his son junk?"

"It's not junk, Aunt Manya." I back away from her fists. "Dad said these are expensive alligator shoes, and the jacket isn't a *schmata*, it's better than the ones they make now."

I sit on the edge of my cot. Everything is spoiled.

Chapter 12

Egg Cream

We ride the subway to Queens to visit Grandpa, who's ninety-five, has twinkly eyes, thinning white hair, and a Viennese accent stronger than Dad's. There are lots of clocks in the apartment he shares with Aunt Ellie and Larry, her sourpuss husband. It's on a corner above the candy store that Ellie and Larry own.

Grandpa is sitting at the kitchen table by a sunny window that overlooks the Jackson Heights elevated station. With his left hand, he's holding a giant magnifying glass. With the other, he's oiling the gears of a heavy clock that's also a savings bank. There are always clocks on the table, being repaired, adjusted, and cleaned. I hug him.

Dad tries to open the bank. Grandpa winks at me, and hands me his pocketknife.

"I'll show you how, Dad." I stick the point of the knife into a secret catch in the back of the clock. Grandpa showed me how two years ago. Inside is a new silver dollar.

"The dollar's for you."

"Thank you, Grandpa."

Last time I counted, there were twenty-seven clocks in the kitchen, dining room and living room and thirteen more in the bedrooms. Grandfather clocks, clocks with figures that dance the hour, cuckoo clocks, alarm clocks, clocks in wooden cases, glass cases, silver cases, all ticking away. Every hour they ring, ding, cuckoo, or chime, and it takes two or three minutes before they're done.

"Why don't all the clocks tell the hour at the same time, Grandpa?"

"Some are more accurate than others. They lose time or gain time, and I'd have to spend the entire day adjusting them so they could strike the hour at once."

"I wanna be a clockmaker when I grow up."

"A clockmaker? I'm sure you'll want to be many things before you grow up."

I excuse myself and walk downstairs to the candy store to say hello to

Aunt Ellie. The store is shaded by the elevated station. There's a soda fountain, six stools at the counter, three booths, a white diamond-tiled floor, and the wonderful smell of chocolate. Al Jolson is singing *April Showers* on the radio. His voice gets drowned out when a train goes by.

Aunt Ellie is behind the counter, setting a red cherry on top of a chocolate sundae piled with whipped cream and sprinkled with chopped walnuts. It makes me smack my lips. Customers are eating chocolate sundaes, vanilla malteds, and sugar cones filled with strawberry ice cream, but all Aunt Ellie ever offers me is an egg cream in a glass so small that I need Grandpa's magnifying glass to find it. I wonder why it's called an egg cream when it doesn't have eggs or cream in it, only seltzer, chocolate syrup, and a little milk. She only gives me that if Uncle Larry is in the back room. If he comes up front while I'm drinking it, he curls his lips into a homely frown. He's behind the counter, so I don't get one today.

When he goes in back, I ask, "Aunt Ellie, remember the Lionel train set you promised me? When am I gonna get it?"

"Soon dear. It's in the back room, way up high, surrounded by a thousand packages, and I can't get to it just now."

"That's what you say every time. I can climb up there real easy."

"No, Norman, the ladder's not tall enough, and I don't want you to get hurt. When one of the boys gets here, he'll climb up and get it."

But neither of my cousins, who have outgrown the trains, ever arrive.

I want the train set more than anything. If I get it, Aunt Manya won't let me bring it in her house, but maybe she'd let me store it in her compartment in the basement. Then I could go down, take a car out and bring it upstairs to hold it and draw it. That would be all right with me, even if I couldn't actually run the train on its tracks.

Aunt Ellie tells me not to sit in any of the booths, and she won't let me read any of the comic books on her stand.

"Customers aren't going to pay full price for a used comic book, Norman."

"I won't get it dirty."

"You'll wrinkle it."

I'll ask her for a pencil and paper. No, why torture myself drawing customers eating ice cream that I'll never get. I go back upstairs.

In the china cabinet in the living room are water glasses that are better than Joey's French cards. On the outside of each one is a girl in a bathing suit. When I look inside the glasses, the girls don't have any clothes on. Aunt Manya would never have anything like this in her house.

The clocks go off at noon, the biggest show of the day. Bong, bong, cuckoo, cuckoo, ding, ding, ding. Even the passing trains don't spoil the fun. I'm surrounded by naked ladies and chiming clocks. After the last clock in the living room sings its twelve-note song, another and yet another sings from the bedrooms. I look at the glasses one more time and put them back.

Against one wall is a brown spinet piano where a cabinet used to be. This is new. I move the piano bench back and discover that the green padded seat lifts up, and inside is sheet music. On the top left-hand corner of Bach's *Minuet in G* is Mother's signature. I'm actually holding something that belonged to her. There's a notebook with her name on it. Inside is a list of music stuff: work for evenness of touch, work on hardest passages first, practice hands separately, count aloud the beats per measure, mark your fingering in pencil throughout. Mother's 'o's and 'i's are shaped just like mine. We both have lousy penmanship. I trace over her words with my finger and feel as close to her as I've ever been. Some day I'll learn how to read music, and I'll practice everything on her list. I want to learn how to play Bach's *Minuet in G.*

I try to pick out the first five notes of *April Showers* that I heard on the radio in the candy store, but I'm having trouble with them. Dad comes in, scoots me off the bench, and finds sheet music for Liszt's *Hungarian Rhapsody No. 2.* He wiggles around on the piano bench until he gets comfortable, then begins to play, his huge but nimble fingers flying over the keyboard. I didn't know he could play the piano. The sound is as beautiful as when he played the violin on the street in Brooklyn. He plays for two pages, then quits. Aunt Manya once said that he often begins but seldom finishes things.

"Is this Mother's piano?"

"Yes."

"Why is it here?"

"Ellie is the only one who had room for it."

"How come you never told me Mother knew how to play the piano? How come you never tell me anything about her."

"That's not true. I told you we used to live in Poughkeepsie. I told you that Melvin lived with us one summer."

"I don't want to know about Melvin. I want to know about Mother. But every time I ask about her you change the subject or say you don't know."

"What do you want to know? Ask me."

"What was her favorite color, her favorite song, her favorite book?"

"I'm sorry, Norman, I don't remember."

"Did you ever know?"

"I don't know. I can't answer your questions. It's too painful for me to talk about her."

"What about my pain? How do you think I feel, not knowing anything about her?"

"Doesn't Manya ever talk about her?"

"No. The only one she ever talks about is you, and she never has anything nice to say."

"Do you believe everything she says"

"Sometimes I don't believe what anyone says."

"Do you believe what I say?"

"Not always. When I asked you about violin lessons, you said it was too late, you said I should have started when I was four."

"That's true. That's the proper age to start."

"My music appreciation teacher told me that some famous musicians started at eight or nine years old. Anyway, how was I supposed to know at age four that you or Mother could play musical instruments? You never told me. Maybe if you had arranged for me to take violin or piano lessons when I was four, I'd be real good at it by now. I bet if I started lessons today I'd be good at it in a few years."

"I don't have money for lessons."

"You have money for horses. I saw you give the pawnshop man money to bet on a horse. Are horses more important than me?"

"Of course not, Norman. I'll see about getting you music lessons. Now let's get back to your grandfather."

In the kitchen, I feel important sitting at the table with them.

"Put some Liederkranz on your bread, Norman. It goes good with beer. Benny, pour Norman a glass of Trommers."

Dad reads the *New York Times* aloud. "President Truman is asking Congress to authorize $597 million for aid to France, Italy, and Austria."

"Piss on Austria," Grandpa says.

"Piss on Austria," Dad repeats, raising his glass.

"Piss on Austria," I say, raising my glass high and sloshing beer on the table. They both laugh.

"Austria was not good to us," Grandpa says. "The country didn't like Jews. That's why we came to America."

Aunt Ellie comes upstairs to say hello to Dad. She gives me a chocolate that has turned white at its edges. It doesn't taste good. She's at the sink, and I don't want her to see me throw the chocolate away, so I go to the bathroom and throw it down the toilet.

The bathroom is a place to think. I try to understand why Aunt Manya doesn't approve of Dad's sisters. It's probably because she would never offer me peanut butter and jelly sandwiches for breakfast, pork sausage for a snack, or anything that isn't fresh. She's the greatest cook in the world. She worries about me when I'm sick. She asks how I do on my tests at school. If I get a B+ she says, "You couldn't have gotten an A?" If I get an A she says, "You couldn't have gotten an A+?" She encourages me to read, to study, to become a doctor, a dentist, a lawyer, a CPA, but not an artist.

I once brought home a report card with two B minuses on it, and she wouldn't sign it.

"I only sign report cards that have A's or B pluses on them."

"But Aunt Manya, I can't take it back to school if you don't sign it. How will the teacher know I showed it to you?"

When I told Joey about it, he told me to practice copying her signature upside down. I felt guilty forging her name. It was harder to do that than to get A's on the next report card.

I'm actually thinking nice thoughts about Aunt Manya. Maybe she's not so bad after all. Maybe I can behave better.

I remember my last visit to see Grandpa. It was after a stupid trick I pulled at home one Saturday night. Uncle Irving, Nathan, Sol, and Debbie were playing pinochle. Aunt Manya, Sophie, and Sarah were in the living room in front of the radio, gossiping about Second Cousin Bessie, who had taken up with an Italian. Abraham was asleep on Sarah's bed. I was sprawled on the kitchen floor, drawing, but I was getting uncomfortable. There was no other place to draw and no one to talk to, so I went into Aunt Manya's bedroom and hid under the bed.

Five minutes went by. Ten minutes. I was disappointed that no one missed me. Fifteen minutes. Aunt Manya went into the kitchen. "Has anyone seen Norman?"

"I thought he was in the living room with you," Debbie said.

"Norman," Aunt Manya shouted.

"Norman," Debbie shouted.

"Maybe he's outside," Sarah said.

"At ten o'clock at night?" Sophie asked.

Sol, Nathan, and Sarah went downstairs to look for me, came back upstairs, called for me some more.

"I hope he didn't run away again," Aunt Manya said.

"Maybe he's playing a trick," Sophie said. "Sol, look in the closets. Nathan, look under the beds." When Nathan looked under Aunt Manya's bed, he didn't see me in the shadow.

Everyone was frantic, and by then, I was too embarrassed to make an appearance. So I climbed out from under the bed and crawled under the covers. Eventually, Debbie discovered me in bed, pretending to be asleep. When Nathan shook me, I acted surprised.

No one was amused. Sophie wouldn't speak to me for a month, but then, she hardly ever spoke to me anyway.

When Dad told Grandpa about the "hiding under the bed" business, I felt betrayed.

"You've made the boy cry," Grandpa said. "So what if he played a trick on his aunt? Were you ever without tricks?"

I'm still embarrassed about it. But what about Aunt Manya's tricks? I can't read or study, because she wants to save a penny's worth of electricity. She always hollers at me. She chased away the man from the museum who said I was one in a million. She makes me stutter and blink my eyes. Thank God I don't pee in bed anymore. But worst of all is her complaining about Dad, who I love more than anyone in the world, I think.

I wish I had a mother. Even Joey's mother would do. At least she hugs him once in a while.

"Cuckoo!" says the clock on the bathroom wall. I forgot to count it when I counted clocks. When I look up, the bird is back behind its door, and the other clocks are striking their single notes.

Knock. Knock. "Norman, did you fall in? It's time to go."

"Okay, Dad, I'll be right out." I unbutton my fly and stand over the toilet. "Piss on Aunt Ellie's tiny egg creams, stale chocolate, and the Lionel train set that I'll never get."

CHAPTER 13

HEWITT PLACE

This afternoon Aunt Manya turned the oven to 350 degrees, got out a baking dish, cored six apples that I picked out at Horowitz's market, mixed flour, sugar, cinnamon, nutmeg, cloves, raisins, and chopped walnuts, stuffed it into the apples, and put them in to bake. She doesn't measure anything. I don't think she owns a cookbook.

We're sitting at the dinner table pouring cream on our baked apples. Aunt Manya's food is worth the aggravation she causes me.

The phone rings. Aunt Manya jumps up to answer it, wiping her lips with her apron. She draws a 'Y' in the air for Yentl. She spins her index finger in circles to indicate the non-stop chattering.

"She should only drop dead," Sarah says, rolling her eyes.

"*Shah*, she'll hear you."

"I don't care if she does, Pappa."

"Enough, already, Sarah. I care. She's my sister-in-law."

Not only is Yentl, the *yenta*, married to Uncle Irving's brother, Mendel, she's also the sister of sourpuss Larry, Aunt Ellie's husband. Cousin Sarah once told me why she doesn't like Yentl.

"By me, Yentl is *persona non grata*. She was the matchmaker who arranged for your mother and father to meet. She expected a little present from Mamma for her services. But Mamma said, 'From me, Norma's sister, you expect money? From a stranger you collect a fee. From family, you do it out of the goodness of your heart.' Then Yentl said, 'Manya, please, it's a sin not to give a matchmaker a little gift. If you don't, something bad will happen.' When your mother died thirteen months later, Momma and I blamed Yentl for tempting the devil."

Aunt Manya looks at the clock and taps her foot on the floor. Finally, the conversation is over.

"So, already?" Uncle Irving asks.

"So, already?" Sarah asks.

"So already?" I repeat, just for fun.

Aunt Manya tucks her chin into her chest and spreads her arms wide.

"Yentl, the yenta, says that Norman's father married a woman from the Bronx, named Rebecca."

"Married? When did Benny get married?"

"A year ago, Irving."

"A year ago, Manya? Did you say a year ago?"

"Yes. You heard right."

"How can a man be married a year, and he doesn't tell anyone?"

"You're asking me? Better you should ask him."

"Norman, you don't know about this, do you?"

"No, Uncle Irving, Dad never tells me anything."

"So, how did Yentl know already?"

"She heard it from Ellie who heard it from her sister, Flo."

"Who's Ellie? Who's Flo?" Sarah asks.

"My aunts."

"Norman's aunts," Aunt Manya says, ignoring my answer. Flo's husband, Dave, has a sister, Bertha, who's the mother of Benny's new wife."

"Manya, stop, stop already with all these names. I'm getting all *far-dreyt*. I have no idea who's who."

"I can't keep it straight myself."

"Yentl should still drop dead."

"*Shah*, Sarah," Uncle Irving says. "Don't you tempt the devil."

The next night at dinner Yentl calls again to tell Aunt Manya that Dad and Rebecca live in the Bronx with Rebecca's mother and father in a three-story Victorian house with six bedrooms, a big back yard, and a dog."

I can picture shade trees and a front lawn where Dad and I can play catch, and in back, flowers and a fence around the garden to keep out the dog. My own bedroom, just like Joey's, where I can draw and listen to the radio. There will be a secret hiding place in the closet for private stuff, like French cards. I can have friends over. Maybe there's a room in the attic, with lots of sun, where I can paint in oils.

Rebecca won't holler at me. Her father will be like Edmund Gwenn, who played Santa Claus in *Miracle on 34th Street*, and her mother will be like Dorothy's Auntie Em in *The Wizard of Oz*.

But no one on my mother's side of the family has a good word to say about Rebecca even though they haven't met her. She's the niece of Dave, Aunt Flo's husband, who isn't exactly her husband, since he and Aunt Flo never got married. They have two daughters, my cousins. According to

Dad's ex-brother-in-law, Lou, whose sister is Melvin's mother and whose other sister owned a whorehouse in Vallejo, California during the war, the daughters walk around New York with mattresses on their backs.

Yentl calls for the third night in a row just as we're starting dinner. She says that Dad and Rebecca had a baby girl who died suddenly in her crib. The rumor is that Rebecca dropped the baby on the floor, but Dad said it died because something was wrong with it. Then he got into an argument with the man at the funeral parlor over prices and took the little casket to the cemetery in a cab.

I wonder if all cemeteries have men with beards and dark coats who hound people until they allow prayers to be said for their dead. I think Dad would punch one of those men in the nose.

Aunt Manya and I are drinking tea in the afternoon. She waggles her finger at me. "You should read more, Norman, and I don't mean comic books. Have you read any more of the Charles Dickens books from the bookshelf? No. A complete set at your disposal, and you've only read two. By you, a book has to have pictures in it! And let me tell you something else. If I were you, I'd spend less time playing with Joey, the *schmendrick*, who's not too bright, and who *schleps* around the neighborhood all day with a mop handle, looking to play stickball. Better you should play with Seymour. Seymour's mother says he already knows what he wants to do when he grows up. He wants to be an accountant, a CPA, a *mensch*. And what does Joey want to become? An artist, a *chaim yonkel*, a nothing." There are heavy footsteps on the stairs. Wheezing. A knock on the door. "Yoohoo, Manya."

"It's Joey's mother."

"So unchain the door, Norman. Let her in."

"*Nu*, Rifke, what tragedy brings you here today?"

"Tragedy? What tragedy? A friendly visit."

"I'm honored… Norman, cut a piece of chocolate cake for Rifke It's from Berman's. My Sophie bought it this morning."

"Just tea, Manya. The cake I can do without. I'm not fat enough already?"

"As you wish, Rifke. So tell me… how's Joey? How's by you?"

"We're all fine, thank God."

"So, you walked across the street to tell me you're fine?"

"I'm here because today I'm at the schoolyard, looking for Joey, when a woman comes up to me and asks if I know Norman, so I point him out. Then I thought, maybe I shouldn't have. She could be a kidnapper or who knows what. So I decided I'd better tell you."

"What did she look like, this woman?"

"A *lungeh lucksh*, at least a head higher than me. And dressed like a fashion model, all *ferputzt*, with a fancy brown handbag. But such a face on her, a face that could stop a clock."

"Maybe she's the mother of one of Norman's friends, looking to give him a piece of her mind. You got into some mischief, Norman? You hit someone?"

"No, Aunt Manya. When have I ever hit anyone? You're the one who hits."

"The woman stood there for a long time, watching him. Maybe she was up to no good."

"Rifke, the kidnapper who would steal Norman would bring him back in an hour, because Norman would drive her crazy with all his questions."

One week until summer vacation. I can't stop reading *David Copperfield*. I'm gonna listen to Aunt Manya from now on. I play chess with Seymour. On starry nights, we go up on his roof, look through his telescope, and see the moons of Jupiter. Seymour's father says he'll take me to Coney Island with them in his Buick.

The day after the last day of school, Dad makes a sudden visit, carrying a big empty suitcase. Without looking my aunt in the eye, he says, "I'm taking Norman to live with me."

She chews her lower lip. Her eyes tear up. She packs my clothes in the bedroom while I sit quietly with Dad in the kitchen. I've always wanted to live with him, but now I don't want to go. I'll miss playing stickball with Joey and Seymour. I'll miss my real family on Mother's side. And what about school and my science projects?

"Manya," Dad says with an innocent face, "I know you have a small savings account for Norman. If you transfer it to me, I'll open an account for him at my bank in the Bronx."

Her nostrils flare. Her lips tighten. "What am I, Benny, born yesterday? The account will stay where it is until Norman's of age!"

I can't say goodbye to Uncle Irving, because he's at work, and Sarah is at Sophie's house. I don't get to say goodbye to Joey and Seymour either. Dad is always in a hurry.

We take the train to the Bronx. After midtown Manhattan, it fills mostly with blacks and Puerto Ricans. I keep a tight grip on my satchel. The train climbs out of the tunnel and rumbles along elevated tracks between blackened brick tenements. Laundry is strung on fire escapes. A boy on one fire escape makes believe he's shooting at us. At the second station beyond the tunnel, Dad folds his newspaper into his coat pocket and says, "We get off here."

We walk through the turnstiles and down a stairway into a neighborhood littered with candy wrappers, paper coffee cups, and newspapers printed in Spanish. Garbage cans are overturned. Two dark Puerto Rican men in undershirts swagger down the sidewalk, whistling at women. Boys yell "fuck you" to each other. Will they be my classmates?

A woman and two girls stand by a pile of furniture and clothing on the sidewalk in front of an apartment house. Two men walk out the front door with a kitchen table and throw it on the pile. The woman wipes her eyes and yells in Spanish. The smallest girl kicks one of the men, and he swears at her.

Dad stops at a corner store, buys a pack of Lucky's. A man buys two "loosies" from an open pack. Cooking odors remind me of Rita, the Puerto Rican girl who lives next door to Aunt Lilly on Livingston Street in Brooklyn. Loud music is playing from windows. People argue on the street just like they do in Brooklyn. Is this a nightmare?

We cross a street into a black neighborhood. I hear unfamiliar music. "That's jazz," Dad says. It's the first thing he has said since we got off the train. Old people sit on folding chairs on the sidewalk. Mothers rock baby carriages. Children dodge cars, run from shopkeepers. People turn to watch us pass. Dad walks erect as a prince, ignoring them. I want to be back in Brooklyn. I think about Aunt Manya, standing stiffly at her kitchen door, pulling away from me when I tried to give her a goodbye hug. I'm afraid she'll never take me back like she did when I ran away. I hope my new home is far away from this awful place, but I feel that it isn't.

We cross a busy street, walk one block and turn down Hewitt Place, a narrow, treeless street of rundown wooden houses and an old synagogue with peeling paint. I look up at the houses and expect to see pale faces looking out from behind curtains, like in spooky movies. There's a face, a mean looking one.

"This is it," Dad says. The face disappears. Dad opens a low iron gate. An old man with a pipe in his mouth jumps out of his rocker and goes inside. I follow Dad through a tiny front yard and up worn wooden steps to the porch. A woman, the one I saw in the window, comes out the front door. Her eyes travel up and down, examining me as I would examine a ball I found in the street, looking for flaws. She's taller than Dad, and she doesn't look Jewish.

"Hello Norman," she says in a Mae West voice. "I'm Becca, your new mother."

She turns away without giving me a hug or even a handshake. So this is Rebecca, Dad's wife, who calls herself Becca, the *ferputzt, lungeh lucksh* woman that Joey's mother described, who spied on me at the playground. I feel like puking. I want to run to the elevated station, take the train back to Brooklyn, wake up in my cot, but I'd be running away from Dad. So I go inside with her. I look for Dad. He dropped the suitcase at the door and is headed upstairs. I follow Becca through a long hallway that echoes our footsteps. On the right is the living room, then the dining room. There's a heavy table and tall-backed chairs inside the unlit room. It wouldn't surprise me to see cobwebs hanging from the ceiling or a butler who looks like Bela Lugosi. The old man I had seen on the porch is sitting in one of the dining room chairs.

"Leave your satchel here," Becca says.

A dog growls as we walk by the cellar door. I feel a chill. I wish I were carrying my satchel so I could protect myself if the dog attacks. But the dog is downstairs, and this is, after all, the house of Dad's new wife. Everything will be okay, I hope. I follow Becca past a telephone stand and into a kitchen with green linoleum and yellowish-green walls that make me feel like puking again.

A gray-haired woman reeking of perfume is at the kitchen table, buttering toast. She looks like Becca, with thick lips and unblinking eyes. She looks me over the same way Becca did.

"Hello," I say, and she turns away. She's nothing like the grandmothers in movies.

"Howard, come in the kitchen," she says, "Benny's boy is here."

He shuffles in from the dining room with a pipe in his mouth. His lower lip is flecked with tobacco.

"Hello." I reach out my hand to give him a manly handshake.

"Hello," he answers, shaking my hand limply and clicking his pipe on his yellow teeth. "Bertha, fix something for the boy. He's probably hungry."

"Let Becca do it. It's her kid, not mine."

"How about bacon and eggs?" Becca asks.

"No. No thank you. I can't eat food that isn't kosher."

"This isn't a restaurant, boy," Bertha says. "In this house you'll eat what's offered."

"Ma, he's used to kosher food. I'll fix him some oatmeal."

No one offers me a seat, but I sit down at the table. Howard pulls up a chair next to me, takes out a pocketknife, and cleans his pipe. No one talks. I don't know how to address anyone. I wouldn't feel comfortable calling Becca mother, or her parents, grandma and grandpa. And I can't call them by their first names. I wish Dad would rescue me.

"My grandpa smokes a pipe, too."

"Eh, what did the boy say, Bertha?"

"I don't know. I wasn't listening to him."

"He said his grandfather smokes a pipe," Becca says from the stove.

The silence continues. Becca sets a bowl of oatmeal and a spoon in front of me. Howard's breath, Bertha's perfume, and the color of the kitchen walls make me lose my appetite.

"How do you like it?" Becca asks.

"It's fine." Aunt Manya's oatmeal with raisins, brown sugar, cream and two pats of butter is delicious. This is tasteless mush.

When I finish, she says, "I'll take you to your room."

I follow her to the foot of the stairs, picking up my satchel on the way. She picks up the big suitcase as if it weighs nothing and leads me up two flights to my bedroom on the third floor. My very own bedroom, with a real bed, dresser, and desk. On the desk is a big tan blotter with brown leather corners. Everything is new. I feel important.

"How do you like your room?"

"I like it a lot."

"Let me help you put your things away."

She opens the closet, hangs up three long-sleeved shirts, three pairs of knickers, two with ragged knees, and my blue mackinaw. Everything else fits in one drawer.

She screws up her face. "I'm taking you to Barney's Boy's Town to buy some decent clothes."

I have on the ones I wear on high holidays. After Becca goes downstairs, I open my satchel and put away my baseball glove, a deck of cards, *David Copperfield*, a *Superman* comic book, a new Spaldine, arithmetic cards, and a box of crayons.

There's shouting outside the window. Seven boys all in different shades of black are playing basketball in the dirt backyard of the house next door. They're shooting the ball into a bushel basket nailed to a tree. I'll have kids to play with.

The dog is yelping when I go downstairs. The cellar door is open, and below, Bertha is whipping the dog with its leash. "That'll teach you to piss on the floor, you mangy son of a bitch."

Howard brushes by me, heads downstairs. "Bertha, don't be so mean. Spotty can't help it. He's getting old like me. We'll have to walk him more often."

"I'm tired of walking that damned dog."

"Norman's here. He can walk Spotty. How'd you like that?"

"I'd like it a lot." I reach down to pet him.

"Careful, he'll bite you," Bertha says.

"No he won't. He likes me."

"A smart mouth, like his father." She mops the floor and then goes upstairs.

"What kind of dog is he?"

"A Staffordshire bull terrier."

"Why is he tied up?"

"So he won't jump into the coal bin and get dirty."

"Can't he go upstairs?"

"Bertha doesn't want him in the house."

"You mean he's tied up all day and all night?"

"Well, yes. We need a watch dog."

"What could he do if someone broke in?"

"He'd bark."

"I think he'd be happy to see a robber. He'd jump up and lick him."

"That's a good one."

I hold onto Spotty's leash and let him pull me down the street. I've never walked a dog before, and this one's powerful. Howard says he weighs forty-five pounds. Some of the boys I saw from my room are now on their front porch being scolded by a fat woman in a rocking chair. One of the boys, with kinky hair and freckles, walks over to pet Spotty.

"I'm Cecil."

"I'm Norman."

"My brothers are afraid of Spotty, but not me. Where do you come from?"

"Brooklyn. I just moved in this morning."

"Cecil, get your black ass back over here. I'm not done with you," the woman shouts.

"See you later, Norman."

We walk for three blocks, and people move out of our way. Spotty sniffs at every tire and telephone pole. I didn't know a dog could pee so much.

A man asks, "Does your dog bite?"

"I don't know. It's my first time out with him."

Another man judges the length of the leash. "I ain't afraid of your dog." Spotty growls, and the man backs off.

At the window of a pawnshop, I look through the steel bars at a silver clock made in Germany and wish I could buy it for Grandpa. The two guns next to it bother me. It's okay to play cowboys and Indians on the street in Brooklyn, where shooting is make-believe, but these guns are real.

Spotty licks my hand. I rub his head. He's my friend. On the way back, I stop at the synagogue. A bulletin board behind cracked glass says *cheder*. I won't have to go far to Hebrew school.

Becca is on the phone when I walk through the door. I take Spotty downstairs and feel bad about having to tie him up. It would be great if he could sleep in my bedroom.

Becca hangs up when I close the basement door. "I think I'll go up-stairs and try out my new desk. Can I have a pencil and paper to draw on?"

"*May I* have a pencil and paper. *May I* is better than *can I*."

"May I…"

"Take these." She tears off three sheets from the telephone stand note pad. "You can have this pencil, too."

"Thank you."

"Don't you have anything better to do than draw pictures?"

"I can read my book."

"What book?"

David Copperfield. My aunt lent it to me. She has a whole set of Charles Dickens' books."

I feel like David Copperfield, not sure what's going to happen to me next. I climb the carpeted stairs two at a time. The door to the bathroom on my floor is wide open, and a naked lady is drying her hair with a yellow bath towel. It's covering her face. I stand in the hallway and watch. When she sees me, she covers her front with the towel and says, "Please close the door."

At my desk, I draw the woman's flabby arms, rolls of tummy fat, and blotchy thighs. When I forget what some part of her looks like, I close my eyes and the image appears. I cover both sides of the three pages with drawings.

"Who's the lady in the room next to mine?" I ask Becca that afternoon.

"Janet's our boarder."

She looks better with clothes on. She sits next to me at dinner, talks even when her mouth is full, and she moves her arms a lot, just missing my face with her fork.

All Howard says during our chicken dinner is, "Yes dear." Bertha seems to know better than he does about every subject.

"Norman, you're not a very big eater," Becca says. "Don't you like my cooking?"

Janet stops talking, Bertha scowls at me, and Howard twists the knob on his hearing aid.

"Your cooking is great. I'm just not hungry." I don't like to lie, and I hope God won't punish me for it. I'm really very hungry, but the food is tasteless. Blindfolded, I wouldn't know if I were eating potatoes, string beans, or corn.

Becca serves cheesecake for dessert, a definite no-no at Aunt Manya's, because dairy and meat at the same meal isn't kosher. But the cheesecake tastes better than anything else. From the identical flowered patterns on

Becca's plates, I'm sure she doesn't use separate dishes for dairy and meat. I'm living among Jewish gentiles.

"I'm tired of Harvey's goddamned cheesecake," Bertha says.

"So don't eat it Ma. No one's forcing you."

"Is Harvey's the name of the bakery?"

"No, Norman. Harvey's our roomer. He doesn't eat with us. He rents a room on our floor."

"He works at a bakery?"

"Right. And every Saturday he brings us a large cheesecake."

"I'd never get tired of cheesecake."

"You will," Bertha says. "Mark my words, you will."

CHAPTER 14

THE FOUR-SEWER MAN

Becca's mom and dad aren't up yet, so I can eat her tasteless breakfast without smelling Bertha's perfume and Howard's bad breath. "I'd like to go to the library today. Is it far?"

"It's somewhere on the other side of the el. You'll have to ask someone."

Without Spotty, the neighborhood doesn't seem safe. From a second story window, a woman shakes out a carpet, and dirt falls on my head. Children ride tricycles straight at me, and I have to dodge. I'm the only boy on the street wearing knickers.

A silver delivery truck is stuck between the pavement and the steel superstructure of the el. A tow truck is tugging it with a chain. A man says to the people watching, "If the chain snaps, it'll take your head off." They all take three steps back.

"Hey Mister, I got a good idea."

"Keep your ideas to yourself kid. We're busy here."

"Are you too busy to let some air out of the tires?"

The man hollers to the tow truck driver, "Hey Joe, I got a good idea. Let some air out of the tires!"

It works! The delivery truck slides out real easy.

Another man shakes my hand and says, "Nice goin' kid." He's wearing a tight tee shirt that shows off his muscles.

"Are you Charles Atlas?"

"No kid, but I took his bodybuilding course… Hey, you guys, ain't ya gonna give the kid a tip fer helping ya?"

"Yeah, all right." The tow-truck driver tosses me a silver dollar, says, "Keep the change."

I walk down the street, feeling the weight of it, flipping it up in the air, catching it, flipping it again, but it doesn't come down. The body-builder has it in his fist.

"You say anything kid, and you're dead."

Easy come, easy go, I say to myself. That's Dad's expression.

I cross the street and go into an *A&P*, the first supermarket I've ever been in. It has lines of silver carts, and the people at the counters don't have pencils on their ears. The cash registers do all the adding. Customers take cans from the shelves without a grocer hollering at them. In Brownsville, Mr. Berg never lets anyone touch the boxes or cans of food on his shelves. He picks them up himself. It's fun to watch him snag a box from the top of a high shelf with a special grabber. But here, the shelves are low, and even I can reach the top shelf, almost.

At the checkout counter, I spend all the money I have on a Mound's Bar. "Mister, where's the library?"

"I don't know, kid. I'm not from this neighborhood. Lemme ask the other checker. Hey Wanda, where's the library?"

"How should I know?" she says with a mouth full of gum, "Do I look like a librarian?"

"Young man," says a black woman in line behind me. "Wait by the door. I'll show you the way."

I carry her grocery bag for two blocks under the el. The sun shining through the tracks makes zebra patterns on passing trucks and busses. Screeching tires echo off the rusty steel beams. I look up when a train rumbles by.

"Don't do that. My son looked up one day, and a sliver of metal fell into his eye. I had to take him to the hospital."

I rub my eye. "Is he okay?"

"It damaged his cornea."

"I'm sorry. Thanks for warning me."

"Turn right and go four blocks. You can't miss the library. It's on the corner and has huge lamps on both sides of the door."

"Let me carry these bags to your house."

"Thank you, but I'll manage."

In the sunlight of the quiet street, the brick buildings have hints of different colors, earthy yellows, oranges, reds, and browns, like the builders were experimenting to see which one looks best. I'm glad they're different. If they weren't, the buildings would be boring.

Coming up the stairs of a basement pool hall are two Puerto Rican boys with dark, greasy hair. They walk next to me. When I slow down, they slow down. When I walk fast, they walk fast. I wish I had Spotty. There aren't any stores to run into. One boy lunges at the other, and I duck and put my arms up. They laugh. I keep on walking, listening to the sound of their footsteps, hoping they won't attack me, but I make it to the library okay.

"Excuse me, what would be good books for me to read?"

The librarian's face brightens. "How old are you?"

"Ten."

"Follow me. I think you'd like *Tom Sawyer*."

I read at a table in front of a barred window. Outside is a sooty tenement where the two boys I saw earlier are sitting on chairs on the fire escape, passing a cigarette back and forth. They're lucky to live next door to a library.

I have the whole day to look at volumes of paintings by Rembrandt. Halfway through the first book, I discover *An Old Man in an Armchair*. He looks just like Prayer Man, who I saw at Mount Hebron cemetery when I visited Mother's grave. I can almost hear him say, "I'll make prayers for the dead."

I say to him aloud, in Yiddish, "Peace be with you, man from Pinsk." The red garment in the picture blends into the red background; the hands and bearded face pop off the page. The real painting is at the Hermitage, in Russia.

The librarian tells me that these big art books are only for reference and can't be checked out. When they close at five, I leave with a brand new library card, four books, and a hug from the librarian.

A boy in knickers with an armload of books is fair game on the streets in this neighborhood, so I walk home like a hiker in rattlesnake country, expecting the worst.

At dinner, I try to tell everyone where I went today, but Janet keeps talking.

"I think I'll look for a new job. You can't tell those bosses anything. You can't get a word in edgewise," she says and knocks over my glass of milk.

After dinner, I try to tell Becca about the library, Howard about the tow truck, even Bertha about the supermarket, but they have more important things to do.

Next morning, while I'm finishing breakfast, Becca answers the hall telephone. "Hello... Norman? He's not here. Who is this? Sophie? Sophie who? A play?"

I walk behind Becca. I can hear Cousin Sophie's voice on the line, telling her she has tickets to *Finian's Rainbow*, and can I meet her and Cousin

Sarah at the 46th Street Theater in Manhattan tomorrow?

"No, he can't go tomorrow." She hangs up.

This can't be happening. Sophie, who never takes me anywhere, was going to take me to my first Broadway play! If I had a nickel, I'd call her back from the pay phone at the candy store. If Becca leaves, I'll use her phone. No chance, she stays in the house all day. I'm afraid to ask her if I can call Sophie. I feel empty. I could run away. I should run away. But I'd be running away from Dad.

Next day, instead of seeing *Finian's Rainbow* with Sophie and Sarah, I'm trying on gray corduroy slacks at Barney's Boy's Town in Manhattan. Becca tells me to be sure they fit right, and they don't have to be one size too big, as Aunt Manya would have insisted. Aside from the tuxedo pants I wore at Sophie's and Nathan's weddings, these are the first pair of long pants I've ever owned. I won't miss the knickers.

The salesman pokes at the toes of a pair of shoes I picked out, and Becca tells me to walk around the store to make sure they don't hurt. I leave with three shirts, three pairs of pants, socks, underwear, and a nice pair of shoes. I thank Becca, but I'm still mad at her for not letting me go with Sophie.

I want to be friends with Cecil next door. When I walk Spotty, Cecil comes out to pet him.

"You're wearing long pants now."

"Yeah."

"You a Dodgers fan?"

"Nah, I've always been for the Yankees."

He smiles. We talk about the Yankees and Joe DiMaggio. Cecil knows as many baseball statistics as I do. He's even been to a Yankee's game.

"My father used to be a prizefighter. He once knocked down Joe Louis."

"Wow. Did he really?"

"Honest. My father was his sparring partner."

"Cecil, come back to the house," his mother shouts.

Whenever she sees Cecil talking to me, she calls him back inside. Sometimes, his oldest brother, Willy, does it. Willy has a way of looking at me that tells me for sure that he doesn't like whites.

The first time I knock on Cecil's door, his mother says, "He's busy. He can't go out." She shuts the door in my face. The second time I knock, no one answers, even though I know the family is home. I stop going to his house, but we both nod if he's on his porch when I go by.

I walk the eight blocks to the library at least once a week to look at art books and to copy my favorite paintings. The librarian gives me pencils, paper, and an eraser. One day, when I show her a sketch that I've done of her, she reaches under her desk and brings out a big drawing pad and some number one pencils wrapped in a rubber band.

I spend a lot of time on Becca's porch, reading library books or drawing the Puerto Rican kids who roller-skate on the street. Bertha comes out of the house and chases me off her favorite chair by clearing her throat and pointing her thumb upwards, like a hitchhiker. She sits and knits and hardly ever talks to me. She never says anything about my drawings. Neither do Becca or Howard or Dad. I know they'd have something to say about my drawings of Janet, naked in the bathroom, but I hid those inside a comic book.

The Puerto Ricans use terrible language. Bertha doesn't like it even though hers is just as bad. "Why do those goddamned Spics have to play on our street?"

"It's their street, too."

"I've a good mind to call the police on them."

"They play here because there's hardly any traffic."

"You're just like your father. An answer for everything."

They call up to me, asking if I'd like to play, but I make excuses. They're not the kind of kids I want for friends, yet I can see that they're having a lot of fun.

Today, they roller-skate up to the front gate and wave me over, and because I'm lonely, I give in.

"What's your name?" their leader asks.

"Norman."

"I'm Felipe, but they call me El Duque. You got a nickname?"

I've never been called anything other than Norman or Norm, but since he expects me to have a nickname I think one up in a hurry and hope it doesn't already belong to one of them. "My friends call me Butch." I remember that name from a movie.

They yell out their names and add their nicknames, which I think is unusual: Pedro-Skunk, Juan-Gordo, Oscar-Moreno, Jose-Chico, Ramon-Diablo, and Rafael-El Toro.

"Ya wanna roller-skate with us?" El Duque asks.

"I don't have any skates."

"Chico, go home and get Butch a pair," El Duque orders.

We sit on the curb and wait for Chico. It's a hot day, and I can smell the fresh tar from a street repair in front of the house. Gordo takes out a switch-blade, slices off a piece of soft tar, and plops it into his mouth.

"Yuck, Gordo's eating tar," Moreno says.

"Gordo likes to eat tar," Diablo says.

"Gordo will eat anything," El Duque says.

El Duque's hair is slicked back, shiny like tar.

"Is that old lady on the porch your grandmother?" Moreno asks.

"Not exactly. She's not my real grandmother."

"She calls us Spics," Skunk says.

"Sorry about that."

"You must be rich, living in a three-story house," El Duque says.

"Yeah," Skunk says. "Only rich people can afford a house like that."

"You got a father?" El Duque asks.

"Yeah."

"How come I never see him around?"

"He doesn't come home till real late."

"He better watch out. Stuff goes on in this neighborhood after dark."

"A man got knifed last night," El Toro says. "He lives around the corner."

A siren blares, and a police car with its red light on speeds past our street.

"Stuff happens in the daytime, too," Skunk says. "There's robberies almost every day."

"Does your father carry a lot of money on him when he comes home from work?" El Duque asks.

"No, he carries a forty-five, and he works for the FBI. He's also knows jujitsu."

Chico comes back. I slide my shoes into the skates and turn the key tight. I've borrowed Seymour's skates before in Brooklyn. I skate across the street and back three times. Keeping my balance is easy. Stopping is a problem.

"Let's play Crack-the-Whip," El Duque says.

I don't know what Crack-the-Whip is, but it doesn't sound good. I think of cowboy movies at the Bluebird in Brooklyn, where springs stick out of the seats, but where they show five cartoons before the movie starts. And there's Whip Wilson, the tip of his whip wrapping around the bad guy's ankle or his gun hand, sending him flying off his horse. I think I know what this game is about.

The eight of us hold hands and skate down the tarred street in a single line. I'm in the middle, behind Gordo, who's still chewing tar. The kid behind me lets go of my hand, and the tail end of the line skates ahead of me and reattaches in front of Gordo. Now I'm on the end, and they're skating faster. We're a block from the end of the street where there's cross traffic. I try to pull away from Gordo before we get up to full speed, but he has a tight grip. I reach over with my other hand, grab his pinkie, and twist. He screams and I'm free of him, but there's the busy intersection, and I can't stop. I put both arms in front of me to cushion the blow as I slam into a parked car. Wham!

I pick myself off the ground and check to see if I'm still in one piece, as Sarah would say.

"Why did you let go?" El Duque asks.

"You think I wanna get killed?"

"The kid's smart," he says. "Not bad for a whitey."

I sit on the curb and unscrew the skates. I thought that lending them to me was a friendly thing to do, but they planned for me to get hurt or even killed. They aren't like my friends in Brooklyn.

"You can have your skates back, Chico." I limp back to the porch and go right to my library books. I'm on the last chapter of Gulliver's Travels, and the Bronx is my weird place. I don't ever want to play with those Puerto Rican kids again.

They're back the next day, calling me out for stickball. I can't stand them, but I can't turn down a chance to play the sweetest game in the world. I don't give any excuses. In ten seconds, I'm in the middle of the street.

Pow. I blast a homer past the synagogue, over four sewer-covers away. Next time up I blast one further. I've gained El Duque's respect. In Brooklyn, I was known as a four-sewer man. I wish Dad were on the porch, watching. He'd think I was a regular Joe DiMaggio, if he even knows who Joe DiMaggio is.

I sure don't know much about Dad. Did he play stickball in Vienna? Was he a four-sewer man? I don't see him any more now than I did when I lived in Brooklyn. I'm asleep when he comes home at night, and he's asleep when I wake up in the morning. I'm out playing when he dashes out of the house to make it to work in time for the lunch crowd.

I miss my friends in Brooklyn, especially Joey. For years I've envied his room, but now I have one of my own, and it's not so great. Today, when I come home from the library, Becca is showing my room to her friend, Flora Nelson, who lives in the house next to the synagogue.

"This is the oak bedroom set I told you about. Look, here in the closet, these are the new clothes I bought for him at Barney's Boy's Town. I'm sending him to Hebrew School."

"You're a good mother, Becca. Oh, hello Norman. Nice room you have here. You're a very lucky boy."

I'd rather be in my old army cot at Aunt Manya's even if she does holler a lot.

On Sundays, Becca gives me a quarter for the only movie house in the neighborhood. I enjoy the smells of spicy Puerto Rican food, chocolate, and beer from the cafes, candy stores, and bars on the way. There's music from almost every storefront. Puerto Rican voices are musical, too. Women dress in bright yellows, reds, and purples, and men wear tight black trousers with pegged cuffs and high waists. Gold chains hang from the men's pockets. I've seen a man flash a straight-edged razor, a boy show off his brass knuckles, and a woman punch a man in the face. The police hauled him away for knocking her down even though it was his nose that was bloody.

Today, there's a crowd watching two snarling Puerto Rican men being held back by their friends. They're pointing switchblades at each other, and their friends are pleading with them to settle their differences peacefully. It's hard to watch, but I can't stop. I hope the police come before someone gets hurt.

An old man shouts, "Hey *estupidos*, you want a scar like mine, fighting over a woman?" He traces the scar that goes from his ear to his chin. "You want to be blind, or dead? You want to spend your lives in prison?"

Other people speak up. "It's not worth fighting over a woman." "After your faces are cut up, she won't like either of you." "No woman is worth being cut up for." When the police come, the enemies are walking into a bar with their arms over each other's shoulders.

It's three more blocks to the movie. The shops are closed on Sundays. Two Puerto Rican guys a little older than I am keep pace with me.

"Hey man, can we borrow a quarter?"

"I don't have any money on me." There are no adults who I can walk beside as if I belonged with them. What would Melvin do? Dad said Melvin was "hard as nails" when he was my age. And when he was a boxer in the Navy, he never lost a fight. But I'm not Melvin. I'm scared.

"All we find we keep?"

That's a common expression in this neighborhood. I hope they don't have razors on them. I keep walking. The movie house is a long block and a half away. I wipe sweat off my forehead. A police car passes. I open my mouth to yell, but if the officers don't hear me, things could get worse. They don't try to slow me down. We pass a black man holding a paper bag with the neck of a brown bottle poking through. He's talking to himself.

One block to go. "There's a cop car," I shout and run fast, expecting to be tackled to the hard sidewalk and lose my quarter, my watch, and maybe a lot of blood. But I make it to the ticket booth, and shove my quarter under the glass cage. The cashier gives me a dime change. Now, I have to get to the ticket taker at the front door.

"You said you didn't have any money on you. You lied to us."

"I only had enough on me for a movie and a candy bar."

"I think you got more quarters."

"You better share with us."

"Get lost," the ticket taker says and threatens them with his fist. I hand him my ticket and go inside.

"We're gonna wait here 'till the movie's over."

"Yeah, we're gonna get you later."

I worry through the newsreel, the cartoons, and *The Ghost and Mrs. Muir.* I make sure to sit between two people, because if those guys sneak inside, they'll sit on either side of me, and I won't be able to get away.

After the show, a different ticket taker is on duty, so I can't ask him if he's seen those guys. All the way home I imagine footsteps behind me. I wish Melvin, my big brother, were with me.

At home, I look at the map of the United States in the back of my geography book and find Vallejo, California. It's near San Francisco. How long would it take to get there by bicycle? But even if I owned a bike, how would I eat? Where would I sleep? I won't go to that movie house again, even if *The Wizard of Oz* is playing.

Now, on Sundays, with a pencil and sketchbook, I take the train to Manhattan and walk to Fifth Avenue and the Metropolitan Museum of Art. The guards know me, and I know some of them by name. I ask about Joshua Mellancamp, the curator, but I'm told that he doesn't work here anymore.

The Rembrandt room is hushed, as it should be. The paintings here are as sacred as the *Torah* in my *shul*. There's *Man in Fanciful Costume*, *Hendrickje as Flora*, *The Standard Bearer*, *Juno*, but my favorite is *The Framemaker, Herman Doomer*. He looks real enough to breathe. I rough in the outlines of his face from the bench in the middle of the gallery, and I stand in front of him to copy the details.

Before I leave, I walk over to Rembrandt's self-portrait for one last peek. The eyes twinkle, and the lips seem to move. A feeling comes over me like the one I get when I look at mother's photographs. It's kinda like if I could say the magic word, then Mother or Rembrandt would talk to me.

Phil, the guard, comes over. "Lets see what you drew… Great work, Norman. Your drawings are improving. I bet your mother is really proud of you."

"I don't have a mother."

"Oh, I'm sorry… I bet your father is really proud of you."

"I don't know. I hardly ever see him."

"I see… well, I wonder what your pal, Rembrandt, would say if he were alive."

"He'd probably say, 'Out of the way, kid. You're blocking the view. Other people wanna see, too.'"

"If you don't make it as an artist, you can always go into stand-up comedy."

I will make it. I'd rather be an artist than a comic or even a four-sewer man.

CHAPTER 15

HAPPY HOLIDAYS IN THE BRONX

Kids hang around in the streets, waiting for the bell to ring. They don't line up in quiet rows like in the schoolyard in Brooklyn. There's no grass between the black iron fence and the school. Paint on the green doors is peeling. Eggs are splattered over the graffiti on the brick walls.

Alex twists my arm behind my back, jerks it upwards, and threatens to break it unless I give him my Waterman fountain pen. I hate to part with it. Its wide point makes my handwriting almost good. My new plan is to arrive at school when the first bell is ringing.

Mrs. Fernandez is on the alert to stop kids from looking at my test papers. The school doesn't have a Mrs. Hartman, like PS 165. She'd pass out three-by-five cards and make the cheaters learn arithmetic the hard way.

Cecil is in my class. He walks to school with his brother, who threatens to tell his mother if he walks with me. Aunt Manya used to forbid me to play with gentiles. My friend Vincent and I had the same birthday and were in the same class, but we weren't allowed into each other's houses.

"You shouldn't play with Italians," Aunt Manya warned.

"You shouldn't play with Jews," Vincent's mother said to him.

I sit next to Daniel, a Jewish boy, who lives as far away on one side of the school as I do on the other. He isn't allowed to walk the thirteen blocks that separate us, because his mother says my neighborhood is too dangerous. Daniel has a Band-Aid on his forehead and a black eye.

"What happened?"

He looks around the room, then whispers, "Puerto Ricans on roller skates asked me for money, and when I said I didn't have any, they searched me and found twenty cents. Then they beat me up."

"What did they look like?"

"Spics," he whispers. "They all look alike to me. Except one, who was real fat. I think they called him Gordon."

We eat on the school steps. "I wish your mother would let you come to my house. I'd show you my dog, Spotty. He's a bulldog. Almost everyone is afraid of him. We could take him with us when we go to the candy store."

"You're lucky, Norman. I wish I had a dog."

"Hey, I'll trade you my cheesecake for your pickled herring."

"Cheesecake? Who ever heard of trading cheesecake? I'll give you my whole lunch for it."

"No. Just give me the herring. I haven't had any since I left Brooklyn."

After school on the day before Halloween boys are armed with nylon stockings filled with powdered chalk. They swing them like war clubs, hit their victims, and streak them with chalk. On the way home from school, I buy a box of chalk at the candy store. I also have a pocket full of broken sticks from the blackboard at school. By the time I reach the house, neighborhood kids have streaked me with chalk.

Becca gives me an old pair of nylons. I go down to the basement, spread newspaper on the floor, and Spotty watches me crush the chalk with a hammer and load a stocking. Now, I can protect myself.

After school on Halloween, I put my loaded stocking in my jacket pocket and take a long walk. It feels good to get out of the neighborhood even though I feel safer there lately. People accept me even though we never speak to each other. In new neighborhoods, people look at me suspiciously, and storekeepers are extra vigilant. But I like to explore the streets.

I take out my stocking and twirl it around for no reason at all while counting the lines in the sidewalk. At a street corner, a little boy sees me and starts to cry.

"I'm not gonna hurt you." I stuff the stocking in my pocket. But the boy keeps crying, and a woman shouts from her porch, "Leave him alone. Go pick on someone your own size." I'm about to tell her that I'm not picking on him, when a man flies down the steps. So I run fast for three blocks before I even look back. I'm safe now. No, I'm not! Out from a side street, swinging chalk weapons like mine, four boys rush me. I swing my stocking at them, but they surround me and knock me into the gutter, where I curl up in a ball and wrap my arms around my head. They keep pelting me until a woman yells at them in Spanish and chases them away.

"Your nose is bleeding. Hold your head back. That's right."

She wipes my nose with her handkerchief. "Are you all right? I mean, besides your bloody nose, are you all right?"

"Yes. I'm okay. Thank you for stopping the bleeding."

"You're a polite young man. Where do you live?"

"Hewitt Place, near the IRT station."

"Oh, dear!"

On the way home, I'm worried that I'll run into the same gang or that angry man. In my reflection in a store window, I'm a snowman with a red nose.

Halloween in the Bronx is different from the way it is in Brooklyn.

In art class, Cecil is watching me draw Mrs. Fernandez.

"Sorry we can't walk to school together. My little brother will tell on me."

"At least he can't spy on us here."

"A white man killed my uncle last year. That's why my mother won't let me play with you."

"I understand. I'm sorry about your uncle. What happened?"

"He was at a party with his girlfriend, and a drunk guy was hassling him, so they tried to leave. They were at the top of the staircase when the guy charged into my uncle and knocked him down the stairs. My uncle's neck broke."

"I hope they put that guy away forever."

"Me too... Norman, how can you draw the teacher when she's not posing for you?"

"I memorize her face in a certain position, and if I forget some detail, I wait 'till she's in that position again."

"I wish I could do that. Hey, I almost forgot. Here's your Waterman pen. I told that bully, Alex, that if he ever messes with you again, I'll tell my father. Alex knows he used to spar with Joe Louis."

I put my arm around Cecil. "Thank you."

Snow is falling. I'm touching up a picture I drew on the blackboard of Santa Claus and his reindeer. There are pine trees in the background and snow under the sleigh.

"It looks so real that I can feel the cold," Cecil says, "even though it's seventy-five degrees in the classroom."

I don't have to use an eraser very much. It's as if the picture is already completed in my head, and all I have to do is transfer the image to the blackboard. I use green chalk for the trees and red chalk for Santa's suit and for pinking up his cheeks.

Mrs. Fernandez and the class think the picture is perfect. The principal comes in and writes "Do not erase!" all around it. Then, just before the last bell rings, a man with a flash camera comes in and snaps photos of my drawing. Not bad, I say to myself, for a four-sewer man.

Next day, in arithmetic class, I keep staring at the picture, not because it's so great, but because something is wrong with it. I figure out what it is by the time art class begins. "Hey Cecil, something about Santa bothers me."

"That's because you're Jewish."

"It's not that. He's too flat. He looks like he's pasted on the black-board."

"He looks great to me."

"Not to me, he doesn't. I have to make him three dimensional." I pick up an eraser.

"No, Norman, don't touch it, please."

"Norman's erasing Santa Claus," one girl shouts.

"What are you doing, Norman?" Mrs. Fernandez asks.

"I'm not happy with this Santa." I make him shorter and plumper, and they clap.

Since Daniel isn't allowed to come to my house, I go to his on a Saturday morning. The streets are slushy, and the sidewalks, slippery. Store windows are painted with Merry Xmas, *Feliz Navidad*, and Santas that aren't drawn as well as mine. The neighborhood is cheerful, and I feel safer.

Families are picking out Christmas trees at a busy lot. I walk through the lot, touching the sharp green needles and smelling the pines. I'm as happy as if I were in a real forest.

A man in a red woolen cap huddles over an oil drum full of fiery coals. He makes change from a large wad of bills. "Okay, okay, I'll knock off a buck, but I can't go any lower," he says to a young couple. "Merry Christmas." The scene is strange to me. I love it and hate it. What a waste to cut down all these trees and spend the next week watching them die.

I'm gonna have to deduct the six minutes I spent at the Christmas tree lot. I'm timing my walk on the neat watch Howard gave me. The hands glow in the dark, and the chrome wristband stretches over my hand. Howard is a janitor at a high school, and he keeps me supplied with sneakers, pens, pencils, and other things he finds in the classrooms. I'm keeping warm with the blue woolen muffler he gave me.

Two boys wearing black ski masks step in front of me one block before I get to Daniel's house. They're not planning to wish me a Merry Christmas.

"Lend me some money."

"I don't have any."

"Come on, man. I know you got some."

"No, I don't. I spent my last nickel on a candy bar." I know what happened to Daniel. I wish I had a quarter to buy my way out of trouble. "Hey, there's the police."

I run around them. I plan to keep running until I see a grownup or an open store. I'm slipping on the ice. I can't catch myself. I land on my behind and slide to a stop. Now they're standing over me, laughing. I know that one laugh. I've heard it from my bedroom window. I hope they don't start kicking me and not know when to quit. One boy grabs my arm and pulls me up.

"Fine lookin' watch you got."

That voice. It's definitely Willy, Cecil's brother. He rips off the watch, and they run away.

Easy come, easy go. I'm glad I didn't get beat up.

I find Daniel's apartment house, ring his bell, and get buzzed inside.

"Too bad about your watch, Norman. My father says the sooner we get out of New York City, the better off we'll be. We're gonna go to Connecticut. Come see my models."

Five solid-model airplanes, painted in camouflage colors, sit on a shelf. The wingspans are nine inches. The P-38 is my favorite. Daniel's lucky to have parents who appreciate his work and display it in a place of honor right below a portrait.

"They're real nice. You did a good job. Is that a picture of your grandmother?"

"Yeah. My father painted it. He paints on weekends."

"Well, the painting is real nice."

Aunt Manya once told me that I'm a diplomat, able to hold my tongue and not say what's really on my mind. Other times I'm just the opposite, like when I hollered cockroach in front of the rabbi's wife or told Aunt Manya she looked like a witch. Actually, the airplanes aren't that great. It's like Daniel rushed through the modeling without paying enough attention to details like the contour of the wings or the smoothness of the fuselage. And the colors of the painting of his grandmother grate on my nerves. Aunt Manya uses that expression a lot. Of course, it doesn't take much for anything to grate on her nerves. The colors fight with each other, and the woman's face is flat, but I'm not going to tell Daniel this. I don't want to lose my only friend in the Bronx.

We play chess until his mother comes home and fixes us chicken sandwiches. She's very nice. I wish Dad had married someone like her.

On the way home it's colder, and there's more ice to slide on, but I make it to Hewitt Place without being attacked.

When I come home from school and put my books down, I think I've walked into the wrong house. There's a Christmas tree in the living room. It makes me queasy. I'll pretend it's a Hanukkah bush. It doesn't help.

Christmas morning I hear laughter. The boys next door, silhouetted against the overnight snow, are having a snowball fight. Except for Willie, I wish I could play with them. It would be better than playing with El Duque and his friends. Their idea of fun is to throw snowballs with rocks inside.

I open the window, breathe in the cold air, scoop up snow from the windowsill, and make three heavy wet snowballs. Cecil waves to me from across the yard, and Willy throws a snowball in his face.

I squeeze one of my snowballs, trying to turn it into a smooth crystal ball, but it doesn't work. I leave them on the ledge, shut the window of my lonely room, and walk down to the second floor past the bedroom where Dad is having a Lucky Strike cigarette cough. No sense going in to talk to him while he spits phlegm for twenty minutes. Downstairs, the radio is on, and Bing Crosby is singing.

> I'm dreaming of a white Christmas
> Just like the ones I used to know
> Where the treetops glisten
> And children listen
> To hear sleigh bells in the snow...

I'd like to be in Brooklyn, playing in the snow with Joey and Seymour, having tea and cake with Aunt Manya on icy afternoons while she talks about the importance of a college education. I'd like to go to 34th Street with Sarah to look in Macy's windows, to Rockefeller Center to watch the ice-skaters, and to Radio City Music Hall to see Danny Kaye. I miss my real family.

Becca calls me into the living room. Mean-faced Bertha, in her pink robe, sits in a straight-backed chair next to the Christmas tree like a sentry guarding a fort. Howard sits in a brown leather chair, smoking his stinking pipe. Dad comes in with a cigarette in his mouth, still coughing, and sits next to Becca on the couch. He pats her watermelon tummy.

"Merry Christmas," she says. Howard and Bertha mouth the words. Dad yawns.

"Merry Christmas," I whisper. I wish I could gargle out those words. I stand there not knowing what else to say.

"Well, aren't you going to open your presents?" Becca asks, handing me a red package. Inside, there's a brown sweater from Barney's Boy's Town. She gives me a two-volume encyclopedia and three drawing pads. She's not so bad. But Dad's name isn't on the labels.

"Thank you for the presents." I try to hug her, but she pushes me away.

"Be careful of the baby."

Dad says nothing.

There are presents from Bertha and Howard. I feel awkward opening them. I don't like Bertha, and she doesn't like me. I don't like Becca either. Howard is okay. No, he isn't okay. He followed Dad and me when we went for a walk around the neighborhood. He's not good at spying. I bet he couldn't protect me from bullies.

I part the white tissue paper in one box and find a vomit-colored shirt. The lost and found at Howard's school must have run out of nice ones. I hold it up to me and pretend to like it. I also get a used wallet and a Bulova wristwatch with a scratched glass.

I shake Howard's dead-fish hand. "Thank you for the watch. I really like it."

"I hope you don't lose this one, too."

"I didn't lose the other one. Willy stole it."

"Don't argue with Howard," Bertha says. "You have a bad habit of contradicting people. I talked to Willy's mother. Her family is religious. They don't steal."

"They do, too."

"Now you're contradicting me. See Benny? What did I tell you?"

"Bertha, Norman is sticking up for his rights. Why shouldn't his word be as good as your neighbor's?"

"It's Christmas, Benny, can't we talk happy?" Becca asks.

"You're right… Norman, thank Bertha for your presents?"

"Thank you for the presents," I say as politely as I can. I try to give her a hug, but she pulls away, which is okay by me. Bertha is colder than Aunt Manya and her perfume doesn't cover the bad odor. I can finally go to my room to read.

A couple of weeks later, Dad says, "Your grandfather died in his sleep. He shrunk down to nothing. He weighed sixty-five pounds."

"What did he die of?"

"Old age. He was ninety-six."

I hadn't seen Grandfather for almost a year. Aunt Ellie had to feed him and bathe him like a baby.

It's drizzling as Dad and I enter the funeral parlor in Queens. We sit in a pew behind Aunt Ellie and her two sons. The sons are talking about business. Sourpuss Larry isn't here. He's tending to the candy store. Aunt Lilly and Aunt Flo are on the other side of Dad. Uncle Tim died six months ago. He had no faith in doctors or hospitals. I bet he'd still be alive if he'd gone to a good doctor, like Dr. Apfel, when he first came down with consumption. I hope I don't come down with it after all the times Aunt Manya wished it on me.

"Where are the girls?" Dad asks Aunt Flo.

"They couldn't get time off."

I know she's lying. Anyone can get off when a grandfather dies. Are Aunt Flo's daughters really walking around the city with mattresses on their backs, in the rain? Why aren't my other aunts and their families in the funeral parlor? Half of Grandfather's family is missing.

After the rabbi says prayers for the dead, he gives a sermon and praises Grandfather so much that anyone would think they were best friends. "He was a wise man who was descended from the *Kohanim*, the high priests. He brought his wife and children from Austria to the United States to escape religious persecution. His hobby was the restoration of old clocks."

During the sermon, Aunt Ellie's sons quietly talk to each other nonstop, and I hear stuff like, "I paid him under the table." "Now is the wrong time to buy that stock." "Do you think the crabby bastard left us anything?" Dad is bent forward, listening to them, chewing his lip, and moving his head from side to side. With his big hands, he reaches in front and slams their heads together with a clunk loud enough for the rabbi to hear.

"Come with me Norman to see your grandfather one last time."

"I'll wait here."

"It would be a sin not to see him."

I know it isn't a sin, but to please Dad I follow him to the casket. Tiny Grandfather looks as if he's sleeping. I keep looking for his chest to move. I wish he'd wake up and say, "Piss on Austria."

My aunts are crying. Dad is gritting his teeth. The rabbi is hammering the pine casket shut. My cousins are rubbing their heads. A flash of lightning lights up the chapel window, and there's the rumble of thunder.

In a black limousine, we follow the hearse to the cemetery.

"It's good luck when it rains on a funeral," Aunt Lilly says.

I wonder if it rained when Mother was buried. And if it did rain, who got the good luck? Dad is sitting next to me in the back seat, and he's still gritting his teeth. Aunt Manya says that people who grit their teeth all the time are *ferbissoners*, grouches, but Dad isn't a *ferbissoner* today. He's just sad.

There's more lightning and thunder. The limousine pulls into the cemetery with windshield wipers going full speed. I don't see any prayer men around. The casket is sitting over the grave on top of iron pipes. A mound of earth next to it is covered by a green tarp. Aunt Ellie and my cousins are wearing raincoats and rain hats. Aunt Lilly, Aunt Flo, and I are huddled under Aunt Lilly's black umbrella that has holes in it, listening to the rabbi's long prayer. Water is dripping from the brim of the rabbi's hat onto his prayer book. Dad's hands are folded over the front of his coat, and he's saying by heart the same words the rabbi is reading from his prayer book. The rain lets up, and a little bit of sun shows through the clouds, lighting up the grave. Aunt Flo gasps.

"It's a sign," Aunt Lilly says.

This is a Rembrandt painting. I'm going to memorize this moment and draw it at home.

Cemetery workers in high rubber boots lower the casket. When they take off the tarp, Dad tosses in the first shovelful of earth. This is the saddest part of all. Goodbye, Grandpa.

Dad wakes me up to tell me that the baby came. I wonder if there's some link between births and deaths. Mother died three days after I was born, and Grandfather's funeral was three days before the new baby boy was born. Do old people die to make room for new babies? Why did Mother have to die? She wasn't very old.

I'm not allowed near the new baby. I don't know what Becca thinks I would do to him. I wasn't allowed to go near Sophie's baby when I had the whooping cough, but I'm not sick now.

He sleeps a lot, and I'm told to tiptoe up the stairs, to speak softly, to not slam the door. Becca and her mother are busy with the baby, and I'm ignored, but it's all right with me.

I've been looking forward to my special day for weeks, but this Groundhog Day is the first time no one says happy birthday to me at the breakfast table. Instead, when I lean over to get a better look at my new brother, Becca says, "Don't breathe on my baby."

The phone rings. I answer it, because Becca is nursing the baby. Did Mother nurse me at least once before she died?

"Happy birthday, Norman," Cousin Sarah says from Brooklyn. It's good to hear her voice.

"Thank you, Sarah."

"Imagine, our little Norman, eleven years old. Tell me, how are they treating you there?"

"Okay. They treat me okay." What else can I say within earshot of Becca?

"Here's Momma."

"Happy birthday."

"Thank you, Aunt Manya."

"Eleven years old. How time flies. You're doing well in school, Norman?"

"Of course Aunt Manya, I always do well in school."

"In Hebrew school, too, you're doing well?"

"Not as good as in public school."

"So you'll have to study harder. Remember, your bar mitzvah is coming up in two years."

"Who's on the phone?" Becca asks, standing over me, burping the baby.

"My Aunt Manya."

"Well, cut it short. I'm expecting a call."

"I heard what she said, the witch. May she roast in hell." I imagine Aunt Manya's red face, her clenched fist, the spit spraying from her mouth. I hold the receiver tight against my ear so Becca can't hear. "Goodbye Norman, be well, and call me from a pay phone if you need anything."

"Goodbye Aunt Manya, and say hello to Uncle Irving and Nathan and Debbie and Sol and Sophie and Joey."

"Hang up the goddamned phone, Norman."

"Goodbye, Aunt Manya."

Dad comes downstairs as I leave the house with schoolbooks under my arm.

"Bye-bye, Norman."

"Bye, Dad." I don't remind him that it's my birthday.

Weeks pass. I've never held my baby brother or touched his chubby fingers. I tiptoe into Becca's room, stand next to his crib, watch him sleep. Becca comes in and says, "What are you doing here?" Before I can answer, she grabs my arm and yanks me into the hallway. "Don't you ever sneak into my room again, Mister."

"I just wanted to see him."

"You stay away from him. Do you hear me?"

"Yes. I'll stay away."

From then on, I spend as little time as possible in the house.

CHAPTER 16

LOSS OF INNOCENCE

It's spring. Boys are playing marbles in Daniel's neighborhood. Potso has cut three openings in a cardboard box that look like mouse holes in a Tom and Jerry cartoon. One opening is slightly wider than a marble, one is half again as wide, and one is twice as wide. He sits on the curb while boys ten feet away take turns trying to roll their marbles into one of the openings. The largest opening pays two marbles to one, the next smaller, five to one, and the smallest, ten to one. Potso gets to keep the ones that miss.

Daniel lends me twenty marbles, and I try my luck, rolling them at the biggest opening. I get through almost every time and win all of Potso's marbles. I pay Daniel back and give him a few extras. Then I find a box behind a grocery store and make a game of my own, cutting out the openings with a pocketknife that Howard gave me, but I cut the medium and big openings a little bit smaller than Potso did. I set up my box where the surface of the street is slightly rough. Sitting at the curb with the box between my legs, I win a sack full of marbles from boys on the street.

Daniel gets bored and goes home, and I'm about to go home myself when Potso comes up to me and introduces his older brother, Marco, who says, "I wanna play."

"Okay by me."

"But first I need to borrow a few marbles."

"Don't you have any of your own?"

"Not yet, but I will pretty soon."

"It's getting late. I have to go home for dinner."

He grabs my wrist and says, "It wouldn't kill you to play another five minutes. My kid brother didn't leave while you were winning his marbles."

"Okay. Just five minutes."

"Good. Now lend me twenty-five marbles."

While I'm thinking about how to get out of this situation, Marco keeps slapping his right fist into the palm of his left hand, so I give him the marbles. He walks ten feet away to my chalk line in the street, rolls three marbles at the box and misses.

"Hey, the street ain't smooth here. Scoot down that way about five feet. Yeah. That's better."

He loses the next fifteen marbles. The *schmuck* will lose his last seven, and I can go home.

Potso whispers to his brother.

"Good idea," Marco says. He stands off to one side and rolls his marbles in an arc so they slide across the front of my box, hitting an opening every time. He starts to win like crazy.

"Hey, you have to stand in front of the box."

"Who says?"

"I say. It's the rule."

"Show me your rule book."

"I don't have it on me."

"Well, until you show it to me, I'll do it my way."

"It's been over five minutes. I gotta go."

"Not until I'm done playing." He pushes his fist into my chest. I stay until he wins all my marbles.

"What about the ones I lent you?"

"Oh yeah. I forgot about them." He picks out chipped ones to pay me back.

Easy come, easy go. On the way home I find a sewer, and one by one, roll my marbles along the curb until they all disappear down the grate.

Too bad "tough as nails" Melvin is in California. Well, maybe my little brother can look up to me some day, if Becca ever lets him be my little brother.

On one of my after-school walks, I find a condemned school surrounded by a rusty cyclone fence. On the fence is a sign that says Boys' Club. Boys are playing softball in the yard, on rough blacktop, the kind that gashes your knees if you fall on it. I have these scars as proof. I walk through the gate, hoping to get in a game.

"Are you a member here?" asks a wiry man wearing a Yankees cap. His badge reads "Mr. Gonzalez."

"No, but I'd like to be."

"Go to the office, first door on your left, and they'll give you a form to fill out."

Now I'm a member of the Boys' Club. The first time softball sides are chosen, I'm picked last and have to catch. I don't like catching. It's easy to get hit by the bat. But after the guys see me hit the ball, I'm the first to be picked, and I get my favorite position, shortstop. It's fun to scoop up grounders and throw batters out at first. I have the highest batting average on the team. A softball coming at me looks as big as a basketball, and I can hit it a mile whether it's high or low, fast or slow, or even if I have to stretch to reach it. Playing stickball in Brooklyn paid off. I used to hit tiny Spaldines with a broomstick and hardly ever struck out.

"Nice going, Norman," Mr. Gonzalez says when I make a good play. His powerful hands remind me of Dad's, only Dad never played ball with me.

On rainy days, we play inside. Boxing is the most popular indoor sport at the club, but it looks like a good way to get hurt. A few boys work on jigsaw puzzles. Manuel always hides one of the pieces so he can put in the last one, and he cheats at chess and checkers. I don't know how he can enjoy winning a game that way. I get annoyed with him and go into the gym to watch the fights. The room is hot and smells of sweat and garlic. The Puerto Ricans are good boxers, and they ask me if I want to try, but I shake my head, no. It doesn't look like fun.

Mr. Gonzalez urges me to try.

"C'mon Norman, put on the gloves. Let's see what you can do."

"No thank you, Mr. Gonzalez."

The boys start calling me *maricon* and *pendejo* and shame me into putting on the gloves. I've never worn them before. I've never been in a fight.

The boxing ring is a white square painted on the wooden floor. I stand in the middle with my hands to my face, fending off Francisco's punches. He's smaller than me and moves around the floor like a dancer while his friends shout, "Hit 'em." "Knock Norman down."

The referee is Mr. Gonzalez. He tells me to start punching, but I've never hit anyone in my life. I stand stiffly and protect myself for two rounds. At last, he stops the fight and says he'll box with me to show me how it's done.

Just him and me in a small room. He kneels on the floor and throws lots of quick punches at me that are so soft that I barely feel the ones I can't block.

"You can protect yourself fairly well, but that's not going to win a fight unless you know how to punch, too. When you hit an opponent, it has to be more than a love tap, or you won't gain his respect. So here's what you have to do, Norman. Make believe he's two feet further away than he really is. Then, when you connect, he'll feel it… C'mon, throw a punch."

I can't hit him any more than I can hit Dad. Jews are supposed to honor their elders. Mr. Gonzalez is making me fight when I don't want to. His glove slaps across my face. He's getting impatient with me.

"Well, Norman, I guess if you won't box, you might as well forget about playing softball with us."

I throw a bunch of punches to his head, and he blocks them.

"Now we're getting somewhere." He's grinning one of those "ear to ear" grins that tells me he's gotten what he wants. "Listen up. Your left hand is just as important as your right. If you jab off to one side, like this, your opponent's eyes will follow that jab, and in the split second he's distracted you come in with a killer punch and knock him on his ass. Now get in the ring again."

Francisco is faster and more aggressive this time. I can't avoid his blows. I throw a couple of punches to his head, but he ducks. His puffy-looking gloves feel like stones crashing into my head.

"Keep your guard up, protect your face," Mr. Gonzalez says.

The boys shout, "Beat up Norman." "Kill *El Blanco*." "Murder the Jew Boy."

"Ignore the racist talk, I'll deal with that," Mr. Gonzalez says.

Francisco is hurting me, but I can't give up and be called a fag. If Melvin was a "hard as nails" boxer in the Navy, I can try to be one right here in this ring even if I get the shit knocked out of me, which is what is happening. I feint with my left, way out to the side, and sure enough, Francisco is distracted. With all the anger inside me, I swing at his unprotected mid-section, making believe it's two feet farther away. WHAP. I hit him in what I learn is his solar plexus. He lowers his gloves and stares at me, his mouth open. I throw another punch at his chin. Something pops. Everything is happening in slow motion. I have time to land another punch to his nose. His knees collapse, and now he's on the floor. I back away. Am I tough? Am I violent? Look what I've done to him.

"We're gonna get you, Jew Boy," I hear as Mr. Gonzalez bends over

Francisco with a towel, trying to stop the bleeding from his nose. My stomach is turning over. Manuel, the cheater, takes off my gloves and tells me how great I looked when I connected. I run home, looking back once in a while to make sure that Francisco's friends aren't following me.

I'm panting when I get to Becca's porch. My brother is in his playpen, sucking on a baby bottle that's propped up on a pillow. I catch my breath and watch him. His bottle rolls away, and he cries. I reach into the playpen for it. Becca rushes out the front door and yells, "Don't touch my baby!"

"I didn't touch him. His bottle rolled away, and I was just gonna give it to him."

"You leave his bottle alone, and you leave him alone."

"But he's my baby brother. What's so terrible about giving him his bottle?"

"I won't stand here and allow you to question me. I told you before to stay away from him, and now I'm telling you for the last time. Do you hear me, Mister?"

"Yes, I hear you. I promise I won't go near your baby again."

I also don't go anywhere near the Boys' Club.

I'm glad Hebrew School is only a half-block away. Mrs. Norotsky patiently corrects me when I make a mistake reading a Hebrew passage, but she considers it her duty to slap my face if I make the same mistake twice. It's another mistake to duck, because her slaps always land somewhere. Barry, who sits next to me, winds up with a black eye when he ducks. At home, he winds up with a bruised cheek when his father finds out why Mrs. Norotsky slapped him. Cheating on a test. But we get hugs from her when we do well. I want to be prepared for my *bar mitzvah* lessons, so I figure her crude way of teaching works.

I win a portable radio for collecting the most money for the *United Jewish Appeal*. Black neighborhoods are the most generous. One man gives me a five-dollar bill and doesn't even want any tickets. At the same time, I collect money for the *March of Dimes*, and I go back home with lots of coins in my collection box.

On Saturday, I'm walking past the synagogue when a big black girl comes up to me and shouts, "The Jews killed Jesus, the Jews killed Jesus."

She punches me so hard that I fall down on the sidewalk. Here comes big trouble. I grab her shoe in mid-kick, twist it hard, and she lands next to me, which gives me time to get up, throw her shoe across the street, and run to the door.

"I be wait'n for you right here," she says as I close the door in her face.

The Saturday service is going on. I take a yarmulke from the pile on the table and sit in the last row. I've heard that the rabbi is a young freedom fighter from Israel. He comes to me after the service, concerned about the blood that I don't realize has dried on my forehead. I tell him what the girl said and worry if he'll get mad if say the name, Jesus. When he finds out that I go to Hebrew school here and that I live just a few houses down the block, he gets mad at me for not attending services regularly. Then he tells me never to run from a fight.

"It's okay for you to say that. You're a war hero, but how am I supposed to defend myself against a girl who's twice as big as I am?"

People come up to him to shake his hand, and I don't get an answer.

There's no use telling anyone at home about it. They don't care what happens to me on the streets or how I do in Hebrew School.

"There's no *mezuzah* on their front door," I tell Aunt Manya at a pay phone three blocks away. I've spent my last nickel on a phone call instead of a candy bar. The street is crowded. Loud music is playing. It's hard to hear.

Bang, bang, bang. "If you're not done in ten seconds boy, I'm pullin' you out of this fuckin' phone booth by your hair," a fat woman shouts.

"I have to go now, Aunt Manya. A lady wants to use the phone."

It bothers me that there's no *mezuzah* on Becca's door. In Hebrew school, Mrs. Norotsky told me that a *mezuzah* invites all who enter to bring with them a spirit of love, so that the home will remain a sanctuary of God. And it tells all who leave to carry that spirit of love into their daily affairs. There are *mezuzahs* on the doorposts of every house on Mother's side of the family.

Harvey the lodger is missing.

"This is the first time in three years we don't have fresh cheesecake on the table on Sunday morning," Bertha says.

"That should make you happy, Ma. Maybe Harvey heard you complain."

"Where's he been for three days?"

"That's what his boss wants to know."

"Maybe he's visiting his sister on Long Island."

"He always tells us when he'll be gone."

"So call his sister. It's not like Harvey not to tell us."

Now I'm worried about Harvey, too. Becca calls his sister, but she doesn't know where he is. Bertha calls the police, and after thirty minutes of red tape, she's told that the morgue has two unidentified males that fit Harvey's description. Dad offers to go to the morgue.

"Can I go with you, Dad?"

"No, Norman. You'd better stay here."

At the morgue, he identifies Harvey's body.

"They killed him for the five dollars he had in his pocket."

"How did he die?" Howard asks.

"He was stabbed on his way home, two blocks from here."

"Two blocks from here?"

"Yes, Norman."

I wish I were back in Brooklyn.

"They counted twenty slashes. The coroner said that from the slashes on his wrist, he must have put up a good fight."

"Dad, how do you know he only had five dollars on him?"

"One of his friends at the bakery told the police he had lunch with Harvey the day he was murdered, and when he paid the bill, he only had five dollars left in his wallet."

"I'll miss the rent, but I won't miss his cheesecake," Bertha says.

I wonder whether she'll miss Harvey and whether the murderers started off by robbing other boys on their way to the movies.

The school term is coming to an end, and that means I'll be going to Junior High School in the Bronx. I heard that new kids get beat up as an initiation. It's bad enough at my school with Alex the bully and other dangerous characters, like Gonzo, who stabbed a boy in the arm for looking at him the "wrong way." Gonzo went to reform school. When I told Becca, she said Gonzo would now learn how to be a real killer. I think I'll run away before I go to Junior High in the Bronx.

Dad comes into my room late one night when I'm half-asleep. "Here's the train Ellie promised you."

I thought I was dreaming, but in the morning a big cardboard carton is on the floor. I jump out of bed, open it, take a long tan box from the carton, open the end flaps, and slide out a green New York Central passenger car that looks like the real thing. I've wanted this train set since I was six years old. I imagine the layout I'll build: switchbacks, a freight yard, buildings, trestles, tunnels, water towers, all in proper scale.

Becca comes through the door. She smiles an evil smile. "Just what do you think you're doing?"

"Opening up my train set."

"Your train set? Ha, ha. Not today Mister."

"Why not?"

"You'll open it at Christmas and set it up around the tree."

"I just want to see the trains."

"I said no!" She grabs the car out of my hands, puts it back in the box, and slides it into the carton. She slaps the carton closed, puts it over her shoulder, and carries it downstairs.

I grit my teeth just like Dad does. That's it with Becca and me. I know I'll never see the trains again, because I don't plan to stick around until Christmas. Now is as good a time as ever to escape from this nightmare. Becca is probably going to give the train set to her son anyway.

I stick my toothbrush in my back pocket, take out my pocketknife, fish out a nickel from my coin bank, tiptoe down the stairs, open the front door quietly, and fly to the elevated station so I'll lose Howard if he tries to follow.

No sneaking under the turnstile today. I'd gladly pay five dollars for the forty-minute ride to Brooklyn. When the train rolls in, I take a seat, and the doors hiss shut. A little black boy is sitting in his father's lap, holding tight to a teddy bear. His mother kisses his forehead. I'm envious. I walk through the cars to the front of the train, but looking out the front window makes me think of the Lionel train set and all the things I had planned to do with it. I wait years for a train set, then Becca won't even let me look at the cars. Watching a train go around a Christmas tree once a year, how boring. And what kind of Jews would have a Christmas tree anyway? Becca and her foul-mouthed mother should get consumption! They should roast in hell!

I'll miss Spotty. I feel sorry for him. Becca's father doesn't seem to be much better off than the dog. He was nice to me when he wasn't spying. He gave me a watch, books, and pairs of almost new sneakers.

I'm thinking so hard that I miss my stop and have to double back to the Saratoga Avenue station. I love my old neighborhood. There are tiny storefront synagogues, shops with Hebrew writing on the windows, and Meyer's deli, next door to the Ambassador, with the best knishes in Brooklyn. I wish I had fished more nickels from my coin bank so I could buy one. I wish I took the coin bank with me, but it wouldn't fit in my pocket, and I didn't have a bag to put it in.

Two women, wearing black babushkas, are carrying shopping bags down Saratoga Avenue. They raise their voices at the end of each sentence and complain about their aches and pains.

"Hello, Mrs. Z. Hello, Mrs. Schmall. Can I help you with your bags?"

"We can manage, thank you. We're not cripples yet," says Mrs. Z, the rabbi's wife.

"You've been sick, Norman?" Mrs. Schmall asks. "You look, *keyn eine hore*, so thin."

"No, I feel fine."

They don't feed you in the Bronx?" Mrs. Z asks.

"How could they feed him when he's so skinny? When he lived by Manya he had some meat on him. Now he looks like from a concentration camp."

"Maybe he should see a doctor. You have a doctor in the Bronx, Norman?"

"No, Mrs. Z. But I'm fine. I'm just growing."

"A growing boy should have some meat on him."

"Mrs. Schmall, you sound like Aunt Manya. I will have some meat on me soon. I'm going back home."

"*Zay gesunt*, be healthy," both women say. I usually find their conversation tiresome, but not today. Today they are sweet little old ladies with Brownsville Jewish accents who care about me and make me feel at home.

The crippled boy's house is on the next block. I'll walk right up to him, introduce myself, and shake his hand no matter how many of his friends or relatives are there. I should have done that last time. That's odd. Even though it's a sunny day, his cot isn't out on the sidewalk. I hope he's okay.

Aunt Manya is on the stoop, talking to Mrs. Katzman, when I walk up to the house. I've never been so happy to see her. She must be happy, too, because she gives me a tight hug. So does Mrs. Katzman.

"I ran away."

"You what?"

"I ran away from Becca's house, Aunt Manya."

In the kitchen, I'm eating a bagel and lox. I haven't had one since Dad took me away in June. Aunt Manya pours a glass of coffee for Mrs. Katzman. I tell them about my awful year in the Bronx. They cry.

That afternoon, Becca calls, and Aunt Manya tells her that she hasn't seen me. She calls again at dinnertime. Sarah says the same thing. When Dad calls at nine, Aunt Manya tells him where I am. He says he's relieved to know I'm safe.

He calls again a week later. "Meet me here so you can pick up your things."

"I'd rather not go to the Bronx."

"You have to. You'll need your clothes."

"Will Becca be there?"

"Yes."

"Can I go when she's not there?"

"Come tomorrow at ten. I'll be here."

"But she might hit me."

"I won't let her."

"Okay, but I don't think it's a good idea."

When I get there at ten, Dad isn't waiting for me on the porch like he said he would. I swallow hard and knock on the door. Becca opens it. She looks as if she's just eaten something sour. I back up a step.

"So this is how you treat me? After all I've done for you?"

I've heard those words before on the radio and in movies. I can't think up a good answer, so I don't say anything.

Dad comes down the stairs. "Go up to your room and pack."

I stuff as much as I can into the suitcase and kneel on it to close it. My drawings aren't under the bed, in the closet, or in the dresser. The coin bank on the dresser is empty, so are the two March of Dimes cards I was supposed to return to school. There was a dime in every slot. God should punish people who steal from cripples.

Making two trips, I leave the suitcase and the satchel by the front door. Spotty is barking in the cellar. I walk to the kitchen, where Dad, Becca, Bertha, and Howard are arguing. Howard is holding the baby.

"He didn't appreciate anything I did for him, not one thing."

"What did you do for him? Take away his trains?"

"I'm happy to be rid of him."

"Not as happy as he is to be rid of you."

"The ingrate never once called me mother."

"I'm not an ingrate, and you're not my mother."

"No one's talking to you," Bertha says.

"He lost the watch I gave him," Howard shouts. He's brave with the baby in his arms.

"Are you talking about the watch you took from the high school lost and found?" Dad asks.

"Willie has it. He pulled it off my wrist."

"He's lying, Bertha says.

"I'm telling the truth."

"Don't contradict me."

"I'm not contradicting you."

"Don't answer me back. You're always answering me back, goddamn it."

"Don't use your gutter language around my son, you foul-mouthed hag."

"Don't call my mother a hag."

"Good riddance. I'm glad Norman ran away. We'll finally have some peace and quiet around here," Bertha says.

"Where's my train set?"

She doesn't answer.

"Where's my train set?"

She smirks.

"Where's Norman's train set?" Dad asks.

"It's not his. It's the baby's."

"Ellie promised it to Norman."

"Norman, Norman, all I ever hear about is Norman." Becca lunges at Dad, claws his forehead with her long nails. He pushes her away and bumps into Howard. "Don't hurt my baby." She grabs a fistful of his hair. Bertha runs out of the room. I remember Mr. Gonzalez's instructions. I kick Becca's shin, making believe it's two feet farther away than it really is. She screams, lets go of his hair. He knocks her down with a backhand to the side of her head. She's on the floor in the doorway between the kitchen and the hall. There's blood on Dad's forehead. Spotty is barking and scratching on the cellar door. Bertha is dialing the phone.

Dad tries to get to the phone, but he can't get past Becca. She groans, gets up, limps to her mother, twists the phone out of her hand, raises the receiver over her shoulder, moves it up and down like a weapon. Bertha is hollering at Spotty as she opens the cellar door. He runs past her with a loose end of rope hanging from his collar and leaps for Becca's wrist. She's on the floor again.

"Get him off me. Get him off me," she screams.

Bertha kicks Spotty and curses, but he doesn't let go.

"Come Norman, this is a good time to leave."

A police car screeches up to the house as Dad pulls me onto the porch. How can this be? When someone is lying on the street with blood oozing out of his head from a knife fight, the police take a half-hour to come. People are gathering in front of the house. Two policemen come up on the porch.

"Okay, what's the problem here?"

"My stepmother attacked my father, and..."

Becca screams again. One of the officers draws his gun.

"Come inside, all of you, and shut the door," Becca yells. "I don't want the neighbors to know our business."

The officer puts his gun back in the holster. Spotty is barking. Becca is holding a wet towel to her wrist. Bertha grabs the loose end of rope, drags Spotty to the cellar door, kicks him down the stairs, and slams the door.

"He started it all," Bertha says, pointing her finger at me.

A second police car arrives. Becca and Bertha ride to the police station in one car, Dad and I, in the other.

"If they lock me up, go to Manya's and tell her what happened," Dad says.

The police station is neat. There are cells with prisoners inside. From one cell a man is singing a dirty song. A policeman leads Dad and me into a small room. There aren't any bright lights shining in our faces like in the movies. I start to explain before the officer has a chance to introduce himself. Now I'm a character from the movies. I'm all my heroes rolled into one, only this is real life.

"I saw it all Mr. Policeman. I came to pick up my clothes, and my stepmother attacked Dad in cold blood. She scratched him and pulled out a handful of his hair. Here's the evidence. I picked some of it up from the kitchen floor. Assault and battery. It's an open and shut case. Dad had to knock her down in self-defense. She stole the money in my coin bank and the March of Dimes money that I had to turn in at school. She also stole the drawings I did at the museum, and my electric train set. You should throw the book at her, then lock her up and throw away the key."

"How old are you, son"?

"Eleven."

"You're going to make a fine lawyer some day."

"That's what my Aunt Manya says."

In the evening, I say to Aunt Manya, Uncle Irving, and Sarah at dinner, "I think the policeman let us go because he was tired of listening to me talk. Anyway, we beat the rap, and I'm glad to be back home."

CHAPTER 17

GROWING UP

I'm sitting on the cool gray cement stoop, wrapped up in my new *Superman* comic book. Two girls are playing hopscotch on the sidewalk. A little boy rides his tricycle in circles over their chalk lines, and they scream at him. From the corner of my eye, I see Max, the school bully, my personal terrorist, sneaking up. He stops when I look his way, and he raises his eyebrows, probably wondering why I don't run inside. He comes closer, puts his hands out like a zombie, fingers poised like vulture claws, buckteeth bared. I stand up, mimic his gestures, walk like a zombie down the stairs toward him. Max's eyes widen. He spins on his right heel, dodges the boy on the trike, runs down the block past Gussie's delicatessen and Berg's grocery store and crosses the street to PS 165, but I'm faster. I grab the back of his burgundy shirt, push him into the black, iron fence, and twist his arm behind his back.

Is this trembling *schmuck* the same Max who used to rough me up and mimic my stuttering and blinking?

"Don't hit me, please don't hit me, Norman."

"I won't this time." I jerk his arm upward but not as much as Alex, the bully in the Bronx does. "Don't ever come near me again or I'll break some bones."

"I promise I won't. I promise."

"Don't even walk in the street in front of my house."

"Okay, Norman. I won't."

I let go, and he runs home. I cross the street and sit on the refrigerated box in front of Mr. Berg's grocery store. Long ago, it replaced the icebox that Joey and I used to sit on to watch the neighborhood. Life is more complicated now. There's candy, baseball cards, and drawing pads to buy, and I'll need money to pay for them.

Almost every morning during summer vacation, I sit on the box, draw pictures in my mind, and wait for shoppers to come out. Then I hop down, ask if they need help with their groceries, and carry bags to their apartments, sometimes up five flights of stairs. Instead of considering me a nuisance for hanging around his store, Mr. Berg is happy to see me invest my tips in candy.

I borrow a hammer and a saw from Mr. Mirsky. Using roller skates for wheels, I build a cart out of wooden vegetable crates so I can haul big grocery bags. The cart sounds like a garbage can being dragged down the sidewalk, and the neighbors complain. Next day Mr. Berg brings a red wagon with big wheels and solid rubber tires to the store. Now, I'm making enough money to put some in my school bank account.

"Sometimes, boys come around, hoping to steal some of my regular customers, but the women pick me over them because I'm polite," I brag to Aunt Manya.

"You're just like your father. You know how to flatter the ladies."

She doesn't mean it kindly, but I consider any similarity between Dad and me a high compliment.

One of my regulars comes out of the store with two big grocery bags, and another boy begs to help. I let him pull the wagon to her apartment, and I give him the heaviest bag to carry to the fourth floor. Before we leave, she hands me a quarter and a nickel, which I put in my pocket. Downstairs, I tell the boy the lady was a cheapskate and only gave me two nickels. I give him one, and that's the last time he comes around the grocery store.

When it's too dark to play ball, Joey and I go around the corner to the vacant lot on Herzl Street. It's surrounded by tall buildings that we pretend are mountains. Tonight, a crescent moon sits on the tallest peak. We build a campfire, using vegetable crates for firewood, and we're cowboys out west, squatting on the ground, roasting marshmallows. Other boys are on the lot, squatting around their campfires.

"Hey, Joey, don't waste so much wood. Remember that movie last week at the Bluebird? Remember the Indian who said that white men make a big fire and have to sit far away from it? They're too hot in front and too cold in back."

"Yeah, I remember. That's why I'm making a big fire. Because we're supposed to be cowboys."

"Well, it's ninety degrees out. Let's be Indians, instead."

"But Indians don't roast marshmallows."

"Neither do cowboys."

"Look what I bought today, Norman, cigarette paper."

We can buy a pack of cigarettes if we tell the clerk it's for our father, but we don't want to waste our money. This morning, I found an empty Band-Aid can in the junk drawer at home and walked down the street, picking up cigarette butts from the sidewalk. Our deal was that Joey would get the paper, and I'd get the tobacco. It's as if I'm trying to make Aunt Manya's consumption curses come true. We stuff the papers with tobacco, roll them, and lick them shut like cowboys, but they come apart after a few puffs, and we throw them in the fire.

The next night on the lot, we sit at a small campfire, playing blackjack on a big hunk of concrete when Seymour shows up, proudly puffing on a cigarette.

"Hi, guys. I checked three other fires before I found you. Everyone's on the lot tonight."

He takes a pack of Camels out of his pocket. We use a twig from the fire to light them.

"This is how you inhale."

Joey starts to cough. Then I start to cough. We throw our cigarettes in the fire.

"Maybe you sissies should try a pipe."

I buy a corncob pipe from a store on Hegeman Avenue and fill it from my can of tobacco. It tastes like burning tires. On the way to baby-sit for Sophie and Sol, I splurge and buy a pocket-sized can of sweet-smelling pipe tobacco. When Abraham goes to sleep, I take out my pipe. It looks neat when Spencer Tracy smokes one. I tamp down the tobacco, light up, take a few puffs, and open *Great Expectations*. It's almost three hours before my eleven o'clock show. When the pipe goes out, I light it and puff some more. I'm sophisticated, then I'm nauseated. My face in the bathroom mirror isn't green like I expected it to be. I'm definitely not "hard as nails." I open the living room window, throw the pipe and tobacco onto the courtyard three stories below, then sink into Sophie's sofa and hope I live through this.

I miss my eleven o'clock show, the highlight of Saturday night babysitting, an event so wonderful that I would come here even if Sophie and Sol didn't pay me. I'm too miserable to get up, shut off the kitchen light, open the Venetian blinds, and watch the woman in the apartment across the courtyard get undressed. She does this at exactly eleven o'clock every Saturday night. Once, I invited Joey over. It cost him his deck of French cards.

On my 12th birthday Sarah gives me money to buy a pastrami sandwich and cream soda at Gussie's. As long as the deli isn't busy, it's okay to sit and draw all day. It's good to be in Brooklyn, to live with people who remember my birthday. Even Henry the handyman knows.

"Happy Birthday Nor-Man. May I share your table?"

"You sure can."

"How is your art coming along?"

"Here's my sketchbook."

He puts his coffee and corned beef sandwich aside, reaches into his shirt pocket for his eyeglass case, and takes out a pair of gold-rimmed bifocals, which he polishes with the tiny cloth from inside the case. He lingers on the pages, nods his large head.

"Nice, Nor-Man, very nice."

"Thank you, Hen-Ry. I draw every day."

"Would you like to draw me?"

"Draw you? I'd love to."

Between bites, I rough in Henry's features with light lines so I won't have to use an eraser. I darken the lines I want to keep, varying their thickness. Henry's the perfect model, keeping the same pose while he slowly eats his sandwich and sips coffee.

"All done. Do you like it?"

He pats his lips with a napkin and smiles.

"Nor-Man, you spent a lot of time on my eyes, and they're the least interesting part of your drawing. Don't make them identical. One eye should be dominant."

"What does that mean?"

"It means that your attention should go to the stronger eye before it goes to the other or you won't know which one to look at first. You never want to confuse the viewer."

"Both of your eyes look the same to me."

"That's because you're looking but not seeing. My left eye is not the same as my right. Examine the upper lids."

"You're right, Hen-Ry."

"Even if they were identical, you should make one different, especially if you're drawing me straight on. It helps if the head is tilted, if the light comes from one side, if there are shadows, if part of one eye is hidden because the bridge of the nose is in front of it."

"There sure is a lot to know to be an artist."

"You're right, Nor-Man. And we're just talking about eyes. In this drawing and in your others, I see good things. Your handling of line is excellent. You're a natural at composition. Your work has a freshness and a naïveté that I wish I had. But from now on, you need to work on solidity. Think of the head as a sphere, like a Spaldine. Do you mind if I make a few corrections?"

"I'd mind if someone else drew in my book, but not you."

He takes a fountain pen out of his pocket and draws an oval around my sketch at the level of the eyes.

"Honor the direction of this ellipse when you draw the eyes."

He corrects the placement of the eyes that I spent too much time on. Now they seem to wrap around the sphere.

"The same with the mouth."

He draws another ellipse at the level of the mouth and corrects the position of the corners of the lips.

"Let me show you something else."

On another page, he draws my head in three-quarter view without looking at me. When he cuts one line across another, my ear overlaps the side of my head and my upper lip overlaps the lower. The picture looks alive.

"This overlapping is called 'form over form.' It gives a painting depth. I suggest that you go to the Central Library at Grand Army Plaza and look at drawings by Michelangelo, Raphael, and Cambiaso. Always consult the masters to see how they handled form over form."

Henry has just given me the world's best birthday present. This is a turning point in my life!

With pencils, pad, and tracing paper, I spend every Saturday at the Central Library. There are tons of art books with pictures by famous artists in color. Cambiaso has become one of my favorites. He simplified the figure, representing arms, hands, and fingers as boxes. I trace his drawings and paintings and those of Michelangelo and Raphael.

One Saturday, while I'm talking to Rembrandt's *An Old Man in an Armchair*, an overhead light flashes and burns out. In the reduced light, the middle tones are eliminated, and I discover that the painting is composed of overlapping rectangles. I put tracing paper over the face and draw all the rectangles I can find. At another table, where the light is better, squinting gives me the same effect. I look at other Rembrandt paintings, and also those of Michelangelo and Raphael and discover that rectangles are in their work, too.

On a lunch break on the steps in front of the library, eating a bagel from Berg's grocery, I wonder why the masters have rectangles in their works. Where did they get that idea? I think about squinting and remember reading that Indians squint when they track animals through the forest. It makes the hoof prints sharper and easier to see. I squint at the tree-lined street. There are rectangles everywhere, connecting buildings to buildings, trees to buildings, trees to trees. They're part of nature. They tie things together and take my eyes on a journey.

"Sarah, Uncle Irving is going to give me my first *bar mitzvah* lesson tonight. Do I really have to have a *bar mitzvah*? I'll feel like a freak, standing in front of the *shul*, blinking and stuttering."

"Calm down. Listen to me. Have I ever given you bad advice?"

"Yes. When you wanted me to taste pork at the Chinese restaurant."

"I'll never live that down. But seriously, it would be a sin to not have a *bar mitzvah*. It's what your mother, may she rest in peace, would have wanted."

"But... "

"Just listen for a minute. Remember when you told me about your science project in school? You went into great detail about materials that absorb light. And when you tell me about the discoveries you make in art, you explain in detail things like overlapping rectangles and form over form. You don't stutter or blink when you talk about things you know a lot about? So what I'm saying is that by the time your birthday comes you'll be so good at the reading that you won't blink or stutter."

"But I'm still worried. I'm the worst student in Hebrew School."

"How can you be the worst student in *cheder* when you can read the *Daily Forward*? Oh, I know. You get in trouble, drawing the teacher, right?

"Yeah."

"Well, your *bar mitzvah* isn't until February. I'm sure Pappa will have enough time to teach you all you need to know to become an expert reader.

Sitting on the top step of the sunny stoop, I check the gold Bulova wristwatch Howard gave me: 3:46, 4:02, 4:29. Joey walks across the street with his broom handle. "Norman, they're playing stickball at the playground. Let's get in a game."

"You go, Joey. I'm waiting for my father. He promised he'd be here at 3:30."

"You sit there every week and he never shows up."

"I know, but he said he'd be here today for sure."

Now the stoop is shadowy. It's dinnertime and still no Dad.

"I'll be there this Saturday," Dad says on the phone, "ten sharp."

On Saturday at eleven-thirty, I'm still on the stoop when Joey and Seymour come by.

"Hey Norman, *Little Caesar's* playing at the Bluebird. Let's sneak in."

"C'mon, Edward G. Robinson's in it."

"I like him almost as much as James Cagney. But I'm waiting for my Dad."

I'm still here at 4:00 when they come back from the movies.

"Did your father ever show up?"

"Yeah," I lie, "but he couldn't stay long. He had to get back to work."

"Uh huh," Seymour grunts and elbows Joey.

On the day Dad actually shows up, my sadness goes away in a second. I forget about all the times I sat on the stoop, looking at my watch, being disappointed. I run up and hug him.

He doesn't want to go in the house in case Aunt Manya asks him about money, so we take a walk around the block.

"How is Manya treating you?"

"Okay, but she keeps saying bad things about you. It makes me mad."

"I understand how you feel, Melvin."

"I'm Norman."

"Yes, Norman. Manya is difficult, but she means well."

"How can she mean well? She says you're a bad father?"

"Don't believe everything she says. She's a neurotic."

"What's a neurotic?"

"Someone who over reacts."

"How did she get that way?"

"I don't know."

But I think he does know. Sarah and I were playing cribbage one night.

"Why the long face?"

"Aunt Manya's been hollering at me all day."

"What did you do wrong?"

"Nothing. She was hollering about Dad. I know she hates him, but why does she take it out on me?"

"I'm sure she doesn't mean to. She's frustrated. Not with you, but with the situation."

"What situation?"

"Let me explain. She's almost done raising her own children when your mother dies. Then, from the goodness of her heart she takes you in. I mean, how can she not take you in, her own sister's baby? The apartment is crowded, no room to turn around, and Pappa is barely making a living. On top of that, your father pays very little support, sometimes none. He promises next week, next week, next week, but promises don't buy groceries. I know you don't like to hear complaints about your father, but maybe now you'll understand why Momma is the way she is."

A snarling dog wakes me up from my daydream. It's baring its fangs. I reach for Dad's hand.

"Nice doggie, good doggie." Dad tousles its gray fur. The dog rolls on its back. Dad lets me pet it. I feel safe with Dad and hardly ever stutter.

"I almost forgot. Here's a present for you."

"A present?"

He reaches into his pocket and hands me a brown wooden box the size of a pack of cigarettes. "Press the button and you'll hear music."

"I know this trick. If you press the button a pin sticks you." I press the edge of the button, making the pin pop out. Dad is disappointed but not as much as I am.

At the dinner table, after Dad is gone, I talk about the dog and about the "music box" with the pin.

"You shouldn't pet a stray dog," Aunt Manya says. "It might have rabies."

"Dad said it wouldn't bite if I spoke nice to it."

"Your father says lots of things: the dog won't bite, I'll pay you back the money I owe, I'll be back next week to visit. For every true thing he says, ten are false."

"And the pin," Uncle Irving says, "how can a father enjoy seeing his son stuck by a pin?"

"He should know better," Sarah says. "Who knows what disease you could catch from the last person who stuck his finger on that pin."

"He was trained as a pharmacist, and he doesn't know from infection?" Uncle Irving says.

"My sister dies from an infection, and Benny, the genius, gives Norman something he should stick his finger on. Benny should get an infection. He should have tubes sticking out of his body to drain the pus."

A pimply-faced teenager comes to the schoolyard to sell fuck books for fifty cents. That's what we call them at PS 165. For fifty cents, I can buy five comic books! Joey says that last year the same boy sold these eight-page books for thirty-five cents. Now I understand why Aunt Manya complains about inflation.

Joey and I can't afford to buy one, but we'd love to own one and look through its pages of naked men and women doing it. It would be better than looking for naked women in the National Geographics or the photography books in the Stone Avenue library that are stacked right where the librarian sits and are impossible to pick up when she's there.

Joey's friend, Arnie, lends him two books. The vacant lot is a good place to look at them. They're wrinkled from being in his back pocket.

"Hey Joey, did you spill something on this page? It's all stained."

"No… yeah, I was drinking milk and spilled some."

"Did you make copies yet?"

I'm gonna do it tomorrow. My mother will be gone all day."

A week goes by. "Norman," Joey says, "you gotta help me. Arnie says he's gonna beat me up if I don't give him back his books. I tried a bunch of times, but I couldn't copy them so good. And I spilled India ink on them."

"I bet if the drawings were airplanes, you would have copied them perfectly."

"Yeah, but people are hard to draw. You gotta help me."

"Calm down. Cut a bunch of papers to size, get some India ink, a pen, and thin and medium pen points. I'll go up on your roof and make copies."

I draw three copies of each page, and Joey staples them together. Thanks to studying the masters, drawing form over form makes them much better than the originals.

"Hey, Norman. We could go into the fuck book business. You draw 'em and I'll sell 'em. Thirty-five cents each."

"No thanks, Joey."

His mother catches him reading them in his bedroom and for a week he's not allowed to go out after school.

"Let's play stickball," Joey says when he's back on the streets. He's got his broom handle with him.

"You got a Spaldine, Joey?"

"No, I got a nickel. Let's go to Mrs. Rothman's and buy one."

"She'll sell you a dead ball for a nickel. Good ones are a whole dime."

The roof of Mrs. Rothman's two-story apartment house next to the school playground is a magnet for foul balls. Once, I hit a brand new Spaldine up there, and she made me pay fifteen cents to get it back. She comes to the door, carrying a cardboard box full of balls.

"Hello Mrs. Rothman," Joey says. "We'd like to buy a ball, but I only have a nickel."

I pick out a good one. "Can we have this one?"

"What are you talking, Norman? This is a fifteen-cent ball... but it's for free if you draw me."

"What are you talking, Mrs. Rothman? My pictures are two dollars."

"That's highway robbery."

"Okay. A dollar, and two more balls. This one... and that one."

"You drive a hard bargain, Norman. It's a deal."

"Come to my stoop this Wednesday at four. I'll save you a spot."

Stickball is played at the schoolyard, three on a side, a pitcher, and two fielders. We don't need a catcher. The handball wall is the backdrop. If the ball goes past the second iron pole that holds up the cyclone fence, it's a single, past the fourth pole, a double, and so forth. This is my favorite game. I play it so much that I imagine I can hit the ball if I were blindfolded. We're tied in the bottom of the ninth with two outs. My count is three balls, two strikes. I swing at a fast one and connect. The ball sails over the far fence, across wide Hopkinson Street and up over the top of the four story apartment house where Sol and Sophie live. A gigantic home run. It's worth losing that ball. I wish Dad could have seen me hit it.

Gloria is beautiful, like an actress, and every weekday she gets ready for bed at exactly 9:45. So I go into my darkened bedroom a few minutes before 9:45, get comfortable at the window, and wait for her lights to go on. Peeking between the slats of the Venetian blinds, I watch her take off her blouse and skirt and lay them on a chair. She takes off her brassiere and admires herself in her dresser mirror, pulling back her shoulders and turning to the right and to the left. Just as she begins to pull down her panties, Sarah walks in, snaps on the light, and hollers, "What are you doing"? Gloria's lights go out, Aunt Manya runs in, and the show is over.

"Norman was watching Gloria get undressed."

"He's a boy. What do you expect? Gloria shouldn't undress in front of a window without a curtain."

"He probably watches me, too."

"I do not. Anyway, it's always dark."

"What did I tell you, Mamma?"

"Sarah, quit pinching my arm."

"Enough already, both of you. We'll put the cot in the living room."

Pesach, Passover, the Independence Day of the Jewish people, is coming up. Sophie's Abraham is now old enough to ask the four questions. I'll miss being the one to do it. It made me feel important.

Why is this night different from all other nights?
Tonight we eat no bread, only matzah, symbol of enslavement;
Tonight we eat bitter herbs, symbol of enslavement;

Yet tonight also, we dip our herbs in condiments, symbol of freedom;
And tonight we sit on cushioned chairs, symbol of freedom.

To get ready for this holiday, all the Jewish families in Brownsville clean their houses like crazy. It scares me to see Aunt Manya sit on the second-story window ledges of the apartment with a soapy rag in her hand, washing the grime off each window frame. She wads up pages from the *Daily Forward*, sprinkles ammonia on them, and polishes the window-panes to squeaky perfection. Uncle Irving climbs on a stepladder to take down the Passover silverware and dishes from the highest cupboard in the kitchen. There's a *milkhig*, dairy, and a *fleishig*, meat, set of dishes for every day and two other sets for Passover. Large pots and pans, carving knives, and other utensils that are not duplicated by those used for Passover, are made clean by ritually soaking them in a bathtub full of water for several days. Every metal surface shines. I can see my reflection in the waxed linoleum. Cockroaches are not welcome on Passover.

The wonderful day arrives. Aunt Manya is up early to prepare for the Seder. Already, cooking odors fill the apartment. We keep out of her way. I sit on the top stair, drawing pictures near the kitchen door, so I'll be handy.

"Norman, here's money. Run to Berg's for another box of egg matzah." "Norman, go by Sophie's and ask for her big black frying pan. She knows the one I want." "Norman, pick up my eye drops from the drugstore, and tell Mr. Gibalowitz that I hope his wife is feeling better."

At sundown Uncle Irving is at the head of the table with a black *yar-mulke* over his thinning hair and a yellowed *talis* on his shoulders. Abraham sits on one side of him. I sit on the other on a cushioned seat, wearing my *talis*. Aunt Manya lights the candles, covers her face with her hands, and says the blessing. We raise our glasses together and drink the wine. Behind me, on the sewing machine, flickering candles drip white wax. The candles are reflected in the crystal decanter filled with Mogen David Concord grape wine.

"Aunt Manya, make Sarah stop pinching me."

"I can't help it Mamma. He's so sweet I can't resist."

Across the table are Nathan and Debbie, and Sophie and Sol. They treat me as if I'm someone special, except for Sophie. They remember my birthday and give me presents, sometimes money. I like Debbie much better than Sophie, even though Sophie's my Godmother. Debbie taught me how to play pinochle, and blackjack, and I taught Joey and Seymour. I carry a pack of pinochle cards in my back pocket, and we play on the vacant lot. I remember every card that's played.

"Nathan, your wife's a card shark," Aunt Manya said once when Debbie wanted to play for pennies.

"When you play for money, it eliminates all sorts of foolishness."

Debbie was right. Since then, every time I play a card I pretend I have money riding on it.

"Norman, Norman, you're daydreaming," Sarah says. Her hand is waving in front of my face.

"How can I be daydreaming when it's nighttime?"

"An answer for everything," Sophie says, "like his father."

Abraham points to Sophie's belly. "New baby," he says.

Debbie looks sad. Once I overheard Mrs. Katzman say to Aunt Manya that she's sorry that Debbie and Nathan can't have children. I'm sad for her, too. She's Aunt Manya's main helper, getting up and down, serving the food, encouraging everyone to eat more than they should.

"Whatsamatter, Sol, you don't like your mother-in-law's cooking?"

In my case, I don't need any encouragement. I've missed out on a whole year's worth of good cooking, living with Becca in the Bronx.

As busy as Aunt Manya is, she's mellower at holiday time and seldom hollers. Tonight, at the far end of the table, her face is glowing. She smiles when Sol compliments her on her cooking. She looks younger without her moustache.

On the counter in back of Mr. Gibalowitz's drugstore is a silver-colored cash register that says ka-ching when he makes a sale. Next to it is a candy case with a sliding glass cover, and inside are rows of Lifesavers, Jujubes, and Good & Plenty's. Good & Plenty's are just okay. I like the name better than the candy inside.

I have lots of good and plenty. Good food upstairs at Aunt Manya's and plenty of it. I also get plenty of hollering and cursing when I stick up for Dad. I wonder if he's worth sticking up for.

The drugstore is small but looks bigger because of the mirror on the back wall. On one side of the mirror are three telephone booths. On the other side, behind the cash register, is a Dutch door with the top part open.

Mr. Gibalowitz is on his stool behind the Dutch door. With tweezers, he picks up silver weights, some as tiny as a pin, and sets them on a silver pan on the left side of a balancing scale. He spoons yellow powder from a gray glass jar onto the right side until the pans are level. He makes a funnel out of paper, holds it over a smaller jar, and pours the yellow powder into the funnel. I don't think Dad is patient enough to do that. No wonder he's a waiter.

I've been coming here for years to pick up Uncle Irving's pills and Aunt Manya's eye drops. When I was five, I saw a man with a tack hammer in his hand and a row of tacks between his lips put up a Flit display, cardboard cutouts of the enemy as bugs to be killed by the orange Flit sprayer. Those fiends were scary, especially Hitler, who Aunt Manya cursed even more than she cursed me.

Except for the Flit display and Mr. Gibalowitz not looking as tall as he used to, the store is the same as it was when I was a little kid. He steps away from the Dutch door. I slide open the candy case cover, reach inside, snatch a box of Good & Plenty, and put it in my back pocket. Mr. Gibalowitz is so nice to me. How can I do this to him? He's the one I used to go to when I had something in my eye. He's thorough in everything he does. I want to be a pharmacist when I grow up.

"Norman."

Now I'm in trouble.

"How would you like to work for me a few hours a week?"

"I'd like to, Mr. Gibalowitz, but what about your daughter?"

"Arlene can't work here anymore. Lots of homework in high school, and she needs time for violin lessons."

"Violin lessons? Has she been taking them long?"

"Since she was nine."

"I bet she's real good at it."

"Yes, she is."

I stand on a ladder that slides along a railing attached to the top shelf and dust off the medicine bottles with a feather duster. I'm neat and careful not to drop anything. It's fun to watch Mr. Gibalowitz measure vials of foul-smelling liquids and count out tablets of all sizes and colors. With a spatula, he fills small tin cans with salves and ointments.

"Mr. Gibalowitz, what's the difference between a salve and an ointment?"

"Nothing. The terms are synonymous."

"You mean the black salve you gave me to draw out the pus from my thumb when I poked it with a fork could be called an ointment?"

"Yes, Norman."

This job is better than *schlepping* heavy grocery bags up the stairs of apartment houses. When the pay phone rings, I take messages or run to nearby apartments to call people to the phone. I deliver medicines, wash windows, and go to Gussie's deli to pick up a pastrami on rye for Mr. Gibalowitz.

While he's typing a label, I'm up on the ladder, dusting. I can see the whole store through the big two-way mirror. A boy comes in with a prescription in his hand. At the candy counter, he looks around, slides back the glass, swipes a box of Jujubes, puts it in his pocket.

"Did you see that, Mr. Gibalowitz?"

"Yes, Norman, I did. I'll just have to charge his mother a nickel more for her medicine next time she comes in."

I wonder how many extra nickels Aunt Manya has paid over the years.

CHAPTER 18

HENYE GITTEL

Uncle Irving's cousin, Henye Gittel, never says a harsh word to me, but I'm embarrassed to be around her even though she buys me birthday presents and gives me money for the gumball and polly-seed machines in front of Shirley's candy store. She and her sourpuss husband, Jacob, were in the taxi with us on the way to Sophie's wedding. They still smell like wet chickens. Friends and even family call Henye Gittel Fat Annie, just not to her face.

When she and Jacob come across the street with their folding chairs to sit with Aunt Manya, Uncle Irving, and the Mirsky's on the sidewalk in front of the lighted window of Gibalowitz's drugstore, I go upstairs to get my drawing pad. The neighbors pull up their chairs, too, and talk about Israel and the politics of President Truman, interrupted with occasional curses against *anti-semitten*. The sidewalks are filled with chairs on warm nights. Sometimes, I can't walk to Gussie's deli without bumping into a chair.

Jacob only speaks in Yiddish. He reminds me of Charles Laughton in *Mutiny on the Bounty*. Aunt Manya says he looks like death warmed over. He's looked that way for as long as I can remember. I'm scared to draw his picture, but I draw Fat Annie a lot. I can draw her from memory, but I prefer to draw her live so I can select different angles and shadows and get the effect I want. Tonight she's wearing a faded housedress that ends up above her knees when she sits. I draw her rolled up stockings and her behind that overflows the chair. I exaggerate her piggish face and fleshy arms and legs, but I leave out the bumps on her chin that have hairs growing out of them. She reminds me of the fat lady at the circus. I interrupt the talkers to show my drawings to everyone except Jacob. Some neighbors laugh out loud, the Mirskys snicker, Aunt Manya smiles a thin smile, but Uncle Irving isn't amused.

Fat Annie stops giving me money to spend at the candy store.

I'm face down on the sidewalk with my chin touching the grate in front of Fat Annie's apartment house, looking into the dark hole for my Spaldine, which landed on the only place that's big enough for a ball to go through. I couldn't have tossed the ball in there if I tried. I see it on the black tarry bottom between a Milky Way wrapper and a yellow comb. There's a quarter down there, too. It'll take priority. Coins are easy. I run home to get chewing gum, a wire coat hanger, and the mop handle I use for stickball.

I enjoy the act of lifting a coin out of a grate, especially a quarter. I pry it from the gum I stuck on the end of the mop handle and put it in my pocket. Now for the Spaldine. I slide the mop handle through the grate, lower it so it reaches the ball, and nudge the ball across the bottom until it's directly under the hole. I pull out the mop handle, twist apart the coat hanger, wrap it around the mop handle, and make a ring for the ball to rest on. I lower it, slide it under the ball, and pull it up slowly, trying not to jar it. But just as the ball is within reach, it bounces back down and comes to rest in a corner where the mop handle can't bend to reach it. So I stretch out the hangar in an "ell" shape, reach the ball and nudge it under the hole again. This time, as I'm lifting up the ball, a rat runs across the bottom. I jump, and the ball falls off. One more try and I get it.

I didn't know Fat Annie was watching. She's clapping her hands at my success. She's clapping so hard that her glasses fall off and drop down the grate in the same place the ball did.

"*Oy Gotenyu.*"

"Don't worry, I'll get them out." I bend the wire loop into a hook, lower it, and haul up the glasses. "See Henye, they're not even broken."

"Norman, you're such an expert at fishing things out of sewers. For this, I'll treat you to something at Shirley's, anything you want."

"You don't have to treat me just for getting your glasses."

"I insist. Come."

"You're going, too?"

"Yes, of course."

Oh boy. Now I'm in a spot. "Uh, I already had an ice cream cone. I'm full."

"A growing boy full? Who ever heard of such a thing? Come, I'll buy you a chocolate malted. At Shirley's they're so thick you can cut them with a knife."

It's hard to refuse a chocolate malted at Shirley's. They come with two long pretzels and a seltzer, and there's enough in the can for two and a half glasses. But Fat Annie has to spoil my treat by actually going there with me.

"There's a booth in the back, Henye."

"In the back? Who wants to sit in the back? I want to sit in front, in the window booth, so I can see out."

Now the whole neighborhood will see in.

"Why the long face, Norman? The malted doesn't taste good?"

"It tastes fine. Thanks a lot for treating me."

When Joey walks by the candy store, carrying a pair of shoes to Bloom's shoe repair shop next door, I dive for the floor.

"Norman, what are you doing under there?"

"I dropped my handkerchief."

"How long does it take to pick up a handkerchief?"

"I was looking for coins under the booth." I sit back on the seat, bite off a piece of pretzel, take a long sip of chocolate malted through double straws.

Joey walks by in the other direction, and I dive again.

"Now what did you drop?"

"I'm tying my shoe."

"You can quit tying it. Your friend is gone."

At school, Joey asks me who my girlfriend is. I call him a *momser* and don't talk to him for a week.

"Jacob died in his sleep. Henye will need someone to stay by her."

"Not me," Sarah says fiercely. "Don't even think about it."

"Me neither." I was in Fat Annie's apartment once. She and Jacob were boring, and their place stunk like a hamper full of dirty laundry. I wouldn't drink from her glass.

I know that mirrors are covered over when someone dies, and I know that a grieving person shouldn't be left alone overnight. When Aunt Manya talks nice to me, I know I'm stuck with Fat Annie for three nights of mourning.

After dinner, I take my time walking up the stairs of Fat Annie's apartment house, carrying my history book, my pajamas, and my toothbrush. I'm terrified of being in a place where someone has just died and hope that my good deed will be noticed in heaven. I ring the bell, and the awful odor hits me when she opens the door.

"Come in Norman. Don't stand there in the hallway."

The iron door slams behind me. She fastens the deadbolt and secures both chains with a clack and a rattle. It's like scenes where a prisoner enters his cell for the first time. She pulls out a chair from under the kitchen table. "Sit here, Norman, in Jacob's place." Her eyes are red and wet. Her hair is mussed. "You must be hungry. What can I fix you?"

"Nothing. I just ate. Thank you anyway."

"Maybe some milk and cookies?"

"No thanks."

"A glass of water?"

"No, thank you."

She sits down on the other side of the table and asks me about school. I give short answers. I feel sorry that she's lost Jacob, but I wish I were anywhere but here. While she wipes her tears with a tiny handkerchief, I look out the open window across the narrow courtyard and see a family eating dinner. I hear laughter and conversation and see the father get up from his chair to hug his daughter.

At bedtime Fat Annie says, "Norman, you can sleep in Jacob's room, may he rest in peace."

"No! I want to sleep on the sofa."

But over the green sofa in the living room there's a big biblical tapestry that scares me. A man with a huge knife in one hand holds a baby by its feet. I know the story about the two women who both claim that the child is theirs. Solomon orders that the baby be cut in half and one-half given to each woman. When one woman cries out to spare the baby, saying it belongs to the other woman, Solomon knows who the real mother is. Even with the tapestry, I'd still rather sleep here than in Jacob's room.

In the bathroom, I put toilet paper on the seat before sitting down with my history book. The mirror on the medicine chest is covered with paper. So is the one on the wall in the living room across from the sofa.

It's no fun being stuck in this smelly house, afraid of eating, drinking, or breathing, thinking I'll catch a disease from Fat Annie's cracked dishes, her water-stained glasses, or the foul odor that fills every room. I read so long that she knocks on the door.

"Hello, Norman, are you all right?"

"I'm okay. I'll be right out."

After I wash my hands, I dry them on my pants.

Bedding is on the sofa. I undress, put on my pajamas, and climb under the covers. She comes in from the kitchen, kneels at my side, and fluffs up my pillow, things my aunt has never done.

"You're the image of your mother, may she rest in peace. Your hair and eyes are black as coal."

It thrills me when someone compares me to Mother. Fat Annie again asks if I want anything to eat, but I pretend to be asleep. She kisses my forehead and whispers in Yiddish, "God bless you."

When I hear her walk back into the kitchen, I rub off her kiss, then stare at the tapestry in the dim light. As scary as it is, I can't take my eyes from it. Like Rembrandt's paintings at the Met, it has the power to grab me and not let go.

Fat Annie is sobbing back in the kitchen. I think about her kiss, her kindness, and her blessing.

Chapter 19

Grand Slam

Thirty-five hours a week are used up in seventh grade. Then there's five hours dusting off bottles and washing windows at Mr. Gibalowitz's. Eight hours at Hebrew school, reading Hebrew but not understanding it. At least six hours, studying for my bar mitzvah with Uncle Irving. On Saturday, I hang out all day in the Central Library, in my special cubbyhole by the window, copying pictures of Rembrandt's paintings.

Mr. Gibalowitz goes home early on Wednesdays, so I have extra time in my schedule to sit on the top step of the stoop and sketch portraits of my customers.

"Turn toward me a little. Not that much. Lower your chin. A little more. There, stay like that."

Using a fat stick of charcoal, I draw the outline of Mrs. Rothman's face on the pad balanced on my lap. With the side of the stick, I darken the area where the eyes will be. I'm used to neighbors standing behind me, kibbitzing, and Mrs. Mirsky watching from her ground floor window. I don't draw the bridge of Mrs. Rothman's nose, and I don't define her eyes too early. With my pinky, I smudge a line that's too strong, and with a pointed charcoal pencil, define a line that needs to be stronger. Her pout is hard to draw.

Henry's basso profundo startles me. "Nice job, Nor-Man, except for connections. That's what the problem is. You have to look at your subject like an artist does."

"I don't understand."

"You will. Here's my address. Come study with me. I think you're free on Sundays."

The rest of the week, all I can think about is studying with Henry. Saturday night I'm so excited I can hardly get to sleep. On Sunday morning I gobble down breakfast and take off without telling Aunt Manya where I'm going.

On the way to Henry's house, an empty Ralph and Rockaway trolley goes by, clanging its bell at kids playing in the street. "Hey, look at my squashed penny," one boy says.

I used to put pennies on the track, too.

A Hasidic family passes by. Father, pregnant mother with a baby in her arms, and four more children march in single file, the tallest in front and smallest in back. Oscar, the meanest boy at PS 165, is with his family, carrying a Bible. His mother is in a blue silk dress, and his sisters are wearing bright dresses tied at the waist with bows. The bright colors make their black skin darker. They're all wearing their hats to church.

"Nice suit, Oscar."

"Thank you, Norman. On your way to Henry's?"

"How do you know?"

"We live in his building. He said I have to be nice to you."

"It's about time."

In the eight-block walk to Henry's there are enough colorful things to draw to keep an artist busy forever.

The bricks on Henry's basement apartment are painted blue. I knock on the door at the bottom of the steps. The lady who opens it is white, and she has on a paint-splattered white shirt with rolled up sleeves. On her neck is a silver chain with a Star of David. Her eyes are opened wide and her mouth is open too, like she's seen a ghost.

"You're the image of your mother, may she rest in peace."

"You met Mother?"

"Yes. Come on in. I'm Lola, Henry's wife."

The kitchen smells of chicken cooking and apple pie baking. In the living room are three sculptures of her in red clay and one in bronze. On the wall are five watercolors of New York City skyscrapers and bridges, two oil paintings of Henry, and one of a tailor at his sewing machine.

"That's your grandfather. Your mother painted it."

"Mother painted it? Mother was a painter?"

"Yes."

"Aunt Manya never told me that Mother painted."

"What about Benny? Surely your father must have told you."

"No one tells me anything."

"Henry didn't tell you?"

"No."

"I guess he assumed you always knew."

"I have a million questions to ask about Mother."

"I'm sure you do. I'll answer them, but right now Henry's waiting for you." She opens a heavy metal door at the far end of the living room, and we go into a basement studio.

A giant furnace hisses. Pipes painted in pastel colors crisscross the ceiling. Unlike Mr. Mirsky's dark basement, this one is lit by small windows just below the ceiling and by bare light bulbs. Henry can fix anything. He's the maintenance man here. He's standing by a work counter with seashells on it, tearing hot-dog shaped chunks from a block of brown clay.

"Hi Hen-Ry. Thanks for inviting me."

"You're welcome. Let's get busy with these shells."

"I thought we were going to draw."

"Sorry to disappoint you."

"What about connections?"

"That's why you're here... This is a giant Pacific scallop."

"The kind you eat"?

"Yes, but it's not kosher... And this is a triton's trumpet, and that's a pink conch. Lola got it in Florida."

"It was in the water at low tide thirty feet offshore, and I pulled it off of some eelgrass," Lola says.

"It made the best chowder we've ever eaten," Henry says. "Now let's get busy. We'll start with the scallop."

It's the smallest shell on the counter, eight inches across, with seventeen low, rounded ribs. While I knead the clay Lola is at her easel by a sunlit window, painting me. She looks like she's in a Vermeer painting.

"Feel into the shell, really see the shell, become the shell. As you sculpt the bowl, go deep into it, exaggerate. The flutings curve to the left and to the right and have different shapes, different widths. Carve into the flutings, like this, because that's where the deep shadows will be."

It's easy to work here with all the wood and the metal sculpture tools hanging from hooks on the wall behind the counter. I liked making mud pies when I was four, but this is even more fun. Damp clay is cool and smells earthy. It feels good to shape it.

"What do shells have to do with drawing people?"

"You'll see."

"Norman, wash up. It's time for lunch."

The kitchen table is a wooden cable reel covered with a red and white checkered tablecloth. On it are plates of roasted chicken, chard, baked potatoes, and a basket of pumpernickel bread.

"Look, Henry, how Norman handles the silverware just like his mother did. She had a special way to cut meat, raise a fork to her mouth, or gather up crumbs with the side of her hand. I wish you had seen his face when he saw his mother's painting."

"Is your mother's fishing boat painting still hanging in your bathroom?"

"Mother painted it?"

"Your aunt never told you?"

"She never told me anything about her."

"I see we have some catching up to do. Your mother and Lola were best friends. After your grandmother died, Norma moved in with Manya. When Lola and I met, Manya's door was closed to us, and your mother was heartbroken."

"My aunt won't let my friend, Vincent, in the house, because he's Italian."

"Let's have some apple pie and then get back to work."

My face is magically appearing on Lola's canvas, and I feel special. As she paints, I sculpt the triton and the conch, and Henry sits at the end of the counter, sculpting my head in side view. Once in a while, he gives me a few tips.

"Don't lick the sculpture!"

"I never licked it."

"Sure you did."

"What Henry means, Norman, is that the surface is too smooth. It's as if you actually put your tongue to it."

"Well said, Lola. Smooth is okay around the lip, where it's shiny, but not on the outer shell, where you need texture."

From a cabinet, he takes out clay sculptures of the very shells I'm working on. They're perfect. "Study these. Study Lola's painting of you. Notice that in sculpture, painting, or drawing, there are connections. The artist uses these connections to control how the viewer sees a work of art. Lines are meant to go somewhere. They are not haphazard. Your assignment is to look for these lines at the library, at the museum, and in your mother's watercolor. Then ask yourself if your lines are meaningful."

"But I still don't know where they're supposed to go."

"You will. Consult your friend, Rembrandt."

"How do you know I like Rembrandt?"

He smiles. "And one more thing. Before you go, tear down these sculptures. I don't want you to fall in love with your work."

That's okay. Aunt Manya won't let me bring them into her house.

The dishes are washed, dried, and put away. Aunt Manya hangs up her apron and sits across from me, drinking a cup of tea. Uncle Irving and Sarah have gone across the street to check on Fat Annie. "If looks could kill, I'd be dead by now."

"Aunt Manya, is it a sin to lie?"

"Of course it's a sin. So who lied to you, already?"

"Remember when that man from the museum came to the house?"

"So what about it?"

"When he asked if my mother or father were artists, you told him that there aren't any artists in my family."

She pounds her fist. Tea sloshes onto the table. "There will be no more talk about art in my house."

I bang my fist on the table. I can't believe I'm doing such a thing. "There will be talk about art!"

Aunt Manya's eyes open wide, as if she's afraid of me for a change. She pushes her denture back up with her thumb.

"You lied to the man, and that was the same as lying to me. How would you like it if I wished that you would roast in hell for not telling me that Mother was an artist? How would you like it if I wished consumption on you for having cheated me all these years out of the pleasure of knowing that the painting in the bathroom was done by her?"

"Stop shouting. I did it for your own good, so you won't become a bohemian or whatever they call people like Lola, the *Schvartze's* wife, or your

Aunt Lilly, the fortune teller, or your father, the big spender, the gambler, the man who neglects his son, and who buys him second-hand clothes from a pawnshop."

"Okay, I can see why you don't like Dad, but what's so bad about Aunt Lillie, and Lola?"

"One marries a drunk and lives in a slum. The other marries a *Schvartze* and lives in a basement. I want better for you, Norman."

A week goes by.

"I went to the library to study lines."

"What did you learn?"

"Well, Lola, I learned that when I look at the work of master painters, lines lead me around the paintings like train lines on a subway map. In one, there's a lady in a real neat black and white dress, watching an opera or something. The man behind her is looking through his opera glasses, but his mind isn't on the opera. He's probably looking at some other lady. It's Renoir's *La Loge.*"

"Yes. We know that painting."

"I laid a ruler next to the lines on the front of her dress and could see that they went somewhere important. My eyes were led around the painting. And interesting things were happening. I guess they were artistic tricks. The edge of the man's right shoulder connects to the edge of her dress. They blend together."

"Yes. The man becomes part of the woman," Henry says. "These tricks, as you call them, were done on purpose."

"Norma was fond of that painting."

"What was my mother like, Lola?"

"You couldn't keep her out of museums or art exhibits. She went to plays, recitals, concerts, you name it. She had an almost encyclopedic memory, and she could read fast, I mean book-a-day fast, and a year later, she could tell you all about any book she ever read. She worked as an office manager for a piano firm near Livingston Street where I believe your Aunt Lillie lives. She took lessons upstairs from the piano store, and she played in the store every day on her lunch break. She played the *Wedding March* when we got married."

Henry has me sculpt my right hand and wrist. I spread it out on a slab of wet clay, and with a stiff piece of wire, trace around my fingers, palm, and forearm.

"Pay attention to bony landmarks. Lay strips of clay down quickly, and don't think about it too much, or your art will come from the rational side of your brain, and that's not good. It must come from your heart."

It's awkward to work with the same hand I'm sculpting. I look at my right hand and try to memorize the pose. I make the fingers too thick and have to carve them down. Henry makes me start over and build up the fingers gradually. It's a sticky mess.

"You've let the clay take over. It'll do that. You have to be rough with it, show it who's boss. Let me show you."

He sculpts my hand, starting with the large forms. He talks about hands in such detail that I realize I've never really seen them at all.

"There are spirals in all living things. Everything in nature breathes. Hands breathe. Did you ever notice that only your middle finger is straight? The others are slightly curved toward it."

Seeing him do it was all I needed. I sculpt my hand and wrist in different positions and pay attention to the insertions of forearm muscles that he points out. I make sure to keep the work thin so that clay can be added rather than removed. And I don't let the clay take over.

Hebrew school is in the basement of a small apartment house on Chester Street, five blocks from home. I go there after dinner, and on the way, I sometimes stop at Mr. Berg's grocery store to buy fifteen cents worth of halvah for a *nosh*. I'm not a good student, but I can read the Hebrew writing upside down like the ancient scholars did when they sat around a table with only one book.

Reb Isaacson is a bearded man with eyes in back of his head as Aunt Manya would say. He raps my knuckles with a ruler if he catches me drawing, but the time I drew his face as he sat napping at his desk, he had me sign it before he put it in his drawer. And he actually smiled. By rights, I should have my knuckles rapped more often, but he's too busy rapping other knuckles.

This evening I'm late. No time to stop for halvah. I run to Hebrew School with my books and a writing pad in one hand and a sharp pencil in the other. I trip, fall on the sidewalk, and break off the pencil point in the heel of my hand. It hurts worse than the knee I just skinned. The pencil point is deep inside. In Hebrew school I pick at it with my pocketknife.

The next day I show my hand to Mr. Gibalowitz, and he says the point is in too deep and a doctor should look at it. So I walk three blocks to Beth-El hospital even though I've been warned by Aunt Manya never to go there. When she has shopping to do beyond the hospital she walks blocks out of her way to avoid "that place of death." I tell the doctor in the emergency room that I have a pencil point stuck in my hand. He has on a white coat with a stethoscope sticking out of one pocket. He's pale like Bela Lugosi, the scariest villain in the movies. He comes toward me with a scalpel in his hand and a smile on his face. Maybe he's teasing, but I don't wait to find out. I run and don't stop until I get home.

One cold Saturday in the first week of January Aunt Manya comes to the lot on Herzl Street where I'm having a snowball fight with my friends.

"Norman, Norman," she hollers so loud that you can hear her a block away. She's such an embarrassment. And she says I have a big mouth. "Come with us to Pitkin Avenue."

"Pitkin Avenue? Why do I have to go?"

"Don't worry why. Run home, wash your hands and face, and put on a clean shirt."

I wave goodbye to my friends. At home, I make sure I do a good job washing up. I remember Aunt Manya's Fels Naphtha soap face-washing.

"Why are we going to Pitkin Avenue, Uncle Irving?"

"We're going. There has to be a reason?"

I never get straight answers. Pitkin Avenue is a long way from the house, and the streets are covered with ice. If my friends wanted to go, I'd be happy to join them, but I'm ashamed to be seen with Aunt Manya, who's shorter than me, and her moustache has grown back.

"I'm tired of walking." "I'm hungry." "I don't know why we're going."

Busy Pitkin Avenue is the shopping center of Brownsville. We pass my fa-vorite pizza store, where they sell it by the slice, but I don't tell Aunt Manya that Sarah and I eat there. The Lional train in the window of the toy store up the block makes me think about the one Becca stole from me. I stop to look at a blue Schwinn bicycle.

"Come on, Norman, we don't have time for bicycles."

They go into a clothing store, and I feel like a *schmuck* before we even reach the boys' department. They're buying me a suit for my *bar mitzvah*. The salesman measures my chest and my waist and pushes away suits on each side of a rack to get to ones that are my size. Uncle Irving examines the material and every seam. "These three are good quality. So pick already."

"I like this one."

"Good. You'll try on the *pents*, you'll try on the *coit*, we'll see if they fit."

"Irving, better the suit should be big enough so he can wear it next year."

"What are you talking? At his *bar mitzvah* he should look like a *sch-lep*?"

"I'm not saying it should be two sizes too big, just a little."

"Stop *hocking mir a chaynik*, Manya. I'll tell the tailor to leave extra in the cuffs, for next year."

I thank them for the nice blue suit, and I'm very well behaved on the walk home.

Three weeks to go, and I still haven't memorized all the pages. Every night, Uncle Irving tutors me. He's patient. We put on our *yarmulkes*, and he guides me through the text, which doesn't have diacritical marks. The marks make it easy to sound out the words, but without them, it seems like an impossible task. He makes me repeat the text until I'm hoarse. I need glasses of water to get through the readings.

"I'm really nervous. What if I don't learn it in time?"

"Practice while you're sculpting," Henry says.

"Wouldn't he be better off taking a break from sculpture?"

"No, Lola, and I'll tell you why. The problem is that he thinks too much."

"Thinks too much?"

"Yes. When he's spontaneous, his work has more life."

"What does that have to do with his bar mitzvah lessons?"

"The bar mitzvah ceremony, as far as I'm concerned, is an incredible piece of performance art. When you do art without thinking about it, great things happen."

"I think a lot about my art," Lola says.

"You do in the planning stages."

"You know, you're right, Henry. When I'm putting paint on canvas, I don't think about it at all. I just do it."

"So if I just do it, I'll be able to memorize my reading?"

"It's worth a try, Nor-Man."

Lola poses for us on a rotating stand with my bar mitzvah text open on her lap.

"Let's get busy. Make Lola's head life-size. If a head is to be larger than life-size, it must be much larger or else it'll be disturbing. Add the clay evenly on all sides. A sculpture is 360 profiles."

With difficulty, Lola reads each paragraph of the text, and I repeat after her.

Henry rotates the modeling stand, and I rotate the lazy Susan that holds my sculpture.

"Pay attention to the profiles, Nor-man. Just keep adding clay, and no carving down."

Lola stumbles over a passage. "Sorry, Norman, I'm a little rusty. It's been a while since your mother and I went to Hebrew school."

Henry keeps rotating the stand. I keep adding moist, cool clay. At the end of the day, Henry says, "Very nice. Now tear it down."

The next week, Lola poses again. Working with the clay, it only takes me a little while to get back to the same stage. Lola chants a paragraph, and I chant. Henry puts a pad of newsprint on an easel. "If Lola were sitting by the fountain in Prospect Park you'd be able to recognize her even though you might not see her features. If your cousin, Sarah, were walking down the street, a block away, you'd be able to recognize her, too. We're dealing with gait, posture, and a few bony landmarks."

"What bony landmarks?"

"I'll show you."

Lola chants with me while Henry draws front and side views of her skull. He measures dimensions on her head with an aluminum caliper and marks my clay sculpture in the same places.

"From the side, the highest point of the skull is directly over the hole of the ear, and the front of the nose, as it tapers toward the brow, lines up with that point. Looking from the front, the broadest points are over and slightly behind the ear canals. Here's the caliper, Nor-man. Measure us and see if I'm right."

By the end of the session, I feel really good about what I've accomplished, and I'm flattered when Henry says to me, "Don't tear this one down. Wrap it in wet rags."

Today's the last weekend before my *bar mitzvah*. Henry puts me in the teacher's role. It's fun to show off. On his easel, I draw a side view of Lola's head, and on this view I superimpose a five-sided figure that Henry calls a pentahedron.

"The sides of this figure connect the highest point of Lola's head, the widest point of her head, the corner of her cheekbone, the angle of her jaw, and the Moses horn, which is the highest point of her eyebrow. This geometric figure, according to Henry's teacher, is as good as a fingerprint in identifying a person. Do you want to hear about the Fibonacci Series or the Golden Section?"

"No thank you, Nor-Man."

I walk to the far end of the basement, as far from my sculpture as I can get. It doesn't have ears or eyes or lips, but still, it looks like Lola. I feel like I've hit a homerun.

I drink a glass of water, and Lola and Henry join me in chanting the Hebrew text. Bass, alto, and boy soprano. The basement echoes with the joyous sound. Every paragraph is memorized. I've just hit a grand slam.

My *bar mitzvah* is in Rabbi Zimmerman's synagogue in the basement of a small apartment house on Herzl Street two blocks from where I live. I wish it were in the big synagogue on Hopkinson Street where Seymour and Joey had their *bar mitzvahs*. I immediately apologize to God, since what I'm thinking sounds sinful.

As we enter the *shul* Sarah tucks a few stray hairs under my white *yarmulke* and kisses my forehead. I don't wipe it off. I sit in the first row next to Uncle Irving.

"Don't slouch," he says as he adjusts my *talis*.

I'm nervous when Rabbi Zimmerman, with his fiery blue eyes, motions me to the Torah. His hair is now completely white, and he looks like Michelangelo's version of God on the ceiling of the Sistine Chapel.

Aunt Manya, in the women's section, has on a new light blue dress. Her face is powdered and her moustache is gone. Dad, wearing a fedora, is in the second row, looking at his watch. I didn't really expect him, but I'm glad he's here for a change. Joey gives me a thumbs up, Seymour waves. Abraham squirms in his seat.

With a shaky hand, Rabbi Zimmerman aims his silver pointer at the text. I stutter on the first word, stop, take a deep breath, and as he slowly slides the pointer under the words, I chant them smoothly and melodically, like I did in Henry and Lola's studio. When I finish the reading, I duck, and cellophane-wrapped hard candy comes flying. Now I am a man. The rabbi shakes my hand and reminds me that this is not the end but the beginning of Jewish studies and responsibilities.

Joey's mother kisses my cheek. Her moustache tickles. Joey and Seymour shake my hand. All my relatives on Mother's side of the family are here, including Fat Annie, now over three hundred and fifty pounds. Also here is second cousin, Bessie, who crushed me into her perfumed breasts and danced with me at Sophie's wedding. Nathan, Debbie, Sol, Sophie, Sarah, Uncle Irving, Aunt Manya, Mrs. Katzman, and the Mirskys hug me and give me envelopes with tens and twenties inside. It looks like all the women in the shul are wiping their eyes with hankies.

Aunt Lilly is the only one on Dad's side of the family who came, and he's standing next to her, eyeing the envelopes in my hand. Henry and Lola congratulate me.

"Our Nor-man is finally a man."

"I'm glad you're here. You two are the most important people in my life."

"It's nice of you to say that. This is for you." He hands me a heavy package.

The rabbi's wife comes over.

"Hello, Mrs. Z."

"Hello, Norman the artist, who studies with Henry and Lola. How's by you Henry and you, Lola? Norma, may she rest in peace, would've been so proud to see this day. Her son, thirteen, a man, and what a blessing to be able to study with you. What a blessing. On my living room wall, in frames mind you, are pictures Norman drew when he was nine, but what am I talking, you'll see them at the buffet, in my house, in the rumpus room, a little party for Norman, it's the least I can do, Manya's place is too small. Do you know that from blocks away people come to Norman for their portraits? In line they stand and wait their turn. Like Mrs. Katzman has told me a hundred times, a young Rembrandt we have in Brooklyn, on Lott Avenue no less."

Chapter 20

Strike Three

Lola is Vermeer, sitting by a sunny window, painting us in watercolor as we work on separate sculptures of her head. Henry rolls out string bean-sized strips of clay and models the helix and the lobe of her ear.

"Lola, the curve of your ear is like a small portrait of your skull."

"Good observation, Norman."

Other strips of clay become the concha, the tragus and the antitragus. Henry's fingers are fast. In less than a minute he produces a believable ear, and in a few minutes more, an outstanding ear. I do too. I'm slow but proud of what I accomplish.

Henry fashions Lola's upper lip with one strip of clay. He curves the ends well around her face so that the corners of her eyes and lips share a vertical axis in side view. The lower lip is made with two strips of clay that are wrapped around, into, and under the upper lip. He presses in the corners with a thin tool to create dark shadows. He presses in a groove in the midline of the upper lip, and he's done.

"Hen-Ry, look at these lips I'm working on. They don't look real, and I don't know why."

He pinches them together a little to puff out the lower lip.

"How did you know what to do?"

"It's a matter of experience. You see what you know, and the more you know, the more you see. But it's more than just seeing; it's a knowledge of anatomy; it's being able to visualize; and it's having a high degree of esthetic sensibility, which, by the way, you have in abundance, Nor-Man, or I wouldn't have asked you here."

We change roles. I'm the teacher. Henry says a person doesn't really know a thing unless he can teach it.

"Okay, class," I begin, "the eyes are not straight across. They wrap around the head. There's a space the width of one eye between the eyes, but the space is narrower if you're French. The high and low edges of the eyes are not at the center but catty-corner from one another. To keep the eyes in focus, make their white spaces the same size. On side view, a line drawn from the upper to the lower lid will be on a forty-five degree angle."

"Good, Nor-Man. You have the technical stuff down."

Henry builds up Lola's eyes almost as fast as I can lecture. I've learned to look at things more critically. I fashion Lola's eyes in no time, her Jewish nose, too. It's a miniature of Dad's eagle beak. Now I can sculpt eyes, ears, lips and noses on my own, but Henry says he's going to lower the bar. He can lower it all he wants. I'm still going to dance right under it.

I'm ready to tackle Henry's torso. He's sitting shirtless on a stool.

"Nor-Man. You've studied Michelangelo and Rodin at the library. Now let's see what you can do."

I turn the platform until he's in three-quarter view. "Twist your right shoulder to the front. That's enough. Now raise it a little. A little more. Are you comfortable, Hen-Ry? Okay. Here goes."

To build his torso, I press hot-dog-sized slabs of clay onto a wire armature. So that my work will be uniform, I rotate the turntable he sits on and the lazy Susan holding my sculpture every fifteen minutes. I'm concerned only with his neck, chest, and upper arms. When I've gotten his figure roughed in, I adjust the lamps so the light is the same on him as it is on my sculpture. It's important to get the maximum effect of light and shadow.

The following week and the one after that I perfect the anatomy, taking great pains to reproduce Henry's bulging muscles. I deepen triangles of clay and fill in others, making sure not to destroy the clarity of my composition. I don't want my marks to call attention to themselves. Did I just use the words "clarity of composition" and "marks that call attention to themselves?" I'm starting to think like Henry. But it gets harder to please him. Good. I don't want to be a mediocre artist.

"You need color," he says.

"You mean I've got to paint it?"

"The Minoans did at Knossos," Lola says.

"Really?"

"Yes, Nor-Man. We've been to Crete. Spent five glorious weeks in Greece going from island to island."

"We went to every museum there, I think," Lola says. "There's nothing like seeing the *Charioteer* in person. He looked alive."

"Like Rembrandt's portraits?"

"Yes. Between light and shade, there's a range of half tones, which the sculptor thinks of as sculptural color." Henry picks up a slender wooden carver from the table and points it at the deltoid muscle I've just built up. "One plane is no longer enough to represent a surface. From now on, minor planes are needed. They'll add life and movement to your work."

"And I'll have sculptural color?"

"Right. Just like Michelangelo and Bernini have in their work."

I spend weeks at the library studying books on sculpture. My favorite sculptor is Bernini. Talk about color! Talk about work that lives and breathes. Someday I'll go to Rome and see his *Apollo and Daphne* at the Villa Borghese.

At the Met, I set off the alarm when I stand too close to Degas' *The Little Fourteen Year-Old Dancer*. The guard comes. Instead of warning me, he sees my drawings and gives me a compliment.

With Novocaine there's no electric yellow pain. Dr. Bass squashes the silver into my tooth, carves it down, and removes the Tofflemire. His younger daughter works for him now. She takes off the paper bib. My little white lie about writing a school paper on dentistry pays off.

"Okay already. Can you come back tonight at seven?"

I'll miss some study time, but it'll be worth it.

In the evening, he's wearing a polo shirt and dungarees and looks like a regular guy. He checks his watch and says, "Seven on the dot. It's good to be prompt, Norman."

The lab is hot and cluttered.

"I'm about to cast a gold crown. Here, put on these goggles and watch."

He picks up tongs, opens the door to his electric oven, takes out a metal cylinder, and puts it on his casting machine.

"A half-hour ago this cylinder contained a wax replica of the crown that goes on Mr. Berg's bicuspid. Do you know him, the grocer? This morning, I poured heat-resistant dental stone around the wax. The stone is hard now. The oven burned out the wax and left a hollow chamber in the stone. This casting machine is a spring-loaded centrifuge. I'll wind it up with one, two, three turns."

He places a grape-sized chunk of gold in the melting pot next to the cylinder, opens the valve on his acetylene tank, lights the torch, and heats the gold. The torch roars.

"Gold melts at 1,945 degrees."

"What did you say, Norman?"

I shout over the sound of the torch, "Gold melts at 1,945 degrees."

"How do you know?"

"I read a lot."

When the gold becomes a pool of yellow liquid, he turns off the torch, releases the catch on the casting machine, and it whips around, forcing the melted gold into the space where the wax used to be.

"When it cools, I'll slide the stone out of the cylinder, break away the stone, and expose the crown. Now let's have a *nosh*."

At his workbench, I drink cocoa and eat macaroons from Yellin's bakery. Dr. Bass sips his cocoa, then lubricates with oil a stone model of another bicuspid crown preparation. Using a small metal spatula, he melts blue wax over a Bunsen burner and slowly drips it onto the model until it fills up the space between the adjacent teeth. Without carving or melting away wax, he's able to reproduce the anatomy of the tooth. His attention to details reminds me of Henry and Lola.

"Most dentists send their crown preps to a dental lab, but I enjoy lab work. Everything I do in dentistry is fun. It's like playing stickball all day and getting paid for it."

"Lab work looks easy."

"Oh yeah?" He hands me a box with Rabbi Zimmerman's name on it. Inside is a molar prep. He takes a dental anatomy book down from a shelf, opens it to a picture of a first molar, and plops it in front of me on the workbench. "You try it, wise guy."

I lubricate the stone model, hold a spatula over the Bunsen burner to heat it, melt the wax, and drip it onto the molar prep. In a half-hour, I've reproduced the tooth in wax.

"Norman, sometimes it gets so busy here that I don't have time for lab work. Would you like to earn some money waxing up crowns for me? I bet you'd be good at setting denture teeth, too."

Tilden High School is a half-hour walk from my house. If it rains, Joey and I and five other boys share the cost of a giant DeSoto taxi with jump seats in back like the one I rode in to Sophie's wedding when I was seven.

It's cheaper than taking the green trolley up Church Avenue and still having to walk four blocks. The school is named for Samuel Jones Tilden, a Democrat who won the popular vote in 1876 but lost the presidency to Rutherford B. Hayes. That wasn't fair.

Except for algebra and gym, I like high school. Gym would be all right if the kids were allowed to play basketball, use the horses, ropes, and exercise equipment, or run around the indoor track that encircles the upper level. Instead, we spend most of the time standing at attention, listening to an instructor tell us how brave he was in the war and how he'll make an example of any student who gets out of line. "Only veterans will get an 'A' in my class; the others will get no higher than a 'B'," he said the first day before ordering us to do calisthenics.

The indoor pool is as warm as bath water. We have to swim naked, and I'm shy. It's like sitting in the candy store with Fat Annie or being called to the blackboard at an inconvenient time and having to walk there with my hand in my pocket to conjugate an irregular Spanish verb.

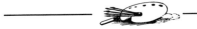

Lola takes over my art education. She's going to teach me how to paint.

"Let's start with watercolor. It's the medium of the masters."

"Why watercolor first? I want to paint in oils!"

"Watercolor is more difficult than oil. Because it's unforgiving, it will teach you to think before you touch brush to paper. When we get to oil painting, it'll be easy."

She uncaps large tubes of watercolor and squeezes luscious colors onto a white porcelain butcher tray. She arranges the colors on all four sides, like those on her tray, bright ones separated from dull, and warm separated from cool. My throat tickles as the colors ooze out. It's the feeling I had when I was four, opening a new box of Crayolas. They had a fresh waxy smell. These paints don't smell, but the colors sure excite me.

Alongside her table is a claw-footed bathtub for soaking sheets of watercolor paper. She staples the wet sheets to plywood boards and I help her carry them out to shrink in the sunny back yard. When the paper is dry, she lays a board on her table and raises it in back with a brick. She shows me how to lay on a wash and gradate it. Holding a rag in one hand and painting with the other, she snaps orders like a drill sergeant. "Use the biggest brush possible." "Wipe it clean before you put it back into the paint pot." "Feather dust so you won't leave a hard edge."

She has me mix and experiment with transparent non-staining colors, opaque sedimentary colors, and staining colors. "Be particularly careful with stains. They'll get away from you." What she does looks easy, but it isn't.

"Use a light touch. Don't wipe and paw at your marks. Place them and leave them."

"Watercolor is harder than I thought."

"If it was easy, everyone would be doing it well."

On Sunday we draw for an hour, and for the rest of the day we paint. After the first few weeks with the basics of watercolor, I paint Lola at her easel and Henry, chiseling a hunk of marble, his forehead glistening. It gets easier to control the amount of water in my brush. My washes don't have blooms from too watery a mix or hard lines from mixes that are too dry.

Her instruction gets more intense. She critiques my first paintings.

"There's more to painting than copying what's in front of you. That would be better done with a camera. However, you have a great sense of composition. The best technique in the world can't make up for poor composition, but good composition can overcome poor technique. That's why these first pictures of yours are better than you think they are. But you have to pay more attention to values and complementary colors."

Henry reviews my figure drawings. His instruction gets more intense. I draw Lola in a variety of poses. Henry insists that I use only straight lines. Curves are forbidden. When it's necessary to go from point A to point B to point C, he tells me to go from A to C without thinking about B. He wants me to look where I'm going, not where I've been, to see the whole all at once.

"Give it a soft-eyed look," he says, and I know he wants me to squint a lot to eliminate middle tones. It makes me look weird, but not any weirder than I look when I blink my eyes, which I've been doing less and less since I've been studying here.

When I exaggerate the angles of the pose, the completed drawing is pleasing. When I don't, the drawing straightens itself out and looks weak.

"You're almost ready for oils," Lola says. "We'll start when school lets out for summer vacation. Then, if you'd like, you can come more often. Tuesdays and Thursdays would be fine. We have great plans for you, Norman."

Since I'm great with numbers, I thought algebra would be easy. After all, I understand the Fibonacci Series, which among other things describes the curvatures of shells and the lengths of the bones of the back of the hand and fingers. Each number is the sum of the two preceding numbers. (1,1,2,3,5,8,13…) But my young brain is not ready for abstract x's, y's, and z's.

"I don't understand algebra, Mr. Garf."

"It's easy. X is an unknown quantity. It stands for a number."

"What number?"

"That's for you to find out."

Seymour, the future accountant, spends an hour with me. I don't understand a thing he says. I go to Joey who still counts on his fingers but gets an 'A' on every test. I can't understand him either. I can add a column of figures in my head faster than Mr. Berg can on a grocery bag with the little yellow pencil he keeps on his ear, but I can't pass an algebra test. Sarah, Aunt Manya, and Uncle Irving have never taken algebra. Mr. Garf tries to help me in class, between periods, after class, even at his home on a rainy night. I don't understand a thing.

"Uncle Irving, Mr. Garf said that for me an 'F' is better than a 'D'."

"What are you talking? How is it possible? What kind of *meshuggas* is that?"

"He told me that a 'D' is for a student who's not very bright or who's too lazy to study, and an 'F' is for a student who's not mature enough to grasp the concepts."

"Speak English, Norman. Manya, what is he saying?"

"He's saying that his teacher is going to give him an 'F' because he doesn't understand algebra."

"If he was a good teacher, he would make Norman understand."

"He should get consumption, this Mr. Garf. He's probably an anti-Semite."

"He wears a Star of David, Aunt Manya."

"Garf. What kind of name is Garf? Is he a foreigner?"

"He said he was born in Manhattan. I heard that he changed his name from Garfinkle."

"Aha, so it doesn't sound Jewish. What respect does he show his parents? A man like that shouldn't be allowed to teach."

"He told me to take algebra again next year."

"I would take it by another teacher if I were you," Uncle Irving says.

The first day of summer vacation Joey, Seymour, and I line up enough guys for a ten-man softball team. I'm elected manager, and of course, I'll get to play shortstop.

"What'll we call ourselves?" Seymour asks.

"Well," Joey says, "since most of the team lives on Herzl Street, we'll call ourselves the Herzl Street Tigers."

"I don't like that name."

"Why not, Norman?"

"Because I live on Lott Avenue."

"I don't like that name either," Seymour says.

"Why not?"

"Because when we put letters on our caps, people will think we're the Harry S Trumans. "

"Okay. How about the Barracudas?"

"Yeah. Barracudas. I like that name."

"Me, too."

"So it's agreed, and we'll only have to buy one letter for our caps."

We're one inning into our first game at Betsy Head Park. We're playing the Amboy Street Dukes, a name they got from some book. Two outs. Seymour's on third. I'm at bat. Sarah comes to the fence, waves me over. I'm so excited that she's here to watch us play.

"Norman, your father's at the house. He brought a suitcase, and he's making Mamma pack all your clothes in it. I don't want you to go."

"I don't want to go either."

"Hey Norman, you gonna talk or play."

"Sarah, watch me drive in a run."

Where to now? A place with cruel people, uncaring people, food that's tasteless mush, another dangerous neighborhood, another dangerous school?

"Strike one."

I hope Dad's not taking me back to the Bronx. Maybe I should run to Henry's and hide out there.

"Strike two."

What about my art lessons? My job waxing up crowns for Dr. Bass? My softball team? My real family?

"Strike three."

CHAPTER 21

RIVER PEOPLE

The yellow iron-on 'B' is already half off my blue baseball cap. It won't stay when I try to squeeze it back on, but I wear the cap anyway. Aunt Manya doesn't kiss me goodbye. She stands in her spotless kitchen and glares at Dad. He picks up the suitcase. I pick up my satchel, follow him down the stairs, out the front door, and up the block. I feel empty.

Four-foot-eight-inch Sarah runs alongside of us, shouting over and over, "Don't take him away, Benny. Please don't take Norman away."

He ignores her.

Heads turn on Lott Avenue. Three old women, sitting on folding chairs on the sunny side of the street in front of Shirley's candy store, stop talking and stare. Mr. Bloom, with a hunk of leather in his hand, peeks through the window of his shoe repair shop. A woman sticks her head out of her ground floor window to see what the commotion is. Manny, in his yellow straw hat and blood-splattered white apron, watches from the doorway of his butcher shop. Dad yanks me along by one arm. Sarah tugs me back by the other. They're pulling me apart. She curses and kicks the side of the suitcase. He puts the suitcase down and raises his hand. She backs away, defeated. I look back and see the saddest face I've ever seen. I blow her a kiss goodbye.

We're at the Saratoga Avenue station. "Melvin, here's a dollar. Get nickels for the turnstile."

I feel like kicking his suitcase when he doesn't call me by my name.

We ride in the first car with the suitcase and the satchel on the floor between us. Dad is reading *The Daily News*. He'll read it all the way to Manhattan. The buildings of Brownsville are passing fast, and the train is going into the dark underground. So are my hopes. What about the game at Betsy Head park, going to the Central library afterward, and Henry and Lola wondering about me not showing up for my lessons tomorrow? A very sad face is reflected back at me from the train window.

Manhattan is noisier and busier than Brooklyn. Car exhaust mixes with the odor of hot dogs, mustard and warm pretzels from street vendors.

There are honking horns, sirens, and jackhammers. Crowded sidewalks. A woman with a big package bumps into me.

"Watch where you're going, young man."

Steam comes out of sidewalk vents. Elevators come up through the sidewalk. I used to be scared to step on the iron plates that cover the elevator openings, thinking I'd fall in.

We walk down Madison Avenue to the office building where Uncle Lou works. He's Dad's ex brother-in-law, which makes him Melvin's uncle, not mine, but I call him uncle. Since I'm now taller than Dad, I don't have to run to keep up or worry that I'll lose him in the crowd. There were other trips to Manhattan with him. When I was eight, I stood with my nose pressed against a toy store window. When I turned around, he was gone. I looked up, down, across the busy street, walked in one direction, then another, looking over my shoulder, afraid to move too far from the spot. Something in my mouth tasted metallic. I was afraid I'd never see him again. Then he appeared with a grin on his face, enjoying his joke.

Uncle Lou is standing in the lobby next to the open express elevator. He has on a gray uniform with brass buttons. He chews on a toothpick and speaks out of the side of his mouth like a racetrack tout I saw in the movies.

"Hello, Benny. Hello, Norman." He shakes my hand.

Bong. Bong. "Back to work." He motions us inside the elevator, closes the door, and turns a lever. We go up twenty-eight stories. My stomach is still on the first floor. A woman gets in. Uncle Lou nudges Dad with his elbow. On the stops on the way down, he nudges Dad three more times.

In the lobby, there's a woman wearing thick makeup who smells like she just took a bath in gardenia perfume. She looks and dresses and smells like my cousins, Aunt Flo's daughters, who carry mattresses on their backs all over New York City. She walks into the elevator, squeezes up against Uncle Lou, and whispers something in his ear. After she gets off, he rubs his crotch. I bet he had to walk to the blackboard with his hand in his pocket when he was in high school.

When there aren't passengers, Dad and Uncle Lou talk about Pimlico, Saratoga, Belmont, and Aqueduct. Uncle Lou is an expert on racehorses. He talks about Johnny Longden and about Eddie Arcaro, who rode Citation when he won the Triple Crown in 1948. I hear about tips, touts, racing forms, odds, mudders, and long shots. Uncle Lou takes a racing form out of his uniform pocket, points to Shady Lady, and frowns.

"How could we lose, Benny? It was a sure thing."

Aunt Manya said, "Your father follows the horses, but the horses he follows follow other horses." Now I know what she was talking about.

"Norman, don't mention horses in front of Ruby. She's allergic to them."

"Don't worry, Uncle Lou, I won't."

In the basement locker room, Uncle Lou changes into a suit and tie. He's a sharp dresser like Dad. He takes a handkerchief out of his pocket and bends down to polish the toe of his shoe.

"Hey, Benny, I'm hungry. Let's go to the spaghetti joint."

We walk to a restaurant with steamed up windows that serves only spaghetti and meatballs. Behind the counter, a fat man is stirring a huge pot of spaghetti. Sweat is pouring off his face.

"Where's the ketchup, Uncle Lou?"

"Ketchup?"

"Yeah, to put on the spaghetti. That's what we do at Aunt Manya's."

Uncle Lou roars. "Hey Sam," he says to the cook, "did you hear that? The kid's aunt uses ketchup for spaghetti sauce."

Now everyone in the joint is laughing, Dad, too. I wish I were back at Aunt Manya's.

Sam dips his tongs into the pot, picks up a strand of spaghetti, and plops it into his mouth. "It's ready." He fills three plates, and from another pot ladles out the sauce. "Here you go fellas."

"Well, how does it taste with real sauce?"

"Real good, Uncle Lou. I like it."

"Is it better than your aunt's spaghetti?"

"Yeah, Dad. It is."

"Don't say 'yeah,' Norman. Say 'yes.'"

"Give the boy another helping, Sam. He likes your cooking."

"No thanks, Uncle Lou. I'm full." With everyone laughing and with Dad correcting my English, I'm not hungry anymore.

The buildings we pass on the way to the bus station have urine stains on the sidewalk and bums sitting in doorways, bottle necks poking out of the brown paper bags in their hands. A man is sprawled on the sidewalk. I look to see if his chest is moving. One doorway smells of vomit. In a bar, a woman is sitting on a stool with her red dress pulled up over her knees. She blows me a kiss. Now I have to walk with my hand in my pocket. Lou buys a *Daily Mirror* at a newsstand. I peek into a store and see a shelf with pink, brown, and black penises on it. A woman takes one down, squeezes it, and puts it back.

We go inside the Elgin Hotel. There are fingerprints on the glass door. To the left is a lobby with a sagging pink couch along one wall. A man is snoozing behind a counter, and behind him is an unpainted plywood board with keys dangling from it. Straight ahead is a ramp that leads to the basement bus terminal. A black man is shining the brown wingtips of two customers on his shoeshine stand. He uses his bare fingers to scoop polish from a can of Shinola. I don't want to rush through this neighborhood. I want to be like Toulouse-Lautrec and sketch the spaghetti joint, the shoeshine man, the bums sleeping in doorways, the woman in the bar, the seedy hotel, and later, to capture these scenes in my studio in oil paint.

"Hurry up, Norman, the bus is leaving!"

I take a window seat on the brown bus. Dad slides in beside me. Uncle Lou stretches out his legs on the seat in front of us, puts on his glasses, and opens his newspaper to the sports section. The driver backs out of the stall onto a turntable. It revolves and points the bus to a steep exit ramp. The bus climbs up the ramp to street level, honks its way into heavy traffic, crawls through the West Side of Manhattan, and gets stuck in traffic across from an art supply store. It's tempting to get off and go inside. Someday I'll have an art studio and easels and canvasses and brushes and paints that are all the colors of the rainbow.

Cars honk in the Lincoln Tunnel. Someone told me that they're not supposed to, because the tunnel might break. I'm nervous in here with the Hudson River ready to burst through. There's daylight again. It's the first time I've ever been in New Jersey. Out the back window, across the river, is the Empire State Building and the Chrysler Building. I'm leaving my favorite art deco buildings behind.

"Dad, where exactly does Uncle Lou live?"

"Mountain View. His house is on a river. You'll like it there."

"Which river?"

"I don't know. Lou, what's the name of the river you live on?"

"The Pequannock," he says and returns to the sports section.

"What's that smell outside, Dad?"

"Lou, what's that smell?"

"Secaucus. They raise pigs here. It always stinks."

Uncle Lou, Ruby, and their two kids, Richie and Jody, used to live in Manhattan in a neighborhood like the one I lived in, in the Bronx. I was there once with Dad. Ruby had a big cross drooping from her neck, and there was a cross on her kitchen wall with Jesus hanging on it. It gave me the creeps.

Now, Uncle Lou lives in New Jersey and goes to Manhattan five days a week. Once, I heard Dad tell Aunt Lilly that every few months Lou misses his bus and has to stay over in the city. He and Ruby have a big fight when he comes home. She accuses him of going out with "who-ers," but they always make up. I'm sure that perfumed lady in the elevator was a "who-er."

It's twenty-three miles from Manhattan to Mountain View, but that's a long way from my friends, my school, and my family. Forty-five minutes later, we get off the bus and walk across the highway.

"There's the Mountain View Diner," Uncle Lou says. "Great hamburgers and waitresses." He cups his hands in front of his chest and makes like he's lifting something heavy. He's as bad as Joey. At a dusty gravel parking lot, we climb into his midnight blue '37 Packard and drive across the Pequannock River. "Norman, it's a lazy river now, but wait 'til the rain starts. And here's our two-block-long town."

Dad is yawning. We pass an old-fashioned candy store with a pink and white striped awning. A sign painted on the brick building says, "Home of the best Fizzician in town." A man with a handlebar moustache is sitting on a bench in front of a one-chair barbershop. A sign next to the barber pole says Scissors Joe. I can't wait to paint Mountain View.

The pavement ends, and the Packard bumps along two miles of potholed road to the edge of the river and Uncle Lou's white house with green trim. Ruby waves to us from the front porch. She's wearing the same cross.

"Hello Norman, hello Benny. Come inside. Norman, put your satchel down."

Jesus is on the cross on her kitchen wall. I remember once asking Aunt Manya who Jesus was. She got red in the face, shook her fist at me, and hollered, "Don't you ever say that word in my house again." I had to wash her spit off my face.

Friends say that in Aunt Manya's house you can eat off the floor. I wouldn't eat off Ruby's floor.

"Richie, Jody, come say hello."

Richie is one year older than I am, and Jody's one year younger. They're as skinny as they were the last time I saw them in Manhattan, and from what I see when we have dinner, it doesn't take much to fill them up. It takes a lot to fill me up. Ruby serves dinner in dollops the size of a scoop of ice cream, three dollops per person, and there's nothing extra in her pot.

Dad spends the night. I haven't slept in the same bed with him since I ran away from Aunt Manya's.

"Dad, I'm hungry. If we hadn't had spaghetti this afternoon, I'd be starving."

"Maybe Ruby didn't know I'd be staying over the weekend."

"Could be, Dad, but I don't think there was enough food for four people.

"I'll talk to Lou about it."

"Dad, I wish you could live here, too."

"Norman, I'm still with Becca. I have to make sure she takes good care of the baby."

Things are going around in my mind. How will I get to Henry's place, the Central Library where all the great art books are, and the Met? When will I see Sarah, my friends, and the rest of my real family?

Breakfast is as big as one of Aunt Ellie's egg creams. Where's Grandfather's magnifying glass? I'm gonna starve.

Monday morning, Dad gives me two dollars and leaves with Uncle Lou to catch the seven o'clock bus. This money and the dollar in the secret hiding place in my wallet are all I have.

Richie doesn't like to play ball, hike, or fish. He stays in his room, listening to the radio. Jody spends her days down the road at her girlfriend's house. That's okay with me. This place is beautiful. It's in the country, on a river, with trees and birds. I can walk along the bank, skip stones in the water, and fish for the first time in my life.

On the other side of the river is a tiny island, and there's a wooden bridge from the island to a big log cabin on the far shore.

"Ruby, what's that log cabin over there?"

"It's the Casino. People play cards there. They have classes, too. Quilting, embroidery, watercolor… "

"That's a good scene to draw. What about painting it from inside your back porch? Would that be okay?"

"Yes, Norman."

I get the drawing pad and pencils from my satchel. But I still need to go to Brooklyn on Sundays. Let's see, how long will it take to go to Henry's? Ten minutes in the car to the bus stop. Wait ten minutes for the bus. The trip to Manhattan is 45 minutes. Then it's a ten-minute walk to the subway, another 30 minutes to Brooklyn, and a 15-minute walk to Henry's from the Saratoga Avenue station. Two hours total. I'll have to get up real early.

By the time Uncle Lou comes home, I have five landscapes to show him.

"Nice work, kid. I've seen drawings in art gallery windows that weren't near as good."

"Uncle Lou, can you take me to town real early on Sunday morning?"

"Sunday morning? Why?"

"So I can take the bus to New York. So I can go to my art lesson."

"Sure. You can catch the eleven o'clock bus when I take Ruby and the kids to Mass."

"But I need to be in town to catch the seven o'clock bus."

"I can't afford to make two trips to town. You'll have to walk. It'll do you good. Richie can show you the short cut."

I get up at six on Sunday, walk a quarter mile through the woods, and cross a creek by jumping from rock to slippery rock. Oops, I'm in water up to my knees and my shin is gashed. In squishy shoes, I walk a mile to town on a dirt road along the river. The houses here have neat lawns, picket fences, and no rusty cars lying around. Maybe I can find a job mowing lawns, or painting fences.

Mountain View is deserted. The bench in front of Scissors Joe's barbershop has names cut into the wood. There aren't stacks of comic books inside like there are at Sal's. Is there even a place to buy a comic book in this town? Why did Dad take me away from Brooklyn?

The bus doesn't come. There's a schedule taped to the window of the diner. On Sundays, the first bus is at nine. A man comes out, and the smell of potatoes and onions frying on the grill draws me inside. My stomach was never empty at Aunt Manya's. I take a seat at the counter, order, and chomp on the most delicious hamburger I've ever eaten. There's room in my stomach for another one and a slice of apple pie and a cup of coffee, which uses up the money that was for round-trip bus fare.

There's a grocery store, hardware store, candy store, diner, nursery, and gas stations on the highway, but no one has a job for me. Scissors Joe doesn't need anyone to wash his windows or sweep his floor, but he tells me that they're always looking for pinsetters at the bowling alley in the next town. It feels strange standing alongside the highway in front of the diner with my thumb out. A car stops and the driver asks how far I'm going. Hitchhiking is easy.

The job's mine. Seven to ten Tuesdays through Fridays and two to ten on Sundays. There will be money for hamburgers at the diner and for brushes and oil paint at the stationery store next to the bowling alley.

Dear Henry and Lola,

I'm fine and hope you are too. The reason I haven't been around is because Dad took me away from Brooklyn and dumped me here in Mountain View, New Jersey. The whole downtown is only two blocks long. I live with Dad's ex-brother-in-law, Lou, and his family in a house next to a river.

I miss your house, the great lunches, the great apple pies, and the sculpture and drawing and painting lessons. Thanks for giving me the Rembrandt book. When I paint studies of my favorite pictures in oils, I forget that I'm lonely.

My studio is a screened-in back porch where the turpentine doesn't stink up the house. What can be done with a tube of white, a tube of black, and a piece of cardboard is amazing.

I thought I could take the bus to Manhattan on Sundays and continue my lessons, but I have to work. I got a job as a pinsetter at a bowling alley, and I make 35 cents an hour plus tips, but no one has tipped me yet. They need me on Sundays, so that eliminates my time with you.

Your friend,
Norman

Bread for bait works better than worms. Ruby screws up her face and hands me a slice. Half of it goes into my mouth. There's a concrete dock behind the house. It's cracked and tilted and rebar is exposed, but sitting on the edge with Richie's fishing rod, I haul in a shiny black catfish. It's too beautiful to kill. It floats belly-up before it rights itself and swims away. If it weren't for my art studio I'd swim away, too.

Uncle Lou's old green rowboat is upside down on the bank.

"Is it okay if I use the rowboat, Uncle Lou?"

"It leaks."

"We could fix it."

"Some other time."

The old inner tube under the house is just right for floating down the river. Paddling with my hands close to the bank, out of the current, it isn't hard to go back upstream. To get to the island, I have to go way upstream before paddling across so the current doesn't take me down river before the inner tube reaches the island.

A big snapping turtle is in shallow water under the footbridge. It disappears below half of a yellow canoe that's floating over reeds. I can't tell if it's the front or the back half, but after climbing inside and hauling in the inner tube, the broken mid-section rises above the waterline and the half-canoe floats just fine. Two boys on the footbridge are watching me paddle the canoe with my hands. They run to the beach and come back with stones. It doesn't take a genius to figure out what they have in mind. The only way out is under the bridge. The other direction is blocked with reeds. When they see that I'm not going to go under the bridge and be a target for their bombs, they throw the stones at me. One hits my shin. Another hits my shoulder. I grab the inner tube, jump out of the canoe, and slog my way through the reeds. By the time I get through and paddle home, I'm out of breath, and my arms are sore. Those boys are as bad as El Duque and his henchmen in the Bronx. Too bad big brother Melvin isn't here to protect me. He'd make them eat those stones.

Back at the bridge the next day, the canoe is busted into a dozen yellow pieces. Easy come, easy go.

The job at the bowling alley gives me enough money to buy model airplanes, razor blades, and glue, and catch up on the stuff I wasn't allowed to do at Aunt Manya's. The Supermarine MK 1A Spitfire on the table on the back porch is finished. I add it to my squadron. There's a silver Grumman Hellcat, a camouflage-green P-47 Thunderbolt, and a North American Aviation silver-blue P-51 Mustang with a red cowling and a four-bladed prop. They hang from my bedroom ceiling by strings, diving, climbing, banking to the left and to the right.

I clean the balsa wood scraps off the table. I've finally gotten plane building out of my system as Cousin Sarah would say. Now I can concentrate on painting for the rest of the summer.

It's fun to work on Rembrandt's self-portraits from the book Henry and Lola gave me. Over the weeks, after copying tons of them on pieces of cardboard, my handling of values is getting better. It doesn't take much difference in value to turn a plane, to give cheeks, lips, even eyelids three-dimensionality. When copying Rembrandt's lips, they seem to vibrate. Music vibrates, color vibrates, but this vibration, it's like… it's like Rembrandt is trying to speak to me, but he can't, not yet, not until his lips are painted perfectly.

His *Young Girl Leaning on a Windowsill,* is finished. The hard part was making the face look like Cousin Sarah. Oil paints are much better for portraits than watercolors. If Aunt Manya had let me paint in oils, I'd be good at it by now. But I'm gonna be good, better than good, excellent. Gazing at Rembrandt's work, like Aunt Lilly gazes at her crystal ball, makes it easier to see how he tackled sad lips, expressive eyes, and jewels. My copies of four of his self-portraits are hanging on the wall behind the table. The originals of three of them are at the Kunsthistoriches Museum in Vienna. Did Dad ever go there to see Rembrandt's work? But who cares where he went? The original of one of them is at the Frick, in Manhattan. I've never been there. Rembrandt looks serious in these paintings. He looks like a tough guy, a "hard-as-nails" guy like Humphrey Bogart. The Frick self-portrait is my best copy, even the lips, because the picture in the book is bigger and clearer than the others. Some day I'll go to the Frick to see the original, but for now, my copy, hanging on the wall, will have to do.

Turning the pages, looking for something else to copy, I pause at *The Standard Bearer, Saskia as Flora, The Man with the Golden Helmet.* Look at those feathers and that fancy metalwork. If I could only paint like that.

"YOU CAN PAINT LIKE THAT."

What? Did Rembrandt's picture from the Frick speak? Rembrandt has a voice like thunder, a voice God might have used when he gave Moses the Ten Commandments.

It takes a few days to copy *The Man with the Golden Helmet* in black and white. These are the only colors I have. The painting shines. It pops off the canvas, or in my case, cardboard. It's almost as three-dimensional as Henry's sculptures. I don't know how I did it.

Dear Henry and Lola,

I'm fine and hope you are too. Thanks for the oil paints and brushes. The eight by ten canvasses you sent me are perfect for portraits and so much better than cardboard. I promise to wash with soap and water after using the lead white.

Lou's wife, Ruby, is pretty, and I draw her even though she starves me. Her son, Richie, is a year older than me and stays in his room all day, so he's no fun. The only other boys around here, my age, live on the other side of the river, and it's a good thing, too, because they're not very nice. So I'm still lonely in New Jersey.

There's a building across the river called the Casino, where they have watercolor classes on Wednesday mornings. I paddled over there on my inner tube, and boy, was I disappointed. There were just a bunch of grandmas sitting around, gossiping. Their paintings of flowers weren't up to our standards, so I'm not going back. Anyway, I like oil painting better.

I hope you don't think I'm weird, but Rembrandt talks to me. Henry, you told me that Michelangelo talks to you through his work, so I guess I'm in good company. Anyway, I miss you both a lot.

Your friend,
Norman

It would be nice to paint twice as many pictures and read more books from the tiny library in town, but school starts tomorrow. I'm lucky to have a job at the bowling alley and five lawns to mow and two fences to paint and maybe even a whole house. I bought two pairs of dungarees for school.

Richie, Jody, and I jump from stone to stone across the creek, walk to town, cross the highway, and wait for the yellow school bus to take us three miles further to Wayne High School. Every morning, in homeroom, the class stands and recites *The Lord's Prayer*. Some kids wear crosses around their necks. No one wears a Star of David. I don't belong here, but at least algebra is easy now.

It rains on and off for weeks. At times it sounds like gravel being dumped on the roof. The gray river widens, rises, spills over its banks. The house is surrounded by water. What was once a lazy, narrow stream is now an awesome, fast moving river a hundred and fifty feet wide. It's scary in the dark to hear rushing water but not see it until lightning streaks down. In the morning, trees and fences float by. To be safe, all my paintings and drawings are piled on the table in the porch.

The floor of the house is four feet above ground, but the flood is a couple of inches below the front door. The tilted back porch is under water. Uncle Lou has an excuse to stay overnight in the city with his who-er.

A motorboat comes to the front of the house with two men in orange life jackets. One of them throws me a line, cups his hands over his mouth, and shouts above the noise of the engine, "The river's still rising. Better come with us." I pull the boat to the door and help Ruby into the middle seat. Her face is chalky white. Jody and Richie climb in. The bottoms of their dungarees are wet and their shoes are squishy even though there's no water in the house. As we head across the river, our house looks as if it's floating. Ruby keeps her eyes closed until we reach shore.

"Climb up to that school bus," we're told.

As we wait, a woman tells each new arrival that the living room set she bought last month is ruined. When the bus fills up, we ride to town to the Phillips elementary school gymnasium where the Red Cross has provided cots and blankets. There are giant stainless steel pots full of beef stew and baskets full of bread, and I eat 'til I'm stuffed. There are people to talk to, and my school bus stop is across the street.

The flood makes the front page of the newspaper in Paterson, eight miles away. The rescued families are referred to as river people. I like being a river person.

When we go back to the house three days later, I measure the scummy waterline with my ruler. There had been almost four inches of water inside the kitchen and nine inches inside the back porch. I didn't realize the house sloped that much. All my art is ruined. Richie and Jody put my paintings and drawings on the lowest part of the floor while I was pulling the rescue boat to the front door.

The green rowboat is wedged between two trees down river. When Uncle Lou returns from Manhattan, he, Richie, two neighbors and I carry it back home. Uncle Lou doesn't strain himself with his share of the load. He's more concerned about his shoes.

From day one of my stay here Dad promised to visit every two weeks, on Mondays, at four o'clock. I've heard that story before, lots of times, but I'm lonely and he's all I have. I wait in front of the Mountain View Diner. He's not on the four o'clock bus. Maybe he'll be on the next one. Maybe we can talk in the diner, have hamburgers, coffee, apple pie. Maybe he'll give me money for painting supplies. Maybe he can buy an easel for me in Manhattan, but if he says he will, I might have to wait a year.

Six people get off the five o'clock bus. I stare at it as it leaves. Maybe Dad fell asleep. Maybe he'll wake up and make the driver stop the bus to let him off. The bus disappears over the last hill. When am I going to stop kidding myself?

A month passes. I hitchhike to Manhattan and walk to Longchamps, the fancy restaurant where Dad works.

"May I help you?" The tuxedoed headwaiter wrinkles his nose.

"I want to see Benny. He's my Dad."

"Wait here."

I stand by a clay vase, hidden from the customers by a plant whose leaves look like the ears of an elephant. Dad comes right away, not smiling. He exhales strongly, as I've heard him do when he reads something in the newspaper that makes him angry. He leads me upstairs to an empty dining area.

"I'll be right back."

His face is sour. I walk to the shiny brass balcony railing and look down on the elegant main dining room. Classical music is playing. The tables have vases filled with flowers. Oil paintings, each with its own attached light, hang on the mahogany walls. The scene could be a Manet painting.

There's George Burns and Gracie Allen! I remember them from the movies. Dad is pouring their coffee. Other diners turn around to watch them. George lights a cigar. Gracie is serious, not silly like she is on the radio.

Dad comes back up the stairs, balancing a silver tray over his shoulder. He sets it down on the table, lifts a silver lid, says *voila*, and fills my plate with more Hungarian goulash than Ruby would have served to the whole family. Dad leaves, and two cooks in white uniforms sit down at the next table. One is wearing a chef's hat that looks like a white umbrella stand turned upside down. After I take a few mouthfuls, the man in the chef's hat asks, "What do you think of my goulash?" I give him a thumbs-up. Dad comes back at just the right time, with bread pudding and two cups of coffee. He sits down with me and wipes an imaginary speck from my spoon with the white towel he carries on his sleeve just like I saw him do when he handed George Burns his spoon.

Dad sips coffee, lights up a cigarette, and looks me over.

"Norman, the way you're dressed… don't ever come to this restaurant, or for that matter, to Manhattan, in dungarees."

"But the only other thing I have to wear is my suit, and it barely fits."

"Shh, not so loud. We'll talk later."

Dad gives me money for a pair of pants and for bus fare and waves goodbye. I walk past the bus station, stop at the art supply store I spotted from the bus months ago, spend all the money there, and hitchhike home with a big bag of art supplies.

On Sundays, work at the bowling alley doesn't start 'til two. I help Uncle Lou wash and wax his huge midnight blue Packard. I'm in charge of polishing the chrome, and there's lots of it. When I'm done, the bumpers and the grille gleam. We finish in time to take Ruby, Richie, and Jody to Mass at the Catholic church in town. On the way, Uncle Lou buys the New York *Daily News*. While we wait in the car, I read the headlines and the funnies, and he reads the sports section. At the horse-racing page, he talks to himself most Sundays and says some "oh shits" and "fucking son-of-a-bitches." Today, he's pleased and whistles through his teeth. For sure he'll miss the bus tomorrow night.

After Mass, Ruby says, "Drive to the market. I have to pick up a few things." She doesn't begin her sentence with "could you" or "would you" or "please." He parks in front and Ruby and the kids go inside. I feel sorry for Uncle Lou. His kids, who are half-Jewish, are being raised Catholic. They don't know the beauty of the Passover ceremony. It's as if Jody and Richie belong only to Ruby and not to Uncle Lou.

Ruby is on the other side of the window, in the produce section. She picks up a bulb of garlic and two lemons, looks around, stuffs them into her coat pocket, but neglects to look out the window to see if anyone's watching. I stole milk bottles, candy bars, and comic books when I was younger but not anymore. I'm shocked to see her steal, especially right after church.

If I ever hear anyone say, "I'm going to pick up a few things at the store," I'll think of Ruby.

Back home I tell her that if the river ever floods again we'll need a way to get out sooner. She hires a man to caulk the rowboat. I don't tell her that by the time we row to shore the current will carry us a mile downstream.

It's fun, trying out the boat, rowing with the current, enjoying the cool, peaceful river, pretty houses with boats tied to their docks, fishermen, birds and ducks. A stone lands in the water in front of the boat. Then another comes flying. It's the boys who were at the Casino footbridge. I row to the opposite shore, out of range. It would be great to go all the way to the ocean to get away from Lou and Ruby and their sneaky children. Why did they ruin my art?

The sun tells me to head home. Rowing against the current takes longer. My hands blister. The blisters break open, ooze, and stick to the oars. Dunking my hands in the cool water helps. It's dark when I tie up at the house.

Next day there are gloves on my hands when I row to town with Ruby's grocery list and haul the boat up on the gravelly bank near the bridge. An artist is standing at his easel on the water's edge with me behind him, watching. With oils, he paints the bridge and its fuzzy reflection in the water. I like the way he handles shadows, the way he simplifies the bridge's intricate architecture. He adds a figure on the bridge, in just the right place, to give a sense of dimension. His impressionistic painting looks more inviting than the real scene, yet something about it bothers me.

"Excuse me, Mister. What if you put some blue on the shoreline to go with the blue of the sky and the blue of the water."

He smacks his forehead with the palm of his hand, then dips his brush into a glob of cerulean blue, adds turpentine, and paints a thin blue wash over the brown shoreline. He makes a thumbs-up sign.

On the way home, I think of lots of questions he could have answered, but that's okay, I'll ask Rembrandt instead.

CHAPTER 22

HUNGER

It's six in the evening. When moonlight reflects off the snow, it's easy to see my way through the quarter mile of woods, across the frozen creek, and down the icy road that leads to town, but tonight it's dark, and I depend on house lights to find the road. On the highway in front of the Mountain View Diner, I stick out my thumb and hitch a ride to the next town three miles away. Rides are easy to get at this hour. Ruby doesn't think a fourteen year-old boy should be hitchhiking, but how else am I going to get to work?

"Thanks for the ride, Mister."

It's snowing. There's a half-mile to go past the Armstrong Carpet Mill and the Capri Cinema. *Cyrano de Bergerac* is playing, with José Ferrer. It would be nice to sit in a cozy theater and see a movie for a change. I haven't seen one since I left Brooklyn. There's Dr. Payne's dental office. All dentists should be called Dr. Payne. I should have him look at the lower right molar that Dr. Bass filled last year. It twinges sometimes.

Maple Lanes is hot and stinks of cigarettes. The cheapskate league bowlers hardly ever leave a tip. There's Georgie.

"Geez Norman, the pin that hit me in the head yesterday didn't hurt near as bad as the one that got me on the shin a little while ago. See my bump? Them lady bowlers, they're dangerous."

"Sorry about that, Georgie. I'm still black and blue from Tuesday."

For three hours, I hop from lane five to lane six, pick up pins, rack them, and pull the cords to set the racks. Sometimes, balls crash into the rack before I have it raised, or a bowler sends a ball screaming down a gutter, and I have to jump out of the way. When pins fly, I get beaned.

At ten o'clock, with a dollar and a nickel in my pocket, I stomp through the snow to the highway. I'm usually home by eleven, but tonight, there's no traffic. It's after twelve when I get to Mountain View. There are no streetlights on the dirt road, but a few porch lights are on. It's pitch-black where the road ends. Branches poke at me as I stumble through the woods, looking for my porch light but someone turned it off.

Dad didn't come around on my birthday last week. He never does. Saturday, I walk to town in the rain on slushy snow, hitchhike to New York, and head to Longchamps. The same headwaiter is there, with a black eye.

"Your father is no longer employed here."

"How come?"

"We had a disagreement."

"Where does he work now?"

"Nowhere, I hope."

I take the subway to Brooklyn and drop into the drugstore to say hello. The new owner tells me Mr. Gibalowitz has retired. Upstairs, Aunt Manya unchains the door, opens it. No smile. No hug.

"How skinny you are. They don't feed you, Norman, in New Jersey?"

She opens a green can of Del Monte sardines in tomato sauce, cuts thick slices of rye bread from Yellin's bakery.

"You'll have a glass of coffee with lunch?"

"Yes, Aunt Manya, thank you."

She looks tinier. So do the refrigerator and the apartment.

"Where's Sarah?"

"She went to the Saturday matinee with Harry, her new gentleman friend."

"What's playing?"

"*The Father of the Bride*, with Spencer Tracy."

"Where's Uncle Irving?"

"By his brother's."

"Maybe I can stay overnight?"

"We sold your cot. Where will I put you?"

I don't ask to sleep on the couch.

"I haven't seen Dad in a long time. I stopped at Longchamps, but the headwaiter said he doesn't work there anymore. Do you know where he works?"

"How should I know? I don't keep track of your father's comings and goings."

There's no place I can call home. In New Jersey, I think a lot about the only family that feels real. Now I'm in Brooklyn, but Sarah's not home, I don't get to see Uncle Irving, and I'm not invited to stay over. Aunt Manya doesn't let me kiss her cheek when I leave and head for Henry and Lola's.

Nobody's home there, so I slip a note under their door and go back to the Saratoga Avenue station. I don't feel like looking out the front window of the empty train as it rushes toward Manhattan. I'm empty, too.

Dear Henry and Lola,

    Thanks for sending me the salami from Katz's deli. Sarah took me there once after a movie in Manhattan. Their pastrami sandwiches are five inches thick. Too bad there isn't a deli in Mountain View.

    My studio is freezing, so I have to paint with gloves on. I made an easel out of scrap wood. It's better than painting on the table.

    It's hard to concentrate when it's noisy. In the summer, people run motorboats on the river, and in the winter, they cut down trees for firewood with chainsaws. But when Rembrandt talks to me, I go into a trance and don't hear anything except him.

    Lola, I've painted seventeen different winter scenes, all of them within two blocks of my house. I've kept in mind everything you've told me, like for instance, that snow is mostly gray or blue with very little white in it. And I'm better at composition now that I keep things simple, like Pissarro does in his French snow scenes. Did you know he was Jewish?

    Neither the town library nor the one at school have many art books, but the librarians get me the ones I want from other libraries, even the one at Harvard University. Right now, I'm reading The Art Spirit, by Robert Henri and waiting for books of Moses Soyer's and Tamara de Lempicka's paintings. Their work speaks to me, as you would say, Henry.

    Sorry I missed you. Well, it's real late now, and I better go to bed so I won't fall asleep in class tomorrow.

    Your friend,
    Norman

Four pm. The bus from Manhattan pulls in on time. Dad may not be on it, but there's always a possibility. There he is in a long black overcoat, strutting across the highway. He kisses my cheek, and there's the familiar smell of Camay soap and cigarettes. I don't want to go home just yet. I don't want to share him.

"Dad, let's go to the diner. The hamburgers are great."

We sit at the counter. I introduce Beth, the waitress. Dad orders a hamburger, fries, coffee, and apple pie for me. He gives me a nickel for the jukebox. I play *Kisses Sweeter Than Wine*. It's great to be with Dad and to sit here and smell hamburgers and onions frying.

"How are Lou and Ruby treating you, Norman?"

"Fine. They're nice people. No one ever hollers at me."

"How's school?"

"I get A's in everything."

"Algebra, too?"

"Yes. Now I understand x's and y's. They're unknowns, and they're easy to figure out."

"Good. So you're okay, happy here?"

"Not exactly."

"What? What's the problem?"

"Well, Uncle Lou, Ruby, they're nice and all, but I'm never full, like I was at Aunt Manya's."

"They don't feed you enough?"

"Ruby serves us all the same exact amount of food. It's like she's a pharmacist, dispensing it in measured doses."

"Measured doses, Norman? The word doses means that they're measured. How do you come to use words like dispensing and doses?"

"I worked for Mr. Gibalowitz last year, in the drug store downstairs from Aunt Manya's… Anyway, when Ruby pours a glass of milk, it's half full, and there are no seconds. I'd gladly trade Aunt's Manya's curses for a full stomach."

"I'll talk to Lou about it."

I don't think Dad ever talked to Lou. Today's breakfast is as skimpy as ever. It seems like Richie and Jody are never hungry. Sometimes, they even leave food on their plates, which I make sure never goes to waste. After breakfast, we bundle up and walk to town to catch the yellow school bus.

It wasn't fun to walk in slush yesterday, and today the slush is frozen into craters. We slide around in our rubber boots and grab each other's arms to keep from falling.

We cross the highway to Phillips elementary school, where we stayed during the flood, and wait for the school bus. I hope it won't make it up the steep icy bridge over the railroad tracks. I'd like to walk home and go back to bed, but the bus, with tire chains jingling, is unstoppable.

I return some books to the school library, run to my homeroom, stand quietly while everyone else recites *The Lord's Prayer*.

In the overheated history class, Mr. Porter drones on about the Civil War, Harriet Tubman, Frederick Douglass, and the Underground Railroad, making an interesting subject a boring one. I think about black people riding the subway from Manhattan to the Bronx. That's another kind of underground railroad. I think about cooking odors in the Puerto Rican and black neighborhoods. I'm at the Mountain View Diner, watching Dad's new wife, Beth, cook giant beef patties on the grill. Onions sizzle. She lifts a patty and an onion with her spatula, slides them onto a bun, adds lettuce and tomatoes, and plops the burger onto a plate. She sets the plate in front of me and hands me a bottle of ketchup.

"Here you are, Norman, Norman, Norman... " It isn't the first time Mr. Porter has caught me asleep in his class. He sends me to the counselor.

"Mr. Porter tells me you often fall asleep in class".

"I'm tired, Mrs. O'Brien, and his talking hypnotizes me."

She smiles. "Do you get enough sleep at night?"

"I get plenty of sleep on weekends, but not during the week."

"Why is that?"

"I work nights at Maple Lanes. It's a bowling alley."

"I know. I've been there. Is it wise to work when it interferes with your schooling?"

"But the money. I need the money, Mrs. O'Brien."

"Ah, you're saving up for something. A bicycle, maybe?"

"No. To buy food."

She reaches for her gold crucifix.

"Your mother... "

"I don't have a mother."

"Your father... "

"I hardly ever see him."

"Who do you… "

"I live with my Uncle Lou and his family."

I explain my hunger and my loneliness, and her hand goes to her crucifix again. She writes notes. She picks up a folder with my name on it, compliments me on my good grades.

"Here's a memo from the librarian. You check out seven times as many books as the average student. What do you read? When do you find time to read?"

"I read Dickens, Steinbeck, Jack London, Herman Melville, Mark Twain. I read during the lunch hour, on the bus, in the bathroom, and in bed."

"See if you can cut down on the number of days you work. Show this note to the cashier in the cafeteria, and you won't have to pay for your lunches."

Winter is over. I can leave the gloves off when I'm painting. It's easy to walk to the school bus on a dry road. Mrs. Clark, my English teacher, calls me over to her desk after class.

"Would you be interested in working for the *Herald News*?"

"The Paterson newspaper? Sure. But there's no bus between Mountain View and Paterson."

"You won't have to go there. Your job will be to record box scores at the baseball games and write about what you see on the ball field. The paper will pick up your report at the principal's office."

I'm a sports reporter! With a byline! I ride to the games with the team on a yellow school bus, but there isn't much to report about Wayne High, because we lose every time. I've never seen more strikeouts in my life. It's more interesting to write about the teams that are crushing us.

The *Herald News* sends me checks, which I deposit in my savings account. I didn't know I'd get paid.

Jack, one of the older boys on the team, becomes my friend after he reads my story about his heroics: *Speedy left-handed Passaic High second baseman, Dwight Curry, on a 2-2 fastball, pounded a towering fly into the right field corner, 325 feet away. The ball, fair by inches, bounced off the wall and into the glove of Right Fielder, Jackson Waddell, who spun around, double*

clutched, and let loose a bomb, a perfect strike to third baseman Scott McBride
to tag out Curry, who was trying to make a triple out of a double.

I laid it on thick, as Aunt Manya would say, even though we lost, 13-2.

Jack invites me to his home for dinner. I go to town, walk along rail-road tracks for a half-mile, turn down a dirt road, and see his house, sur-rounded by rusty cars and piles of old tires like at my house. I sit with him, his parents, and his younger brother and help myself to corn on the cob, salad, homemade bread, string beans, baked potatoes, and fried chicken. I fill my plate again. There's enough on the table for twenty people. They stop to watch me eat. They might not invite me back again, but I can't stop. On the way home, on the railroad tracks, I lose some of the food that my stomach is too small to hold. I wish I could eat a decent meal every night. I'd settle for once a week.

CHAPTER 23

ON THE MOVE AGAIN

On Saturday morning I'm playing with a heavy green turtle crawling on the riverbank. It's six inches across the shell, and it's head doesn't retract when I tap it, but it opens its mouth wide, as if to say, "Get away, don't bother me."

"HELP! HELP!"

I put the turtle down, run to the rowboat, jump in, drop the oars into the oarlocks, and try to shove off, but the boat doesn't move. Maybe it's caught on the rebar that's sticking out from the broken concrete dock.

"HELP! HELP!"

Into the water I go in sneakers and dungarees. The boat's too heavy to lift off.

Uncle Lou walks over from the back porch.

"The boat's stuck, Uncle Lou. Help me lift it off the rebar."

He unties his black Florsheim's.

"Someone in the river is in trouble."

He eases off his Florsheim's, rolls off his socks, and tucks them in his shoes.

"HELP! HELP!"

Two people are being dragged down the river in the strong current. I yank on the boat, but it won't move.

Uncle Lou rolls up his pant legs, gets in the water, and helps lift the boat.

"Come with me, Uncle Lou."

"No, you go."

I row furiously in the direction of the cries. I'll never get there in time. That stupid Lou. He should get consumption. He should roast in hell.

"HELP! HELP!"

"I'm coming. I'm coming. I'm right behind you!"

I reach the victim and the rescuer. They grab onto the side of the rowboat, cough, spit and pant. They're too exhausted to climb inside.

"You're a life saver, kid."

"Yeah, you got to me just in time."

People are cheering on the shore as I row toward them with the two men hanging on.

"Thanks again, kid."

Alice is in my Spanish class. I've wanted to ask her to the school dance, but I'm shy around girls. Now it's too late. Some guy named Brad is taking her. Jody will go with me even though she knows that the last dancing I did was as a seven-year-old at my cousin's wedding. She and Ruby give me lessons. Lou shows me some steps, too.

"Don't just move your feet, Norman, move your ass. Yeah, that's right, your ass. And loosen up. You're stiff as a board. That's better. Hey, get the hell off my shoes. The lesson's over."

Scissors Joe gives me a five-minute, fifty-cent haircut. I swore after my last haircut never to go back there, but the other barbershop across the highway charges a dollar.

It's the night of the dance. In my tight bar mitzvah suit with its now very short pant legs I feel like a hillbilly. Jody spends most of the night dancing with other boys. It's okay with me. My belly aches, and these tight pants aren't helping.

At the punch bowl, Alice introduces me to Brad. He's wearing gray slacks and a blue blazer with gold buttons. He has gold cufflinks, new shoes, and a great haircut.

"Happy to meet you, Norman. Bet you're from Mountain View."

"How do you know?"

"You've been to Scissors Joe."

There's nowhere to hide.

Alice asks me to dance. I've just hit a homerun. As we dance around the crowded gymnasium, I wish I hadn't been too shy to ask her out or too cheap to go to the good barbershop. She's soft and smells good. Brad cuts in, and that's the end of that, as Cousin Sarah would say.

My bellyache is worse. It's a long night.

For days, the pain comes and goes. Now it comes back with a wallop. "Ruby, it's really bad today."

"How bad?"

"Like someone stabbing me with a butcher knife."

"Do you want me to take you to my doctor when Lou comes home?"

"Maybe you should."

Lou frowns when Ruby insists that he take me to see Dr. Carson. On the way, she says, "Give it some gas, the kid's sick."

"Don't tell me how to drive. The road's bumpy here. You want I should get the wheels out of line, or break a spring?"

Do you think it's appendicitis, Ruby?"

"It goddamn better not be," Lou says.

Doctor Carson presses the middle of my belly. When he lifts his hand I yell.

"It might be your appendix. How does it feel right now?"

"Not as bad as it did a minute ago."

"Go home and rest, but let me know if the pain gets worse."

Lou is in a much better humor on the way home. The pain goes away, and I don't think about it any more.

My tooth has been aching all day. It's worse than the bellyache was and hard to ignore. Ruby tells me to find a dentist. Since there isn't one in town, I go to a neighbor's and call Doctor Payne. He tells me come right over. Lou won't take me, says he's low on gas, but I know he's afraid he'll get stuck with the bill. I hitchhike and get there at eight o'clock at night. Doctor Payne takes an x-ray, has me bite on a stick, taps on my tooth. The tapping almost makes me jump out of the chair.

"It needs a root canal."

I don't feel the shot in my jaw or the drilling. He says he used arsenic in the canals, but who cares what he used, after three days of agony I'm free of pain. It's midnight when I get back. Dad will have a fit when he sees Dr. Payne's bill.

The money I earn setting pins, writing the school's sports column, weeding yards, and mowing lawns goes into a savings account. So far, I've saved up two hundred and thirty-six dollars. The free school lunches helped. There would be a lot more money in the bank, but I spent a fortune, as Aunt Manya would say, on food, art supplies, and clothes.

Ruby asks Dad for more money for my care, and they get into an argument. He tells me he's been writing to Melvin, who agrees to take me in as soon as school is out. I'll finally get to meet my hero, my big brother, who survived Pearl Harbor. He's all I think about these last weeks of school. I'll meet my sister-in-law, and nephew and nieces and see wide-open spaces, cowboys, Hollywood, and the Golden Gate Bridge.

The morning after the last day of school, the brown bus from Manhattan pulls up and Dad gets off. On the way to the house, we walk by Lou's Packard in the gravel parking lot. The car is dusty and the chrome is dull. I stopped polishing it after the river rescue.

"Look Dad, down there on the river, that's where I watched an artist paint a picture. I helped him make it better."

"That's nice."

He doesn't ask for details.

"There's Scissors Joe's. He's the fastest and the lousiest barber in the world." Dad grunts. The heck with pointing things out. He's not interested in me. When Melvin was a kid, did Dad see him any more than he's seen me? Was Dad interested in the things Melvin did? Did he remember Melvin's birthday? Can he imagine that going to California worries me? It's so far away from Brooklyn and my real family.

Into my satchel and ragged suitcase go everything I own. Ruby gives me tape to wind over a broken hinge. Dad doesn't want me to take my model P-51 Mustang fighter plane to California to show to Melvin. He says there's no room on the bus, so the planes go to Richie.

We walk back to town, carrying the luggage. There's no time for a last hamburger at the diner. Lou's at work in his elevator in Manhattan, but he's supposed to meet us at the Greyhound station. What about my savings account at the bank? How will I get my money when I'm in California?

"Dad, I'll be right back. I have to go to the bank to take out my money. We've got fifteen minutes."

I fly across the highway to the bank and get back in seven minutes.

"How much do you have?" Dad asks.

"Two hundred thirty-six dollars."

He rubs his palms together. His tongue pooches out his cheek.

"Where'd you get all that money?"

"Working at the bowling alley. Mowing lawns."

He licks his lips as if he's about to bite into chocolate cake.

We're the only passengers on the brown bus.

Dad looks up from his paper. "I can sure use that money, Norman."

Look at him, sleazy like the guy last year at the bus station in Manhattan who grabbed my satchel when I got up to get on the bus.

"I'll carry this for you."

"No thanks, mister. Give it back."

I looked around, hoping to find a cop before he ran off, but he walked to the bus fast, and I had to run to keep up. He dropped the satchel and extended his palm. I just stood there. He made a fist with his other hand. I reached into my pocket, took out a nickel, and dropped it into his hand. He flipped it into the air, caught it, put it in his pocket, and strutted away.

There's that pig smell. We're passing Secaucus. Dad folds his paper, puts it in his coat pocket.

"Norman, I could sure use some of that money. You know, your bus ticket to California, it wasn't cheap." He rubs his hands together like Peter Lorre.

The Manhattan skyline is out my window. Inside is the cold wind, the spit in my face, the bowling pins crashing into my shin, slipping on frozen paths, falling asleep in heated classrooms, the growling stomach, the clothes that don't fit, the loneliness, the violin music I will never play, the metallic taste in my mouth.

The bus comes out of the Lincoln Tunnel, heads uptown, and turns down the steep ramp that leads to the carousel of the bus station under the Elgin Hotel. It's hot and humid on Tenth Avenue. My shirt sticks to me. Nothing is said as we walk the crowded streets to the Greyhound station. I don't belong to Dad anymore.

Lou stands with his perfumed elevator floozy, waiting for us. Instead of a hello, he says, "The tape on your suitcase is coming off."

"Norman, now how can you travel with that old suitcase? If the other hinge breaks, you'll lose everything, all your clothes."

"But Dad, you said you'd pick one up for me, remember, at a pawn shop."

"I did? Well, I've been so busy, you know, arranging for your ticket."

Sure, busy arranging for my ticket. How long does it take to buy a ticket? Five minutes? Lou is eyeing the winter jacket I'm carrying, the one

Sarah bought for me on Pitkin Avenue the last time I saw her. It wouldn't fit in the suitcase.

"Norman, it's warm in California. Nobody wears a jacket there."

"You're wrong Lou. Ever hear of the Donner Party?"

Cleveland-Chicago-Des Moines-Omaha-Cheyenne-Salt Lake City-Reno- Sacramento-San Francisco. I can barely make out the blaring baritone names of cities en route to California. The woman behind me in line is staring at my suitcase and shaking her head. The driver opens the cargo doors and loads the luggage. Mine will be easy to find.

Lou yawns. The floozy reaches into her dress to adjust her bra strap. Dad smiles a phony smile.

"I could sure use that money... son."

Son? He doesn't know when my birthday is, but he's still my Dad. I pull my wallet out and hand him three twenties.

"Sixty dollars? Be realistic, Norman. The bus ticket, it cost me more, much more than that."

"Okay, okay already. Here's a hundred."

"Norman, don't be such a cheapskate."

Cheapskate? Look who's talking. People are getting on the bus. I could run away, but where to? Henry's maybe. It's real tempting. But Melvin, I've wanted to be with him for as long as I can remember. I don't want to be a cheapskate. I give Dad all the money.

He wets his fingers with his tongue, counts my twenties like a banker, making sure Jackson's face is right side up on every bill. He stuffs two hundred dollars into his billfold, hands me my ticket and thirty-six dollars.

I grab Lou's clammy hand, shake it goodbye, and step hard on his shiny shoes and twist.

"Sorry, Lou, lost my balance."

Dad approaches with a big phony smile on his monkey face and puckers up his lips. I turn my back, climb aboard, and sit in the right front seat of a silver Greyhound bus bound for San Francisco.

Chapter 24

Never Climb in Your Glide

The bus comes out of the New Jersey end of the tunnel. It's my chance for a long last look at the Manhattan skyline. Goodbye Empire State Building, goodbye Chrysler Building, I'm going to California!

I can't wait to meet Melvin, his wife, Denise, and their three children. From what Dad told me about him over the years, he must be awesome. A Pearl Harbor survivor, a boatswain's mate, a boxer. And he's "hard as nails," like Cagney and Bogart.

The Greyhound crawls through picture-book towns then speeds along the open road. I'm reminded of happy-ending movies, where the hero has overcome difficulties and is going on to better things, like college maybe. The bus will stop in cities with exotic names, like Omaha and Cheyenne. I imagine getting off the bus and losing myself in those places. Would some kind family take me in? But real life is not the movies. California will be different. Melvin will take me to Hollywood to see movie stars, to Yosemite National Park to see the second highest waterfall in the world, and to giant redwood trees that you can drive a car through.

The woman who was staring at my suitcase at the bus station in Manhattan sits next to me on a red swivel stool at a rest stop in Ohio.

"Where are you headed, son?"

I reach for a napkin, wipe ketchup off my lips. "California. I'm gonna live with my brother in Vallejo, near San Francisco."

"I'm going to Salt Lake City to visit my daughter. She's a genealogist."

"There are lots of them in Salt Lake City."

"How do you know?"

"I read a lot."

"Well, my daughter traced our family, the Steeres, back to England. There are more William Steeres than you can shake a stick at, but the William Steere who was my great, great... heavens, I lost track of how many greats there are, came over shortly after the Mayflower... "

There's no way to tell her about my art or my brother. She doesn't stop talking. It would be nice to know who my ancestors were, but no one on my father's side of the family or my mother's side will tell me about any-one further back than my grandparents. They say my grandparents didn't want to talk about the old country. All they've told me is that they came to America from Austria and from Russia to escape prejudice against Jews.

She sits next to me when we get back on the bus, never stops talking about her family tree, and all the time she's talking, my belly aches, the molar that Dr. Payne worked on throbs, and my bladder wants to burst. The bus travels for hours before pulling into a rest stop. I run to the toilet, and there's a long line, because other buses are there, too, so I have to go behind the building to pee. It's hard to avoid the woman at rest stop cafes. She plops down next to me and talks non-stop even when her mouth is full of food. The urge to pee hits me again as soon as the bus gets back on the highway.

"The Steere Family Association was founded in 1931. We have reun-ions every August in Chepachet, Rhode Island. It's an historic village, at least for us Steere's. My daughter and I took a walking tour of the village last year, and we stepped into the Freewill Baptist Church... "

As she drones on across Iowa, the scenery outside becomes more im-portant. This flat state is one huge cornfield dotted with white farmhouses, silos, and windmills, but the windmills aren't as pretty as the ones Rem-brandt painted in Holland. He talks to me in a voice like Grandfather's.

"Few places are flatter than Holland, yet my landscapes are not flat. See how I cross my horizons with windmills? Can you feel the power of a footpath or a road slicing diagonally across a field? Be aware of these things when you paint Iowa in your mind."

"I don't know what the corn is like here in Iowa, but they sure have enough of it. Back in Chepachet on the Steere farm they grow white corn. I took home a sack of it, and my gracious, it was the sweetest corn I ever ate. Oh, and the hayride, but before I tell you about it, let me tell you about the cookout dinner... "

After we cross the Rockies and pull into Salt Lake City she gets off, and I enjoy some peace and quiet, as Aunt Manya would say. It's fun to fill a page with sketches of the bus driver's hands on the steering wheel and another page with a woman curled up on the seat across the aisle, sleep-ing. She reminds me of Lola. The last time I saw her, she said, "Norman, when you talk about school or baseball or anything that isn't about art, you sound like a high school student. But when you talk about art, you sound like a college student."

"Lola's right, Nor-man. When you talk about art, you use the language of art."

"Well, Hen-ry, I have you and Lola to thank for that."

On the high desert of Utah, there are long stretches of highway without a single house. I paint it in my mind with the same earth colors I used, sitting on Aunt Lilly's fire escape, sketching the brick tenements in downtown Brooklyn. There are wildflowers with cadmium yellows and reds that give the landscape the artist's touch that Rembrandt told me about.

The road sound lulls me to sleep and wakes me to a sky full of stars, and I'm back on Aunt Lilly's fire escape, connecting the dots in the night sky, seeing the animals that Uncle Tim told me are there. My tooth and my gut and my need to pee keep me awake. The pain comes and goes. We pull into Reno, which sparkles with colored lights that remind me of the circus Dad took me to. I'm on the high wire, alone, riding that bicycle through life, but there are no clowns below to catch me in a safety net.

There's a half-hour layover, time for a hamburger and coffee at the café in the bus station. I used to enjoy being with Dad at hamburger joints in Coney Island, Manhattan, and Mountain View. That memory gives me no pleasure now. I finish my coffee and dig in my pocket for a nickel to drop in a slot machine. Three sevens come up on the first pull, and coins clunk into the metal box. That's a good sign. I fill my pocket with nickels and climb back on the bus.

The sun is peeking over the eastern horizon by the time we reach the green "Welcome to California" sign. We pick up two passengers in Truckee. Long freight trains are coming into town from both directions with horns blaring. A truck carrying five giant logs is parked in front of a café. We drive by the north shore of Donner Lake. I imagine the lake surrounded by snow, the Donner Party in trouble, and Lou eyeing my winter jacket. We start to climb and pass semis that are struggling uphill, Diesel smoke pouring from their shiny exhaust pipes. Highway 40 narrows, becomes steep, and winds around rocky cliffs. There's barely enough room for trucks to pass in the opposite direction. A freight train, heading west up the mountain, is partially hidden by the snow sheds that protect the track in winter. A thousand feet below, Donner Lake is shimmering in the morning sun. Near the 7,239 foot summit, climbers are scaling School Rock.

We head down the western slope of the Sierra. Each side of the highway is a solid wall of tall evergreen trees. There are turnouts for runaway trucks. This Greyhound is going fast enough to be a runaway bus. The driver said we were over an hour late leaving Reno, and he'll try to make up lost time. Soon, I'll be with Melvin and his family. I'll have good meals. I'll get my high school diploma and go on to college to study art. Melvin will give me good advice, like the best books to read and the best elective classes to take in high school. Most important of all, I'll be wanted.

We've run out of evergreens. The foothills are covered with oaks. Below, is the hazy Sacramento Valley. It won't be long now. I spot the Capitol dome before we pull into the Sacramento Greyhound station. I know the names of all the state capitols and that gold was discovered at Sutter's Mill, not too far from here, in 1848. In one more hour, I'll be with my big brother.

Melvin is waiting outside at the Vallejo Greyhound station. He folds his newspaper and puts it in his jacket pocket. He's a young version of Dad, short, wiry, a gap between his upper front teeth, and large hands. I walk up to him, expecting a brotherly hug, but he doesn't even shake my hand. His first words are, "It's about time you got here. I've been waiting a fucking hour."

As we head to his house with my luggage in the back of the station wagon, he gives me some sort of grand tour, driving up and down city streets, pointing to apartment houses and stores. "My mother owns this one... my mother owns that one, and some day, all these will be mine."

He drives up a hill to an area of fancy homes with manicured lawns. "There's my mother's house, the white one. It's the biggest house on the hill."

By the time we get to his house, I know that he has an airplane and that his Ford station wagon is brand new and fully loaded, whatever that means. Denise, and the kids hug me.

"How was your trip?" Denise asks.

"Fine. It was great seeing the country, but I wish they had bathrooms on buses."

"I'm hungry. Let's eat," Melvin says.

Denise serves hot bowls of chili con carne, which I've never eaten. It tastes wonderful. Melvin tastes his, twists his lips and growls, "It's not hot enough. Gimme some hot sauce."

Denise brings it to the table. He shakes it on his chili and then on mine.

I pull my bowl away. "I don't like hot stuff, Melvin."

"Chili's no good unless it's hot." He shakes more onto my chili. "Whatsamatter? Why aren't you eating?"

"It burns my tongue."

"Oh for Christsake, I didn't put that much on."

"I'll get you another bowl, Norman," Denise says.

"No, goddamn it," Melvin shouts and pounds his fist on the table. "It isn't right to waste food. Let him finish what he has."

I try another bite, but my tongue is on fire, and my belly aches. I push the bowl away. Melvin adds more hot sauce to his own chili and eats it, grunting like a pig.

Is this my hero? I rub my eyes. It's hard to keep them open.

"Let's go for a ride."

"Mel, Norman just rode three thousand miles. I think he'd rather take a nap."

"Naps are for kids, Denise. I want to show him the Cessna."

Melvin speeds to the Napa airport, passing cars, weaving. I pump the non-existent brakes on my side of the car.

"Don't slow down when you get to a curve. Speed up half way through it," he hollers over the sound of the engine and the air blowing through the open windows. At the airport, he screeches to a stop in front of a sign that says Jonesy's Restaurant.

He starts his green four-passenger Cessna, which he says is the best, warms it up, taxies to the runway, and takes off. The ground feels as if it's falling away from us. I've never been in a plane, and I don't want to be in this one, even if it does have metal covered wings instead of cloth covered ones, and even if Melvin did get a fantastic deal on it. My stomach is upset from the chili, and I'm sleepy. Below is a river, looking like a shiny ribbon.

"That's the Napa River. It goes to Vallejo and empties into San Pablo Bay."

We follow it. Melvin flies low over Vallejo and does a lot of pointing. "That's Mare Island on the right. We're not allowed to fly over it. See those two destroyers in dry dock and the three submarines along the seawall? There's my mother's store. The apartment houses across the street are gonna be mine some day. See her white house on the hill, the one with the big swimming pool?"

"Sure, Melvin, everything's real nice." I can't tell the houses apart.

"There's my house. Damn it to hell, I told Denise and the kids to be out in front, on the lawn. Where the fuck are they? That woman never listens."

"Should you be this flying this low?"

"Don't worry about it. The guys in the control tower are all in the Twenty Thirsty Club."

"What's the Twenty Thirsty Club?"

"It's really the Twenty-Thirty Club, a service club for members between the ages of twenty and thirty." We gain altitude and fly over Carquinez Strait. He points out the Carquinez Bridge, the C & H Sugar Refinery, and San Pablo Bay. Then we circle back to Vallejo and fly over his house again. This time, Denise and the kids are outside, waving to us. He dips his wing at them. I'll be glad when the flight is over.

"Time to head back. Here, you take over. It's easy to fly a Cessna. The only thing you have to know is never to climb in your glide."

"What does that mean?"

"It means that if the engine quits, and you have to glide back to the airport, you better be sure your landing trajectory is just right, because you can't increase altitude without power."

Well, at least he's capable of giving me an intelligent answer. I grab the yoke, feel the plane tilt slightly, but level it out. Flying is fun even though I'm not feeling too good. Maybe Melvin's not so bad. He's showing off, trying to impress his kid brother. Hey, flying an airplane my first day in California? How many fifteen year-olds get to do this? Wait 'till I tell Joey. Oh, oh, there's the airport.

"Melvin." Looks like he's asleep. "Melvin, wake up. We're past the airport. Are you okay?"

I poke him. He doesn't move. That metallic taste is in my mouth, the same one I used to have when Dad hid and made me think I'd lost him. I lean over to shake his shoulder, and the plane banks to the left.

"Hey, what the hell are you doing?" he growls. "You want us to crash? I better take over."

"You scared the shit out of me."

He sits at the controls with an inane look on his face, playing tricks on his admirer, his 15-year-old kid brother, who adores him.

My eyes close. My stomach hurts. I'm sleepy. I want to be back in

Brooklyn.

He shakes me. "Wake up Norman. I thought you'd appreciate me taking you flying your first day here. You have a fine way of showing it. Hold on, I'm gonna dive… goddamn it to hell, you puked all over the cockpit."

"Goddamn it to hell, you're lucky I don't puke all over you."

CHAPTER 25

THE INVALID

For breakfast, Denise serves orange juice, bacon and eggs, toast and coffee, and lots of it. I pass on the bacon.

"Come to Benicia with me," my brother says.

"Who's Benicia?"

"It's a city eight miles away," Denise says. "It's named after the wife of General Mariano Guadalupe Vallejo, who founded this city. Benicia and Vallejo were once state capitols... Mel, why don't you take Norman on a tour while you're there?"

"I don't have time for bullshit like that."

Melvin's a shoe salesman at Renee's, his mother's store. He also delivers dresses to whorehouses that have been in the area since the Second World War. He claims to know all the high-class whores in the area and swears that they only buy dresses from his mother, because she sells the best merchandise. After breakfast, we go to the store, load the station wagon full of fancy frilly dresses, and drive to Benicia.

"How did you wind up in Vallejo?"

"Aunt Peggy, my mother's older sister, came here from New York in the early thirties and established a classy whorehouse on Georgia Street. Like my mother, she was born in Hungary, and she had an accent that drove men wild. People thought she was from France, so they called her Frenchy. She made out like a bandit catering to shipbuilders and also sailors stationed at Mare Island. Business was so good that she opened two more houses. She wrote to my mother in New York and told her to come to California, where she could make a lot of money no matter what she sold, but Benny didn't want to leave New York. Then John, my stepfather, came on the scene. You'll meet him sooner or later. He wears hearing aids in both ears, because Benny came home from work early one night and found John hiding in their closet. Benny kicked the living shit out of him while my mother screamed for the police. Anyway, my mother and Benny got divorced, she married John, and they moved to Vallejo in the mid thirties and opened a dress store that was a great success. They changed location three times, moving into bigger and bigger stores. Today they're in a choice area two blocks up from Lower Georgia Street. Now let me give you some history that's better than the state capitol crap that Denise likes. Lower Georgia Street was the district where all the bars had gambling rooms in back and whorehouses upstairs. There were more bars per block on lower Georgia during the war than anyplace in the world."

"I didn't know that. There are lots of things I don't know, like for instance, how come you changed your last name?"

"I wouldn't inherit shit if I didn't change my name. You should change yours too. As for me," he says, pointing to himself, "I don't want people to know I'm Jewish."

"Well, I'm proud to be Jewish. I'm never gonna change my name."

"You don't have to shout in my fucking ear."

I better switch topics. "What was the Navy like?"

"I liked it until the Japs bombed Pearl Harbor. I was on the *Curtis*, a seaplane tender, on the other side of Oahu away from the main action, but we still got hit. I lost three buddies, but the ship didn't go down."

His eyes tear up. It's the first sign of humanity I've seen, but it only lasts a few seconds.

"Did Dad tell you that I boxed in the Navy before the war? I was a flyweight believe it of not, not a lard ass like I am now. I never lost a fight. I was "tough as nails" and still am. I'm not afraid of any man. And I don't give a fucking shit how big he is."

"Now you're shouting in my ear."

"We're in my car. I can shout all I want."

We drive across two sets of tracks and pull into a dirt parking lot in front of a faded yellow building that was once a railroad station. The Carquinez Strait is a few yards away. Melvin opens the back door, scoops up an armload of dresses, tells me to wait in the car, and slams the door shut. At the seawall, a lone fisherman casts his line out, sits on his folding chair, and lights up a cigarette. In the middle of the strait, a huge oil tanker, low in the water, is heading east. I wish I were heading east, back to Brooklyn, back to my Jewish neighborhood where people are proud of who they are, where people think of others rather than just themselves, where people don't have foul mouths. I'm lonelier here than I was in New Jersey. There, Aunt Manya's was only two hours away.

On the way home, it's more of the same.

"Business must be good in Benicia. I just delivered $300 worth of dresses. Talk about whorehouses, my shipmates wanted to get laid one night in Oahu. I was the only one who wasn't interested. They all got the clap, but not me, ha ha."

"Tell me about when you were my age. Did you see Dad much?"

"Hardly ever. He was always working."

"How long did you live with my mother?"

"Six months. You look just like her."

"Did you play stickball?"

"Nah. I had better things to do, but I remember hiking in the woods with some friends. I saw a clump of poison ivy, took off my shirt, and rubbed the leaves on my chest. The guys copied me, and they all had terrible rashes the next day, but not me, 'cause I'm immune to poison ivy, ha ha."

"Why did you live with my mother? Where was yours?"

"She didn't have time for me. I was in her way. I was in Aunt Lilly's way. I was in everyone's way, except your mother's. She was good to me. But I started to get into trouble, so my mother sent me to a military academy in upstate New York."

"Like West Point?"

"Not exactly. A military academy, in my case, was a glorified name for a school that was one step above a reformatory."

I sleep in the laundry room off the kitchen on a folding cot like the one at Aunt Manya's. Since I'm older than Melvin's children, I'm appointed baby-sitter. I'm also put in charge of painting the house. The older children paint too, but correcting their careless work makes my job harder. Melvin brags that he's the one who painted the walls and the trim so precisely.

I mow the front and side lawns with a push mower and use an edger next to the sidewalks. I like the smell of fresh cut grass. Melvin's lawn is now the neatest one on Florida Street. He also has a power mower, a dinosaur according to Mr. Mendoza, our Filipino neighbor, but I can't get it started.

"You fucked it up," Melvin says. "It worked fine until you touched it."

Mr. Mendoza overhears Melvin's remark. "Norman didn't puck up da lawnmower. Da only ting pucked up is you. You can't start it either."

In the back yard, I till the black soil with a shovel and take out rocks and chunks of adobe. Following the depth and spacing instructions on seed packets Denise bought, I poke holes in the raised rows with a rake handle and plant corn, string beans, bell peppers, zucchini squash, tomatoes, onions, and lettuce. I weed, water, and wait.

"Nothing's coming up," Melvin says. "You should have let me plant the goddamn seeds."

They don't come up overnight, Melvin."

My belly is aching again, but this time the pain doesn't go away. I have dry heaves like the ones I had with the whooping cough. At eleven-thirty at night, Denise makes Melvin take me to the hospital. On the way, he stops for a pack of cigarettes at a convenience store and gets into a conversation with one of his friends. I holler from the car window, "Melvin, I don't feel good." When he gets back to the car, he takes his time lighting up and blows the smoke in my face.

He glares as I ring the bell at the emergency room door of Vallejo General Hospital on Tennessee Street. I lean against the concrete wall until an orderly in blue unlocks the door. Soon, I'm lying in bed, shaved and drugged for an emergency appendectomy.

"Count to ten," the anesthesiologist says.

"Will it hurt?"

"No."

"One, two, three… "

I'm in Brooklyn, lying on my cot, and I have to pee, but if I do, Aunt Manya will accuse me of doing it on purpose. Then I'm standing over the toilet in the bathroom, but still I don't pee, because I might be dreaming. If I am, I'll surely pee in bed, and Aunt Manya will take the sheets to school. I hate her. She makes me stutter and blink. Suddenly, I feel relief and sleep soundly. When I open my eyes Denise is by my bed with her hand on mine.

"I'm glad you're finally awake. You were out a long time. The doctor said you made it to the hospital just in time. Your appendix was close to bursting."

"The garden. How's the garden?"

"I weeded and watered it this morning."

An aide comes in. "My goodness. I ain't never seen a boy pee so much, and a good thing, because they was goin' to stick a tube up your thingy."

When I get home from the hospital two days later, Melvin shows me his payment schedule. John paid for the operation, three hundred dollars, and Melvin has to pay his stepfather back in ten installments.

"Why didn't you tell me you needed an appendectomy?" Melvin grits his teeth like Dad does when he's annoyed.

A week after coming home from the hospital, my tooth is aching again. The pain is worse than my appendicitis. "Melvin, I've got a really bad toothache."

"What do you want me to do about it?"

"I need to go to a dentist."

"Shit. You're costing me a fucking fortune. I pay for your bus fare from New York, I pay for your appendectomy, and now you have a toothache."

"Dad said he paid for the bus."

"The fucking hell he did! Here, look in my checkbook. I mailed the ticket to him, and I purposely had them stamp "no refund" on it.

Melvin drives me to his dentist, Dr. George Berger.

"The root canal has to be redone."

"I'm not paying for his root canal."

"But I want to save my tooth."

"It's a back tooth. You don't need it. Pull the damned thing out, George."

Aunt Manya, as stingy as she was, wouldn't have allowed a dentist to pull a tooth that could be saved.

"I'm going to work," Melvin says. "When George is done with you, you can walk home. It'll do you good."

Dr. Berger sticks a needle in my jaw and disappears. "Is your tongue numb yet?" he asks when he returns.

"No."

He gives me another shot and disappears again. "You numb yet?"

"No."

"You have to be. Let me try."

When he touches an instrument to the tooth, I recoil.

Another shot, but it doesn't work either. "I'll have to send you to the oral surgeon. Your brother's going to have a fit."

An hour later, I'm unconscious for the second time in two weeks. When I wake up, my tooth is gone.

The extraction site is no longer sore, and my appetite is back. Denise and the children are visiting her sister. I'm at the dining room table, reading the *Vallejo Times-Herald* and thinking about fixing a peanut butter and jelly sandwich for lunch, but Melvin comes in with a grocery bag that he sets on the table right under my nose. Slowly, he takes out two plain bagels, Philadelphia cream cheese, and a package of lox. From the kitchen, he brings a plate, a cutting board, and a knife. He checks the knife with his thumb. He slices one bagel, smears cream cheese over both halves, and positions the lox on the halves just so before setting them on the plate. I admire the deft way he prepares the bagel and smack my lips. I haven't had a bagel and lox for a very long time.

He hands me the plate, then pulls it back. His monkey face is the same as Dad's was when he folded my two hundred dollars into his wallet. He sits across from me and leisurely eats both halves of the bagel, smacking his lips and saying ummm. He pops the last crumb into his mouth, burps, and wipes his lips on a napkin.

Okay. He's having fun. Let him enjoy his little trick, sadistic as it is. But I'm an invalid, and surely my brother is not going to deprive me of the world's greatest Jewish treat. He slices the other bagel and adds cream cheese and lox. I'm drooling. I knew he wasn't going to let me down. He hands the plate to me. I reach for it, but he pulls it back fast. He eats the second bagel and lox. Melvin, my great hero, whom I've longed to see for years, finishes it and goes back to work after farting an ugly goodbye at the door.

CHAPTER 26

NORMAN'S FRIENDS

I call Denise out to the back yard to show her the plants poking through the soil. "Keep the ground moist," she says. "Occasional deep soakings are better than frequent light sprinklings. That'll prevent mildew." I follow her advice, and soon, all the vegetables in my first garden are growing in abundance.

Melvin shows the garden to his mother, Renee, whose fingers are heavy with diamond rings. I'm standing next to them with a basket of string beans. I'm invisible. Nobody bothers to say hello.

"I told Norman what to do."

"I understand you also taught him how to fly an airplane. I'm surprised they let you rent one with an expired license. Grow up, Melvin."

While he looks down at his shoes, his jaw muscles twitch like Dad's.

"Dinner's at my house, tomorrow. You can bring Norman."

The bushes in the front yard of her white stucco house are as manicured as the lawns, not natural like the ones in yards farther down the hill. The inside is a crowded antique store filled with gaudy chairs, couches, chandeliers, and musty oriental carpets. On the dining room table is a porcelain platter filled with apples, grapes, and bananas made of wax.

Melvin doesn't poke around his mother's kitchen or taste things in the pot like he does at home. I consider Denise second only to Aunt Manya in cooking, but Melvin has to add a pinch of salt or cayenne to her food so he can say he cooked it. Denise is helping Renee in the kitchen. Melvin is sitting on the brick hearth in the corner of the dining room, playing with Hansel and Gretel, his mother's black and white Scottie dogs. The children are watching television in the living room. I'm sitting across from John, looking at the big brown hearing aids sticking out of his ears. I try to start a conversation but get one-word answers, which puts me back in Becca's house in the Bronx when I tried to talk to her mother and father. Does John resent me for what Dad did to his hearing?

During dinner, I pick out a hot sweet potato from a gold-rimmed bowl. John gives me a dirty look. Renee grabs my sweet potato, puts it on

John's plate, picks up the bowl, and sets it down next to him. "These sweet potatoes are only for him," she says.

Melvin is sitting across from me. He writes out a check, an installment on my appendectomy/tooth extraction loan. In a wide arc, he offers it to John, but makes sure to hesitate when it passes in front of my face.

Neither Renee nor John ask if I like California or what I want to be when I grow up. They know I can draw, but they don't mention art. I'm lonelier than ever. I won't come here again even if they do have a swimming pool. Next time I'm invited over, if there is a next time, I'll stay home and read or paint.

Melvin takes me to a bicycle shop. "Try this red one." "Try that blue one." He's actually going to buy me a bike. He's a good brother after all. He picks the one he likes, a black three-speed. "You can ride it home."

"Thanks, Melvin." I'm not sure what I'm thanking him for. I'm not sure he bought the bike for me. Sounds like he's just lending it. But so what? I've never had a bike. After the salesman has me straddle it so he can adjust the seat to the right height, he tells me how to shift gears. I walk the bike out of the store, hop on, and take off. They say you never forget how to ride one. I learned on Seymour's, in Brooklyn, when I was nine. Dad was over that day, holding onto the seat to steady me while I pedaled down the middle of Herzl Street. Seymour was running alongside me, making sure I wouldn't drop the bike on the street. "Don't let go, don't let go." When I got halfway down the block, I was pedaling all by myself.

Florida Street is steep, but it's easy to make it to the top with a three speed. Nice view of the eastern hills. I can coast all the way home. There's lots of traffic at the intersection below. I squeeze the hand brakes, and the brake shoes fly into the street. I'm going faster. Sliding my shoes on the rough blacktop doesn't slow me down. A car is starting across the street, but he stops when he sees me. I shoot through the intersection, swerving around a car that just made a right turn into Florida Street ahead of me. Horns honk and tires screech. I don't know how I managed to get through the intersection in one piece, as Aunt Manya would say.

I walk the bike back to the store determined to chew out whoever installed those brakes backward. Aunt Manya would have said that Mother was watching over me. When I get home with properly installed brake shoes and tell Melvin what happened, he says, "I hope you didn't hurt the bike."

On my next ride, I go to Savage's on Sonoma Boulevard. Tied to the bike rack on a long rope is an English bulldog that reminds me of Spotty. I rub his head. "Hey, I know a doggy like you, and I miss him."

Mr. Mendoza told me about Savage's and the friendly bulldog. The store is a combination ice cream parlor and hobby shop. In a glass case are model airplanes, boats, and cars. Next to them are fishing reels and lures. On top of the case is a very big selection of balsa wood. A silver Boeing B-29 "Superfortress" long-range bomber is hanging from the ceiling. With a four-foot wingspan, it's the biggest model I've ever seen. I want to build another one.

I treat myself to a chocolate ice cream cone. A tall, skinny kid, my age, with an ice cream cone in his hand, is buying a .029 engine for his model airplane.

"It's for my Grumman Hellcat," he says to me.

"I built one once."

"Did you fly it?"

"Yes. It crashed and burned."

"I've never seen one catch on fire."

"I set it on fire."

"I get it. The control wires got crossed, and it hit the ground so hard that it busted into a million pieces and wasn't worth trying to salvage. So you pulled the engine out and lit a match to your poor Hellcat."

"Something like that."

"Ever go fishing? They've been catching stripers by the Sperry Flour Mill."

"What's a striper?"

"It's a striped bass. I can tell you're not from here."

"Everyone can tell that from my New York accent."

"Hey, you're right. I thought you talked funny… So, you wanna go fishing tomorrow morning?"

"My brother has some rods and reels in his garage. Maybe he'll lend me one." I give him my address and find out that he lives three blocks from me.

Melvin lends me a fishing rod that has seen better days, as Aunt Manya would say.

"Don't break it. It's very expensive. It's the best rod money can buy."

It's strange that the best rod money can buy comes with a squeaky Penn reel, frayed line, and rusty hooks.

In the morning, Ralph and I tie our fishing rods to our bikes and pedal to the Sperry Flour Mill across from the south end of Mare Island. There are black Norway rats as big as cats on the seawall. We hear chipping guns from the shipyard. There are giant cranes lifting their loads alongside gray ammunition ships.

"I'll never work at that noisy place," Ralph says, casting his line carelessly close to a fishing boat. "My dad's been a safety inspector there for years, and he's always complaining. Says he wishes he had gone to school like his brother, Paul. I'm going to college when I graduate. I want to be a doctor like Uncle Paul."

"I want to go to art school. Hey, I got a bite." The reel jams, so I pull in the line by hand. I've landed a six-inch fish that Ralph calls a bullhead.

Another day we pedal over to Glen Cove, Ralph's favorite place to fish. Attached to my rod is a new Penn reel with twenty-pound test monofilament line that I bought at Savage's with money I earned by painting Mr. Mendoza's new fence. Melvin wouldn't let me use one of the good reels on the shelf in his garage. We ride our bikes right up to the water's edge.

"Look, Norm, there's the black Sugar Boat coming in under the Carquinez Bridge."

The C and H sugar refinery is in Crockett, on the other side of the Carquinez Strait. That's another scene I'm gonna paint someday. I read that it's the biggest sugar refinery in the United States.

Our hooks are baited with tasty hunks of sardines. Since the current here is strong, we use four-ounce lead weights and cast our lines far from shore. I hope the stripers are hungry.

"Ralph, look at that oil tanker. The deck's bigger than a football field."

My reel starts clicking, and there's a terrific tug on the line. "It's a big one!" I start to reel in, but now there's no tension on the line. "I lost him."

"Too bad."

Another tug on the line. "He's still on. It feels like a whale."

"Loosen the drag a little, so the line won't break. Don't jerk on the line. Tighten the drag a little. Don't let the line go slack. Keep the end of the rod high. Higher. Let him get tired."

I play the fish for ten minutes before landing him. It's a beautiful striped bass.

"Nice goin', Norm. I got a tape measure somewhere. Here it is. Let's see. This baby is twenty-eight and a half inches long."

At home, Mr. Mendoza takes a picture of me, holding the fish by its gills. He weighs it. Eight pounds. Ralph is invited to dinner, Mr. Mendoza, too. Denise bakes the striper and serves it with vegetables from the garden. Melvin tells Mr. Mendoza that he taught me how to fish, and Mr. Mendoza tells Melvin that he's full of shit.

Ralph's mother is an elementary school teacher. I knock on their door. Ralph lets me in. There's a living room with tons of books on the shelves. His parents are reading. His younger sister, Irma, is reading. They get up and shake my hand. They're interested in what I have to say, whether it's about fishing, baseball, my life in New York, even Rembrandt.

I go with them to high school football games, Stinson Beach, and ice skating in Berkeley. They know about Melvin's mother and her notorious family, but they never embarrass me about it.

I love the bike. I'm used to it. It's part of me. In six weeks I've ridden it to Glen Cove, Blue Rock Springs, Sandy Beach, even Benicia. It's my limo. Fast, smooth, comfortable, and no hill is too steep for it.

I come home from school one day and see a man loading it onto a pickup truck. Out of the truck he lifts a gray, rusty one-speed with balloon tires and bounces it to the ground. He hands Melvin some money.

"What's going on?"

"I made a deal with Gene, here. This is your new bike."

Easy come, easy go. I say it to myself a few times, but it doesn't make the pain go away. There's something defective about my father's side of the family. I hope I haven't inherited their bad traits.

"Don't sit there," Melvin orders Denise. "Sit in the other chair." "What the hell are you watching that for, Norman? There's a better program on Channel 7."

I wish I could live with Ralph and his family. But things could be worse, as Aunt Manya would say. I'm allowed to use the garage to paint. I build an easel out of scrap wood. My Rembrandt book looks like a king size version of Uncle Irving's prayer book, well worn, with bookmarks sticking out. I find jobs in the neighborhood and buy more brushes, canvases and paints. At night, when the family is at the television, I have the garage to myself, and Rembrandt and I talk. I've got it made, as Melvin says. I better say *keyn eyne hore* to ward off the evil eye, because every time a Jew takes his good fortune for granted, something bad happens.

My pal, Michael, is a tough looking but gentle kid, who lives with his mother in the old, hilly part of town, in a blue two-story house on the top of Carolina Street. You can see most of Mare Island from their living room. Their back porch reminds me of Aunt Lilly's fire escape in Brooklyn. Michael's mother reads tealeaves and Tarot cards, but she doesn't bathe in perfume or have Aunt Lilly's gypsy voice.

Ralph and Michael and I play touch football with the girls in Michael's neighborhood. We all play Monopoly in Ralph's house. For his sixteenth birthday, Ralph's father buys him a black '41 Packard gas hog. If we can come up with a dollar or two for gas, we cruise Georgia Street. Sometimes we splurge and go to a drive-in restaurant. It's 1952, and hamburgers are seven for a dollar.

We take the Packard to the drive-in to see *The African Queen*, with Humphrey Bogart and Katherine Hepburn. Michael and I and our dates squeeze into the back seat. Ralph and his date have the front seat to themselves. After Ralph pulls in and out of three slots, he finds one with a speaker that works. We pool our money for big bags of popcorn. Michael's date moves to the front seat when he gets fresh. When I get close to my date, she sticks an inhaler up her nose and honks. Our windows steam up, and we have to crank them down to clear the air.

At eleven thirty, we drop the girls off and head home. The Packard runs out of gas a dark couple of miles from any phone booth or gas station.

"Let's sleep in the car and hitchhike to the gas station when the sun comes up," Ralph says.

At 2:00 am, Ralph's dad raps on the windshield. Melvin is with him. I'm sure he came along to see what kind of trouble I've gotten into.

On Halloween, Michael and Ralph come over. "Norm, there's an all night horror show downtown. Wanna go?"

"Sure… Melvin, can I borrow a dollar?"

"Fuck no."

"I'll pay you back. Your mom owes me ten dollars for writing post card advertisements at her store."

"That's between you and her."

"Aw come on, Melvin, it's Halloween."

"Yeah, it's Halloween," Michael says.

"If you jokers want Norman to go with you so bad, why don't you lend him the money?"

"I only got a dollar," Michael says.

"And I only got a dollar fifteen," Ralph says.

"Let me see your money." They take their dollars out of their wallets, and Melvin goes into his bedroom and comes back with a pink piggy bank and a hammer. "Tell you what. I'll trade you my pennies for those singles. There must be six or seven bucks in here. He breaks open the bank, and pours pennies and broken plaster into a brown bag. "Bring me back the change."

Ralph tries to start his car. No luck, he's out of gas again. So we walk to town. I carry the sack of pennies.

"How can you stand him?"

"He's not so bad, Michael. He feeds me and gives me a place to sleep."

"Big deal! You painted his house, inside and out."

"And you baby-sit," Ralph says.

It's eleven thirty, and we're walking down Georgia Street when three police cars pull up. Cops come out, draw their guns, and circle us. "Hands up, all of you."

I raise my hands, the sack tears open, and the pennies fall to the sidewalk. I can't say to myself, easy come, easy go, because the pennies weren't easy to come by. This is an odd thing to be thinking while staring into a gun barrel as big as a water pipe.

We answer questions with hands in the air and shoes covered with pennies. They let us go without an apology. We fish pennies out of our shoes, pick up all the ones we can find, stuff them into our pockets, and hurry to the midnight show. The cashier frowns when we dump our pennies on the counter. The customers behind us aren't happy either.

In next day's *Times-Herald*, I read that three men, wearing Halloween masks, robbed a market of a sack full of cash last night.

Vallejo High is my third school in three years. Plane geometry is easy, but I have a 'D' in chemistry going into the Christmas break. I decide to do nothing but study chemistry during the holiday. I start at page one of my textbook and go through all the exercises before classes start up again. I get an 'A' in chemistry and feel that I can do anything if I put in the effort.

I want to know more about my mother and father and grandfather. When Melvin is in a good mood, I try to talk to him, but he gets distracted by the TV. All I ever learn from him is that Dad is a gambler and he's irresponsible, but I already know that.

On February 2, 1953, I turn 16. Denise bakes a chocolate birthday cake. She waits for a TV commercial break so she and the kids can pry Melvin from his chair and drag him into the dining room to sing Happy Birthday. No telephone calls from New York, but I get cards from Sarah and Henry and Lola.

When we aren't going to school or working, Ralph and Michael and I like to hang out at an arcade on lower Georgia Street. I play my favorite pinball machine and hardly ever tilt it. Ralph finds a more practical machine in a pool hall across the street that pays off a penny a point. We play until we rack up enough points for a game of pool. We're playing at the best table when some Filipinos come in and demand the table.

"First come, first served," Michael says.

One of the men takes out a knife to clean his fingernails. We give them the table.

Ralph and Michael talk me into going bowling. I make a strike, pick up a split, make another strike. Bowling is fun from the player's end of the alley.

Georgia Street is exciting. Melvin insists that it's a ghost town compared to what it was during the war. Still, there are busy cafes with juke boxes blasting, a beauty parlor that curls straight hair and straightens curly hair, jewelry stores with diamond earrings, silver bracelets, gold chains and star sapphire pinky rings like the one Melvin wears. His mother's store, Renee's, has a window full of fancy silk dresses and sexy negligees for foxy women. Melvin, the shoe salesman, brags, even in front of Denise, that some of his customers don't wear panties.

I go downtown to capture the daytime and the nighttime colors of Georgia and other streets where things are happening. I save up to buy more paints, brushes, canvasses, painting mediums, canvas-stretching pliers, and a real easel. I add more customers to my busy schedule of mowing lawns, painting houses, and repairing fences. I will definitely stop working for Melvin's mother. Six hours of addressing postcards and then having to wait six weeks for my ten dollars is crazy.

I want to paint the excitement of Georgia Street, not present-day Georgia Street, but the way it must have been during the war. I can picture it. At night, the Shore Patrol, twirling their batons, standing on street corners, keeping law and order, hauling drunken sailors to the brig. Swarms of shipyard workers. Sailors in dress blues, walking six abreast down busy littered sidewalks. Cheap hotels, movie houses, smoky pool halls, whisky-smelling bars, tattoo parlors run by real artists, buzzing colored inks into muscled arms, creating roses, eagles, dragons, and Mom. Melvin's arms are highly decorated.

One night at the arcade, a sailor is playing my favorite pinball machine. A lady says, "There are more enjoyable ways to spend your money, sailor boy." Tilt.

On cobble-stoned Branciforte Street, a black man in a blue silk suit, sitting in a shiny orchid Cadillac convertible, directs sailors to a yellow house at the top of the hill. I follow them up the hill on a clear, starry night and stand on the street in front of the house. The upper windows are lit like a lighthouse overlooking the sea. Below, warships at Mare Island sparkle from welders' arcs.

School vacation is coming up, and I'll have all summer to paint. My studio is just the way I want it, and I'm full of ideas. I'll paint lower Georgia Street, the pimp in his orchid Cadillac, the Yellow House on Branciforte Street, the shipyard, the Carquinez Bridge, and lots of people. I've rigged up lights to shine on the overstuffed red chair in the garage, and I'll light my subjects in Rembrandt's style. People are waiting their turn to sit in the chair and be painted, just like they were on Aunt Manya's stoop in Brooklyn. On my list are Mr. Mendoza, Ralph's mother and sister, Denise, the kids, even Hairy Mary, the girl I took to the drive-in, who sticks an inhaler up her nose and honks. Melvin has other ideas.

"Good morning," he says casually at breakfast. This is the first "good morning" I've heard all year, and I don't like the sickly sweet sound of his voice or the smug expression on his face. What evil thing is coming next?

"Norman, you've been living with us, what, a year now, eating my food and living the good life. I think it's time for you to move on."

"Mel, he has one more year of high school."

"Fuck high school, Denise. He's sixteen, old enough to get a work permit."

"No one's going to hire me without a high school diploma."

"Bullshit. They're looking for apprentices at Mare Island."

He reaches to the cabinet behind him and takes out a thick envelope. He slides the papers out slowly with the same expression he used when he ate the bagels and lox in front of me.

"I just happen to have an application form for you. Fill this out and get your lazy ass down to the Mare Island Employment Office today."

Chapter 27

Afternoon Tea with Perfumed Prostitutes

Michael's mother, Ruth, is thin and pale, and she has a raspy cigarette cough. She's barely able to support herself and Michael by working nights as an aide at a convalescent hospital. How she can lift patients is a mystery. When Michael told her that Melvin kicked me out, she was happy to take me in as a rent-paying boarder.

Attached to the second story of her house on the Carolina Street hill is a rickety glass-enclosed sun porch. In it is a round wringer washing machine and barely enough room for my easel. From here, there's a clear view of Mare Island, the old part of town, and the Yellow House on Branciforte Street.

"Make sure to keep the door closed," Ruth says.

Cigarette smoke stays on one side, turpentine smell stays on the other. We're both happy. My own studio. A job. I'm an apprentice electrician. Money for art supplies, living with people I like.

There's a sleek, midnight blue '37 Oldsmobile at Rosedale's Used Cars on Virginia Street. One hundred dollars, no interest, just a handshake and twenty-dollars a month for five months. Not a bad deal for a sixteen-year-old who's been working at the shipyard for three months.

"Not a scratch on it," Ralph says.

"Looks like a gangster car from the movies," Michael says.

Ralph drives. Michael and I sink deep into the plush rear seats. We're riding on a cloud, the cloud of black smoke that follows us to an empty field along the waterfront. We change seats for my driving lesson. Ralph sits next to me.

"Step on the clutch pedal, shift into first, give it some gas. Too much, hit the brake. Not so hard, you let her die. You have to push down on the clutch when you come to a stop."

"I can't do it all at once."

"You'll get used to it."

Every day after work it's time to practice. The Olds is parked across the street from the house, pointing downhill, with the wheels turned to the curb. Since the starter doesn't always work, I can coast to a start if no one parks in front of me. When the motor dies in the flat part of town, I have to wait for a push. Shifting has become easy.

I drive up steep Branciforte Street and get almost to the top when the car in front of me stops for a pedestrian. The motor dies and the car behind me keeps honking. Despite Ralph's efforts to fix it, the emergency brake doesn't work, so I keep one foot on the brake, shift into neutral, and slowly back down the hill until my bumper touches the bumper of the car behind me. Now I can step on the starter with my left foot and the gas pedal with my right. By a miracle, the car starts. I shift into first and make it over the hill.

I drive to my appointment at the Department of Motor Vehicles and park in a space marked "Driving Test." The license examiner gets in the Olds.

"How did you get here?"

"I drove. My friend was with me. He has a license."

"I see. Turn right at the driveway."

Thankfully, the Olds starts right away. I shift into first, drive to the street, make a hand signal, and turn right when it's safe.

"Turn left at the corner."

I stretch out my left arm to signal, wait for the car coming in the opposite direction to pass, and make my turn. In the rearview mirror, Ralph and Michael are following me in Ralph's car.

"Park up ahead on the right."

I pull alongside the car in front of the empty space, shift into reverse, and start to back in. The clutch chatters, and the car bucks.

The examiner moans. Ralph and Michael are still behind me, laughing and making funny faces. They follow us back to the DMV.

The examiner taps his fingers on the dashboard. Sweat runs down my neck. He rolls his blue eyes, but signs "pass" on my form.

"What were you guys doing back there?"

"We were trying to cheer you on."

My folding cot at Michael's is like the ones at Melvin's and Aunt Manya's. Ruth prepares breakfast for us before she goes to bed in the morning and cooks our dinner before she goes to work. The conversation at the table is sincere. She listens to everything we say. She knows about Renee's notorious sister. With a wink, she points to the apartment downstairs, where Betty and Carla live. During the night, we hear doors opening and beds squeaking. Living above this is an adventure.

On Wednesday, her only day off, after she comes home from her Alcoholics Anonymous meeting, Ruth bakes and invites the girls up for tea and cake. One Wednesday, I join them in a kitchen that smells of cigarettes, perfume, and chocolate cake. Betty, five foot three, is wearing dark mascara that contrasts with her pale skin. She has a Billie Holiday voice and wears a skirt with long slits that expose thighs encircled by rose tattoos. Carla is as tall as I am, five nine, but with the gold braids bobby-pinned on top of her head, she's over six feet. Her voice is low and quivery. She has on a pink dress that shows cleavage. The girls remind me of Aunt Flo's daughters.

Carla walks over to the watercolor taped to the kitchen wall, a nude sitting on the edge of her bed, combing her hair. "Looks just like you, Betty. When did you pose?"

"I never did."

"I copied it from a book of Degas' pastels, and I put your face on it."

"Well, if you'd like to paint me in person, come on down. We can do some sort of exchange."

Ruth clears her throat. "Norman, show the girls your drawings."

I hand them sketches of the Carquinez Bridge, the C&H Sugar refinery, sailboats at the Vallejo Yacht Club, and the *Golden Bear*, a training ship tied up to the wharf at the California Maritime Academy.

"Look Betty, he drew the arcade on lower Georgia Street and the Filipino pool hall across the street."

"Frenchy's old place was upstairs," Betty says. "I worked there when I was fifteen. I lied about my age. She treated her girls right. Her sister, Renee, owns the *Renee Shop* on Georgia Street. I have to be careful not to mention Frenchy when I'm there."

"And how about that shoe salesman who works there?" Carla says.

"The guy with the gapped teeth and the cleft chin. The bug-eyed creep is always looking up my dress."

I'm enjoying my afternoon tea with perfumed prostitutes.

In the middle of the night, we hear pounding downstairs.

"Answer the door, bitch."

"What do you want?"

"Forty dollars is missing from my wallet. I want it back."

"I don't have your money."

"Maybe your friend does."

"We don't do stuff like that," Betty squeaks. "We've got reputations to uphold."

"Well, one of you sluts went through my wallet when I fell asleep."

"Nobody took your money. Now get lost."

He pounds louder.

"I'm calling the police," Michael says.

"No. That would get the girls in trouble."

"He sounds drunk and dangerous."

"Watch this." I open the door, yell down in my best gangster voice, "Hey asshole, I got a shotgun. Get the hell out of here before I blow your fuckin' head off." The front door slams. Feet pound down the front porch steps.

I'm a hero. The girls take me to Munchies for a hamburger, fries, and a milk shake. We sit in a window seat. If only Joey could see me this time.

On my walk to the waterfront every workday, I carry a lunch pail with a tasty sandwich packed by Ruth. A rolled-up sketchbook and drawing pencils take the place of a thermos. Coffee's a dime on the Yard. I turn onto Georgia Street and join the crowds of shipyard workers headed for the ferry.

The *Pelican* appears through the fog and bumps up against the tires lining the floating dock behind the ferry building. Workers pile on. A horn blows. The boat leaves the dock. A latecomer jumps across three feet of open water and lands on the stern next to me. We applaud.

The ferry churns through the gray water on its five-minute crossing of Mare Island Strait. I climb out on the narrow outside deck, hold the railing, smell fishy water and diesel fuel, and feel the fog on my cheeks. We pass the *Heron*, on its way to pick up more workers. Half way across, I can see two destroyer escorts, side by side in a dry dock. Destroyers are tied up to the sea wall. A light cruiser sits in another dry dock. Further down river are the *Able* and the *Baker*, instrument-fitted ships that I heard will be used in an A-Bomb test. Hundred-foot-tall cranes look like prehistoric four-legged birds with their steel-wheeled feet on tracks, their booms hovering over the submarines. Behind the cranes are red brick buildings with gray slate roofs punctuated by a huge black smokestack and waves of yellow, green, and blue hardhats. I'll paint that scene some day in the manner of Whistler.

As the ferry nears the dock, the empty *Robin* motors by on its way to pick up more workers. The sound of paint-removing chipping guns gets louder. It's joined by sirens, horns, the piping of boatswains' whistles, and shouts of Leadingmen, bosses with skunk-like white stripes on their hardhats. Workers, affectionately known as yardbirds, get off and show their badges to United States Marine Corps guards before they climb up the gangplank at the sea wall and head to their time-clock stations.

I spend one week each month at the apprentice school, where, for the next four years, I'll get paid to learn electrical theory, mechanical drawing, and safety in the workplace from instructors who specialize in the art of boring presentations. This is my first day in the Electric Shop, a huge, windowless, concrete building where I have a three-month assignment. I punch in and stop at the workbench of my journeyman instructor.

"Are you Mr. Conrad?"

"No son, I'm Connie. We don't have any misters working here."

Connie is wearing hearing aids. He teaches me to overhaul motors and generators, and there are pallets of them in the shop from DD 537, *The Sullivans*. This destroyer is here for a complete overhaul. Some of the motors are too heavy to lift, so I use the overhead crane to hoist them onto my workbench. I take them apart, loosen screw and bolt heads covered with coats of hard battleship-gray paint, stamp the parts with numbers to identify them for re-assembly, replace bearings, sandblast, paint, and haul them to the drying oven on electric carts. In three weeks, I'm doing it all without supervision.

"Norm, *The Sullivans* is named after five brothers from Waterloo, Iowa. They lost their lives when the *Juneau* was torpedoed at Guadalcanal."

"Five brothers on one ship?"

"Serving on the same ship was a condition they requested before enlistment. The navy doesn't allow that anymore. It was the greatest military loss to an American family in World War II, and I saw it happen."

"You were at the Battle of Guadalcanal?"

"Yes sir, in November of '42. I was there. Black smoke poured out of the Juneau. There were flames, explosions, men jumping overboard. She turned on her side and disappeared. The noise that day, from airplanes, guns, sirens, explosions, it made me crazy. My wife shakes me awake from my nightmares."

My first shipboard job as an apprentice electrician is on the destroyer, *The Sullivans*, where I install electric cables from one end of the ship to the other. The cables are covered with armor, a protective metal meshwork that frays when it rubs against sharp shipboard edges. We wear thick leather gloves for pulling cable. Electricians are stationed in each compartment to pull the cable through bulkhead tubes and make sure it doesn't twist. Karl, the Leadingman, twists a length of cable into a loop. "We call this an asshole."

One of the guys says, "Look, two assholes."

"Very amusing, Fritz. It takes one to know one. I don't want any assholes in my cable or in my gang. If you see one, bang on the bulkhead with a hammer, Norm, so the men on the other side will stop pulling."

We spend weeks pulling cables and fastening them to steel hangars that are welded to the sides of the ship. Then it's time to pack the tubes to make the bulkheads watertight.

"A perfect assignment for apprentices," Karl says. "Fritz, show Norm how it's done."

So begins the ugly task of stuffing coils of semi-solid packing material around the cables that enter the welded tubes that penetrate the bulkheads. On each side of the bulkheads, the ends of the steel tubes are threaded, and screwed into those threads are packing nuts that have holes in them slightly larger than the cables that go through them. I insert thin wooden sticks with curved ends, different sizes according to the size of the cables,

and tamp the coils in with a mallet. Then I tighten the nuts to compress
the material around the cables. Some of the nuts are barely accessible, surrounded by dozens of cables, and can only be tightened a quarter turn at a
time before I have to reapply the crescent wrench.

The engine room is hot and stinks of diesel fuel. I'm on my knees,
bent over and achy, tightening a packing nut that I can barely reach. My
crescent wrench falls into the slimy bilge. On days like this I'm sorry I ever
became an apprentice electrician. Things couldn't be worse. Oh no, there's
a big cable going through that tube, and there's no packing nut around it.
My job just got worse. That cable has to be pulled out, and all the other
tubes it goes through from one end of the ship to the other may already be
packed and compressed.

Weeks later, all the cables are pulled and all the tubes are packed.
When the noon whistle blows, I walk down the gangway, wash up, get my
lunchbox, head for the sea wall, eat a chicken sandwich, and draw. Mare
Island Strait is choppy. A sailboat heading south heels over, exposing its
red bottom. Beyond it is the Yellow House on Branciforte Street and St.
Vincent's steeple standing even higher.

"Not bad, kid. Not bad at all," a worker says.

I'm used to people looking over my shoulder. I draw faster now without sacrificing accuracy. I've filled five sketchbooks with scenes of Vallejo.

I'm on the fantail of *The Sullivans*, sketching the sister ship alongside
it in the dry dock and the cranes and shops in the background. Tomorrow,
water will gush into the dry dock, the destroyers will rise from the bottom,
and they'll be towed to docks down river. After drawing the depth-charge
stands and the five-inch guns, I draw the mast and the pilothouse. They're
splotched yellow with zinc chromate paint that protects the metal from
rusting. I dip a corner of my paper into a shipboard bucket of zinc chromate for a color sample. On the sunny back porch of Ruth's apartment, I'll
paint this scene on a half sheet of D'Arches watercolor paper.

After work I head home for dinner, then go to the library to study
drawings by the great masters. They used light and dark lines, broad and
thin lines, or sometimes, only shading. It's important to return to the masters often to reinforce what I've learned.

At home, I draw thin lips, bushy eyebrows, and the dark brown eyes
looking at me from the mirror. This is my third self-portrait this week.

"Norman, your navy blue watch cap, the way you've captured the texture of the wool, where did you learn to do that?"

"Rembrandt taught me."

Ruth looks at me sideways

Lunchtime, out on the seawall, sketching the Sperry Flour Mill, I'm distracted by a commercial fishing boat, which makes me think about the painting in Aunt Manya's bathroom and how hurt I was that all those years living with her she never told me it was painted by Mother. Then I'm in the bathtub, blowing on the sails of my walnut-shell ships.

"You're a dreamer."

"What?"

"You're a dreamer," Karl says.

"Sorry."

"Don't apologize. Most peoples' minds are elsewhere, either re-living the past or contemplating the future… By the way, congratulations on your Beneficial Suggestion. Who would have thought to cut a packing nut in half lengthwise? How much did they give you?"

"A hundred bucks. You know, I got the idea when I found that cable with no packing nut."

"Well, you know what they say, necessity is the mother of invention."

"I wonder who the father was?"

"It was you… Tell me, Norman, what are your goals?"

"My goals? Well, Karl, I want to get a high school diploma. I want to go to college. I want to become an artist."

"Looking at that sketch, I'd say you already are one."

"I can draw and paint, but I'm not an artist."

"Why do you say that?"

"Rembrandt is an artist. I'm an amateur."

"It's interesting that you refer to Rembrandt in the present tense."

"To me, he's still alive."

"I see… Why are you working here on the Yard, Norm?"

"Making a buck, just like you."

"What I mean is, you shouldn't be here. You should be doing what you want to do, doing art."

"I'm saving up, Karl. I know I'm wasting my time at a job I don't like, but what can I do? A steady paycheck is my only security."

At home, I look at the fuzzy copies of Mother's photographs that Sarah mailed to me. I'm sad every time I think about the mother I've never known. I can see Beth El Hospital looming over my Brooklyn neighborhood, casting a black shadow. I think about Mother's Caesarean operation, her moans as she tries to rip out the drainage tubes, the point of the butcher knife wielded by me when I half-heartedly tried to stab myself, Aunt Manya slicing through the carcass of a chicken with the same knife she used to unlatch the bathroom door, Manny the butcher, with his yellow straw hat, blood-splattered apron and blood-caked fingernails, standing in his doorway, watching Dad drag me away from my family and my Jewish traditions.

Dad took Mother away from her Brownsville family to a *goyisheh* town with no kosher butcher stores and no Jewish writing on store windows, to live in the same apartment house with relatives by marriage, a drunken clown and a stone-faced fortune teller who's as full of shit as a Christmas goose.

I won't paint pain. I'll paint Mother in happy times. I suppose times spent with her best friend, Lola, were happy. And she must have been happy when she married Dad, at least at first.

I try over and over to bring Mother to life, like Rembrandt did his subjects, but I can't. Never mind that my boss, Karl, thinks I'm an artist. Despite having made tons of reasonably good sketches and paintings over the years, when it comes to painting Mother I'm a failure. Sometimes I'm tempted to chuck all my work in Mare Island Strait and be done with art forever. Then I look at the drawings I've made from Mother's photographs and know I have to keep trying. I owe it to her.

There she is, standing on the sidewalk, wearing a short-sleeved, flowered dress with a big bow in front. She looks sweet, healthy, ready for life's challenges. I have to be ready, too.

When painting her, sometimes it's my face on the easel. I paint her shadow on the sidewalk, the building behind her, and the Ford sedan at the curb with the same energy it took to copy Rembrandt's self-portrait. Time escapes. Each painting is better than the last one was at this stage.

Outside, most of the house lights are off. Yellow street lamps glow softly in the mist. On Mare Island, there are a thousand lights and an occasional welder's arc. The only sound is a squeaking bed downstairs. I clean my brushes and go to bed.

CHAPTER 28

SHARON

The closest I'd ever come to loving Aunt Manya was when we had tea together in the afternoon. If she weren't aggravated about something, she'd be kind and caring and talk to me about how important it was to read, study hard, go to college, and make something of myself. She made me feel as if I really counted, really belonged. I think of her every Wednesday afternoon when I have tea with Ruth, Carla and Betty. Working the night shift at Mare Island has its advantages.

On the linen tablecloth is a porcelain vase filled with ferns and roses. The cups and saucers are different colors and different sizes, yet I feel as if I'm at high tea at a ritzy English hotel. Carla is sipping tea with her pinkie extended. Betty lifts a scone to her lips and takes a tiny bite. Ruth hands me a plate of chocolate cake. She looks tired. "Eat, eat. You're too skinny," she says.

Her imitation of Aunt Manya's Jewish accent is getting better.

"Norman, show the girls your latest watercolor."

I tape it to a mat and hold it up. It shows Ruth on the rickety back porch, hanging laundry. Behind her are descending rooftops and the terraced hillside. The girls gush over it.

"You sign your paintings with your first name?"

"Van Gogh and Rembrandt did."

"And look what he's produced in two years," Ruth says, pointing to the pictures on the walls. "Can you believe how talented our Norman is?"

"Seeing is believing," Betty says.

"How long does it take to do a watercolor?" Carla asks.

"My teacher in Brooklyn can do one in an hour."

"I thought it took days."

"It takes me two hours to paint a scene that's ninety per-cent finished. Then I spend some time ruining it. Lola's husband, Henry, he's my teacher also, says it takes two people to do a painting—one to do the work, the other to stand behind the artist with a stick and clobber him if he doesn't stop painting in time."

"Show the girls the portrait of your mother."

"It's not done yet."

"By me it's done."

"Ruth, now you sound exactly like Aunt Manya."

"Manya Schmanya, I learned that from you. Now show them the picture already."

"Yes, Norman, show us the picture already."

"Okay, okay. Stop *hocking mir a chaynik*."

"We know what that means."

"I think we know all of your aunt's expressions."

"But you don't make a fist, get red in the face, or spray me with spit."

"Well, we're not perfect. What do you want from a bunch of *shiksehs*?"

"Okay, here's my painting, but it's a work in progress."

"It's beautiful!"

"I'm going to scrub it out and paint over it. "

"Don't you dare."

"Aren't you ever satisfied?"

"In a museum it should be hanging. Did I say that right, Norman? Do I still sound like Manya? I'll spray on you if you'd like."

"Enough already, Betty," Carla says. "It's more like a sculpture than a painting. Norma is stepping out of the canvas."

"Norman has made us feel his mother's presence."

"You're right, Ruth," Betty says. "I can see kindness, caring... "

"I wish I could have known her," Carla says.

"You do know her, through Norman."

Ruth and the girls are kind and supportive, but they don't see the flaws, the artistic shortcomings, like when I fail to capture the twist of a pelvis or the thrust of a jaw. Sometimes I paint a figure that's technically correct but lacking in feeling. Other times there's feeling but no technical correctness. If only I could do both at the same time.

Ruth picks up my sketchbook. "Show the girls what you were working on this morning."

"It's Norman's mother when she was a teenager."

"No, Betty, it's just a friend."

"Just a friend? For weeks Norman's been walking on air. He hardly eats, he doesn't argue with me, he doesn't fight with Michael."

"I thought he's been acting a little peculiar," Betty says.

"Our Norman's in love."

"Thank you, Carla. My suspicions are confirmed."

Sharon is five foot one with short black hair, dark brown eyes, curves in the right places, and a good head on her shoulders, as Aunt Manya would say. At a party last month at Ralph's, I was across the room from her, talking to Ralph but not paying attention to a word he was saying. Her head was slightly tilted to one side, like in the picture I'm painting. I couldn't stop staring. It was like looking at Mother. She was at the buffet table, filling her paper plate, ignoring the ham and the prawns, which I took as a good sign. She walked toward me and didn't wait for Ralph to introduce us.

"You must be Norman, the artist Ralph told me about. I'm Sharon." We shook hands, and I was in love.

We're lucky to find a parking place four blocks from our destination, U.C. Berkeley. Campus map in hand, we spend the morning walking around the sprawling university.

"You'll like my mom and dad. They're from Brooklyn, too."

"Do they *tawk* like I do? Do they drink *cawfee* with their breakfast?"

"As a matter of fact, they do."

"How could I not like them?"

"I'm so excited about being accepted here."

"I'm happy for you." But I'm sad at the same time. I should be a university student, too.

"I'm hungry."

"I know a place on Telegraph Avenue. Great veggie burgers."

On a street corner, a mime in a white sailor suit is performing. A ceramic bowl at his feet waits for coins. Ethnic restaurants with menus in their windows are packed. Out of doorways, I can smell the whole world's cooking as well as the marijuana that street vendors are smoking.

The restaurant is noisy. There are booths on the sides and tables in the center. Students with backpacks are everywhere. We grab a table when people leave. Sharon is a nurse's aide in the surgical ward at Children's Hospital in Oakland. As she describes her job, I feel that I'm in the ward with her, comforting a sick child. There is the same kindness and caring in Sharon that Ruth and the girls see in my painting of Mother.

Sharon is beautiful. We're both eighteen. She'll be a college freshman. I don't have a high school diploma. How can she be interested in hearing about overhauling electric motors and pulling cables through bulkheads? But she wants to know more about what I do at work.

Five people are sitting around the tiny table to our right, having a conversation about social problems in Argentina, Chinese economic aid to North Vietnam, and Richard J. Daley's rise to power in Chicago. I know nothing about these subjects, just navy ships and art.

I'm in love with the perfect woman sitting by my side. She bites into her veggie burger, pats her lips with a napkin, takes a sip of coffee. Every movement is graceful. I reach for my coffee cup and almost tip it over. In catching it, I tip over a small vase of flowers and water spills on her lap.

"Sorry I'm such a klutz."

"Why, because you spilled some water? It's what makes you perfect."

"What's perfect about being a klutz?"

"It means you're human." She puts her hand on mine. I've just gone to heaven.

At the table to our left, a professor, I think, is talking to three students about Nietzsche. I've memorized a passage by him. Here's a chance to impress Sharon. I blurt out for everyone to hear, "Art is not merely an imitation of the reality of nature, but in truth a metaphysical supplement to the reality of nature, placed alongside thereof for its conquest."

The man turns, raises his index finger, and says to his students, "From The Birth of Tragedy. That lad knows his Nietzsche."

Sharon is awestruck. But I'm jealous. She'll be in this intellectual environment every day, and I won't be part of it. Next semester I'm going to take even more requirements toward my high school diploma.

Outside, we pass a bookstore. There's a book in the window with Rembrandt on the cover, holding a palette and mahlstick. Did he just wink? Is he looking at us approvingly? I wink back.

At another store, there's a human skull in the window.

"Let's go inside."

On glass shelves are skeletons of an alligator, a fox, bats, cats, and snakes. Human bones: femur, pelvis, sacrum, scapula. In a long row stand human skeletons. The one I'm drawn to is designed for artists. It's made in Germany. Plastic, with articulated joints. I twist the skeleton so that the head, chest, and pelvis are on different planes, a pose that Andreas Vesalius used in his book, *De Humani Corporis Fabrica*. It's easy for me to visualize the deltoids, triceps, biceps, and trapeziums, but I don't brag about this to Sharon. I may have already overdone the bragging at the restaurant. We carry the skeleton to the cash register.

"Do you have any human brains in formaldehyde? No madmen please."

"And where can my friend buy an electric generator in this neighborhood? He'll need lots of power for his experiment."

The clerk smiles. "Would you like this delivered to your castle, Dr. Frankenstein?"

"No thanks, I'll take it with me." I'm lucky to have a good job, to be able to afford this pricey skeleton. Carrying it to the car, we're part of the Berkeley scene.

"Norman, when we passed the bookstore, Rembrandt did a double-take."

"I saw that. He winked at us again. If the street wasn't so noisy, you would have heard him say *shalom*."

"Rembrandt was Jewish?"

"Yes. He shortened his name from Van Rijnstein."

"You and my father are going to hit it off."

Next stop is Sharon's two-story white stucco home in the Oakland hills. On the front doorpost is a big brass *mezuzah*. Her father laughs when he looks out the large living room window at the skeleton propped up in the back seat of my Oldsmobile. Her mother cringes.

Sitting on plastic-covered furniture, we have coffee and pastries on fine china. Sharon's mother looks at me suspiciously. When I look at her, she puts on a phony smile. They ask me about my parents, Brooklyn, and how I wound up in California. They're sorry to hear that I grew up without a mother. Sharon's mother brightens when I mention that my father was a pharmacist in Vienna. She makes a *farcrimpte pawnum* when she learns that he's a waiter in Manhattan.

"But he works in high-class restaurants. He's at the Copacabana now," Sharon says. Her mother isn't impressed.

They ask me question after question, a checklist of suitor qualifications. In the middle of telling them about my apprenticeship at the shipyard, Sharon's mother gathers up the china and silverware and goes into the kitchen. She's like Aunt Flo, who was more interested in playing with her cat than listening to me talk about my science project. I hear dishes being washed. Sharon shrugs. I turn to her dad. "Sharon tells me you're a baseball fan. Did you ever go to Ebbets Field when you lived in Brooklyn?"

"You bet I did. I've been to quite a few Dodger games over the years. Let me show you something." He goes to a cabinet and comes back with a baseball. He tosses it to me. "I was in the bleachers and caught it with my bare hands. It stung like hell. A Jackie Robinson homerun."

"He signed it?"

"Yes. His homer tied the score in the bottom of the ninth. I hustled down to the dugout and got there just before the game ended in the tenth. I hollered to him as he was coming off the field. 'Hey Jackie, would you please sign your homerun ball?' And here it is… Have you been to many games?"

"Just two Major League games. At Yankee Stadium, I saw Joe DiMaggio hit a homer off Bob Feller. At Ebbets Field, I saw the Dodgers beat the Cubs three to one. I don't remember who was pitching, but Jackie Robinson stole second twice that day."

"Twice? I saw him steal second twice. We might have been at the same game."

Sharon's mother comes back from the kitchen, her face still sour. I turn the conversation around to books. Surely they'll give me high marks for having read *The Ginger Man*, *The Quiet American*, *A Charmed Life*. Still, I'm a shipyard worker, a high school dropout, and obviously not good enough for their daughter. They look at Sharon with question marks. Now would be the wrong time to tell jokes.

Around the room, except for a mirror and framed sepia photographs of Sharon's grandparents, the walls are bare. There's no sense talking about art; showing might be better. "Sharon, would you please get me a pad of paper to draw on?"

I reach into my pocket for a pencil and draw as I talk. "Let me tell you about the real me. I'm a high school dropout. I used to steal. I ran away from home twice. I broke a boy's nose once. I can add a column of figures in my head faster than you can on your adding machine. If you don't believe it, try me. My father follows the horses, but the horses he follows follow other horses. Two of my cousins are prostitutes who run around New York with mattresses on their backs. I live upstairs from two prostitutes who are my friends. I spend a lot of time painting them in the nude. When I'm not painting or working deep inside the oily engine room of a ship, I take night classes at Vallejo Junior College and sometimes at Napa Junior College. I read books on painting, sculpture, the lives of artists, and at least two novels a week. "

Sharon looks awestruck again, like she did when I quoted Nietzsche. Her parents are sitting with their mouths open. I hand the sketch to Sharon's mother. It was drawn without looking at her, but I softened her pinched face for Sharon's sake. Her mother's mouth opens wider.

At the car, Sharon kisses me goodbye and says, "I love you, Norman."

Blue and red neon tubes encircle the walls near the ceiling. The floor tiles are a checkerboard of black and white. In front of the counter are chrome stools with red plastic cushions. I'm in Munchies with Michael and Ralph, chomping on a hamburger. There are posters of Humphrey Bogart, Marilyn Monroe, and James Dean. Parked in front is my black '47 Ford two-door sedan, another deal from Rosedale's, but this time I had a mechanic check it out. The last trip to Oakland was too much for the Olds. No black cloud of smoke following this car. But there is one hovering over me, like the one that's over Joe Btfsplk in *Li'l Abner*.

"I struck out with Sharon's folks. They gave me an exam, multiple choice and essay, then wired me for a lie detector test. The worst part was the bright light in my eyes."

"Norman, I've told you a million times not to exaggerate."

"He's not exaggerating, Michael. My girlfriend's mom and dad took my fingerprints and ran a rap sheet on me."

"Not to change the subject, but how many classes do you have left before you get your diploma?" Michael asks.

"Physiology, History of the Americas, two semesters of physics."

Michael gives a thumbs up. Ralph says, "Okay for you!"

In the Vallejo library, the regulars sit in their accustomed seats, reading newspapers and magazines. I'm in an alcove on the second floor, copying

Rembrandt's *Seated Nude Woman*. I'm frustrated. Rembrandt groans.

"*Norman. You've been pawing at the paper, attacking it like an enemy to be conquered. I suggest that you sit quietly, with your eyes closed, with no pencil in your hand, and think about drawing.*"

I go to the fountain, guzzle water, splash some on my face, sit down, and do as Rembrandt suggests. Drawing. What is it? Well, there's drawing blood out of a vein. There's drawing a wagon toward me by pulling on the handle. There are drawstrings, drawbridges, and dresser drawers. I get it! Instead of attacking the paper like an enemy, I should draw a pencil along its surface as tenderly as I draw my hand across Sharon's soft cheek.

At home, I use the side of a pencil to capture the gesture of Michelangelo's *Libyan Sibyl*. If I don't think about what I'm doing, if I let it happen, it works better. I copy Michelangelo's God and Adam from the *Creation of Adam* that's on the ceiling of the Sistine Chapel in the Vatican. My drawings of hands are improving, but my progress is slow. I can't see improvement from day to day, but when I put a drawing aside for a month and compare new work to old, there is a happy difference.

Art is constantly on my mind. Sitting on the john, I imagine figures and faces on the rough plaster of the bathroom walls like I did when I was a kid at Aunt Lilly's. Driving through the countryside, there are lions and elephants hidden in the crowns of trees. When I'm fishing, there are ships and islands in the clouds.

I open the book Henry and Lola gave me for my *bar mitzvah* more than six years ago. It's as worn as Uncle Irving's prayer book and has even more bookmarks sticking out from its pages. There's a self-portrait of Rembrandt, painted in 1652. His hands are on his hips, his face is serious, his voice is too pleasant. I know I'm in trouble.

"*Are you planning to live a thousand years?*"

"Why do you ask?"

"*Norman, you're young, and you don't understand that the clock is running. You insist upon wasting time. You don't have enough control to keep your watercolor palette clean or to adjust the amount of water on your brush and on your paper. While you wait for a wash to dry, you stand there, staring at the muddy paints on your palette instead of doing something constructive, like working on another painting that's dry.*"

As always, Rembrandt is right.

Ruth is getting weaker. Even though she doesn't ask for it, I give her more rent. Michael gets a job as a milkman. We take turns cooking. I follow a cookbook recipe for meatloaf. It looks good after one hour, but I cook it for two, because that's what the instructions say. I throw away the burnt meatloaf and the cookbook.

A green oxygen tank stands next to Ruth's bed, and plastic tubes are in her nostrils. I take away the cigarette she's just lit. She used to lift patients, but now she can't lift herself out of bed. Michael changes her nightgown and her bed. I cook oatmeal, bring it to her on a tray, make sure it's cool, and put the spoon to her mouth. She takes a little bit to please me. Carla does the laundry. Betty shops.

I've taken over the lease. Ruth's brother arranged for her and Michael to live with him and his family in Redwood City. Sharon helps me paint and decorate. It's nice without the cigarette smell. She buys me a dressmaker's manikin, colored flowerpots, and a big teddy bear. "Your fortune teller aunt was right. You're never too old for a teddy bear."

Michael calls to tell me that Ruth has passed away. At the funeral in Redwood City I'm self-conscious about speaking of how much she meant to me.

"Ruth gave me a good home for three years. She was like a mother. And I'm not talking about cooking and cleaning and laundry. She was interested in us. She was supportive. She wanted to hear what we had to say. We felt that our opinions counted. And if we had the wrong idea about something, she wouldn't raise her voice or shake her fist. She'd be soft and gentle. I will always remember her."

Betty and Carla share their memories of Ruth, but we can barely understand them, because they're crying.

Wearing a black ankle-length dress and a floppy black hat, Sharon poses in the living room on a modeling stand that she helped build. While drawing her in charcoal almost full-size, I imagine Henry behind me, correcting each unwise line, but there are fewer of those these days. Her hands are clasped in front, a silver bracelet encircles her wrist, and she's looking up with a dreamy expression. While painting Sharon in the manner of Robert Henri, her lips accentuated in bold strokes of red, I imagine Lola looking over my shoulder, correcting me as Henry did.

Today, a new model is coming, one of Betty's associates. Betty says she's Rubenesque. I hear her stomping flat-footed up the stairs.

"Hi, I'm Juanita."

In one motion, she whips off her green tent of a dress and lifts her ample body onto the stand. She's more grotesque than Rubenesque, a quivering mountain of flesh, fiftyish, five foot zero, four hundred pounds, with a pretty face, and pink breasts the shape of water balloons. I ask for twenty minutes of one-minute poses and suffer through them because Rembrandt told me to. There's barely enough time for me to capture gestures. When we drew one minute poses in Brooklyn, Henry's drawings were Michelangelos, Lola's were Käthe Kollwitzes, and mine were infantile scribbles. When I tried to crumple them up, Henry stopped me.

"These drawings are valuable. Keep them awhile, to gauge your progress."

Five-minute poses. Juanita is as graceful as a hula dancer, but she talks about crystals and herbs. It's distracting. I make her head too small. I ask for another minute, which isn't enough time to correct anything. After a break, I ask for ten-minute poses. Out of her bag of props, she pulls a baseball cap and silver pixie shoes. She grunts as she puts on the shoes. Her breasts overhang her bellybutton. I subdue her abdomen in my drawing but can't subdue her constant jabbering.

Betty and Carla bring up coffee and a bag of Scotty's Donuts. While I sharpen pencils, they look through my drawings.

"See how Norman's proportions have improved," Betty says.

"And the quality of his line. It's thick where the weight is and thin where the bone is closest to the skin."

I know they're only repeating what they've heard me say on occasion. On Juanita, there's no place where the bone is close to the skin. But I love listening. They're my family now. We finish our snacks, and Juanita poses for twenty minutes, wearing a tight fitting black and white dress with stripes beginning at the mid-line and going upward at thirty-degree angles to seams at her sides. It holds her mountain of flesh together and defines the contours of her breasts, massive thighs, and colossal butt. I do much better with longer poses.

Juanita changes into a nun's habit and looks as innocent as a Sister of Charity. "I was a novice thirty-one years ago."

"Why didn't you stay?"

"Because I like to f… because I couldn't sublimate my physical urges."

The last pose, reclining. She looks like a beached white whale wearing red gloves and a Phrygian cap like the one on Orozco's mural in Mexico City. She tells me more than I want to know about her quirky boyfriends, but I hope she'll pose for me again.

The next day, I draw Sherry, an associate of Carla, who works at the Yellow House on Branciforte Street. She plays the piano there when business is slow. She's as thin as my skeleton, and I don't have to guess where the muscles are in relation to bone. I invite her back week after week and can now draw her from memory in any pose. She says she'll look for a good used piano for me.

Dear Henry and Lola,

Thanks for the birthday card and the gift certificate. I can't believe I'm nineteen. Sharon started her sophomore year, majoring in sociology. Her parents still aren't crazy about me, but they did invite me to their seder. They hung my painting of Sharon in their living room and didn't skimp on the frame. I know they want more than a blue-collar worker for their daughter. Who can blame them?

When I don't have a model, I draw the skeleton over drawings I've already done of the models. With twine hanging from the hooks I put in the ceiling, I adjust the position of the skeleton's arms and legs to mimic the poses. It's helping.

I'm happy to hear that you're thinking about a trip to California. There's room here, and we're only an hour away from San Francisco, so don't even consider staying anywhere else. Sharon can't wait to meet you.

Norman

At the Vallejo post office on Marin Street, I pick up a cardboard carton from Aunt Ellie filled with Mother's music. I had written to Aunt Ellie months ago, asking her to send it, but never heard from her. A phone call got results.

Sherry tells me about a piano that's for sale, a 1918 Richmond upright grand, cherry wood, yellowed ivory keys, mellow sound. It's in a house two blocks away. I pay the $100 dollar asking price and hire a furniture mover to deliver it. Sherry gives me lessons. I'm finally playing an instrument and learning the exercises that are handwritten by Mother on the front of her J. S. Bach music sheet. It's fun working for evenness of touch, practicing the hardest passages first, practicing with each hand separately, and counting aloud the beats per measure. Mother has already marked the fingering. I practice an hour a day, and it's hard to quit. Bach's *Minuet in G*, and simplified versions of *Oh, What a Beautiful Morning* and *Summertime* are easy to play.

I get my high school diploma. Now, at Vallejo Junior College, I'm taking trigonometry, microbiology, creative writing and A Survey of English Literature. Professor Lesher is encouraging and inspiring. He assigns *Moll Flanders*, *The Return of the Native*, and *Emma*. In an assignment, I write that Emma overuses the words mortify, suffering, and evil to give a false sense of importance to the most trivial incidents or inconveniences. In Professor Lesher's writing class I describe my life in New York, New Jersey, and Vallejo. I should use Emma's words to describe my dealings with Melvin's mother, who I charged the bargain price of fifty dollars for wiring her poolside cabana. She paid me with a fifty dollar war bond that cost thirty-seven fifty and won't mature for ten years.

"Norman, you're the opposite of Jane Austen's Emma. You trivialize incidents that should enrage you."

"I am enraged. I've always been enraged. But I have a dilemma. When I took creative writing with Mrs. X, she told me to play down my feelings so the reader won't think of me as a fellow who constantly bemoans his fate. You know, poor me, poor me."

"Don't tell me her name. I already know who she is. Don't ever water anything down. You don't do that with your paintings, do you? By the way, I saw your one-man show downtown. The review in the paper was right on target. I know you admire the Expressionists, especially that angst-ridden, melancholic Egon Schiele. I saw his influence in the paintings of the skinny model. And the one of your brother? Fantastic! I was enraged when I saw it. With gesture and facial expression you portrayed the evil soul of that selfish bastard better than you do in twenty pages of prose."

After a year of reading classical English prose and poetry, I change into a new Norman and write poems about my life: *Peeing in Bed, Aunt Manya's Farsightedness, The Mountain View Diner*, and *Alligator Shoes*. It brings my demons to the surface. I'm my own exorcist.

Ralph is a pre-med student at Pacific Union College in Angwin, in Napa County. Allison is his steady girlfriend. We load my Ford with two tents, a volleyball net, surfcasting rods, and enough food for a two-night stay at Salmon Beach, north of Bodega Bay. I even brought a folding army shovel for digging holes to secure the poles for the volleyball net. Sharon and I trounce Ralph and Allison at volleyball.

Ralph and I catch six red-snappers and give two away. We won't have to eat frankfurters for dinner.

"Look what we caught."

"Very nice, boys, but how are we going to cook 'em?"

"A little olive oil, a little… "

"We don't have a stove or a grill or a frying pan," Allison says.

Sharon has it figured out. "We'll take Norman's folding shovel to the water and scour it with sand."

We clean the fish, build a driftwood campfire, and grill our catch on a shiny shovel that's flat and shallow and just the right shape for pouring off excess oil.

At the M.H. de Young Memorial Museum in San Francisco, Sharon and I head for Rembrandt's *Joris de Caullery*, painted in 1632.

"There's so much to learn. Look at Rembrandt's masterful use of light. Look how he captured the gleam of the metal."

"I can see why he's your favorite."

"I wish I could paint like that." Did I hear Rembrandt sigh? But he lets Sharon do the talking.

"Tell me, Norman, can you copy one square inch of the clothing on that figure?"

"Yes. I definitely can."

"What about one square inch of the face?"

"I believe I can do that, too."

"I know you can. What you've already done proves it. So why do you say you wish you could paint like that when you already can? Just paint one square inch at a time."

"It's more complicated than you think. You see, Rembrandt did all the work for me. He figured out the composition, the lighting, the tonality, the colors, what to emphasize, what to de-emphasize, and what to leave out."

"That makes sense. Otherwise, a camera would be better for recording a portrait or a landscape."

"You catch on fast. Lola said something like that once."

"I admire your passion for art."

"I'm passionate about everything I do."

"That's where your charm lies."

"It's nice to know I'm charming. But seriously, I hope I'm not boring you by going on about art."

"Not at all. I'm interested in what you have to say about it. I'm interested in what you have to say about other things, too."

"I'm happy to hear that. Let me tell you about my rubber band collection."

"With all this great art around us, I can see why you have a burning desire to become an artist. Watch out Renoir, and Rubens and Rembrandt. Here comes Norman!"

"That's kind of you to say, but I wouldn't be qualified to clean their brushes or sweep their studio floors."

"No, no, no," she says, waggling her finger. "Think positively."

"*Yes Norman, think positively. Examine my painting again. Notice that my background gradation is subtle, and the tonality of the figure is simple, yet exquisite. No picture book in the world can take the place of seeing the real thing. Do you think I had a value plan? Do you think I began the painting haphazardly, like you do sometimes? Why does it look alive? Why do the viewer's eyes go directly to the subject's eyes?*"

"Rembrandt's talking to you, isn't he?"

"He's giving me hell."

"*Norman, remember what Henry and Lola taught you? Don't neglect planes, movement, eye path, crossing lines, stops, arrows, texture. Consider the painting you've been struggling with for over two years, the one of your mother. You've been wasting your time trying to paint a photographic likeness. You already have a photograph. Review your notes. The information you need is all there.*"

We look at landscapes. I don't have to be in the same room with Rembrandt to hear him.

"*The thinking that goes into a painting is the same regardless of who the master painter might be. When you try to do the same things those landscape painters did, you must use the same tools you use for portraiture. Compare these works to ones you see in galleries at home, where you'll find subjects with no mood, no people, overemphasis of reflected light, too much color, too much pattern, too much contrast of warm and cool for their own sake.*"

As usual, when I come home from the de Young I'm invigorated, refreshed, eager to paint. I study my painting of Mother and see it differently. Rembrandt was right about it being a photographic likeness. I haven't been following his advice. I select another sidewalk photograph and start over with four thumbnail sketches of a three-quarter-length portrait of Mother in a sleeveless gray print dress with small white flowers. She looks demure in side view, her hands clasped at her waist, and her head tilted down and slightly to one side. I pick the first one, the best, and do a full-size sketch in charcoal on newsprint. I compare it to the failed painting of Mother, the one that Ruth and the girls thought was so great. I've eliminated the car and the building, which were distracting. Now, it's no longer a copy of the photograph.

I'm walking on air, as Cousin Sarah would say. I always feel this way after Rembrandt talks to me. But now he's standing behind me, cheering. Do Henry or Lola ever feel this way? I'll ask them in two weeks.

In Oakland, I buy expensive bristle brushes, Old-Holland paints, an 86-inch roll of Claessens portrait-grade Belgian linen, and I can't resist, a precious tube of Blockx vermilion paint. There goes another paycheck at this candy store for serious artists.

At home, I stretch an odd-sized canvas that's proportional to the dimensions of the photograph, and with brass artists' tacks, I attach it to homemade stretcher bars. This is going to be a wonderful painting.

Chapter 29

Train Trip

Sophie's son, Abraham, will be thirteen in two weeks, and I'll be part of the family that will be there for him, celebrating his *bar mitzvah*. I'll use up some of the vacation time I've accumulated at the Yard and ride the train to New York. It'll be nice to get away from the shipyard for a couple of weeks even though I'll miss Sharon. Since we've been going together, we've never been apart for more than three days, but she can't miss two weeks of school.

Three and a half days in each direction to paint! I'll take my traveling watercolor kit, twenty or thirty quarter-sheets of D'Arches watercolor paper, a plastic water bottle, extra blocks of color. I'll need a bigger suitcase and a bag for sketchpads, pencils, books, and a camera. I'll get traveler's checks, too.

Joey's studio apartment across the park from the Metropolitan Museum of Art will be the perfect place to stay. To celebrate my arrival, he bought tickets for us to see *The Pleasure of his Company* at the Longacre Theater.

With the money the Yellow House on Branciforte Street gave me for a portrait of their notorious establishment, I'll treat myself to a sleeping compartment.

The girls drive me to Martinez to catch the *City of San Francisco* to Chicago.

"Thanks to you, Norman, we're famous in quite a few bars in town."

"Strangers come up to us in stores and call us by name. You're Carla, the woman in the painting at the Farragut Club. You're Betty. I've seen your painting at the Golden Bubble."

"By the way, the Yellow House on Branciforte Street has offered us positions."

"Horizontal, I take it?"

"Naughty, naughty," Carla says, shaking her finger at me.

"Can we go with you? We can buy tickets on the train and pick up some business on the way."

"Imagine, *shtooping* cross country, customers in every state."

"We'll cut you in if you let us use your compartment."

"Anyway, we'd like to meet your *fekoktah* Aunt Manya. To see if she's as bad as you say."

"Yes, we'd like to meet the *ganse mishpockha*."

"And if business is slow on the train, we can have a *ménage à trois*."

"Thanks for the offer, but I'm happy with the *ménage à deux* with Sharon."

A horn blares in the distance. Red lights flash on and off, signal bells ring, black and white crossing gates come down. A huge yellow Diesel-electric streamlined locomotive, it's nose emblazoned with the red, white and blue Union Pacific shield, whooshes past followed by matching yellow cars with silver trucks, mist-gray tops and bottoms and scarlet striping between the grays and the yellow. I'm as ecstatic as I was the day I slid the green New York Central passenger car out of its box, as short-lived as that feeling of ecstasy was.

We hug goodbye.

"Call us when you get back, but not during working hours."

I climb aboard, find my compartment, and get settled in as the train approaches the black railroad bridge that crosses the Carquinez Strait between Martinez and Benicia. Out the right side of the train a barge towed by a tall red-and-white tugboat is heading upriver. Four fishing boats bounce in the tugboat's wake. We pass the gray Mothball Fleet of retired navy ships. We used to fish for sturgeon there on Mr. Mendoza's sixteen foot skiff, using ghost shrimp for bait, but never caught any.

My compartment has two facing seats that make into a bed. I pull up and out on a handle under the window, and I have a table to paint on, but what can I paint as the train is zooming across the flat Sacramento Valley?

We stop in Davis, the agricultural campus of the University of California, and I think of Sharon and life as a student. But I'm a student, too. I spend just as many hours a week studying master paintings.

After Sacramento, the train climbs the foothills of the Sierra, blowing its mournful horn at railroad crossings. The clackety-clack of the wheels and the side-to-side sway of the train remind me of the trolley car in Queens that took us to the cemetery. In the dining car, I sketch a couple at lunch, leaning toward each other, index fingers extended, almost touching, like God and Adam in Michelangelo's painting on the ceiling of the Sistine

Chapel. Between them is a green vase with a red rose.

Beyond Auburn, there are patches of snow on the ground. It's cozy in my compartment, painting the dining car scene in bright watercolor, suggesting the single rose that's more powerful than a dozen. In paintings, less is often more.

The train is winding its way up the mountains, but the swaying and vibration and the occasional thumps cause me to make a mess. What was I thinking of when I decided to paint on the train? But maybe it's good after all. It'll make me loosen up. Henry and Lola used to say I drill the lines on the paper with a dentist-like precision, like Dr. Bass when he's perfecting the margins of a tooth for a filling.

Icicles at snow shed entrances hang from wooden beams. From an empty compartment on the left side of the train, I snap pictures of Donner Lake below, shining silver in the sun. Trees are sprinkled with snow. The sky is clear cobalt blue. I wish Sharon were here to enjoy this.

At Truckee, I get out to stretch my legs. I'm wearing a heavy wool sweater under my jacket, but that doesn't keep me from shivering. The Donner Memorial is outside Truckee. I've been there with Sharon. A stone monument shows how high the snow was when forty-two people died in the blizzard in 1846-47.

The train pulls into Reno. Sharon and I drove here last month and played blackjack in overheated casinos surrounded by ka-chinging slot machines and air hazy from cigarette smoke. We ate lunch at the counter at the café in the Nevada Club. While she read, I drew everything I saw on a pocket-sized sketch pad. Busty cocktail waitresses, blackjack tables covered with green felt embossed with the club name, card dealers wearing white shirts and black string ties, stacks of red, white, blue, and silver chips. A James Cagney look-alike pit boss was overseeing the dealers and keeping his eye on a cigar-smoking gambler who was constantly counting and recounting, stacking and restacking his chips and winning. A new dealer took over, and the gambler's luck changed. There were enough scenes to keep me drawing for a lifetime. I wrote in color notes, and when I got home, I did a series of gambling paintings. Betty, Carla and Sharon are in many of them.

In the evening, we were about to leave a blackjack table with our small winnings when Sharon nudged me with her elbow. The man on her left was counting out fourteen one-hundred-dollar bills.

"Are you betting it all?" the dealer asked.

"Yes."

With the pit boss looking on and the gamblers around the table hushed, the dealer dealt him two face cards. He smiled. It was one of those ear-to-ear smiles. The dealer showed a pair of fours. She drew a three, a five, and another five for twenty-one. His wad was too thick to go down the slot at one time. I had the same metallic taste in my mouth as when Dad took my two hundred dollars.

Outside the compartment window is the dark Nevada desert and not a light in sight. The train rocks me to sleep, and I dream of Sharon.

On day two, I'm in the observation car, painting in watercolor the woman across the aisle. I can see every plane of her head. Her features are so chiseled that she looks like a living sculpture. She sees me painting her, smiles, and returns to her book. Beyond her window are Utah cliffs that nature has colored with a warm palette of burnt sienna, cadmium yellow, and red. Using these colors on my painting, I block in the planes of the woman's head with my biggest brush. Every major and minor plane gets only one brush stroke, and I make sure that the color contrast between planes is subtle. Such exquisite features. Long, thick jet-black hair blankets her shoulders. She has intelligent eyes, an aquiline nose, the perfect nose for her, and moist red lips, slightly down-turned, slightly pouting.

Now I know the excitement Rembrandt felt when he found the perfect model. I dip into a puddle of cadmium red and tone it down with water. I don't want her lips to overpower the portrait. I'll paint her hair with nine brush strokes. That's all. That's how many I need for Sharon's hair. I used to struggle with hair, but Rembrandt showed me how. He was also right about me being too tight. The unsteady train has enhanced the quality of my work. I'm right on track.

I doze off in the hypnotic embrace of the swaying car and dream that my painting is the centerpiece of an important Manhattan art exhibit. I'm dressed in the new clothes Sharon helped me pick out for the trip. She's at my side, wearing a stunning black dress. Her engagement ring sparkles. A waiter walks through the crowded gallery with a tray of champagne. We clink glasses, take a sip, and our lips touch just as the painting is unveiled. It's called *Woman on the Train*.

The dining car steward comes through, announcing lunch. The woman's gone. Did I only dream her? But there's her painting on the seat beside me, her face captured forever in watercolor.

I walk through the train to the dining car, holding onto the passage-way walls for balance. The steward takes me to my table and seats me across from *Woman on the Train*.

"You're the artist across the aisle from me," she cackles, exposing teeth with black holes.

"Happy to meet you. I'm Norman."

"I'm Veronica," she cackles again and offers me a strong hand with cracked nails. She dog-ears her pulp-fiction paperback, puts it aside, and bores me all through my meal.

I change trains on day three in Chicago. There's not enough time to go to the Chicago Art Institute to see Edward Hopper's *Nighthawks*. I want to put my nose right up to the painting and see how he handled green. I'll do that on another trip, hopefully with Sharon.

By Grand Central Station on day four I have enough paintings in my luggage for a one-man show. I take a taxi to Joey's, leave my suitcase with the super, and ride the subway to Brooklyn. On my walk to Aunt Manya's from the Saratoga Avenue station, I pass barred windows, yards strewn with trash, and restaurants that advertise chitlins and tamales instead of knishes or gefilte fish. Gibalowitz's drugstore is a second-hand store.

Aunt Manya's apartment is as spotless as ever. She let's me hug her.

"Norman, they don't have stamps in California? You begrudge me an occasional letter?"

"I'm here in person, it's better than a letter."

"Always an answer, always, for everything."

Uncle Irving comes home from *shul*. We hug. "This wine is for you. Zinfandel."

"Norman brought it all the way from Napa Valley, in California."

"Thank you, Norman."

Footsteps on the stairs.

"I called everybody to tell them you're here."

My cousins and their spouses and children waltz in the door. Hand-shakes, hugs, kisses. The children are allowed to play in the living room. Things have changed. The kitchen table is full of *nosherai*: pastrami, corned beef, mustard from Gussie's deli, rye bread, pumpernickel, pickled herring, *mandelbrot*, apple turnovers from Berman's, and halvah.

Nathan opens some folding chairs. "Here, sit, eat, enjoy. I know in

California you don't have pastrami and rye like in Brooklyn."

Everyone fires questions at me.

"So how's California?"

"Great."

You see any movie stars?"

"No. They're in Southern California."

"You're still a Yankee fan?"

"Of course."

"Have you been on that curvy street in San Francisco?"

"Lombard Street. Yes. We'll go there when you come visit."

"Are you really an electrician on atomic submarines?"

"Yes."

"So you're not going to a university to make something of yourself?"

"Stop, Papa," Sarah says. "Norman's an electrician. That's making something of himself."

"Have you seen your friend Joey yet? He went to an art academy. He draws fashion ads for Bloomingdales."

"I'm staying with him in Manhattan. We're going to a play tomorrow."

"So tell me Norman, in California, you have a lady friend?"

"Yes. She lives in Oakland."

"Jewish?"

"Mama, leave Norman alone. What's the difference what his girlfriend is?"

"You see your father? I hear he's still living in the Bronx with the witch."

"Manya, enough already," Uncle Irving says.

"You're still staying by your friend, Michael?"

"Michael's mother died. I took over the lease."

"May she rest in peace," everyone says.

"You can't stay by your brother? With Melvin?"

"He made me leave his home."

"A fine brother he is. As bad as his father. He couldn't keep you there until you at least finished high school? He should only roast in hell."

This time, that expression works for me.

Joey is six foot two and wears a suit and tie. In the morning he reheats the potato pancakes his mother carefully wrapped in wax paper and foil for me to take to him so we could eat a proper breakfast. "Take this, too," she said last night. "How can you eat *latkes* without sour cream?"

Joey shows me his studio, introduces me to Cliff and Roger, fellow illustrators. A model in brassiere and panties is posing. Joey doesn't need his deck of French cards anymore. I draw the model in three-quarter view, then draw Joey drawing the model. We have lunch at the Carnegie Deli. I order a bagel and lox, the only decent one I've had since I left Brooklyn. We don't have to talk about our work. We've done that in letters.

"Remember when Seymour and I scared the shit out of you before your appointment with Dr. Bass?"

"Remember when you were making sound effects while drawing airplanes, and our teacher, what's her name, oh yes, Mrs. Frankl with the hairy arms. She sent us to Mrs. Hartman's room. You were shaking."

"What about the time you picked that cigarette butt off the sidewalk with your shoe? My mother couldn't wait to tell the world about that."

"I'll never forget the little eight-paged books you tried to copy. You looked so pitiful with ink all over your hands and all over the books."

"And if it wasn't for you being an expert at pornographic drawing, I would have gotten beat up for sure."

I'll spend today and tomorrow at museums. The Frick Mansion on Fifth Avenue is the grandest house I've ever been in, with an enclosed courtyard, rich oriental carpets, and masterpieces in every room. I'm fascinated by the face of the great master, painted in 1658. Rembrandt has a self-satisfied smirk, barely masking his explosive nature. He's wearing a golden tunic, and he looks like a king, sitting on his throne.

"Look at me in the oriental finery I bought at a flea market in Amsterdam. Looks expensive, doesn't it? So what if my house is filled to bursting with extravagant art props? Didn't you buy a skeleton? Didn't you buy a costly tube of Blockx vermilion? Art comes first."

Was he really speaking to me? Yes, he was, as clearly as Mozart speaks to composers and Shakespeare speaks to playwrights.

I feel confident walking north on Fifth Avenue to the Metropolitan Museum of Art. I climb a long staircase to the lobby and another one to the Rembrandts. I don't see any of the guards I knew when I lived in the

Bronx and took the subway to the museum on Sundays. I spend a long time with Rembrandt, unable to walk away from his self-portrait, a loaner from London, where he's holding a mahlstick, brushes, and a palette. Layers of transparent paint make the surface vibrant. His voice sounds like Grandfather's.

"It's nice of you to visit me at the Met, too. Now move on so someone else can see. Just kidding, Norman. Don't look so sad. You take everything seriously. Lighten up. Have fun. Look at the work of other masters. Learn how Manet, Goya, and Eakins handle the very problems you're faced with in your mother's portrait."

I wander through the museum, studying every painting in the artistic spectrum: Photo-realism, Illustration, Expressionism, Abstraction, and Non-Objectivism. I don't want my work to look like a photograph. I want to create an illusion of reality. Some Abstraction is too whimsical to suit me. Rembrandt wants me to be less serious, but I don't think he wants me to be this much less serious.

"Correct, Norman. I want to see emotion, poetry, character, and symbolism. My work is in the middle of the artistic spectrum. If your work tends toward the abstract, with distortion, decoration, and pattern, it will still be acceptable. Although I have nothing against non-objectivism, which relies almost totally on shape, color, space, and design, I'd like to see it only in your underpaintings, not in your finished work."

I go to some of my favorites, *The Horse Fair*, Sargent's *Madame X*, Hals' paintings. I'm crazy about Hals' portraits. Am I in trouble with Rembrandt again?

"Don't look so guilty. I'm not insulted that you're studying Hals. He's highly underrated, you know, yet he's one of the best portraitists. Too bad for him that he's my contemporary. His work follows the same criteria mine does, but by and large, his work is too gay, too flamboyant. I don't care to capture momentary expression, but I do admire his flashy, spontaneous brushwork. You need a little of that in your work, Norman. And by the way, you're not quite ready to begin painting your mother's portrait. When you get home, study Hals' brushwork and his handling of warm and cool. Study Rubens and El Greco. See how they handle their underpaintings. And don't forget Chardin. He knows how to move the eye. When you have mastered their techniques, then you will be ready for your mother's portrait."

I take a bus to Harlem, where I have a date with some very important people.

Next day I'm in my compartment, heading west on the train, painting watercolor studies from the Hals book I bought at the Metropolitan Museum of Art. What a find! Hals' *Civic Guard Portrait Groups* with color details of hands and faces. I've been hyped-up ever since getting advice straight from Rembrandt's lips. What a blessing! I'm glad I went east for Abraham's *bar mitzvah*.

CHAPTER 30

ART HAPPENS

I'm back on the Yard, in a submarine, bent over a gray electric panel. It's cold on the Building Ways where ships are constructed then launched with the crack of a Champagne bottle. My jacket's zipped tight. They can't pump in enough warm air to heat the area around these massive gray ICBM launching tubes. Shop 64 hasn't yet glued thick cork insulation to the skin of this new nuclear sub.

Other electricians are shouting to be heard over the blowing, sucking, clanking, banging, buzzing, and ringing machinery. On the deck above, a machinist is using a screaming pneumatic grinder to smooth a steel hatch cover. He's been bluing it and grinding it for hours. And there are hissing air ducts, whining electric motors, whirring fans, and the warning whistles of riggers as they guide a heavy electric generator through an opening in the deck.

Now welding sparks are falling on me.

"Hey, I'm working here," I yell up and bang my forehead on an electric panel. Karl says I must wear my hardhat, but then I can't get close enough to the panel to do the work.

One more cable to go. I slice through the braided metal armor and the thick plastic outer sheath, peel them off, and tape the cut end of the armor with black electrician's tape. Frayed armor is wicked stuff. It'll rip the skin off your hand if you're not careful. Sid, at the next panel, has a bandage across his palm. Now I pull the cable into the panel and secure it with a screw-on clamp. The cable is as big around as a silver dollar, with forty-eight individually insulated, color-coded conductors inside. No wonder they checked me for color-blindness at the Mare Island Employment Office. The first ten colors are black, brown, red, orange, yellow, green, blue, violet, gray and white. I'll never forget my instructor's mnemonic for memorizing them: bad boys rape our young girls but violet gives willingly.

The conductors are covered with a sticky substance we call monkey shit, which protects them from rotting, moisture, and gnawing rats. I unwind them, wrap a length of waxed twine around each one, and pull the twine along its length, ridding each wire of a grape-sized glob of monkey shit. By the time I've cleaned a day's worth of conductors, I have gallons of gray monkey shit. After it dries for a couple of days it loses some of its medicinal smell and stickiness and is perfect for sculpting.

Everyone knows when it's break time, even men without watches deep in the bowels of a submarine where you can't tell night from day. The incessant background noise of machinery is still there, but all working noise stops. The guy grinding the hatch cover knows when to stop. Maybe it's his stomach that tells him.

Today, I don't climb up three levels of compartments, squeeze out of a hatch crowded with hoses and cables, and walk down five levels of wood scaffolding to go through the rain and wind to the canteen to stand in line to buy a cup of coffee and a doughnut. Instead, I fling a gallon-sized glob of monkey shit onto the side of the closest ICBM launching tube and press it on tight. It looks like half of a small watermelon.

Monkey shit doesn't handle as well as clay, but it'll do. I've had lots of practice on other submarines. I've memorized Sid's crew-cut hair, bulbous nose, bug eyes, and receding chin. By the end of the coffee break I've produced a sculpture that looks like him although his facial features are barely developed. By the end of the second break, I have a completed sculpture that would make Henry proud. Subtle planes, texture, nuance. It looks alive. How did it happen so fast? Maybe because I didn't think about it. I just did it. Art from shit! I cover it with a shop towel.

Karl comes by on one of his daily rounds. "What's hiding under there? It couldn't be one of Norman's monkey shit creations, could it?" With thumb and index finger he lifts a corner of the towel, grinning like a child playing peek-a-boo. He flips it aside and studies my work from all angles, like a patron in a museum. "Your art work has improved since you made journeyman. That's an incredible likeness of Sid... Norm, you're wasting your life on the Yard. You should be an artist full-time."

"That would be great, but I have to make a living."

"That shouldn't be a problem. What about those paintings you sold to the Farragut Club?"

"I got lucky, Karl."

At the end of the shift, I catch Sid pressing his fingers into my sculpture, ripping out huge chunks, making shit out of art. I was going to pry it off and take it home. It was good enough to cast in bronze.

"Having fun, asshole? How would you like it if I pulled your face apart? Maybe I should start right now on that clown nose of yours. Maybe I should make you eat this monkey shit."

His bug-eyes are wide open. "Sorry Norm. I was afraid if one of the big muck-a-mucks saw it, I'd get fired for fucking off on the job."

"You do fuck off a lot. You could be fired without my help."

Dear Henry and Lola,

Thanks again for taking me on a grand tour of Harlem. The show at the Apollo was great, and so was the restaurant. Now I'm a jazz fan and a soul-food fan, too.

It was hard to go back to work at the shipyard. The pay is good, but working eight hours a day at a job that isn't creative isn't for me.

Sharon and I took a leisurely drive down the coast last week, stopping at every lighthouse, waterfall, state park, and scenic over-look along the way. At the Los Angeles County Museum of Art we saw a fantastic bronze, a brooding, bat-winged Satan, by Jean-Jacques Feuchère. It was just thirty-one inches high, but it was so powerful that each time I tried to walk away from it, it drew me back. I wish you could have seen it. The figure was sitting in the shelter of its clawed wings. The pose, the expression, it all worked. Everything I learned from you, Henry, was obvious on that sculp-ture. Each detail from top to bottom presented as form over form, right down to the beast's talons. Sharon grabbed my arm when she saw it.

On the ten-hour drive home I did a sculpture of Sharon in my head! I fabricated the wire armature, rolled the clay into hotdog size chunks, built up Sharon's nude torso, and modeled her skull and her facial features. I did everything you taught me in Brooklyn and could even feel the moist, red clay. It may sound weird but so is talking to Rembrandt.

At home, in quarter-size, I worked on the sculpture in real life while Sharon sat on the piano bench, torso slightly twisted to the left, head more to the left, right foot forward, left foot back. The piano bench was on a lazy Susan like yours. I turned Sharon and my sculpture every fifteen minutes but hardly had to look at her. I didn't even use calipers.

Sharon says hello. She feels as if she knows you. She's taking piano lessons from Sherry, my skinny model, and is already much better than I am.

Be well.

Norman

Sharon and I are sitting across from each other in a booth in Spenger's, our favorite seafood restaurant in Berkeley. Dark wood, glass enclosed models of ships, portholes, and nautical pictures are everywhere. After we finish our grilled salmon, I excuse myself, go out to my car, and come back with a silver box with a red bow that's too big to fit in my pocket.

"This is for you."

She pulls off the bow and opens the box. Inside is a smaller gift-wrapped box, then a smaller one yet. She knows what's inside the last box.

"It fits perfectly. It's so beautiful. You're so beautiful. I love you, Norman."

She comes to my side of the booth and kisses me.

"I love you, Sharon."

Our waitress comes over. "I was watching. Congratulations. Here's two glasses of Beaulieu Pinot Noir on the house. Wow, what a rock. "

"Mom and Dad won't be thrilled, but they'll get over it. They know it was inevitable. I told them I'd marry you no matter what you do for a living."

Dear Henry and Lola,

I'm glad you like the photos of the sculpture of Sharon. We were reluctant to show it to her parents, but when we finally did, they insisted on paying to have it cast in bronze! Maybe if I show them photographs of my living room carpet, that's full of paint and clay, they might pay for a new one. I hope the landlord doesn't visit.

I was thumbing through a Rubens book and found a full-page detail of the face of a painting I'd never seen before, Old Woman with Pan of Coals. It had the same effect on me as that sculpture by Jean-Jacques Feuchère. It wouldn't let me turn the page. It said, "Paint me. Paint me now." So I propped the book up next to my easel, picked up an eight-by-ten canvas and tinted it with a gray made by mixing ivory black, flake white and a few drops of drying agent so I could work alla prima as you suggested. For me alla prima is a tough process, especially with models that won't sit still. The colors turn muddy if I don't wait for the under-colors to dry. Usually I struggle with features, especially lips, where a millimeter makes the difference between a good likeness and a bad one, but this portrait was haunting, irresistible.

I squeezed out my colors: lead white, burnt sienna, cerulean blue, ultramarine blue, yellow ochre, alizarin crimson. Without laboring over proportions, or the distance between the eyes, I placed the lights, the mids, and the darks but didn't go too light or too dark. I paid attention to differences. One eye was different from the other. One side of the mouth was different from the other. I expected to struggle, but everything came quickly and easily. I mixed burnt sienna and ultramarine blue to make the darkest darks and used pure lead white for the highlights. I started at six in the evening, and by one in the morning, it looked as lifelike as the picture in the book. Oblivious to the passage of time and the difficulties of oil painting, I had some sort of runner's high.

You're right as usual. One should be deeply moved by a subject, or it's not worth sculpting or painting.

My Rubens copy was hung at an art show in town and signed Norman, after Rubens. I liked it enough to put a high price on it, $400, so no one would buy it, but a man bought it and said it was a bargain. I've been sad ever since, not because I can't paint another one, but because the painting was done under some sort of magic spell in which Rubens was guiding my hand. At least that's what I'd like to think. I hope Rembrandt isn't jealous, but he did say that it was all right to study other masters.

These days, I seldom have to erase a line or struggle with the placement of an eye or an ear. My proportions are better. So is my color mixing. I've come a long way—thanks to you two.

It's nice to hear that Aunt Manya is a little friendlier toward you. She's friendlier toward me, too. Sharon says she's mellowing with age. Sharon's parents are mellowing, also. They'd better, because Sharon has an engagement ring. There's going to be a wedding. Now you'll have to come to California.

Thanks for all you've done for me,
Norman

I'm still mad at Sid for destroying my sculpture, but it would have had to come down sooner or later. So what! I can sculpt another one anytime, but not of him.

Other pathetic characters work at the Yard. Many of them are in my sketchbook. Junior, the stock market whiz, has a reputation for throwing switches that are red-tagged while he searches for the circuit he's working on. One night, I catch him at it and slap the head of a crescent wrench into my leather-gloved palm.

"Junior, you stupid son-of-a-bitch, one of these days you're going to kill someone!"

"No one was working on that circuit."

"You're wrong as usual. I was." I slap the wrench harder.

"Sorry Norm. It won't happen again."

I report it to Karl.

"Norm, I chewed out Junior and had him shaking in his boots. I told him that if he ever touches a red-tagged switch again, he'll be packing bulkhead tubes until he retires. I don't know why he's even working. When he opened his locker to put his hard hat away there was a pile of un-cashed paychecks on the shelf a quarter inch thick. The guys say he's a millionaire."

Homer pesters people for their pocket change. When he finds a collectable coin, he makes an even trade, then says, "Wow, this penny is worth twenty-five cents." The gang has quit letting him examine change, but he never runs out of new workers to annoy.

Larry the rigger is an ex-heavyweight boxer who knits. No one makes fun of him. Under his yellow Shop 72 hardhat is a nasty scar.

"It was the first round," he once explained, "and those punches hurt too much. Blood was running down my face. I knocked the bastard out. Broke his jaw before the ref could call a TKO on me. My trainer asked the ref to take the guy's gloves off. He was wearing knucks."

"Well, you must have been a good boxer. Your nose is still straight."

"I wish I stayed with boxing. I coulda trained fighters. I coulda had my own gym."

Tony the pipefitter sings *La Donna e Mobile* while he brazes pipes in the engine room. When he isn't singing, his voice is rough, but when he's belting out an aria, it's smooth and clear. "Ya know, Norm, I shoulda gone to the conservatory when I had the chance."

I hear a lot of couldas and shouldas from guys who dream about the life they might have led had reality not intervened. They jab me with their disappointments.

And there's me, working eight hours a day at a job I don't like.

I still hear Aunt Manya lecturing to me over a cup of tea and apple turnovers from Berman's Bakery in Flatbush. I was thirteen then, a man.

"Look at Mr. Gibalowitz, Dr. Bass, Dr. Apfel. You should take their example, Norman."

"Aunt Manya, I want to be a painter like Mother."

Her face reddens. "Painting is a waste of time."

"I don't agree. Did Rembrandt waste his time? Did Rubens? Did Raphael?"

"You're not Rembrandt or Rubens or that other name you mentioned."

"But I'm me. My painter friends say I have a God-given talent for art."

She raises both fists in the air. "The *Schvartze* he listens to, not his aunt!"

"Henry says that nothing compares to the pursuit of Art."

"Art, schmart. I'm tired of listening to you already. You're making a mistake. You'll wind up like your father."

"I'll go to art school. If I can learn to paint as good as Mother I'll be happy."

"Well, it's your life to waste."

I thought I hated Aunt Manya then, but now I'm sure she meant well. Dr. Apfel was a great healer. He treated Mrs. Katzman's arthritis, Aunt

Manya's nervous breakdown after Mother died, and Fat Annie's asthma. But with his hands, all he did was thump fingers on my back, press a cold stethoscope on my chest, and write prescriptions. Mr. Gibalowitz was precise in weighing powders and filling prescriptions, but the most exciting thing I ever saw him do was remove a speck of dirt from my eye with a Q-tip. It's Dr. Bass, though, who made the biggest impression on me. He was a good healer like Dr. Apfel and as precise as Mr. Gibalowitz. His crowns and dentures were works of art. And he had fun while he worked.

Aunt Manya certainly had a point. But I don't want to follow her dream. All I want is to pick up Mother's art where she left off. Yet, here I am in a submarine, sculpting faces with monkey shit.

"What the hell are you doing on the Yard, Norm?" Karl asks for the thousandth time as he hands me work orders. "You've been here, what, six years now? You should be applying to art schools. I've heard they have some good ones in San Francisco and Oakland. Surely scholarships are available for someone with your talent. Leave this shit hole. You're an artist, for Christ's sake."

I don't think of Mare Island as a shit hole, especially since I earn a steady government paycheck. I complete the jobs on my work orders in half the estimated times printed on them. Then I hide out to study. I often rip out chapters from my Vallejo College textbooks, staple the pages together, and slip them into the back pocket of my coveralls. Today, I'm studying for a philosophy test. But university life will have to wait. I have to work here. How else can I afford to eat and paint and make payments on Sharon's one-carat blue-white gem-quality solitaire?

CHAPTER 31

SPARRING WITH REMBRANDT

At the Met, Rembrandt spoke to me about other masters in the present tense. I refer to them that way too. Why not? They'll always be alive. I took his advice and studied how Rubens, Hals and El Greco handle underpaintings and warms and cools. Their work has depth. Surfaces vibrate. Faces look alive. So will Mother's.

I learned that a museum restorer had cleaned a purported El Greco self-portrait too aggressively, removing several layers of paint from the top of the head. Photographs of this accident gave me a valuable peek at the layers of the underpainting. X-ray studies, accidents—every piece of information is important. I'm Sherlock Holmes with Grandpa's giant magnifying glass, looking for clues in every painting and every book about art.

It's time to paint without thinking about how the masters handle painting problems. That information is in my head, heart, hands, and soul.

Sharon is curled up in bed, her angel face pressed softly into my pillow, like in a Mary Cassatt painting. So that the turpentine won't give us headaches, I've opened wide every window in the house. It's seven a.m. The fog over Mare Island is lifting, letting the Saturday morning light through. I turn my back to the shipyard and face the canvas.

I uncap tubes of burnt sienna, ultramarine blue, and lead white, squeeze them out on a glass palette, and swirl them together in turpentine with a large round bristle brush. This gives a neutral gray to scumble onto the white canvas. So that the background won't be boring, I leave it blotchy. I want the upper left corner of the canvas to be cool, so I add a little more blue there, and as I work my way over to the opposite corner, I add burnt sienna for warmth. I look at it from the window, eight feet away, then walk back to adjust the warms and cools. In an hour, this thin first coat will be dry, but I'm not going to sit around. There are paintings in the studio in various stages of completion, a sculpture of Sharon to finish, library novels, and my poem, *Egg Cream*, waiting for its final touches. Professor Lesher says writing poetry is cathartic, it lets me exorcise my demons, like when I wrote about Dad handing the pawnshop owner money to bet on a horse. Painting is cathartic, too. I was honored when the Golden Bubble bought the Daumier-like painting of Melvin, the shoe salesman, looking up a woman's dress. It won first prize at an art show in Oakland, which didn't surprise me, based on the reputation of the judge.

A tiny photograph of Mother is taped to my new crank-up wooden easel. Her face is fuzzy, but since everyone in my family says I look exactly like she does, like she did, I'll give her my face. I've done enough self-portraits, so I won't have to look in a mirror. I'll paint in an imaginary background and light her face the way Rembrandt lit his subjects. There aren't any useful shadows in the photograph. I'll put in my own.

I dip a small round brush into a puddle of thinned burnt umber and stand in front of the canvas, clearing my mind like a concert pianist does before he begins to play. Now, with one rapid slash of paint, I capture the position of the backbone and the slight twist of the figure. I exaggerate the pose. If I don't, the figure will straighten itself out as the painting proceeds and look stiff. I rough in the torso, the oval of the head, the pelvis, and the weight-bearing leg. Working with the skeleton and with Grant's *Atlas of Anatomy* has helped me visualize insertion points of muscles. I rough in the arms and the hands and stand back. My marks are in the right places. That's enough drawing with the brush.

Sharon is in the kitchen, cooking an omelet. Coffee is perking on the stove. The cooking odors, the painting odors, doing what I've been born to do, sharing life with the woman I love—this is heaven. I turn on the phonograph and load it with a stack of classical records. Before slicing sourdough French bread, I wash my hands thoroughly since I've handled lead paint. While a Tchaikovsky piano concerto is playing, we eat breakfast silently at the table, reading the *San Francisco Chronicle*, as if we're already married. She'll have the day to study for exams. I'll have the day to paint.

Sharon looks over my shoulder. "You're painting rectangles, aren't you?

"Guilty as charged."

"Why those particular ones?"

"Well, Mother's upper arm is long and calls attention to itself, so I de-emphasize it by leading the eye away. I do it by crossing the arm with rectangles that join the arm to the background. Aren't you glad you asked?"

"You're not boring me if that's what you mean. I really do want to know the technical stuff."

"Okay, you asked for it, but I don't think technical is the right word. With me, it's feelings."

"So what exactly are you doing?"

"I'm painting a figure against an imaginary background, but I try not to look at it as a figure or a background, only as warm or cool monochromatic masses that I make lighter or darker. The masses are composed of barely visible overlapping planes made up of points and lines that give depth to the work. They're also responsible for movement, even the speed of movement of the viewers' eyes. I try to develop these masses evenly. I don't put a mark on the canvas unless it makes something happen, and when something isn't right, it grates on me. The most frustrating part is deciding what to emphasize, what to de-emphasize, and what to leave alone. Understand?"

"You know, Norman, I really do. It's like you're a choreographer devising dance steps for a ballet. "

By the next Saturday the forehead, cheeks, nose, and hands are underpainted in lead white made warmer, lighter, brighter, and thicker so they'll stand out. The darker cooler areas are thin and transparent so they'll recede. The image appears on the canvas like a developing Polaroid film and is beginning to look like Mother.

After breakfast, Sharon waves in front of me a copy of the tiny picture of Mother that's taped to my easel. "I took this photograph to antique clothing shops in Berkeley, Oakland, and San Francisco, and no one could come up with anything close to your mother's dress. I tried theatrical costume houses, too. No luck. But look at this." She pulls a dress out of a bag. It's identical to the one mother wore.

"I showed the picture to my mom, and she headed straight to the attic. It was in an old steamer trunk. I didn't want to give it to you when I came in last night. Knowing you, I'd have to pose with it on 'till three in the morning."

Sharon stands in the fragile silk dress, posed to match the picture, and I render the flowered fabric that was fuzzy in the photograph. I paint the dress with a low tonal contrast that's indistinguishable from the background when I squint. This is the right effect.

Sharon's hands, which are holding a small book, won't be difficult to paint. Rembrandt said, *"Don't think about hands at all. Paint the tones and the shapes you see, and if you start to think about hands or fingers, stop. And don't fall into the trap of creating too much detail, or you'll lose feeling."*

I paint the hands his way and they magically appear. And they're large, like his paintings of women's hands, to show power. Darks that separate the fingers are lightened, because the separation has to be subtle. This must be a perfect monochromatic painting before color is added.

In the afternoon, our crowd is gathered in our kitchen for a big Italian feast.

"Sharon, the meat-balls, the sauce, everything is cooked just right."

"Thank you, Betty."

"Your spaghetti is as good as my mother's, and she was born in Sicily."

"Thank you, Carla."

"The Caesar salad's terrific, too. Did you have to leave out the garlic?"

"A favor for the girls."

"Yes, Norman. It was a business decision."

"With your cooking, we'll never be able to tear him away from you."

"Tough luck, girls. You should have taken lessons."

"Not to change the subject," Carla says, "but Norman's been painting his mother for weeks. When will he be done?"

"Why don't you ask him? He's sitting right next to you."

"She's playing like she's my aunt, talking to me without addressing me. I hope she's having fun, more fun than I'm having, struggling with the painting."

"What are you talking about, struggling? It's a perfect likeness," Betty says.

"Something doesn't feel right. I don't know what it is, but I'll figure it out eventually."

I consider all my works studies, which make the mistakes easier to bear. When I turn the painting of Mother to the wall and come back days later, I see things I overlooked. A shadow under the nose needs to be lighter, a shadow behind the ear, darker. I tone down a distracting highlight on the chin. But something still bothers me. Sharon hears me mumbling.

"What's wrong now?"

"The book's too intellectual. It's not helping the picture."

"Well, what if it's a book on poetry?"

"How will the viewer know?"

"Identify the book."

"No, that's too trite. Anyway, the shape, it's too harsh. It doesn't work. A rose in her hands would say love."

"Isn't it too late to change anything?"

"It's never too late."

"These are the most beautiful hands I've ever seen you paint. They look as good from across the room as they do up close. Are you sure you want to paint them out? And the book? And part of the dress?"

"I know it's a major change, but it has to be done. Didn't Rembrandt repaint his *Danae*? He repainted her hand, her arm, and her face! What did he care about how long it took or how painstaking the alteration would be?"

It takes two Saturdays to take out the book, restore the flowered pattern of the dress behind the book and repaint the hands in their new position. You'd need an X-ray to see the changes.

It's time for color! Using viridian, cerulean, yellow ochre, French ultramarine, cadmium orange, and cadmium red, I glaze on thin transparent washes, layer upon layer, making sure what's underneath shows through. It takes a few seconds to apply a glaze but hours to dry. That's okay. I'll practice the piano, Bach's *Minuet in G*, then work on my bawdy poem, *The Yellow House on Branciforte Street*.

I make sure that light comes to the viewer's attention first, then color, middle tones, and dark tones. If color pulled attention away from the light, there would be a burnt look to the painting, but I'm not going to let that happen.

Since Mother's left eye is unclear in the photograph, I'll have to use my eye as a model. With a round magnifying mirror clamped to my easel I see my eye straight on, but it can be rotated to three-quarter view in my mind. With burnt umber I paint in the shadowed iris and use solid black for the pupil. One brushstroke of dark for the upper eyelid. One stroke of a lighter tone for the lower lid. Light bluish-gray for the white of the eye. Four more strokes of increasingly dark gray as the cornea turns toward the nose and dissolves into darkness. My eye becomes Mother's eye. The iris is a deep, dark, syrupy pool achieved after a dozen layers of glazes.

The final highlights on the forehead, nose, and chin are tricky. I paint them in, but they're not right. Out they come with the help of a palette knife and the corner of a rag dipped in turpentine. In they go again, but something else isn't quite right. The red on her lips is too insistent. A darker red on the V-neck of the dress will pull attention away from the lips. In her clasped hands, I paint a red rose. For a moment I think, "That's it." But no, she needs something more, and I'm not sure what. Very frustrating. I lift the painting off the easel and turn it to the wall. Maybe fresh ideas will come in a day or two.

At Mare Island, Karl sets his coffee cup on the cafeteria table next to the philosophy pages that I've torn from my textbook. He sits next to me.

"I've won a scholarship to the University of California. I'll be leaving the Yard next month."

"Congratulations. It's about time you're going to art school."

"I'm taking courses to get into dental school."

"I thought you wanted to be an artist, not that you aren't one already."

"That's the point, Karl. No teacher could possibly be harder on me than Rembrandt."

On the wall behind the bar in The Golden Bubble on Sacramento Street are reclining nudes of Betty and of Carla done in the manner of Velazquez. On a side wall are standing figures of Juanita, my Rubenesque model, and of Sherry, my skinny one. *Greed*, which won first prize at the

Solano County Fair, is on another wall. It depicts a many-armed, green-faced, cigar-smoking Melvin clutching his fully-loaded station wagon, a metal-winged Cessna, a pink piggy bank, a load of fancy dresses from his mother's store, and a handful of deeds to her properties. For some reason, Melvin is no longer a customer here.

Betty, Carla, Sharon and I enter the private back room, which is festooned with blue and gold crepe paper, the colors of the University of California. Michael and Ralph and their girlfriends are here. Karl is here with my friends from the shipyard, including Sid, the sculpture destroyer, whom I can't stay mad at. Professor Lesher is helping himself at a buffet table piled high with Caesar salad, roasted vegetables, baked potatoes, chicken, prime rib and French bread from Passini's bakery. Juanita, dressed in a polar bear-sized white tunic and chef's hat, carves a thick slab of prime rib and places it on his plate. Sherry is at the piano, playing Scott Joplin's *The Entertainer*.

We sit and eat at one huge table while the piano plays by itself. Sherry pours Cabernet Sauvignon and Pinot Noir from Beringer's in Napa Valley. Everyone is talking and gesturing. It's like I'm back in Brooklyn. But Napa Valley is where Sharon and I want to live someday.

"Dr. Bass must have made some impression on him."

"Maybe it was Dr. Payne, the dentist in Mountain View."

"They should trade names. Dr. Bass should be Dr. Payne."

"In Napa, there's a physician named Dr. Slaughter."

"Well, I personally will never go to any of them," Sid says. "Hey, Norm, how come you changed your mind about going to art school?"

"He doesn't need to," Sharon says. "He's been trained by the best artist in the business."

"Huh? Who, Norm?"

"Sid, I've been studying with Rembrandt."

"With him? He died a few hundred years ago."

"He's still alive," Karl says. "Norman has me convinced."

"I'll drink to that."

"We'll all drink to that."

"I wish my mom could have lived to see this day," Michael says.

"I wish Norman's mom could have lived to see this day," Sharon says.

Karl clears his throat and speaks loud enough for everyone to hear. "I've always been curious about Norman the artist. What drives him, what inspires him, what keeps his fire burning? There has to be something more than wanting to follow in his mother's footsteps. Help me here, Norm, was there a person, an experience, something that pointed you in the right direction?"

"Yes there was, Karl. I was five years old, sitting on the stoop in Brooklyn with a coloring book on my lap, filling in the spaces between the lines with crayons. Henry, the neighborhood handyman, came up the stairs and told me to throw away all my coloring books. He said they were bad, because they made me stay inside the lines. He said those lines made for limits and barriers that must be overcome. I didn't realize it at the time, but that was the most solid advice I've ever had."

Professor Lesher taps his wine glass with his knife. "Norman, let's explore this theme. From humble beginnings in Brooklyn at the height of World War II you've made an arduous journey, and you've overcome obstacles. What will you say some day to your children about lessons you've learned?"

I put my hand on Sharon's.

"I'd give our children the same advice Henry gave me. I'd urge them to not be boxed in by barriers. And to make that happen, I'd do everything my father didn't do, like take them to museums, ballparks, the beach, concerts, movies, and the library, especially the library. I'd teach them to play the piano and to paint. And I'd support them in their dreams, even their wildest ones."

Sharon squeezes me, kisses me on the cheek. Total silence. Professor Lesher claps. Everyone claps. Karl shouts a loud bravo. *Bar mitzvah* candy is flying.

I put the painting on the easel, and the answer comes to me. The long vertical of Mother's body needs to be neutralized by a horizontal. I paint a table behind her at the level of her forearm, but now the empty table is too obvious. No matter what I do, something else has to be done.

I have to calm down. Even Rembrandt isn't perfect, at least not all the time. The horse in his *Polish Rider* isn't as alive as Géricault's or the ones in Rosa Bonheur's *The Horse Fair*. Still, Mother should be perfect.

"Enough, Norman. Enough already."

Rembrandt is annoyed.

"*Remember the boys' club in the Bronx? You were in the ring with a boy smaller than you and getting hurt.*"

"That's how I feel now, getting punched out, sparring with... "

"*Rembrandt. That's right, Norman, you're sparring with me, and I'm the best in the business. You almost have me licked this time, only you don't know it, just like you didn't know you could lick that boy. But you knocked him down. You did it by following Mr. Gonzalez's advice, and then going beyond, adding a little something extra to your efforts.*"

"So what do I have to do to finish this portrait?"

"*Oh no you don't. I'm not throwing this fight. You'll have to win it on your own.*"

"But I'm losing. I'm not satisfied with... "

"*How can you possibly be satisfied until a painting is perfect? Not perfect for the Louvre or the Frick or the Met, but for you... Your thinking is right on the mark. You're listening to my suggestions. Don't you realize that you're only a few brushstrokes away from completion?*"

"But... "

"*No buts, Norman. Give your portrait a little more punch. Keep painting until the addition of one more stroke will diminish the effect you wish to achieve.*"

It comes splashing all over me in the shower, where creative ideas show up. I dress, put on a pot of coffee, turn on Vivaldi's *Four Seasons*, mix the paints, call up personnel to say I have more important things to do today. I see it before I even touch brush to canvas. On the table behind Mother there should be a round fishbowl with an undefined goldfish swimming in it. I paint quickly, add a slight smudge of deeper orange to the gills, stand back, scratch my head. Almost there. Almost.

Now Mother's face needs an imperceptible something. I warm up her cheek with precious Blockx vermilion and rub my pinkie on it to spead the paint. The light around the figure vibrates. I'm a boy again, riding to the cemetery on the streetcar, jiggling my marble in my hand. Sparks from the sun make it easy to see what's inside the marble. It's Mother. Now, in my studio, she's alive, painted in total harmony. Every brush stroke is a loving caress. I've captured her wisdom and strength. I feel Rembrandt's arm on my shoulder, giving me a fatherly squeeze.

Glossary

A fier auf dir A fire on you
Anti-semitten Antisemites
Boychik Boy
Challah Usually braided egg bread
Chaim Yonkel Fool, bumkin
Chazer traife Piggishly unkosher
Chuppah Wedding canopy
Chutzpa Gall, audacity
Cheder A school where Hebrew is taught
Clop Hit
Dreyt mir nisht kein kopf Don't make me crazy
Farcrimpte pawnum Sourpuss
Fardreyt Mixed up
Ferbissoner Grouch
Ferkokteh Shitty, crappy
Ferputzt All dressed up
Fleishig Food containing meat
Gantze Mishpokha The whole family
Gey in drerd arayn Go to hell
Gonif Crook
Gornisht Nothing
Gotenyu My God
Goyische Gentile
Groyser Large
Gut morgen Good morning
Halavai If only
Hertzabubba A non-Yiddish German word meaning a large woman
Hocking mir a chaynik Talking nonsense to me non-stop
Hora Jewish circle dance
Ich veys nisht I don't know
Kein eine hore A statement to ward off the evil eye,
Kook Look

Knacker Big shot
Kohanim High priests
Knish Potato dumpling
Kop Head
Kugel Baked noodle or potato pudding
Kvetch Complainer
Latkes Potato pancakes
Lungeh lucksh Tall, thin person
Maricon A non-Yiddish Spanish word meaning faggot
Mazel tov Congratulations
Mensch A decent man
Mezuzah A case with scripture inside affixed to the doorpost of a house
Milkhidik Dairy
Mishugas Crazyness
Momser Untrustworthy person, bastard
Nosh Snack
Oy gevald Oh help
Nu So
Pendejo A non-Yiddish Spanish word meaning asshole or stupid person
Pishach Urine
Pisk Mouth
Schmata Rag
Schmear Spread
Schmeck Smell
Schlemiel Dork, bungler, easily victimized person,
Schlep Pull, drag, tug
Schmendrick Nogoodnik, fool
Schmuck Jerk, asshole
Schmutz Dirt
Schmutzik Dirty
Schtoop Perform sexual intercourse
Schvartze Black person
Seder Passover ceremony
Shah Hush
Shikseh Gentile woman
Shtetl Village
Shul Synagogue

Talis Prayer shawl
Tatelah Little father, an endearing term for little boy
Traife Unkosher
Tsuris Troubles, aggravation
Vos machts du How are you
Vos zol ich machen How should I be
Yarmulke Skull cap
Yenta Busybody
Yenta Kvetch An expert busybody

Breinigsville, PA USA
12 December 2010
251188BV00002B/1/P